She folded her arms across her chest to hide her shaking fingers. "I said I'd like to see how you act when your iron-clad control slips. Looks to me like it's firmly in place." She looked at her watch, realizing that she enjoyed needling him. His eyes darkened, but that didn't unnerve her; no matter what color they happened to be, they lured her to him the way a magnet attracts nails. "Don't you think I'd better finish what I was doing so we can eat? You threatened to punish me if I made you starve. Remember?"

He leaned against the doorjamb, casual-like but exuding an energy she hadn't known he possessed, a sexual energy that encircled and entrapped her, kindling a fire at the edges of her nerves. In his yellow shirt, short-sleeved and open-collared, and with his arms folded across his chest, the sight of his hard biceps and prominent pectorals made her mouth water. She hadn't seen him that way before: a big jungle cat—hot, powerful and ready to pounce.

Why didn't he say something? It was as if he was waiting for her to burn all of her bridges. When she lowered her gaze, it fell on his flat belly and meandered downward to the flap of his tight jeans. Barely half aware of her movements and gestures, her gaze traveled back to his face. Quickly, she shifted her glance, only to see him ball his fists, loosen them and ball them again. She felt his heat then, and tremors streaked through her as the rough male in him jumped out at her, heating her blood and driving it straight to her loins.

After the Loving

Gwynne Forster

ARABESQUE

BET BOOKS

BET Publications, LLC
http://www.bet.com
http://www.arabesquebooks.com

ARABESQUE BOOKS are published by

BET Publications, LLC
c/o BET BOOKS
One BET Plaza
1900 W Place NE
Washington, DC 20018-1211

All Kensington Titles, Imprints and Distributed Lines are available at special quantity discounts for bulk purchases for sales promotions, premiums, fund-raising, and educational or institutional use. Special book excerpts or customized printings can also be created to fit specific needs. For details, write or phone the office of the Kensington special sales manager: Kensington Publishing Corp., 850 Third Avenue, New York, NY 10022, attn: Special Sales Department, Phone: 1-800-221-2647.

First Printing: February 2005
10 9 8 7 6 5 4 3 2 1

Printed in the United States of America

ACKNOWLEDGMENTS

To the memory of my parents who gave me a legacy of faith; instilled in me the efficacy of kindness, integrity, and commitment to good; to the memory of my siblings from whom I learned the art of distinguishing conflict from competition; and I thank my late mother, especially, who wrote the first fiction I ever read and taught me to read and write by the time I was five.

Most of all, I thank God for the talent he has given me and for the opportunities to use it.

Chapter One

Velma Brighton zipped up the mauve-colored, strapless silk and lace gown, fastened a strand of eight millimeter pearls at her neck, and forced herself to look in the floor-length mirror that leaned against the wall. Grimacing at the sight of her more than amply rounded figure in the fitted gown, she cringed with embarrassment.

"Now, he'll know what I really look like," she said to herself, lamenting the fact that she couldn't wear her usual caftan and wishing that she was tall and slender. As she stared at the mirror, she saw not only her own likeness, but a reflection of the groves of snow and icicle-ladened trees on the north side of Harrington House that created an idyllic dream world. For a better look, she walked over to the window of the guest room she occupied and fixed her gaze on the broad expanse of snow-covered beauty, shaking her head in wonder at the sunlight dancing against the icicles. No bride could ask for a more beautiful wedding day.

This was her fifth or sixth visit to Harrington House, an enormous red-brick colonial set off by a great circular driveway, dominating John Brown Drive in Eagle Park, Maryland. She first visited it in order to be with her sister, Alexis, but on each subsequent trip to visit her sister, her heart had fluttered wildly in her eagerness to see Russ Harrington again. And though he always welcomed her, often being especially attentive, she didn't think she'd made much headway with him.

She checked her hair and make-up and went downstairs to the rooms her sister occupied with her five-year-old daughter Tara.

"How do I look, Aunt Velma?" Tara asked the minute Velma walked into the room.

"Beautiful. You'll be the perfect flower girl."

Smiles enveloped Tara's face. "My mummy said I looked uh . . . spec . . . spec what Mummy?"

"Spectacular."

Velma regarded her sister, tall, willowy and beautiful in the ivory-colored silk-satin and lace wedding gown. "I was a little surprised when you said you'd wear white, but I'm glad you did."

"Telford asked if I would; he wanted a traditional wedding. I wasn't going to deny him because of a foolish convention that a divorced or widowed woman shouldn't wear white at a subsequent marriage. Brides wore white traditionally because they were virgins. Honey, that was then. Telford's never been married, and he deserves a good old-fashioned wedding if that's to his liking."

"You're the most beautiful woman I ever saw," Velma said. "Just wait till Telford sees you. The poor man's heart will jump right out of his chest."

"I certainly hope not," Alexis said, adjusting her tiara. "I haven't seen him since last night, and it seems like years."

"You're not supposed to see the groom on your wedding day until you meet him at the altar. You know that."

"I do know it; I just wish I could see him. Velma, I can't believe this is happening to me. I'm . . . I'm so happy. If I'm not careful, I'll bawl."

"You won't. It's not your style." She reached up to Alexis with open arms. "I'm happy for you, sis. After all you suffered with Jack, you deserve this wonderful man. Turn around and let me fasten these buttons. I never could figure out why they put these tiny things on the back of a wedding dress, unless it's to frustrate the groom when he tries to get the gown off the bride."

She loved Alexis' low, sultry laugh when she said, "I hope to have him in such a state that he'll rip 'em off."

Velma stopped her task and wondered aloud, "Would he do *that*? Good Lord, how exciting! I would never have believed him capable of it."

"Can't judge a book by its cover, hon, nor a man by his height. And that's gospel. Seen Russ today?"

Velma shrugged as if didn't matter, but it did. "Not since last night. If he ate breakfast, he did it before I went downstairs. That man is an enigma. Last night, he laughed, joked and teased with me, and this morning, he acted as if I wasn't in the house."

Alexis placed a hand on her sister's arm. "Understanding Russ may prove to be a full-time job, Velma. He's tough and sometimes he seems cynical, but dig deeper. He's loving, caring and if he tells you he'll do something, he does it."

"I believe that, but—"

In the act of inspecting the long white leather gloves she planned to wear, Alexis stopped, threw them on the bed and stared at her older sister. "I want you to listen to me. No buts. Russ is straight. What you see is exactly what you get. Don't bother to look for hidden meanings either in his words or his actions. There won't be any. What you see is exactly what you get."

"Not many people are like that. I guess he's too ornery to be dishonest."

"No," Alexis said. "Russ is too self-assured to lie or to be devious. Pay attention to him if you want him, otherwise forget it; when it comes to Russ, those notions about how to get a man aren't worth the mental energy required to remember them."

"I know he's special," Velma said. She finished buttoning the dress, checked its hem and train. Her happiness for her sister was boundless, but she couldn't help wishing for Alexis' beauty, her flawless figure and her self-confidence.

"I've been a bridesmaid half a dozen times," Velma said, "each of which was increasingly painful for me. This is the last time I'm doing it. It hurts too badly."

"Aunt Velma, has Grant come yet?" Tara asked of Grant Roundtree, her friend and the son of Adam Roundtree and Melissa Grant-Roundtree.

"I didn't see him, but don't worry; it's a bit too early for the Roundtrees."

"My mummy said he's the ring bearer. Can Mr. Telford and my mummy get married if Grant doesn't bring the rings?"

"He'll be there," Alexis said. "Anyway, we can get married without rings, although I wouldn't like to. But relax. Grant will be here on time."

"Yes, ma'am. You already told me to relax four times. How do I do it?"

"Excuse me for a few minutes," Velma said, and made her way down the corridor toward the stairs.

"Well, now don't you look real special?" Henry said as he met her near the bottom of the stairs.

"Thanks, Henry. What about you? You look great. With that tux on, you could snare a princess."

"Yeah? If I believed you, I'd get out of this monkey suit fast as I could."

"Did ... er ... re—" Velma began tentatively, so that Henry wouldn't think her question important.

He second guessed her anyway. "The boys ate breakfast in town this morning. Drake and Russ had to keep a lid on Tel. Never saw anybody so shook up about getting married as Alexis and Tel." With an expression of reverence, he glanced toward the ceiling, then smiled, a rarity for him. "They're meant for each other sure as my name is Henry Wooten."

Velma started up the stairs. "What are you going up there for?" he asked her. "Ain't gonna be nobody up there but you. Stop worrying about him. Can't nobody second guess Russ."

"I'm not worrying about him."

"You are so, and he won't appreciate it. You listen to what I say. You hear?"

First Alexis and now Henry lectured her on how to deal with Russ. Life didn't revolve around that man; not so far, anyway. "Thanks, Henry. I'll ... uh ... see you later."

Inside her room, she closed the door and, for a minute, had an urge to lock it. Fighting back moroseness, she admonished herself sharply.

It's her day, so put a smile on your face and grin if it kills you. For years, you've gone alone to the movies, theaters and concerts. You're used to it, girl, used to having no one to hold you when you hurt, no one to love you when you can't stand being alone. Nothing has changed. Not one damned thing.

No. Everything remained as it had been. Except the joy, the happiness Alexis radiated when she mentioned Telford's name. She wanted that joy, that happiness, that knowledge that she belonged to a man who belonged to her.

"I gotta snap out of this," she told herself as she got a small lavender-colored handkerchief and folded it into the palm of her left hand. She dabbed some Hermès perfume behind her ears and at her wrists, inhaled its elegant scent and went back to Alexis and Tara. She entered the room as Alexis picked up the telephone receiver.

"Hello. Alexis speaking."

"Hello, sweetheart. Russ, Drake and I are leaving for the church.The stretched-out white Lincoln Town Car out front is for you, Velma, Henry and Tara. The Roundtrees will meet us at the church. Can you believe that in an hour and a half you'll be my wife? Baby, I can't wait."

"Me neither. Drive carefully."

"Russ is driving, and you know he wouldn't consider breaking the speed limit."

Alexis treated them to a deep, throaty laugh, a happy laugh. "I know. Tell him I said he's carrying precious cargo, so he shouldn't go beyond sixty."

"I'll tell him that, for all the good it'll do. I love you, woman. See you."

"And I love you."

Velma listened to that side of the conversation and couldn't do one thing about the ache that settled inside of her. An ache that would vanish for all time if she had Russell Harrington and three children who looked just like him.

Henry met them at the front door, handed a bouquet of mauve and pink calla lilies to Velma and a bouquet of white ones to Alexis. "From Tel and Russ. You can figure out who sent what to whom," he said, and added: "Thank you Alexis for the honor of letting me escort you and give you to Tel. You're my daughter now, and it'll be the proudest moment of my life."

An hour and a half later, bells of the Eagle Park Presbyterian Church in Eagle Park, Maryland, began to peal, and Velma stepped behind Alexis, straightened the train of her dress, adjusted Tara's mauve-pink hat and Grant's bow tie, kissed her sister's cheek and headed toward the altar.

Walking up the aisle that was banked on both sides with white calla lilies, she knew her face was devoid of emotion, reflecting neither her happiness for her sister nor the loneliness that was her interminable visitor. She took her place at the altar, made almost surrealistically beautiful and magical with dozens of lighted white candles, white calla lilies and white rosebuds. When she could no longer avoid it, she let her gaze find Russ who, as Telford's older brother, served as best man. Drake served as groom.

She knew Russ heard her audible gasp, for a slow-moving smile formed around his mouth seconds before he greeted her. Granted it was a solemn occasion, but there was no need to behave as if they were in a morgue. Her composure once more in order, she let the smile that came from her heart light up her face.

To her, Russ stood out among men, tall, tough and handsome, but in that black tuxedo and mauve-colored accessories—the uniform for every male in the wedding party, including Grant—he took her breath away. Although he stood with his brothers, themselves imposing men by any standard, she barely looked at them. And when Russ caught her ogling him and winked at her, she lowered her gaze in embarrassment.

Russ shifted his glance from her face to a spot somewhere below her left elbow. She looked down and realized he wanted her to know that Tara and Grant stood beside her solemnly holding hands. She heard the tune, "Here Comes the Bride," held her head up and smiled at Telford, for her heart seemed to overflow with joy.

"Who gives this woman to be wed?" the minister asked.

Henry's voice, strong and not quite steady, replied, "I do." He kissed Alexis, placed her hand in Telford's and took his seat beside Adam Roundtree.

Velma watched Telford and her sister exchange their vows, speaking directly to each other and looking at each other as if they were alone. She realized that in their hearts, they were alone. The minister asked for the rings so that he could bless them, and Grant released Tara's hand, walked up to the minister and said, "Here they are, sir."

Velma's eyebrows shot up. She forced back a grin, took pains to avoid looking at any of the adults who stood around the altar, for no one told Grant to say that. Yet, it seemed so appropriate. He stepped back to Tara, reached for her hand and held it. Finally, the minister pronounced Telford and Alexis husband and wife. Their arms enfolded each other in a joyous embrace, as they laughed, hugged and cried.

As if she didn't want to be left out, Tara tapped on Telford's leg. He looked down at her, grinned, and lifted her into his arms to the applause of the wedding guests.

"Is this what you meant by 'working it out,' Mr. Telford?"

He hugged her. "This is exactly what I meant."

"And we can be together now, you and Mummy and me?"

"Yes. That's what it means."

Her arms tightened around Telford's neck, then she kissed his cheek. "I have to tell Grant I was right." He set her on her feet, and she went back to Grant who immediately reached for her hand. With Tara and Grant walking ahead of them, the bride and groom smiled and waved to their guests as they walked away from the altar. Her eyes glittering with tears of happiness, Velma looked up into Russ Harrington's face as he held out his arm to her, his smile as radiant as she knew her own had to be. She nearly tripped, but he tightened his grip.

"It was the most moving thing I've ever experienced," he said in low tones. "I'm happy for them."

"I am, too. It was . . . I can't describe it." She said silent thanks that he didn't see her face, for she knew that all she felt—happiness, pain and loneliness— were mirrored in her eyes.

I'll be back on track as soon as I can get away from Eagle Park and this man whose arm I'm holding. I don't want his casual friendship. I want him.

Russ held the door of his car, seated Velma in the front passenger's seat, and left Henry and Drake to make themselves comfortable in the back. Tara and Grant rode with the bride and groom.

"You want to offer the first toast, Drake?" Russ asked as he moved the Mercedes away from the curb and headed for the reception.

"That's your job, brother," Drake said. "I'll do the honors when you tie the knot."

"If that ever happens," Henry put in. "You both shoulda seen how happy Tel is. Now maybe you'll figure out how to get some of that happiness for yourselves."

"Don't bring that up, Henry," Drake said. "I'm not interested in walking the remainder of the way to the reception."

"Would he put us out?" Velma asked with a tone of wonder in her voice.

"Maybe not you. I'm taking no chances," Drake said.

Henry sucked his teeth loudly enough for all of them to hear. "He ain't putting nobody out. I raised him to have manners. Just because he can't stand foolishness, don't mean he'd screw up Tel's wedding reception."

"What's going on back there, Velma?" he asked the quiet woman beside him. "After living with me for thirty-some years, you'd think they'd know what a real pussycat I am."

"Which feline family you talking about, brother? Surely not the house variety."

"Do they always meddle with you like this?" Velma asked him, and he got the impression from her tone of voice that she didn't like it.

He turned into the driveway leading to the Eagle Park Palace Hotel. "The three of us jostle all the time, and because Henry practically raised us, he reserves the right to say whatever appears on the tip of his tongue, but if my finger began to bleed, all of them would run to me with Band-Aids. That's what this family is all about, Velma. We're here for each other."

She looked great, and he felt good walking through the hotel lobby with her holding his arm while the crowd of on-lookers waved and smiled. "You should wear this color all the time," he told her. "And this style suits you. I like it better that your caftans. You . . . you look terrific."

"Thanks, but maybe you need glasses."

He stopped and looked hard at her. "You're telling me I don't know my own mind, that I don't know what I like and don't like? I'll tell you this; I do not like those caftans you wear. Dressed like this, you look like a real woman."

If she was posturing for more praise, she could forget it. He wasn't in the business of building egos with empty phrases.

Just what I needed to keep my head straightened out. He walked on with her but didn't offer her his arm. They joined Telford and Alexis in an anteroom, and he watched a subdued Velma embrace her sister and her brother-in-law.

"My mummy is going off with Mr. Telford on a honeymoon. What does a honeymoon look like, Mr. Telford?"

"I'll . . . uh . . . find out while I'm there and explain it when we get back."

Russ snickered. It wasn't often that he saw his older brother squirm and loosen his collar.

"Time for the party to enter the reception room," the manager told them.

They stood around the table laden with the wedding cake, calla lilies and glowing candles. Russ stepped up and raised his glass. "It gives me the greatest pleasure to introduce to you Telford and Alexis Harrington." After the applause, he continued. "To my brother and his wife. May you always be as deeply in love as you are this day." He let the champagne drizzle down his throat, set his glass down and moved aside.

Drake held up his glass. "I thank my brother for giving me such a wonderful sister and a niece who I adore as if she were my own child. Telford and Alexis, God bless you with a long and happy life."

It was Henry's turn. "This is one of the happiest days of my life. Take care of each other, and grow old together in peace and love." He took a few sips and set the glass aside.

Russ motioned to the orchestra, and Telford waltzed onto the center of the floor with his bride in his arms. His turn, but he felt a little shaky about it. He figured it would pay him to keep his distance from Velma, though he didn't discount his strong attraction to her. He preferred independent, self-assured women, and Velma had just showed signs of a lack of self-confidence, at least with him. He liked the company of mature people who knew who they were and where they belonged. However, as custom demanded, he stepped in front of Velma and opened his arms. "Dance with me?" he asked her, for he didn't believe in taking anything for granted.

She smiled, lifted the hem of her gown and rested a hand on his shoulder. "Thanks. I'd love to dance with you." She danced well, he realized, a point in her favor, for he loved to dance.

The manager announced that dinner was served and that dancing would continue later. After dinner, he said to Velma, "Drake's car is in the hotel garage. If you wish to stay, he'll drive you home along with Tara and Henry. I'm driving Telford and Alexis to the airport in Baltimore as soon as they change clothes. I can drop you by Harrington House, but no one will be there with you till Drake gets back."

She thought for a couple of seconds and quickly made up her mind. He liked that. Nothing got on his nerves faster than shilly-shallying.

"I'll go back with Drake," she said. "Drive carefully. Will you come back to Eagle Park tonight?"

"Yes, but it will be late. I'll see you in the morning." To his own surprise, he leaned down and kissed her cheek. "It was fun. Good night."

He could take her with him, and maybe he should, but if he did, it would seem that she was his date, and he wasn't ready for what that would imply. He walked over to Telford and tapped his elbow.

"Alexis will blow a fuse if I speed, so we'd better get started. Check-in time is an hour and a half from now. Say your goodbyes, man."

It amused him when Alexis, who stood within hearing distance, said, "If he spoke to all these people, we'd miss the plane. Everybody thinks newlyweds are off-the-wall anyway, so why don't we just sneak out? I've already prepared Tara. Let's go."

"Woman after my own heart, brother. Meet you in the lobby in ten minutes."

Telford clapped his hands. "Unmarried ladies to the right please." About a dozen women including Velma gathered there. Alexis tossed her bridal bouquet, and Adam Roundtree's cousin caught it.

As Russ was leaving the reception hall, he glanced to his right, toward the spot where he last saw Velma, and noticed that her gaze followed him. His heart battled with his will in a fight to which he was entirely unaccustomed. He stopped, turned and walked over to her.

"Do you want to ride with me? I'll drop them at the airport and head directly to Eagle Park. Do you want to go?"

She gazed steadily up at him, almost as if trying to see inside of him, to divine his motive. He wasn't accustomed to that Velma—serious, standing her ground and doing it without the props of wit and quips. He spread his hands palms out, telling her without words, "what you see is what you get." Suddenly, a smile enveloped her face, and relief flooded him, though he could not imagine why.

"I'd love to go, Russ."

No silliness such as "if you're sure you don't mind" or "if it won't inconvenience you." Straight from the shoulder. She wanted to go with him, and she didn't mind letting him know it. Another point in her favor. He liked a woman who let a man know what she wanted.

He took her hand. "Come on. I'll tell Drake you'll be home later."

"Way to go, man," Drake said, his voice well contained. "It's the simple things that count; they can make you or break you."

"Yeah. It's easy to forget that."

"Would you like me to get a vase for your flowers?" Russ asked Velma.

"Thanks, but each stem is in its own little water cup." She

gazed up at him. "You're a thoughtful man, and it's something I appreciate."

He didn't know what to make of that statement, so he let it go. Fortunately Telford and Alexis appeared, having changed into traveling clothes. To his amazement, neither of them seemed surprised to see Velma with him.

"All right," he said. "Let's get this show moving. If we waste another minute, I'll have to drive ninety miles an hour in order to get you to the airport on time."

"Don't tax yourself, brother," Telford said. "I can get us there driving fifty-five or sixty, so if you'd rather I drove . . ."

Russ couldn't help laughing. "All right. All right." He buckled Velma's seat belt. "You two buckle up back there." He ignited the engine and headed for Route 70. He didn't feel the need to talk; most any subject would take him down from where he was. He didn't want anything to blight his mood. How many times had he feared Telford would let Alexis slip through his hands? It took him a long time to concede Drake's point, that Telford was a different man when he was in Alexis' company, that he had never known Telford to be truly happy until he fell in love with Alexis and Tara. It was an incontestible truth; they belonged together.

He glanced at Velma, who sat beside him serenely with her hands relaxed and the bouquet lying in her lap. "Thank God, she doesn't feel the need to chatter," he said to himself. He flipped on the radio and out came the strains of "Will You Dance This Waltz With Me?" As if of its own volition, his head turned toward Velma and, at the same time, she looked toward him. A grin formed around her lips, and then she laughed. He didn't ask her why she laughed, because he knew. It was the reason why he also laughed. *They could duck it as much and as often as they liked, but something would always remind them.*

"I won't ask what the two of you are laughing about," Telford said.

"Oh, you can ask," Russ replied, "but it won't do you much good."

"What if *I* ask?" Alexis put in.

"Won't do you any good either," Velma said.

That wasn't the first notice she had given that she would support him, that she'd be there for him if he needed her. He recorded it in his mental notebook. A long-term arrangement with her wasn't on his agenda, but he had to reckon with it because her attraction for him was nothing to gainsay. He wanted her, but he wasn't sure he was willing to pay the price.

"You're here with twenty minutes to spare," he said to Telford when they reached the Baltimore International Airport.

"What was his top speed, Velma?" Telford asked.

"My lips are sealed. You two have the time of your lives."

"We'll do our best," Alexis said.

"Thanks, brother, for everything. I'll finish thanking you when we get back."

Driving away from the airport, Russ found himself thinking of a way to end what, for him, had been a perfect day. "We've got about an hour and forty-minute drive ahead of us, Velma. Would you like to stop somewhere for some kind of beverage and a snack? I don't drink anything alcoholic when I have to drive, but I could use some ice tea or a soft drink."

"I'd love to stop," she said. "Any place where this evening dress won't look silly."

He couldn't help laughing. "No matter where we stop, your dress won't look a bit sillier than this tux with mauve-colored accessories."

She seemed disappointed, but she was good at bluffing,

he saw, when she lifted her chin and said, "I remember you said you liked this gown I'm wearing. Well, it's mauve too."

"I like it on you."

She didn't let him drop it. "It's not more outlandish than the brilliant red or royal blue accessories that some men wear with formal dress. Besides, you look fantastic in that getup. I was practically ogling you when we were waiting for the bride to reach the altar."

"Really? Thanks for the compliment." He knew she'd stood there cataloging his assets until he caught her at it and looked her straight in the eye, but he didn't think she'd be comfortable knowing he was aware of her uninhibited admiration.

"What do you say we stop at the first drive-in restaurant on Route 70. Give 'em something to talk about in there."

"Fine with me."

A groan escaped him when he saw the long line. "You have a seat somewhere," she said. "I'll get what you want, and we'll be out of here in twenty minutes."

He stared at her. "I'd like to know how you plan to manage *that*."

"Have a seat and you'll see."

He took out his wallet and handed her a twenty-dollar bill. "I'd like a huge bottle of ginger ale and a blueberry muffin." She saluted him, and he went to find a table, praying that he wouldn't have to spring her from jail. In less than five minutes, she arrived at the table he chose holding her bouquet as if it were a baby, and followed by a busboy who carried their order. The busboy took the food off the tray and placed it on the table. Russ handed the man a five-dollar bill and thanked him.

"No problem, sir. Congratulations and much happiness."

"What was he . . . ?" He stared at Velma who was near convulsion with suppressed laughter. "How did you . . . ?"

"I just went to the busboy and told him we were already late for the wedding. People heard me and it was like the opening of the Red Sea. They assumed I was the bride. The busboy ran behind the counter and collected what I wanted, took it to the cashier, I paid, and you know the rest. Here's your change."

When he could get his breath, he said, "Well, hell," opened a bottle of ginger ale and was about to pour some in a glass for her when the humor of it struck him. He slumped in the chair and gave in to the laughter that rolled out of him. He knew that everybody in the restaurant was looking at them, but that seemed to make it all the funnier.

When they managed to control their laughter, he found her staring at him. "What is it? Did I get some blueberries on my teeth?"

"I never knew you to laugh like this. It is wonderful. Just . . . just wonderful."

He sobered then. "Drake likes to call me 'old sourpuss.' Is that what you think of me?"

"That hadn't occurred to me. In this context, I think of you as a serious-minded man who has a low tolerance for nonsense." She lowered her head a little, and stole a glance at him. "Russ, I've been called a prankster, and I suppose you'd classify that as nonsense."

"Most of it is nonsense, but if it's witty, if it's clever, that's different; then it's a challenge. However, that's not an invitation for you to—"

She held up her right hand. "I know. I stand sufficiently warned. Still . . ." She let him wait for her next words, and he found himself anticipating them with heightened pleasure. "Uh . . . I can't imagine myself not going to great lengths, if necessary, to make you laugh."

"Yeah. A prankster would do that." He pondered her words, but didn't wonder why she enjoyed seeing him laugh. As frank as he was finding her to be, she'd probably tell him without any prompting.

Nonetheless, it gave him something to contemplate. "I never thought much about my personality or how it strikes others," he said. "It's who I am, and I can't see myself pretending to be what I am not."

Her left hand moved toward him, and he thought she would reach for his hand or, at least, touch it. But she almost snatched it back, and he realized that what he'd thought was insecurity could well be an uncertainty as to how to relate to him.

"Velma, I find that it never pays to try to figure out a person."

"You think I'm trying to figure you out?"

"Aren't you? You wanted to touch my hand, maybe even hold it to show the sympathetic understanding that you felt, but you weren't certain how I'd react and you withdrew."

"What would you have done, Russ, if I'd held your hand?"

"How many times tonight did I take your hand? Did I ask permission?"

Her eyes sparkled like a dozen night stars, and her face bloomed into a smile. "Russ, what you're saying is like dangling money and jewels in front of a thief."

He glanced at his watch, poured the remainder of the ginger ale into their glasses and took a sip. "Not quite. It means take a chance. Show me who you are, and I'll reciprocate."

"But not necessarily in a way that I'd like."

He drained the glass. "True. But you have one thing going for you. We Harrington men respect women. Now, if we don't get out of here, that busboy will know you handed him a line."

"Right."

When they stood to leave, the busboy appeared with a tray, cleared the table and let a grin take over his face. "Congratulations again, sir. This made my day."

"You've been very kind," Russ said. He wanted to get out of there before he folded up in another laughing fit. As they walked toward the door, the other diners applauded, and he could feel his lower lip drop when Velma waved and blew kisses to the people.

Deciding to play along, he slipped an arm around Velma's waist, and while he didn't succeed in keeping the grin off his face, he was able to resist howling with laughter until they got into the car.

"I never had so much fun in my life," she said. "My sister wouldn't dream of doing anything like that." She shifted her position until she sat with her back partly against the door. "Wasn't that fun?"

"Probably. I've never been tempted to do anything like that. I don't know which cracked me up more, your arriving at the table with the busboy or blowing kisses at your fans." He ignited the engine and headed for the highway. "Velma, you're full of surprises. I had a very different picture of you, and I'm glad you agreed to come with me." He shook his head in disbelief. "Neither Henry, my brothers nor Alexis would believe I'd participate in any hairbrained thing like that."

"Are you ashamed that we did it?"

"Who, me? No indeed. I don't know when I've had so much fun."

"I'm glad, Russ. I'd like us to be friends."

He came within a breath of asking her what kind of friends, and he was glad he corrected himself before the words slipped out. He finessed a response. "Why shouldn't we be?"

When she didn't answer his question, he considered it another point in her favor; she wouldn't gainsay something was important to her. She stifled a yawn.

"Sleepy?" he asked her.

"Terribly. I was so keyed up when I went to bed that I was still awake at four-thirty this morning."

"I won't feel badly if you sleep."

"But I will. If you talk, I'll stay awake. What was it like being the middle of three boys when you were growing up?"

"Now that's a topic for a cold night. Growing up and being an adult . . . it's all the same. Telford and Drake are closest, because Telford was protective of Drake. So was I, for that matter. That left me to my own devices, and I used it to my advantage. Strange thing is that Drake isn't spoiled; he's one hundred percent man."

"What did you do on your own?" she asked with such sincerity that he know her questions sprang from a genuine interest in him.

"I read the great philosophers, the leading writers of the Harlem Renaissance, Shakespeare, Richard Wright, newspapers, the funnies, whatever I got my hands on. And one day, I read about Frank Lloyd Wright. After that, I read everything about him that I could find."

"So he was your idol and the reason you became an architect?"

"Partly. Telford's the other reason. He had this dream of vindicating our father, and he talked about it so much that . . . Well, it fit with my passion for Wright's work. Drake's a born engineer. From childhood, he was always interested in how to make things work, and it is he and not Telford or I who fixes things around our home."

"The three of you work well together. I assume Telford is the project manager."

"Right. He negotiates contracts, purchases supplies, hires the workers and oversees them. He's responsible for bringing the project in on time. He's the boss, but we take a vote on everything important. If there's disagreement, I always lose."

He heard himself say it, and knew it was true, but it didn't much bother him and never had. When he wanted to get his way, he knew how to do it.

Her reaction didn't surprise him. "You don't seem resentful. How's that? I'd be after their heads all the time."

He slowed down to take a curve on a poorly lighted section of the highway. "Sure I've resented it, but only at the moment and only about the issue in question. When I seriously want to have my way, both Telford and Drake yield. We care about each other, Velma, and neither of us is ever knowingly going to hurt the other."

"All of you have strong, dominant personalities, what we call the alpha males. It's a wonder you're so close."

"Henry's the best leavening agent three young Turks ever had. Even before our father died, Henry was the adult we looked to, because Papa was rarely at home, always off working himself to death."

He swallowed and ran the tip of his tongue over his lips, surprised at his dry mouth. "I don't think I've ever talked this much. We're practically home, and I haven't learned very much about you. What I got, though, was special." He pulled into the circular driveway of Number Ten, John Brown Drive, stopped and cut the motor.

"Here we are, and I didn't speed." He wondered at her nonresponse. They entered the foyer, and after locking the door, he hung up their coats. "I'm going into the kitchen to get some juice. Want some?" he asked her.

She shook her head.

"Thanks for making these last few hours so pleasant. You and your brothers have been fortunate, Russ. You didn't have your parents, but you had peace and love. Alexis and I had our parents, but I think I'd be a happier person today if they had separated or put us in foster care."

He could feel both of his eyebrows shoot up, and his eyes seemed twice their size. "Does Alexis feel this way, too?"

"Alexis is a Quaker. She thinks in terms of a peaceful, serene present and doesn't worry about the past. Furthermore, I'm older than she is, and I understood better what I heard and saw. But let's not end this lovely day talking about my parents."

"Then, we won't." He took her hand and walked with her into the kitchen. They drank the orange juice, and he remembered that they would ascend the stairs together to go to their separate rooms. From the expression on her face, he knew she had already thought of it, and that her nerves were on edge.

"Come on," he said, deciding to make light of what was becoming an embarrassing situation. "We can be trusted to walk up those stairs together."

"Speak for yourself." When she glanced up at him, heat roared through his body. Blatant vulnerability spread across her face. He wanted her. He'd wanted her all evening, from the minute she reached the altar. He reached out to gather her into his arms.

"I . . . Sorry. I shouldn't have come with you. Good night."

"Wait a minute. You can't. Look here, Velma. You're beautiful, intelligent and you've got a wonderful, outrageous sense of humor. Why are you—"

"Thanks for trying to prop up my ego. What happened to all that honesty everybody says you have?"

He stepped back. "Thanks for the reality check. From time to time I need those. Good night."

He went into the den and dropped himself into the big overstuffed leather chair. In another second, he would have kissed her senseless. He didn't remember ever enjoying a woman's company so thoroughly. In the space of two hours, she taught him a lot about himself, and he liked all of it. But he wasn't going to tie himself to a woman who didn't know and appreciate her own assets.

Chapter Two

Velma strolled up the stairs as casually as if the pain she felt wasn't eating a hole in her. He'd opened his arms and taken her into them, but he couldn't lock her to him the way she wanted him to, needed him to. No matter what he said, he had to notice her size and the way her dress fitted. Alexis' gown covered a work of art, but hers covered rolls of flesh, and he didn't need twenty/twenty vision to see it.

"I'm sick of being miserable," she said aloud, "and I'm tired of being embarrassed about the way my dresses fit. If I wear them loose, I look as if I'm middle aged; if I wear them fitted . . ." She didn't finish the thought. "I'm going on a diet."

With that comfort, she made her ablutions and got into bed, but sleep evaded her. She heard every creak, the grandfather clock in the living room and the engine of an automobile in the distance, all the time aware that she waited for the sound of Russ' footsteps on the stairs.

The next morning she awoke early, showered, dressed in a green paisley caftan and went downstairs.

"I thought you'd sleep half a day," Henry said when she walked into the kitchen. "What you want for breakfast?"

"Whatever. Thanks. Where's Tara?"

"Over at Grant Roundtree's house. They're inseparable."

Velma picked up a grape and put it in her mouth. She didn't want to ask Henry, but she knew he'd force her to do it, so she said, "Am I the first one down?"

Henry put a pan of biscuits in the oven, dusted his flour-filled hands on his apron and looked hard at her. "Since you asked, Russ ain't ever the first one to come downstairs." He ran his fingers through the few strands of hair remaining on his head and glared at her. "Today's Sunday. If you're not going to church, you don't come down all dressed up. Go put on some jeans and a sweater."

She sat down in one of the Moroccan chairs at the little kitchen table. "Henry, please don't get on my case. I don't own any jeans, because they don't look right on me."

"They will so. Whatever you're trying to hide in that dress is all in your head. I saw you and Russ last night. He liked what he saw, but he ain't gonna like that thing you got on."

"Too bad. I don't have anything else to put on. I'll set the table."

She'd hardly begun before she heard Drake's voice. "Who's here other than you and me, Henry?"

"Russ and Velma. Tara's visiting her boyfriend."

"This early? Weren't they something to see yesterday? Great-looking kids. That was the best-looking wedding party I've seen. Did you see Velma in that dress? I could hardly believe my eyes. She ought wear more dresses of that type."

Velma stopped setting the table and leaned against the wall. Hadn't Russ said the same thing about her dress? Maybe . . . She shook herself out of it. No more debates and personal recriminations, she was going to take hold of her life and *run it;* she'd had enough of taking what came. She pasted a smile on her face and returned to the kitchen.

"All finished, Henry. Hi, Drake. Do you realize my sister did not tell me where she was going?"

"Hi. You're assuming she knew. She was told only to prepare for a warm climate," Drake said.

"I'll bet you know how to reach Telford in an emergency."

"I don't, but Russ does. Give him a secret and it's safer than if you stored it in Fort Knox. Where is he?"

The quick rise and fall of her right shoulder gave him the answer, but not wanting to seem disinterested, she said, "I don't know. When I went upstairs last night, he was headed for the den." Drake's whistle was barely audible, but she heard it and understood its meaning.

"I say let's eat. Old sourpuss has been known to sleep till three o'clock."

She turned to face him. "Oh, Drake. Is it nice to call him that awful name? Wouldn't you think it makes him feel badly?"

Drake gazed hard at her. "I never thought of it that way; it's always been a joke. I'm sorry."

"'Morning. Is Henry on strike or something? Where's the food?" Russ walked over to her. "I hope you slept well. Thanks for taking my part, but it gives Drake so much pleasure to call me old sourpuss that I wouldn't deprive him of it."

"How long were you standing there?"

"I walked in when Drake said, 'Let's eat.'" His gaze seemed to penetrate her. "I place a high value on loyalty."

"Serve yourselves at the stove, and let's eat in the breakfast room," Henry said. "If we break one of Alexis' rules, she'll know it even if she's not here."

Velma began piling biscuits, sausage and grits on her plate as she usually did, and stopped. She kept the grits, put half a pat of butter on it instead of the usual three pats and got a bowl of mixed fruits from the kitchen counter.

"You not eating my biscuits?" Henry asked.

"I will, if I'm still hungry after I finish this."

Russ eyed her with a frown on his face. "You feel okay?"

She assured him that she did, but she ate as slowly as she could hoping she wouldn't be hungry when she finished. She concentrated on eating, dreading the moment when she would swallow that last spoonful of grits. "I may be hungry," she told herself, "but I'll be happy."

"Ain't nobody talking this morning?" Henry asked.

"I'm eating," Drake said. "You knocked yourself out with these biscuits, Henry. I imagine Telford would put away half a dozen of 'em."

That was the old man's joy in life, Velma realized, when he smiled and passed the plate of biscuits to Russ. "You ain't eating much, either. Alexis found some special flour, and it's right good, if I do say so myself."

When she glanced at Russ, her heart skittered in her chest. The expression on his face, open and—there was no other word for it—adoring as he gazed at her, shook her to the core. She tried to shift her glance, but his eyes, dark and slumberous, trapped her. From their silence, she realized that Henry and Drake watched them and, with effort, she lowered her gaze. But he had stirred her as thoroughly as a spinning bottle mixes what it contains.

She sought safety in the bowl of fruit before her, but the spoonful she intended for her mouth dropped into her lap. "Ex . . . cuse me, please." She pushed back her chair and, forcing herself to walk rather than run as she wanted to do, headed for the stairs. Nobody was going to affect her that way with just a look, robbing her of her aplomb, of the control of her emotions. Nobody, she vowed. Her foot had barely touched the bottom stair when she felt his hand on her arm. She whirled around and into his arms.

"Russ. Please." The feel of his hands through the silk of her caftan, of her breast beaded and aching against his hard chest caused her breathing to quicken.

He stared down at her. "Why didn't you eat a decent breakfast?"

"That's not why you're here," she said, refusing to allow him the upper hand and hating her shortened breath and the rapid rise and fall of her bosom.

"You're right. It's not. I'm here for the same reason that you bolted from the table."

"I spilled food on my dress, and—"

"And we both know why. Did you wear it because I said I didn't like it?"

"Of course not. I didn't bring any other kind of clothes."

His Adam's apple bobbed furiously, his eyes—dark and long lashed—seemed to drag her into him, filling her head with dangerous ideas. If only he would ask no questions, but simply take her to his bed and love her until she couldn't move!

As if he read her thoughts, pure sexual hunger blazed in the stormy orbs that his eyes had become. He held her closer.

"No matter what I want and how badly I want it, I keep my counsel."

Anger diluted the desire that raged in her. "Sure. You want me on the terms that you decide. If you would kindly communicate those terms to me, I'd tell you where you stand."

"I know where I stand, and so do you." As he continued to gaze at her, she could see a change in his demeanor, a softening in him. "Can't you find some pants and a sweater? I thought we might go down to the warehouse. I need to check supplies."

"On Sunday?"

"It's the only day no one's down there."

"Sorry, but this is all I brought along. Don't try to make me into what I'm not, Russ. I don't look right in tight-fitting clothes, so I don't wear them. Case closed."

"Nonsense. You looked terrific in that dress you wore last night."

"And you need glasses."

The daggers from his gaze sent pain piercing through her. "That's the second time in less than twenty-four hours that you told me I don't know my own mind. See you." His shoulder brushed her as he dashed past her up the stairs and, she heard his bedroom door close with a louder than usual or necessary bang.

The remainder of her breakfast forgotten, Velma leaned against the railing for a minute thinking that if she hadn't promised to look after Tara and if she didn't want to investigate property in Baltimore, she'd go home.

"You could have him eating out of your hand. What's wrong?"

Her head snapped up. "I don't know, Drake. One minute, he's wonderful. The next, I'll say or do something that turns him off."

He regarded her intently. "And that happened last night as well as a minute ago. Right?"

She nodded.

"Then figure out what it is, and don't do it. He's straight, Velma. I told you that."

"I know he is. It isn't Russ; it's me. He sees me differently from the way I see myself, but I'm changing that."

He patted her shoulder. "See that you do. And make it up to Henry. Nobody ignores Henry's biscuits unless they want to eat cabbage stew."

"Thanks, Drake." She thought for a second. "Why are you . . . encouraging me? Why are you telling me this?"

"I know my brother. He rarely extends himself to people, and we've all known from the time the two of you met that you were special to him. And your being Alexis' sister has nothing to do with it; if anything, it's a strike against you. Russ is a strong man. If he makes up his mind that nothing should happen between the two of you, he won't change it." He started up the stairs, turned and walked back to her. "I want my brothers to be happy. Whatever works for them, works for me. You understand that?"

"I could use a brother like you," she said, and he treated her to his celebrated charisma with a wide grin.

"Get busy. It just might be one of these days."

Alexis didn't know how fortunate she was to belong to the Harrington family, a part of it, and loved by every person in it. She went up to her room, took her appointments calendar and cellular phone out of her briefcase with the intention of working. She had left the two weeks following her sister's wedding free of engagements so that she could take care of Tara while her sister and brother-in-law enjoyed their honeymoon. But with an agenda of her own, Tara got up early, dressed herself and, with Henry's blessings, left around eight-thirty that morning with Grant Roundtree and his father, Adam, to spend the day with them at the Beaver Ridge Roundtree estate twelve miles away.

Velma began work on the menu for the annual gala and awards dinner of the Society of Environmentalists that would be convened at the Ernest N. Morial Convention Center in New Orleans the first of February. Planning a gala dinner in the food capital of the United States was no cinch, but she knew she could pull it off. Problem was, she needed a test kitchen and a place to store supplies. And she needed office help. The business had become so big that she could no longer manage it with her computer and cell phone.

Five hours later, she drank her fifth glass of water trying

to appease her hunger. "I don't care," she told herself. "One day, he'll say I'm nice looking and mean it."

Russ tempered his urge to slam his bedroom door with all his might. He had gone to her to comfort her, to let her know that he cared, but he was damned if he would settle for less than he knew he deserved. He needed a woman who stood up to him as an equal, who believed him if he said that to him she was the Venus Di Milo incarnate. He snapped his finger. Her preoccupation with the way she looked began with the wedding—at least that was the first time she had revealed it to him. All right, so Alexis was dazzling in that slim white gown, but hardly one in a thousand women looked like Alexis, no matter what she wore.

Feeling inadequate beside her sister probably wasn't new, but he suspected that it had just come to a head. And it obviously explained why she didn't eat her usual breakfast. Maybe . . . Oh, what the hell!! He slipped on his favorite pair of alligator boots, a short mackinaw coat and a pair of wool-lined leather gloves and bumped into Velma as he stepped out of his room.

He grabbed her arm to steady her. "Sorry. Did I shake you up?"

"Not half as much as you did earlier," she said, her wry tone matched by an open, vulnerable facial expression.

She had a way of getting to him without trying, by just being herself. Honest and forthright. And it had been that way since he first saw her.

I'm a sucker for this dame, but I'm not caving in just because everybody expects me to. "Look," he began. "Can't you hem that thing or pin it up so you won't trip on it, put on a coat and come with me down to the warehouse?"

She looked up at him as if divining his motive. "All right.

Maybe Alexis has a pair of sneakers somewhere. They'll be a size too big, but I'll put on a pair of her socks. Twenty minutes?"

He trailed the back of his left hand down her cheek. "Perfect. Meet me at the garage door off the kitchen."

She headed first to her room, and he hoped she would hem that caftan or, better still, cut it off.

"I'm short enough without these sneakers," she said when she stepped into the garage.

He shook his right index finger at her. "I don't want another word of that." After placing a .22-caliber rifle on the floor of the truck, he helped her in and fastened her seat belt, which he had installed after Tara developed a passion for riding with him in the truck. "You're damned perfect just the way you are, and don't dispute me."

She folded her hands in her lap and lowered her head. "Yes, sir, your honor."

Laughter felt good, and she had a way of pulling it out of him. Rolling laughter poured from him only when he was with her, as it did then. "That's more like it," he said, when he could get his breath.

"Why did you bring the rifle?"

"I prefer not to run into a bear if I'm unarmed."

"Oh! Could you . . . uh—?"

"I can, and I have. Self-preservation is the first law of nature. When you're in the jungle, you play by the jungle's rules."

At the warehouse, he knew his pride was evident when he showed her through the ultramodern storage facility, built by Harrington, Inc., Architects, Engineers and Builders.

"What are we going to do?" she asked him.

"Check inventory. You're going to help me?" She nodded. "Telford pays a man to do this, but from time to time one of us double checks. That way, we control every facet of our business. Inventory is one of our most important assets; we don't entrust it to anyone."

He turned on a computer. "You sit at this desk and check the number of unopened boxes in each case against the number on this chart." He pointed to the screen. "Each case and each box in it has a numerical indicator. Okay?"

"Fine. What's in them?"

"Screws, clamps, nails, different types of fasteners." He stacked a dozen cases beside the desk. "I'll be back later," he said, and went to the basement to deal with cables and girders. After what he surmised was an hour had elapsed, he looked at his watch and gasped.

"She must think I'm crazy. I've been down here two hours." He left his coat and gloves on a pile of steel rods and raced up the stairs. At the top, he stopped still. She wasn't pouting or posturing in anger as he had expected, but was bending over a case to inspect its contents.

"I'm sorry, Velma. I'm so used to working here alone, and I got so involved that I . . . I hope you're not annoyed with me."

Still holding a box, she raised up and looked at him. "Why would I be annoyed? We came here to work, didn't we? By the way, I'd love to meet the genius who posted these records."

"Why?"

"'Cause every case is missing two or three boxes. I'd think you'd open a case, use all the boxes in it and then open another one."

He rushed to her. "That's what we're supposed to do. Let me see."

"Hmm. And that is how it looks on this spread sheet," she said, frowning. "Somebody is dipping in the till. Big time, too."

He didn't like the sound of it. To prevent rip-offs, they

built the warehouse on their own property where they could easily oversee it. And now, this. "You mind reading it off to me, beginning with PN3306?"

"Sixty."

He let out a long breath. "Four missing."

For the next three hours, as they rechecked, anger flooded him. Someone had discovered an easy way to increase his salary, but not any longer, he vowed.

"Every order, sealed and unsealed, in this place has to be checked. I don't know how to thank you. You took it seriously, and look what you found. Look, I'm hungry and so are you. Let's go."

"Why wouldn't I take it seriously, Russ? It's important to you."

He stared at her before shaking his head as if that would straighten out his mind. "Don't go there, man," he cautioned himself. To her, he said, "Thanks. I appreciate that. I'll get my coat and gloves and be right back."

When he returned, she had put on her coat—another point in her favor; unlike some women he had known, she didn't wait for him to do for her what she was capable of doing for herself, though he would happily have held her coat for her.

"Well, what do we have here?" she asked of the snow flurries that glided down on them as they stepped out of the warehouse.

He let his gaze roam the sky. "I don't think we'll get much snow." He took out his cellular phone and punched in a number. "Henry, is Tara home?"

"She's here. Adam brought her home soon as it started snowing. I'm gonna take a nap, so you and Velma can make yourselves a sandwich or something. Drake's out on that horse of his, and Tara's playing the piano. See you at supper."

* * *

He drove with care, mindful of the slippery road, and how glad he was when a big brown bear ambled across the truck's pathway.

"Now, you know why I brought along this rifle. If I got stuck on this road, one of those babies could turn this truck over." He let a grin circle his mouth when he looked at her. "Bear meat's good. It is," he added when she shivered.

He stopped the truck at the front door, got out and went around to help her climb down. "Want my baseball cap?" he asked her, deliberately holding her longer than necessary. "Pile your hair up under it so it won't get wet."

"Thanks. I'll keep it as a souvenir." He was about to ask, souvenir of what? when he remembered how candid she could be, so he let a smile suffice for a response.

"I'm sorry about the problems at the warehouse, but I had a good time, and I learned a lot. Thanks for taking me along."

With his fingers tight around her arm, he sprinted with her to the front door, opened it and stepped inside with her. "I'm in *your* debt. I'm not sure I would have opened a sealed case to check its contents."

"Some of those that had been tampered with were sealed, and some had been opened. That's what's mysterious."

"But only temporarily." He shifted his gaze lest he betray himself. "After I wash up, I'm going to the kitchen and see what I can find to eat. Want to meet me there in about ten minutes?"

"Thanks, I sure will. I'm starved."

"I'm not surprised. See you later."

She hated to face him again wearing something he disliked, but what could she do about the caftan? She checked her address book, found the cellular phone number that he gave her during her visit the previous Christmas and called him.

"Russ, this is Velma. Can you wait half an hour? I have to do something."

"All right, but if I starve, be prepared to make amends."

"What kind of amends?"

"Not to worry. Whatever punishment I mete out will be enjoyable. I guarantee it."

"Make it an hour. By that time, your tummy should have begun pinching you, and you'll be eager for vengeance."

"Watch your words, woman. I'm serious even when I'm joking."

"Who's joking?"

She heard him suck in his breath and could barely stifle a laugh. He was a tough man, and he worked hard at hiding his feelings, but she knew when a man wanted her. And he did. The question was whether he'd do anything about it.

"Let's see how you talk when you're not hiding behind a telephone wire," he said.

"Really! And I'd like to see how you act when your iron-clad control slips. Lord, please let me be right there when it happens."

After a telling silence, he said, "Would you say those same words if I was there with you?"

I may regret this, but what the heck! Right now, I'm batting zero. "If you doubt it, honey, step out into the hall."

His labored sigh reached her through the wire. He was two doors away, and he might as well have been in Baltimore. The silence bore into her like a screw tearing through wood. Had she angered him?

"You still there?" Only air and the sound of her own breathing. She lay the phone on the table, but didn't hang up on the chance that he still held the receiver. After brushing her hair, she inspected a navy blue cotton caftan, decided that it would have to suffice and sat on the edge of her bed to put darts at the waist and shorten it.

A knock on her door sent her blood racing like a spooked thoroughbred. She grabbed her chest as if to slow down her heartbeat. Knock. Knock. A greater urgency characterized the second knock, sending the unmistakable message that he would knock until she opened it. With unsteady fingers, she threw the garment on the chair, then got up and walked in her stocking feet to the door. Another knock followed by, "Open the door, Velma," startled her as her hand reached for the knob.

"Hi. I mean, what's the matter?"

He stared down at her. "You got the nerve to ask me that? If I had been dressed, I'd have been here ten minutes earlier. Now, what was that about seeing me without my control?"

Did she dare? She stepped back, the better to see his eyes. "That's not what I said."

"What *did* you say?"

She folded her arms across her chest to hide her shaking fingers. "I said I'd like to see how you act when your iron-clad control slips. Looks to me like it's firmly in place." She looked at her watch, realizing that she enjoyed needling him, that the more she did it, the more secure she felt.

His eyes darkened, but that didn't unnerve her; no matter what color they happened to be, they lured her to him the way a magnet attracts nails. "Don't you think I'd better finish what I was doing so we can eat? You threatened to punish me if I made you starve. Remember?"

He leaned against the doorjamb, casual-like, but exuding an energy she hadn't known he possessed—a sexual energy that encircled and entrapped her, kindling a fire at the edges of her nerves. In his yellow shirt, short-sleeved and open-collared, and with his arms folded across his chest, the sight of his hard biceps and prominent pectorals made her mouth water.

She hadn't seen him that way before: a big jungle cat—hot, powerful and ready to pounce.

Why didn't he say something? It was as if he was waiting for her to burn all of her bridges. When she lowered her gaze, it fell on his flat belly and meandered downward to the flap of his tight jeans. Barely half aware of her movements and gestures, her gaze traveled back to his face. Quickly, she shifted her glance, only to see him ball his fists, loosen them and ball them again. She felt his heat then, and tremors streaked through her as the rough male in him jumped out at her, heating her blood and driving it straight to her loins.

Mesmerized, she couldn't tear her gaze from his face, and as he seemed to drag her into him, she rubbed her hands up and down her sides. Frustrated. Up and down. Up and down. His stance widened and, nearly out of her mind with the sweet and terrible hunger that gripped her, she threw back her head and rimmed her lips with the tip of her tongue.

"Why don't you—?"

He stepped into the room, reached out, brought her to his body and lifted her to fit him, securing one hand on her buttocks and the other on the back of her head.

"Russ!"

He kicked the door closed with the back of his foot. "Open your mouth. My God, I want you!" With a harsh, terrible groan, his mouth came down on hers. Then, she had him inside of her at last, knew his taste, knew the hard thrust of his tongue as he plunged in and out of her simulating the act of loving. More. She had to have more of him. All of him. With her nipples beaded and hard, she moved against his chest, and when she sucked his tongue deeper into her mouth, he let the wall take his weight and his hand tightened on her hips.

Her blood raced. Her mind shut down and she rubbed her left nipple. The hand that had held her head caressed her breast, and teased her nipple, drowning her in a pool of sensuality, and her hips began to undulate against him, leaving no doubt as to what she needed from him. Suddenly, he attempted to push her away, but she wouldn't be denied. She had him at last and didn't want to let go. Her weaving body invited his entrance, and he rose against her, hard and strong. Weakened by the force of her own libido, she slumped against him in what they both recognized as surrender.

Cradling her in his arms, he sank into the lounge chair beside the window. "I can't talk about this right now," he said. "Just . . . I'd like us to stay here like this for a few minutes." She sat on his lap with her head against his shoulder and his arms tight around her, and couldn't have said a word if he had asked her to. She didn't know how long they remained in that position. Her only thought was that she never wanted to leave him. But she understood the decision was not and never would be hers alone, for she had known from the start that Russ charted his own course.

After a long while, he said, "It's been about an hour, and I feel as if something's eating away the lining of my stomach."

She hoped that didn't signal his intention to pretend he'd never kissed her out of her mind.

"And you promised some sweet revenge. If it's anything like what you just meted out, I can't wait."

He set her on her feet and got up. Rubbing the back of his neck with his left hand, he glanced at her from the corner of his eye. "Still like to challenge me, huh? Don't do that, sweetheart. I never accept a challenge unless I am sure I can win, and I won't play games with you."

"That isn't a challenge," she said, a little miffed. "Aren't you used to women telling you the truth?"

"Let's say I'm not used to expecting it. What were you doing that was supposed to take an hour?"

She pointed to the blue caftan that lay across the back of

the desk chair. "Hem that and fit it with darts front and back."

A frown clouded his face before slowly dissolving into a grin. "You're kidding. Because of what I said?"

"I figured if seeing me in these graceful, flowing caftans gave you something akin to gall bladder, I'd better find something else to wear."

The frown returned. "*Gall Bladder?* I didn't—" She stared at him as a grin circled his lips, spread over his face and lighted his eyes seconds before laughter poured out of him. "Ah, Velma. Baby, you're precious." He gathered her to him, looked down into her face and grinned. "I'm too hungry to start that again. Come on. I'll make you a sandwich."

She slipped her feet into her high-heeled shoes and, with her hand in his, tripped down the stairs. At the bottom, she stopped. "Russ, how long has it been since you heard that piano?"

"I don't know. What I've been concentrating on had nothing to do with music. Let's walk down there and see what she's up to."

Just before alarm set in, she saw the note one the piano: "Dear Aunt Velma, I'm over at Mr. Henry's house with Biscuit."

She handed the note to Russ. "Would you believe a five-year-old can write this well?"

"With five teachers in the house, why shouldn't she? Besides, she's smart. I hope she put on some boots before she went down to Henry's place."

"Is she allowed to go there?"

"I think that's the only place she's allowed to go without getting permission. To the kitchen with you, woman."

Their laughter echoed through Harrington House as they raced down the hall, free of pent-up tension and inhibitions, open to each other. He found the makings of sandwiches on a platter in the refrigerator. "Like your bread toasted?" he asked her.

"Yes. Thanks."

He made turkey sandwiches, ham sandwiches and tuna-salad sandwiches, stacked them on a platter, cut some sour pickles, added jars of mustard and horseradish and headed for the breakfast room. "You put out some plates while I get us a couple of bottles of beer. Okay?"

She found place mats and set the table. If anyone had told her that she would be sharing these idyllic moments with Russ, seeing the loving and tender side of him, she might have accused them of idiocy. Yet, although she believed that the wit, tenderness and gentleness he'd showed her defined him as truthfully as did the tough, stoic and solitary side of him, he had not yet acknowledged their passionate exchange, and she wondered if he ever would.

"I'm not going to question it," Russ said to himself, as he searched in the bottom of the beer and soft-drink chest for two bottles of Czech Pilsner beer, his favorite. "I'd been dying to do that since I met her." He reached into his back trouser pocket for a handkerchief and wiped perspiration from his forehead. "Whew! She hit me like a speeding train. I may regret it later, but right now, I'm not sorry."

He walked back into the breakfast room in time to see her nearly trip on the edge of the Turkish carpet his mother fancied and which Alexis brought up from the basement to brighten the room. He rushed to support her.

"Why do you wear those things?" he asked of her spike-heeled shoes. "It's a wonder you don't fall and kill yourself."

"The world loves tall, slim people," she told him. "I'm not slim, but the shoes make me look taller."

He bit into a ham sandwich and chewed the bite carefully

before helping it down with several swallows of beer. "They don't make you taller. Some women put their hair up on top of their head thinking that adds height. Neither makes a speck of difference, so why not be comfortable and"—he told himself to say it even if she got mad—"why not accept yourself? If you don't love yourself, it's damned near impossible for anybody else to love you."

She removed the top slice of bread from the turkey breast sandwich and scraped the mayonnaise off the remaining slice. When she didn't look at him, he knew he had touched a sensitive spot. "Don't smooth it over," he cautioned himself. "This is an issue between us, and if she doesn't solve it, we're not going anywhere."

"You want me to believe that a man like you who can have any woman that appeals to him is so different from all the rest, that these tall, willowy women like Alexis aren't your ideal, the kind you want? You honestly expect me to believe that?"

He put the sandwich aside, leaned back in his chair and looked hard at her. "Whether or not you believe that is immaterial to me. There're your words; not mine." He pointed to her plate. "You ate hardly any breakfast, so you're half-starved, and look at what you're doing to that sandwich."

"I don't like not being able to wear pretty clothes, so I'm going to lose weight."

He felt for her and deeply so, but he knew it was unwise to express it. "To me, at least, you're a beautiful, charming, and witty woman," he said, "but if you want to change yourself into someone I won't recognize, well . . . it's your body and your life. I wish you luck."

She put the glass of beer on the table, untasted. "Those are the nicest . . . the most endearing words that I remember ever having heard. Thank you."

"But you don't believe them."

"I know you mean them."

"But I'm either blind or I've got poor judgment, right?" That kind of talk would solve nothing. He poured the remainder of her beer in her glass, cut a turkey-breast sandwich in half and put it on her plate. When she looked at him with an appeal, an entreaty, he removed the top slice, scraped the mayonnaise off the bottom slice as she had done earlier, and set it in front of her.

"Even if you want to lose weight, don't damage your health."

Her smile, radiant and grateful, affected him like a shot of adrenalin, and he wanted to get her back into his arms and try to soothe away her concerns. However, he wanted to communicate to her trust, caring and reasons why she could hold her own with any woman. He cleaned the table, put the dishes in the dishwasher and left the kitchen as he found it.

"You're neat," she said.

He couldn't help laughing. If Telford, Drake and Henry had heard that, their opinions of Velma would have plummeted. "Neatness is something I never expected anybody to accuse me of. I straightened up the kitchen because I wouldn't like to eat cabbage stew for dinner tomorrow night. That's Henry's favorite form of punishment. Let's go in the den."

He motioned for her to sit in the big brown wing chair, and he sat opposite her on the sofa. "What was it like growing up with Alexis and your parents? You've told me that your home life was unhappy. How did you and Alexis manage to come out of a dysfunctional home as the women you are—educated, successful, professional and refined? You are interesting women. How'd it happen?"

"I'm fifteen months older than Alexis and, even with that little difference, I was protective of her. Our mother taught us how to be ladies, but not how to be women capable of dealing aptly with life. I'm not sure she knew. Our father ev-

idently didn't think it his responsibility to nurture us; he left
the house and us children to our mother and, as I look back,
that was a principal source of their never-ending battles.
Alexis and I got love from each other. She'll tell you they
loved us, but she has never made me believe it.

"I think I told you that our mother ran out of the house
one winter night, escaping the bickering, and froze to death.
Before the funeral, Father left us a note saying he was going
to Canada, but didn't include an address. A man who'd do
that didn't love his daughters."

"You can't be sure of that, because you don't know the
measure of the guilt he felt. How old were you?"

"Eighteen. I'd just finished high school, and Alexis was in
her senior year. We sold the house and everything in it to pay
for our college educations. If there had been a will, we might
have had a nest egg, but the state took a huge chunk of it.
One of these days, I'm going to confront that man."

He understood her bitterness, but he didn't believe in letting such things clog his thinking or his outlook. "Let it lie,
Velma. Harboring ill feelings against anyone is like filling
yourself with poison. Try to drop it."

"That's what Alexis tells me, but she's a Quaker, and it
seems to give her a peacefulness that I wish I had."

"Your father let you down, but you emerged like a newly
minted platinum disc. A lovely woman. Forgive him." He
looked at his watch. "I'm going to check on Tara, Henry and
Biscuit. That little dog trails Tara every place but school.
Thanks for the pleasant company. See you at dinner."

He put on his mackinaw coat, a pair of old boots and a
woolen cap, got his rifle and a pair of gloves and headed
down the hill to Henry's cottage.

Tara opened the door. "Hi, Mr. Russ. We were going to
the house as soon as Mr. Henry finished feeding Biscuit. Mr.
Henry gave Biscuit a red sweater so he won't get cold." He

lifted her, walked into the house, and for the first time, he kissed the child's cheek.

"Biscuit is a lucky little pup," he said, wondering what had just gotten into him. "Henry, it's snowing harder than we'd thought, so why don't you come prepared to spend the night over at the house?"

"I was thinking I'd do that."

Russ realized he was still holding Tara and set her on her feet, but a strange feeling pervaded him, shocking him. He shook his body as a bird flexes its wings after a bath. For the first time in his life, he had a yearning for a child of his own.

Chapter Three

Back in her room, Velma stared at the blue caftan that she had begun to alter before Russ altered *her*. Until the previous evening, he'd never seen her in anything but a caftan, and that hadn't stopped him from liking her and wanting her. She was damned if she'd ruin her dress. She hung it up. If he didn't want to look at her in her green silk caftan, she'd eat her dinner in the kitchen. From the window she saw that the snow had become heavy, and recalled the Christmas Eve just past, the happiest Yuletide of her life. She had thought that night that Russ would at least kiss her with the passion that she knew he felt, but he had settled for putting his arm around her and resting her head against his shoulder.

That night, the Harrington men had sat around the Christmas tree and the lighted fire in the den, each with a woman, along with Henry and Tara in an idyllic family celebration. Everyone, including her, had thought that the men would pair off for the night with their women, but Russ had walked up the stairs with her to her room, kissed her cheek and told her good night. And it was clear to her the next morning that Drake did not spend the night with Pamela. Three extraordinary men governed by their own counsel. She heard the voices on the lower floor, and rushed down to greet Tara.

"Auntie Velma, do you want to hear me play the piano? Mr. Henry gave me my piano, and Mr. Telford teaches me how to play it."

"You're gonna have to stop calling Tel Mr. Telford," Henry said.

"I know. Soon as he comes back, I'm going to call him Daddy."

"Hadn't you better ask your mother about that?" Russ asked. "You have a daddy."

"I know, but I never see him, so I only have to call him that when I see him. I'm going to let Mr. Telford be my daddy." The tears that glistened unshed in her eyes finally dripped down her cheeks. "If he won't be my daddy, I'm going to run away." Her eyes beseeched Russ. "Can't he be my daddy, Mr. Russ? Can't he?"

Russ dropped down on his haunches and pulled Tara into his arms. "He *will* be your daddy. It seems to me he has been ever since you came here. Telford loves you as much as you love him, so no more tears. All right?"

She nodded. "Do you think my mummy will let me call him daddy?"

He hugged Tara and stroked her back. "You're five, going on six, so it seems to me you should call him Dad."

She threw her arms around Russ' neck. "Thanks, Mr. Russ. That's just what I'll call him."

Velma wondered at the significance of that strange conversation with a five-year-old and thought of her father, a man with whom she could never communicate to her satisfaction. Russ understood Tara and knew how to quiet her fears. She looked at Henry who seemed awestruck, with his gaze pinned on Russ. No one had to tell her that to Henry, Russ' behavior was out of character. She mused as to the reason and, especially, whether it could be traced to what had gone on between Russ and her that day. Her heart fluttered, more with joy than with excitement, when she thought he might be softening, that—like her—he had begun to feel the need for love.

"I'll be in and out for the next couple of weeks," Russ told Velma after dinner that evening. "We're thinking of building an annex to the Florence Griffith Joyner Houses in Philadelphia, and I need to work there for a while. If you need me, you have my cell phone."

"Who'll shovel the snow?" She asked the question more to show an indifference to his leaving Harrington House for the remainder of her stay than because she worried about snow removal.

"If it continues after I leave, Henry will call a snow-removal company. Drake's leaving in a couple of days for Barbados. We're building Frenchman's Village there—an apartment, hotel, shopping mall complex—and, as you know, he's the engineer for all our projects."

"You're the architect, Drake's the engineer, and Telford is the builder. How did that happen?"

"We decided on that when we were teenagers, and it suits us."

"Wasn't Drake planning to eat dinner at home tonight?"

"He decided not to risk driving through this snow. He'll be here tomorrow. Join me in the den for some cognac? Henry and Tara will probably have some kind of juice."

She didn't want casual chitchat. As much as she loved her niece and Henry, she didn't want to talk with them right then, and the thought of an hour of impersonal conversation with Russ had about as much attraction for her as poison ivy. Nonetheless, she said, "I won't drink, but I'll sit with you while you enjoy yours."

He leaned against the big walnut commode that had belonged to his maternal grandparents and looked at her. "How is it that you so often manage to surprise me with the right words or behavior?"

She lifted her shoulder in a slight shrug. "It isn't intentional, I assure you."

He straightened up. "Oh, I know it isn't. It's you."

To her relief, Tara began to yawn and nod almost as soon as they went into the den. "I'd better put her to bed," Velma said to Russ and Henry.

"Good night. Sleep well," Russ said, letting her know that their evening was over.

"Good night," Henry said. "As for sleeping well, ain't no point in telling you to do that, cause you're gonna be awake half the night. You young people think you got forever to start living. Dumbest thing I ever heard of."

"You've got my life all laid out, Henry," she heard Russ say as she started down the hall with Tara, "but I will live it my way, not your way or Telford's or Drake's. You listening to me?"

"Yeah, and I ain't heard nothing you haven't said before. You're running from that one just because we think she's good for you. Go ahead. Make yer own bed hard. I ain't the one sleeping in it."

She would have been happier if she hadn't heard that exchange between Russ and Henry. She put Tara to bed, laid out her clothes for school the next day, pulled off her shoes and tiptoed up the stairs to her room. The last thing she wanted was to bump into Russ. He and Henry didn't seem to notice that she ate hardly any supper. Hunger pangs pelted her belly, and she drank two glasses of water in an effort to ease the pain. Still longing for solid food, she eased between the sheets and tried to sleep. Three hours later, she sat up and turned on the light beside her bed, exhausted from dreams of a battle with oversized steaks and spareribs and of trying to hide huge hamburgers from Russ, whose mocking laughter echoed everyplace she went.

Before breakfast the next morning, Russ got the snow-plow and cleaned the circle in front of the house, the road leading to it and the one that connected the house and the warehouse. Sitting in the office at the warehouse, he telephoned Allen Krenner, their foreman, and told him what he and Velma had discovered.

"I haven't got a clue as to how that could happen, Russ," he said, "but from where I sit, at least one of the culprits works for either the manufacturer or the packaging company."

"You don't think the accountant is involved?"

"Hard to say, Russ, but I wouldn't bet on it."

He trusted Allen, a longtime family friend. "Whoever he is, I'll find him." He hung up, made the necessary notes in the daily log and went home to get his breakfast. After eating, he checked the weather on local radio and phoned Velma. "We got about eight inches of snow last night, so I doubt school will open today."

"Oh dear," she said. "I had planned to drive Alexis' car to Baltimore today. I need to take care of some business."

"The roads will be open by ten o'clock, but most businesses will probably be closed. If it can wait until tomorrow, you can drive me to Baltimore, and I'll get a train there to Philadelphia."

Twenty minutes later, he had reason to be thankful that he was at home. "Aunt Velma! Aunt Velma!" he heard Tara screaming, obviously on her way up the stairs.

He bolted from the room and met her as she reached the landing, both hands on her belly. "What is it? What's the matter?"

"My tummy. My tummy. I thought it was candy, and I ate it."

He grabbed her and ran as fast as he could to Alexis' rooms. "What? Show me."

She pointed to the remainder of a substance that he supposed Alexis used either in her sculpting or painting. He tried to force Tara to give up the substance, but she couldn't, and when her eyes widened, he knew that her stomach pains had intensified. He went to a closet.

"Get your coat," he told her.

She pulled one off a hanger, and he sped down the hall still carrying her in his arms. "Velma!" he called. "Get your coat and let's go."

He ran into the kitchen. "Henry, Tara swallowed something toxic, and I'm taking her to the hospital in Frederick this minute."

He pulled out his cellular phone and punched in Velma's number. "Get ready to come with me right now," he said, when she answered. "Tara swallowed something, and we have to take her to the hospital."

Minutes later he put Velma, Tara, blankets, and his first-aid kit in the back seat of his Mercedes and headed for Frederick. "How do you feel, Tara?" he asked the child, more worried that he would let either of them know.

"My tummy hurts, Mr. Russ."

"I know, sweetheart," he said, "and that's why we're taking you to the doctor."

"Did I do bad, Mr. Russ?"

"No, you did not. You made a mistake."

"Do you think she has a fever?" he asked Velma.

"Her forehead is cool, so I don't think so."

"Last time I was in Frederick Hospital, I went there to see my uncle. One of the shocks of my life. Someday, if you're interested, I'll tell you about it."

"If it was important enough to shock you, of course I'm interested."

Her words sank in, even though he didn't want them to impress him. He drove several miles without speaking, but at last he was compelled to respond. "I wish I could see inside of your head, know how your thoughts form and why they seem almost always to fall so nicely on my ears."

"I try to tell the truth. I am not interested in being clever or witty, though some people say I am. I just try to be myself."

He wished he'd been looking at her when she said that. "Including the other night when you blew kisses to your fans in that restaurant? It will be a long time before I let you forget that."

"I told you that I'm a prankster. That came as natural to me as breathing."

"How's she doing? Don't let her go to sleep."

"Right. And that's what she's trying to do."

"Talk to her. Anything to keep her awake. We should be there in about ten minutes, providing a highway patrolman doesn't catch us."

At last, he parked in front of the hospital, jumped out and took Tara from Velma's arms. "If you pray, this would be a good time," he told Velma, slammed the car door shut and raced into the emergency room.

A nurse took Tara from him, but although he knew he had to give the child up for care, a heaviness formed in his chest when he handed her over. "She swallowed some material that her mother uses either for painting or for sculpting, and she complained of terrible stomach pains."

"Thanks. Don't worry. We'll take good care of her."

"Can we go with you?" he asked the nurse.

She shook her head. "Sit here. I'll let you know how she is."

Velma's hand clutched his wrist. Should we put the car in the parking lot?"

"Yeah. I guess so." But leaving the waiting room was like deserting Tara, and he couldn't do that. As if she understood his feelings and divined his thoughts, she held out her hand. "Give me your keys. I'll move the car."

He reached into his pocket, got the keys and handed them to her. "Thanks." Feeling that his heart would break, he stared up at her as she stood over him, her face the picture of compassion. Then, on what was certainly an impulse, she leaned forward and kissed his lips.

"You got her here in time, and she'll be well taken care of," she said. "It's hard for me too, but please try not to worry. You're a wonderful man. I'll be right back."

She left him, and he leaned forward with his knees apart, rested his forearms on his thighs and let his hands dangle in front of him. Useless. Powerless. Unfamiliar feelings. He got up, walked to the other end of the small room and re-traced his steps. Walls white and bare, gray chairs side by side around the room. Why didn't someone put pictures in waiting rooms, or anything to distract a person's atten-tion? He walked back to the other side of the room. If only he could kick something! Thinking that an hour had passed and wondering why Velma hadn't returned, he looked at his watch and grimaced. Less than twenty min-utes had elapsed since he stopped his car in front of hos-pital.

Since he stopped . . . What had he been thinking? He didn't allow anyone to drive his car except Telford and Drake, and he wasn't keen on their doing it. Maybe he should pray, but he didn't know how to begin. He sat down, leaned back in the chair that was too small for his big frame and closed his eyes. He remembered the Lord's Prayer from his childhood, and he said it then in barely whispered tones. When he opened his eyes, Velma stood before him.

She handed him the car keys. "I parked on the side. No news yet?"

He shook his head. "No. She's so little. What could they be doing to her?"

"Probably pumping her stomach."

He sprang forward. "Will that hurt?"

"I'm not sure. I hope not." He started to get up, and she tugged at his hand. "Honey, try to relax. They'll tell us something soon."

She caressed his hand, and he let her do it; he needed the comfort. "That little girl is so much a part of me. If she were my own child, I doubt I could love her more. Telford, Drake and Henry adopted her at once, but it took me a long time. One day late last summer, I saved her life, and she's been in here ever since." He pointed to his heart. "I couldn't bear it if she—"

She sat beside him then and put her arm around his shoulder. "She's going to be fine."

He closed his eyes in a effort to blot out his surroundings and tried to think of his next project, but he failed. He sensed that Velma stood up abruptly and opened his eyes to see the nurse approaching, her face brilliant with a smile. He rushed to meet the woman.

"Is she . . . ? How is she?"

"She's fine, but we want her to rest a couple of hours before you take her home."

"You're sure? You're sure she's all right?" he asked her.

"Absolutely. You got her here in good time, so there won't

be any permanent damage, but there certainly could have been. She said she thought she spit it out when she realized it wasn't chocolate, but she swallowed enough of it to make her very sick. If you want something to eat or drink, there's a cafeteria on the first level down. Take the elevator."

"Can we go in and see her?" he asked. "Just for a second?"

"I'd rather not. It's important that she rest. Are you Mr. Russ?"

"Yes. I'm Russ Harrington, and this is Velma Brighton, Tara's aunt."

I'm glad to meet you. I'm Nurse Parker. She said to tell you she's not sick. She'll be out in two hours."

"Two hours to . . . well at least she'll be all right," he said to Velma. "Let's go downstairs and get something to eat." They got on the elevator and went to the cafeteria. He chose a hamburger, french fries and salad. He put it on the table and stared at it.

"What's wrong?" Velma asked him.

He ran his fingers through his silky curls and then rubbed the back of his neck. "I must be losing it. I don't eat junk like this."

"This chicken fried steak is pretty good, want a sample?"

He tasted it. "Not bad." He dumped his tray of food into the trash bin and returned with the steak, mashed potatoes and a container of milk.

"After we finish, I want to go upstairs and see my uncle. He's terminally ill, and my brothers and I are his only visitors. I'd like you to come with me, if you don't mind."

"I don't mind. I'll be glad to go with you."

He found Fentress Sparkman propped up in bed reading the Bible that Russ had given him as a present the previous Christmas.

"How are you feeling, sir?"

"Some days, I feel pretty good, some not. I'm glad to see you. Telford sent me an invitation to his wedding. Did he marry a woman you like?"

"Yes indeed, and he's on his honeymoon right now. This is Velma Brighton. Velma, my uncle, Fentress Sparkman."

Sparkman nodded his head. "Glad to meet you." He patted the Bible. "It was good of you to give me this, Russ. I read it all the time. You and your brothers have made my last days happy ones."

Russ grasped the frail hand that reached out to him. "It's too bad we couldn't have had a normal relationship all along, sir. I'll be back to see you as soon as I can."

"Don't make it too long. Thanks for coming and bringing your friend."

They told him good-bye and went back to the waiting room. Almost as soon as they sat down, he heard himself telling her the story of his uncle and his father. "I don't know why I'm telling you this," he said, "except maybe because it still surprises me, makes me wonder. That story had a strong effect on me; I pay careful attention to the way I treat people. A stranger, even an enemy, could be a close relative."

He got up and walked toward the door leading to patient care. "What's holding them?" He walked back to Velma. "All I have is that nurse's word."

Velma walked over to where he stood strung out with anxiety. "She's a professional, Russ, and she deals with patients' families all the time. She wouldn't mislead us."

He slapped his left fist in his right palm. "You're right, I know, but it's taking so long. How could she be so weak that she needs to rest for two whole hours?" He remembered to call Henry who he knew was worried about Tara and anxious for her well-being.

"How is she?" Henry asked as he lifted the receiver.

He told Henry as much as he knew. "It appears that she'll be as good as new. I just didn't want you to worry more."

"Worry more? I never been so upset in me life. Thanks for letting me know."

As Russ hung up, the door swung open, and the nurse wheeled Tara through it in a wheelchair. "Mr. Russ! Aunt Velma! They put a tube down my throat, they gave me this big bunny and these balloons, and when I get big, I'm going to play the piano for them."

He raced to the wheelchair, stopped and stared at the nurse. "Can't she walk?"

"Yes, but we always release patients this way."

"Do you have a clerk or someone who I can pay?" he asked her.

"Fill out this form, and we'll send you a bill. After you do that, she may go."

He thanked the nurse, filled out the forms and lifted Tara from the wheelchair. He looked the child in the eyes. "If you ever give me another scare like this one, I'm going to tweak your nose." Her giggles filled his heart with such happiness that he couldn't help hugging her as he walked to his car with her in his arms and Velma holding his hand.

As he drove home, the thought occurred to him time and again that he'd learned much about himself in the last five days, all of it important and some of it life-changing.

After supper, when they had finally tucked the excited little girl in bed, he sat with Velma and Henry in the den musing over what he considered his odd behavior.

"Henry, I had planned to work on a project we have in Philadelphia, but what happened with Tara suggests to me that I ought to work here at home until Telford gets back.

Drake can't stay home; he has to leave for Barbados tomorrow."

"Well, I ain't what I used to be, and I haven't driven a car in years, but Velma here can drive. You don't have to change yer plans. We can manage."

"I know I can count on you, Henry, and that you care as much for our home as I do. After all, it's your home. But my mind tells me to stay here, and I don't mind doing it. My computer and my brain are about all I need in order to work."

Around ten in the morning, two days later, he looked up from his draft board and glanced at his bedroom window just as a silver-gray Lincoln Town Car turned into the circle that graced the front of Harrington House. A familiar car. He got up, went downstairs and opened the door at the first peal of the doorbell.

Jack Stevenson. "What can I do for you, man?" he asked Jack.

"I want to see Alexis." He started past Russ, but didn't get far before he felt the weight of Russ' hand on his shoulder.

"What do you want with her?"

"It's not your business."

Same old Jack. "It may be her husband's business. Would you like me to give him a message?"

"What husband? What the hell are you talking about?"

The pleasure he got from anticipating Jack's reaction to his next words sent tremors through his body. "Didn't anybody tell you? Alexis Harrington is on her honeymoon with Telford Harrington. As we speak, man."

"You're lying to me."

"Sorry. It's a matter of public record. Check it with the minister of the First Presbyterian Church in Frederick, or with me, since I was best man and legal witness. You want to check it with Velma? I think she's playing checkers with your daughter."

Jack stared at him. "The big guy. He got her after all."

"Nobody in this house ever doubted that they would marry. Uh . . . You want me to call Tara?"

"Naah. I'm . . . I'm out of here."

"Really? Yesterday, just before I took Tara to the emergency room in Frederick General Hospital, she asked me if she could call Telford 'daddy,' and I told her she had a daddy. She said she only has to call you daddy when she sees you, and she doesn't see you often. What do you think she should call her stepfather?"

"Damned if I care." Jack moved the few steps toward the front door, but Russ had one more rock to toss and put his hand on the doorknob, effectively imprisoning Jack.

"I got your daughter to the emergency room in time for the doctors to save her life, but since it didn't occur to you to ask how she is, I won't tell you." He opened the door, and with a sweep of his hand, invited the man to leave.

"I see we won't be bothered with you in the future, buddy, and good riddance," he called after Jack.

He went into the kitchen and related the incident to Henry. "There's no telling how he might have behaved if I hadn't been here. Jack learned months ago not to cross me."

Henry raised an eyebrow. "Oh, his type is nothing to worry about. Just put his five-year-old daughter in front of him, and he's ready to go." He stopped kneading dough. "Alexis sent him an invitation to the wedding, but I guess he didn't open it, probably thinking it was something about his daughter. She don't need him. Tel's her daddy, and has been since the day she came here."

Russ stuffed his hands in the back pockets of his jeans

and leaned against the kitchen counter as memories of his mother flooded his mind. "I've often thought that there ought to be some kind of test for parenthood, or at least mandatory classes for people who bring children into this world. My mother and Jack Stevenson would have been prime candidates."

Henry oiled a bowl, put the bread down to rise and covered it with a sheet of plastic. "It ain't good to think like that, Russ. Miss Lizzie was one of those people that needed freedom. She loved her children, but she didn't like being married and having to answer to another person."

"I'm glad she bothered to give birth to me and my brothers, but if she did that, she should have accepted her responsibility to take care of us. Instead, she took off without warning whenever she felt like it. I remember waking up one morning and going in my parents' room and asking my father where she was. He wiped a tear, didn't look at me and said, 'I don't know, Son. I don't know where she went.' That was the day before I started first grade. She came back, and she left again. When dad died, she came back and stayed, but I didn't give a damn. I was eight."

"I know. It affected you more than it did Telford and Drake. Since Mr. Josh died, your brothers and me are the only people you let get close to you. Best thing that could have happened to you, Son, was finding out how much Alexis loves her child. She come here that day, she told me later, with a total of thirty-eight dollars to her name right after she signed away twelve million in exchange for full custody of Tara."

He released a sharp whistle. "I didn't know it was that much. Jack Stevenson is a jerk. I don't see how any human being could fail to love Tara. Well, if I'm going to stay home, I'd better get to work." And he'd have to find a way to avoid Velma except at breakfast and supper when it would be impossible. As it was, thoughts of her interfered with his concentration, and that was a first.

His mind made up, he told Henry, "I think I'll work in the office at the warehouse. Less distraction."

"Yeah," Henry said. "She ain't likely to go down there. If I need you for anything, I'll call you on your cell phone."

He didn't bother to answer. As long as Henry could breathe, he'd say whatever came to his mind. "See you at supper. I'll get a sandwich out of the vending machine in the basement at the warehouse."

"Won't taste like nothing."

"Right, but it will serve the purpose."

At the same time, Velma was considering ways to avoid encountering Russ. She knew that it was mandatory that they all eat supper together, for Alexis had made that a house rule. However, nothing prevented her from leaving before breakfast. That evening after supper, she laid out Tara's clothes for school, read stories to her niece and went to her room early. She heard Russ's steps as he mounted the stairs and her breathing stopped until she heard his bedroom door close. She had known that he wouldn't knock on her door, and she hadn't wanted him to, but in her heart she longed for him to come to her.

She slept fitfully, rose early and got Tara ready for school. She'd never been efficient at braiding hair, and Tara didn't like the result. "Aunt Velma, I'm going to learn how to braid my hair," she said after looking in the mirror.

"I don't blame you. The school bus will be here in ten minutes, so let's hurry." At the front door, to her surprise, Russ was waiting for them.

"Hi," he said. "I'll walk with her out to the bus. It stops

almost directly in front of the house, but the walkway may be a little slippery."

She stood in the foyer beside the big oval window watching as Russ lifted Tara, hugged and kissed her and set her on the bus. She hadn't known him to be so affectionate with the child and wondered again at the reason. He seemed surprised to find her still standing there when he returned.

"I had planned to work in Philadelphia for a few days, but with both Telford and Drake away, I think I'd better stay close to home." He told her about Jack's visit the previous afternoon. "I wouldn't put it past him to do something to upset Telford, who he detests. I told the bus driver not to release her to any man but me, and I've just this second decided to go to the school and warn the principal."

"Surely, he wouldn't—"

"A principled man wouldn't treat his daughter as Jack treats Tara. He didn't want Alexis when she was his wife, but as soon as she divorced him for philandering, he wanted her back. Telford got in his way. I'd better get moving."

"I'm driving to Baltimore today. I hope to be back before supper time." It was on the tip of her tongue to add: so you won't need to work in the warehouse.

As if making the connection himself, his left eyebrow shot up. "Driving Alexis's car?" She nodded. "Better let me check it out."

He opened the closet beside the door leading to the downstairs game room and got a bunch of keys. "Be back in a few minutes."

She sat on a stair step, waiting for him and ruminating about his protectiveness. He was responsible for the house and the family in Telford's absence. Maybe that accounted for it.

"It's okay. Be sure and take my cell phone number in case you need me for something."

"Thanks."

He stood at the bottom of the stairs, and she sat on the third step, but he still towered over her. She looked up at him, seeing his long-lashed and slumberous dark eyes, full bottom lip and square but dimpled chin; the muscled chest that emphasized his six-foot-three-and-a half-inch height, his long legs, flat belly and the aura of power that he exuded. She sucked in her breath and knew he saw and heard her.

His breathing accelerated, and she could see his Adam's apple bobbing furiously. Her tongue rimmed her bottom lip, and he seemed to gulp air. He wanted her, and she wanted him inside of her. Disgusted with herself for having started it and for her inability to control her passion for him, she jumped up and raced up the stairs. But he reached the landing when she did, pulled her into his arms and lifted her hungry body to his, chest to chest and loins to loins.

"Russ. Oh, my Lord."

He stared down at her, his nostrils flaring, his eyes telling her what she knew his mouth wouldn't say. His lips were so close that she breathed his breath, and her senses swirled dizzily as her nostrils caught the odor of his heat. Spirals of unbearable tension snaked through her and, frustrated beyond reason, she put her hands behind his head and brought his lips to meet hers, open and waiting.

He plunged his tongue into her mouth, and she took all that he would give her, as he tested and tasted every centimeter, swirling and tantalizing until she moaned the agony of her desire.

Recovering as best she could, she rested her head against his shoulder. "Stop playing with me, Russ. You give in to your feelings when they overwhelm you, but you don't want this to go anywhere."

"I am not playing with you. Whether you were aware of it

or not, you gave me one of the most seductive invitations a man could get. You know how things are with us. What was I supposed to do? Pretend you weren't there?"

His arms tightened around her and she kissed the side of his neck. "You're famous for your self-control, so—"

"So I decide when to use it. Is that what you're accusing me of?"

She leaned back and gazed into his face. So close and so precious. "Don't you?"

His rough half-laugh almost startled her. "I would have gotten to you if I'd had to jump over a mile-deep ravine. Decision had nothing to do with it." A grin spread over his face. "I suppose I ought to put you down."

"Yes, considering how much I weigh."

"It probably gets less every day, considering how little you're eating."

"That's the problem. I haven't lost an ounce, and I'm hungry all the time."

"Then stop being vain and eat. Losing weight won't change your personality and probably not your face. They're what I find most attractive in you or any other woman. I'd better get dressed if I'm going to Tara's school." He leaned forward and kissed her forehead. "Be careful driving."

She had told him she hadn't lost weight, but she had actually gained a pound. "If this continues, I'm going to see a nutritionist," she vowed to herself. "Henry, I'll be in Baltimore most of the day," she called to him from the kitchen door.

"Ain't no need for that. Russ is working at the warehouse today."

"Henry, I am not going to Baltimore to avoid Russ."

"You are so. He's running from you, and you're running from him, though I can't for the life of me see what the two of you are running *for*. Any adult who's around you for ten minutes can slice the heat with a knife, it's so thick."

"That's not very consoling, Henry."

"I ain't supposed to console you. That's Russ's job. I'm just watching the two of you postpone the inevitable. Soon as Tel and Alexis get back here and start showing you how nice it can be . . . You just watch. I ain't saying no more."

After determining that Henry didn't need anything from Baltimore, she started on her journey, shocked to have discovered that Russ had driven the car out of the garage and positioned it so that she wouldn't have to back out.

"I could love that guy," she said to herself, and not for the first time. "He's everything I need, but I don't believe he's even thinking about developing a relationship with me, to say nothing of marrying me."

In Baltimore, she made her first stop at a real estate company that specialized in small business needs. After settling with the agent as to what she wanted, she headed for Layne Bryant's, intent on seeing how she would look in jeans.

She didn't like the jeans, stretch or otherwise, and settled on two pairs of pants, one oxford gray and the other dark tan. She looked around until she found a sweater, below-hip length and very loose with one side tucked and held up with a self bow. She liked the design and bought lavender and burnt-orange versions of it. Then, she gathered her courage and went into the dress department, trying not to notice the beautiful caftans as she passed them. She saw a navy blue silk-crepe dress that had three-quarter-length sleeves, a fitted silhouette and flared ruffles at the hem. She tried it on and, encouraged, found a burnt orange replica and bought both of them.

Maybe I'll never wear them, she thought, unless Alexis says they look all right. But what did her svelte sister know about what did or didn't look right on a short, overweight woman. She put her parcels in the trunk of the car, bought a bag of miniature snickers to make herself feel better and headed back to Eagle Park, munching as she drove, diet forgotten.

She arrived at Harrington House half an hour before seven, heard Tara practicing the piano and rushed to her room to shower and change. She expected comments from Henry and Tara, but she prayed that Russ at least would keep his opinions to himself.

When she got downstairs, feeling self-conscious in her brown pants and burnt-orange sweater, Tara greeted her, "Aunt Velma, Mr. Russ came to my school today and talked to my teachers and he brought me home from school, so I didn't have to ride the bus. Mr. Russ loves me."

She knelt before the little girl and wrapped her arms around her. "Of course he loves you, all of us love you."

"You look pretty, Aunt Velma. Is Mr. Drake coming home tonight?"

"No, dear. He's gone to Barbados for a few weeks."

"Oh. He likes to go there a lot."

Tara took her hand and walked with her to the breakfast room where Russ and Henry waited for them. As soon as they sat down, Russ said grace.

"Mr. Russ says my grace takes too long," Tara said, blessing them all with her smiles and giggles.

"Henry, this food is first class," Russ said of the medallions of pork, saffron rice, artichoke hearts in cream sauce, and asparagus.

"I made a brown Betty for desert. Alexis left a slew of recipes, and I'm using 'em. I suppose you know how to cook, Velma."

At least he hadn't mentioned her clothes. "Henry, I have two degrees in home economics, and I make a living catering galas and other affairs. And you ask me if I can cook."

"Well, you don't have to do the cooking yourself. You can hire somebody."

She glanced at Russ, and found his gaze pinned on her. "If you want a sample, I'll cook one day this weekend."

"I'd like a sample," Russ said almost before the words left her mouth. "Make it Sunday. One of my college buddies is having supper with us. I was going to take him out to dinner because I don't like adding to Henry's burdens, but since you're cooking—"

"Ain't no burden to add an extra plate. He ain't on a special diet is he?"

Russ shook his head. "Tara, did you finish your homework?"

"Yes, sir. I did my whole workbook."

"What about your reading?"

"I read that yesterday. Can I go play the piano?"

"After your Aunt Velma or I checks your homework, you may."

"And after Mr. Henry gives me some black-cherry ice cream," she said, bringing a laugh from the adults.

Once more, she left the table feeling as if she hadn't eaten in weeks. She took the plates into the kitchen, rinsed them and opened the dishwasher. As she raised up to get the plates off the counter, she glimpsed Russ' gray pinstriped pants.

"You could at least make some noise when you walk. Scare the bejeebers out of a person."

His hands gripped her shoulders, his lips covered hers, and she tasted him. "Russ!" His fingers sent fiery ripples spiraling along her arms, and she pulled his tongue into her mouth, loving him, shaken by the terrible sweet hunger he stirred in her.

When he released her, she gripped his arms for support. "Russ. Honey, would you please leave me down here on planet earth. I want to stay off this seesaw of yours."

"I like the way you look, and I wanted you to know it. Warm and sweet." He kissed her nose. "Nice nose, too."

In the days that followed, she planned her time carefully and managed not to be alone with Russ except on the rare occasions when he surprised her, as he said, "Just so you'll know I'm here and that I know what you're doing."

She didn't ask him what he meant, because she knew. She also knew that until he indicated that he wanted more from her than hot kisses, more that a casual relationship, she intended to stay out of his way.

"If you're going to let me cook tomorrow, Henry, I'd better run into Eagle Park and do some shopping."

"Guess you'd better. If you told Russ you'd do it, that settles it. He don't break his word for nothing, and he expects the same of everybody else. Check the pantry before you make yer list."

She returned from shopping, made a large bowl of créme Courvoisier, put it in the deep freezer, made raspberry sauce for it, marinaded a pork roast and called Henry.

"The kitchen's yours till around one tomorrow," she told him.

"If you need from one to seven to get dinner together, you must think the president's coming."

She winked. "What makes you think he isn't?"

Not to be outdone, Henry called to her as she walked down the hall, "If that's the case, it's high time you started acting like it. If a man's head honcho, his woman lets him and everybody else know it."

Russ turned the corner with Tara holding his hand. "Who's head honcho?"

Henry didn't look at him. "Humph. Since you don't know, telling ya won't do a bit of good."

She hurried up the stairs, went to her room and busied herself with plans for the gala she had contracted to service in New Orleans. The more she thought about it, the less attractive the venture appeared.

Darkness had already set in that Sunday afternoon around five-thirty when she began setting the dining room table. She decorated it with a large crystal bowl of pink and white rose buds that she had bought in town the previous day, and pink candles in crystal candle holders. She used a white damask cloth and napkins, white porcelain that had a tiny pink floral design, heirloom silver and crystal goblets.

At the last minute she decided to wear her new navy blue dress, added rose quartz beads and earrings, combed out her hair, remembered his comment about short women piling their hair on their heads to look taller and pinned hers up on top of her head.

"I'm not going to remake myself for him, and I want him to know it," she said aloud and she walked down the stairs.

She dressed Tara in a red-and-white-checkered pinafore and secured her hair with two red clamps. "Sorry, honey," she said, "braids will have to wait till your mother gets back."

"How many more days?"

"Five."

She clapped her hands and exuded happiness as giggles poured out of her. "And then Mr. Telford will be my daddy . . . I mean my dad."

"He's been your dad ever since the wedding."

Tara's wide eyes stared up at her. "Will he like being my dad?"

"He will love it, because he loves you. Let's go. It's supper time."

"Who's she?" Velma heard a male voice ask, looked in

the direction from which the voice came and saw a tall man-
for-the-ages sexual dynamite staring at her.

"She's Velma Brighton. Why?" Russ asked his guest.

"Why? You have to ask why? Is she yours?"

"No, she isn't," Russ replied. "Dinner's ready."

Chapter Four

Russ steered Velma away from her usual place at the table, beside Tara, and sat her opposite him. With Telford away, he sat at the head of the table.

"That's my mummy's seat, Aunt Velma."

"Not tonight," Russ said. After saying grace, he looked at Velma. "Ms. Brighton, this is Dolphe Andrews. We were roommates for a while when I was in graduate school."

"Delighted to meet you, Ms. Brighton. He told you about me, but hasn't said a word about who you are."

To his surprise and delight, Velma answered, "Glad to meet you. Russ will get around to it. He takes his time with just about everything."

"But I'll only be here overnight," Dolphe said.

Velma passed Henry the tiny crab cakes that served as the first course. "That's plenty of time for him to tell you whatever he wants you to know."

Dolphe looked from Velma to Russ and back at Velma. "Am I missing something here? I don't want to louse up my welcome."

"Keep on the way you're heading, and you're gonna do a first-class job of it," Henry said. "Russ, you mind carving this roast? I'm enjoying having nothing to do to this meal but eat it."

Russ served Henry a slice of pork roast, and then served the others at the table. Henry tasted a small piece and chewed it slowly. "Now this is what I call a pork roast."

"Yeah," Russ said, glad that Henry had moved Dolphe away from the subject of Velma, "It's delicious." Although Dolphe was a good student, he also had a reputation as a stud. Women clamored over him, and he had always seemed to relish the adulation. However, Velma treated him as if he was just another human being, and he'd bet it had been years since Dolphe Andrews met a woman who looked straight through him.

"This is *some* meal," Dolphe said. "I haven't had a meal like this since I left home to go to college. Who cooked it?"

"My aunt Velma," Tara said. "Most of the time Mr. Henry cooks, but sometimes my mummy cooks, too. I loved the crab cakes, Aunt Velma."

Russ pushed back a laugh. First Henry and then Tara had thwarted Dolphe's attempt to make Velma the center of conversation. He wondered what his friend would try next. He knew he could end the game by telling Dolphe that Velma was important to him, but how he felt about Velma was none of the man's business. After all, *she* didn't even know what she meant to him.

"I don't see how you can top off this meal," Henry said to Velma.

"I was thinking the same thing," Dolphe said. He looked at Russ. "Man, you live like a prince."

Returning from the kitchen with servings of crème Courvoisier, Velma said, "Why shouldn't a prince live like a prince?"

The visitor's whistle was barely audible, but Russ knew Dolphe could be dense when it suited him.

"I stand corrected," Dolphe said.

"And not a bit too soon," Henry interjected, put a spoonful of dessert in his mouth and gasped. "Taste it, Russ. I've died and gone to heaven. I just know it."

"Can't I have some, Aunt Velma?"

"It's full of cognac, Tara," Russ said. He went into the kitchen, got a spoon and let her taste his. "Well?"

"Oooh. It's so good."

"But you'll have black-cherry ice cream," he said. She nodded. Such an easy child to manage. Her wants were so simple. Give her love, and she radiated happiness. He put two scoops of ice cream in a double cone and gave it to her.

"Thank you, Mr. Russ. I like ice cream in the cone."

Have a seat in the den with Henry and Tara while Velma and I straighten up here. Cognacs and liqueurs are in the bar," Russ told Dolphe.

"You don't like him?" Russ asked her as they worked together.

"I neither like nor dislike him. Generally, I don't like men who advertise their sexuality. They're usually immature."

"What kind of men *do* you like?"

If he had the courage to ask, she had the guts to tell him. "Well . . . since you ask . . . A man with a great physique, tall, muscular and lean." She pretended not to see his eyes narrow. "Clean shaven, square chin, nice dark eyes, full bottom lip, dimpled chin, long tapered fingers, thick chest, long silky lashes, curly hair. I like a man who loves children, is tough with life but gentle with women, children and weaklings, who's honest and loyal. A man who talks when he has something to say."

She put the pot lids in the pantry, hung the pots on the rack and threw the towel at him. "If you know one like that, tell him to come up and see me sometime, to quote that queen of old black-and-white movies, Mae West." She didn't wait for his reaction, but headed for the den, certain that she had rung his bell. If he didn't know what he looked like, he had to be one humble brother, and she didn't believe that. Beaming with pleasure at having rocked him, at least for the moment, she strolled into the den, took a seat in the corner of the sofa and crossed her knees, something she rarely did owing to her conviction that her legs were too large.

"Where did you learn to cook like that?" Dolphe asked her the minute she walked into the room.

I thought he'd given up. "Food is my business, although I'm not usually cooking it."

"Anybody who can read can cook," Henry said. "All you need is common sense and a little imagination. Velma here has it down to an art."

"My mummy can cook."

"She sure can do that," Henry said.

Dolphe sipped his Tia Maria quietly, ever so often glancing at her from the corner of his eye, and she knew he had something to say as well as the courage to say it.

"This is an unusual household," he said, and she sat forward waiting for the sally that she knew would follow. "It's an extremely tightly knit group, but as I've figured it out, only Tara and Miss Brighton are related. Who's absent?"

"My two brothers and my sister-in-law."

Her head shot up, for she hadn't realized Russ was in the room. "And you're right, Dolphe. We are a very close family."

Dolphe looked at Velma. "Are you part of this family? I mean, do you live here?"

"I'm visiting. And I suppose you'd say I'm a part of this family because my sister and my niece belong to it."

He drained the glass. "I don't know any more than I did when I entered this house."

"Then quit fishing," Henry said. "If you want to know whether there's anything between Velma and your friend, there is. Plenty. Or my name ain't Henry. And it don't take Mr. Einstein to figure it out."

Apparently dissatisfied with Henry's answer, he looked at Velma. "Is there any truth to what he just said?"

She leaned back against the sofa and swung her right foot. "Mr. Andrews, I cannot imagine Henry telling a lie. He's both too proud and too arrogant to even consider lying. That answer your question?"

He made no attempt to hide his disappointment. "Yeah. Too bad. I was beginning to think that, but I had to be sure."

She wondered what kind of man made his pitch to a woman in the presence of two men and a five-year-old. She'd have to remember to get Henry's view on that. As she sat there, happy that the conversation had shifted from her, it occurred to her that the man's apparent interest hadn't impressed her. It certainly hadn't flattered her. Tara began to yawn, so Velma asked to be excused, took Tara's hand and started out of the room.

"You're not telling me good night, Tara?" Russ asked, then took her hand, lifted her into his arms and smiled at Velma. "I'll carry her." She walked along with him, afraid to say a word, for she'd learned that he had a reason for everything he did. He opened the door and sat Tara on her bed.

"Is it too late to read something from your book?" he asked Tara. Although she said it wasn't, her head slumped to his shoulder. "She's too sleepy. Let's get her to bed."

She prepared Tara for bed, threw back the bed cover and Russ lifted the little girl and tucked her in.

Although barely awake, Tara smiled up at him. "'Nite, Mr. Russ." He placed the teddy bear in her arms, kissed her cheek, turned out her light, opened the bathroom door and clicked that light on so that she wouldn't be afraid if she awoke.

"Now, young lady. I'm assuming you're aware that I know what I look like."

She raised an eyebrow and started for the door. "Really. You're the last person I'd have thought would be self-centered. I can't believe you spend time looking at yourself in a mirror." She opened the door and dashed out of the room.

"Go ahead. Run. I always get what I go after."

She sprinted up the stairs and into her room, closed the door and leaned against it. She couldn't risk another of those sizzling sessions with Russ. The last one had nearly gotten out of hand. She'd been on the verge of putting his hand on her breast when he set her on her feet. Nobody had to tell her that, considering how fast and how thoroughly he could heat her up, if he ever put his mouth on her body, whatever he wanted would be his.

If she was going to have an intimate relationship with a man, she preferred it on her terms. At present, Russ defined and engineered their relationship, or at least it seemed that way to her. If she were svelte and beautiful like Alexis, she'd be the one calling the shots. She performed her ablutions, got in bed and waited for sleep. After about an hour, she heard Russ and Dolphe come upstairs and nearly laughed aloud when she realized that Russ walked with Dolphe to his room before going to his own room on the other end of the hall. Russ once told her that he left nothing to chance. She put the pillow over her head and went to sleep, comforted by the thought.

The next morning, after weighing herself, she called a nutritionist, a college classmate who lived in Baltimore.

"What's up, girl?" Lydia Swindell asked after an enthusiastic greeting. "Where are you?"

"I'm in Eagle Park, Maryland, not too far from Frederick, and I've decided to settle in Baltimore. I'm going to establish my business there, and I can be closer to Alexis and Tara. They're my only relatives, and I want to see them as often as I can."

"No tall, dark and handsome on the scene?"

How did she answer that? "There's a possibility. Lydia, I've got to lose weight. Knowing that I'm shortchanging myself and probably ruining my health is getting me down. You should have seen Alexis in her wedding dress. She was—"

"Now, now. Haven't I been telling you since our college days not to compare yourself with anybody else? And especially not your sister. She puts half the female population of this country in the shade."

"I know that, but why can't I look at myself in the mirror and be proud of the way I look? How would you feel if a man couldn't get his arms all the way around you? Huh?"

"For goodness sake, stop exaggerating, and find a guy with longer arms."

"Finding a guy is enough of a problem without having to worry about the length of his arms. I'm serious, Lydia. I've been eating practically nothing for a week without losing an ounce. I ate a decent meal last night and gained three pounds. I want you to work out a diet for me."

"Okay. When are you coming to Baltimore?"

"Tomorrow. I'll stop by your office."

She entered the brick-faced building around eleven o'clock that morning and walked through the expansive, marble-columned lobby wishing she could afford such a regal address for her own business. However, that was out of the question; she'd be lucky to find the kind of place she needed at any price. Lydia's office impressed her with its spaciousness, carpeted floor, living room-type furnishings and atmosphere of comfort and warmth.

"You've arrived," Velma told Lydia. "I'm happy for you."

"Thanks. I was afraid to take this place, but I'm glad I did. The better looking your surroundings, the more willing people are to pay what you ask. I was making chicken feed before I moved here."

Velma made a mental note of that, sat down, took out her notebook and pen and asked Lydia, "Do you think you can help me?"

Lydia stared at her. "No small talk, eh? This *is* serious. All right. First thing, I want you to pack up all your caftans and store them someplace where you can't easily reach them, for example, with a storage company. Weigh yourself on the same scale once a week only. Drink a minimum of eight glasses of water a day."

"That will certainly keep me busy."

"I'm serious, Velma. Please fill this out. I need some information about your medical history."

"Medical history? I just want to—"

"I'm not interested in your sex life, just your health. Besides, unless you changed a lot, I pretty much know what your secret life is like." She laughed. "Nothing happening with you that you couldn't tell a ten-year-old."

"Now who's exaggerating? I want to buy a house or an apartment, preferably a house. What part of town should I look in?"

"I like the Druid Hill Park area, but there are others as nice."

"I'll drive through that area this afternoon. After years of living like a vagabond, seeing my Wilmington, Delaware, apartment about every three months, I want a normal life."

"That will be good for your weight, too. Follow this." Lydia gave her a folder. "Do everything written here, and don't even call me for one month. Then, come back to see me."

"Thanks. I see you haven't lost your crowd-control, school-marm personality."

"You bet. If I hugged you and told you to *try* to follow these instructions, you wouldn't take me seriously. Would you?"

"Probably not. See you in a month."

She drove through the residential sections around Druid Hill Park, noted houses for sale and co-op buildings that advertised vacancies and made her next stop, her real estate agent.

"Finding a house or an apartment will be much simpler than getting what you need for your business," he said. "Warehouses that can be modernized without spending a fortune are hard to find, unless you don't mind being located in a low-income neighborhood."

"I certainly don't expect to find a warehouse in an upper-class residential area," she said. "I'll be in touch."

She made Macy's her last stop before leaving the city. After three hours, she had four daytime dresses, two suits, four blouses, three sweaters and a tailored leather skirt. No more hiding behind caftans, and she hoped Russ Harrington wouldn't assume she'd changed her style of dress for him. She was doing it for herself.

She avoided Russ at breakfast because she knew that, unless he had to catch a plane, he wouldn't eat before seven-thirty, and usually not before eight. The morning before Alexis and Telford were to return, he was sitting at the table when she got there at seven o'clock.

"With the newlyweds back here tomorrow, you'll find it much easier to pretend I'm not around, though I doubt your present eating habits will go unnoticed. Henry said you have half a grapefruit, a soft-boiled egg and black coffee for breakfast, and almost the same for lunch. I don't know how long you plan to continue this, but it's not healthful."

"I'm following the advice of a nutritionist."

"What? What for?"

"Because I want to lose weight. Neither you nor any other man ignores women who look like Alexis."

"Is that what this is all about? You've had her for a sister all your life, and all of a sudden you're—"

"I don't expect you to understand. Even you gasped when she arrived at the altar in that sleek wedding gown."

"You listen to me," he said, waving his fork at her, "Alexis is Telford's kind of woman. She's the type he's always been attracted to. *But she is not my type.* And while we're at it, what did you mean by telling me that I am the kind of man you like, describing me and then pretending you said nothing out of the ordinary? That wasn't a pass; that was an invitation."

"Was not. You asked me, and I told you the truth. Besides, I didn't expect you to do anything about it; that would be out of character."

He leaned toward her. "This isn't the first time you've challenged me to show you who I am. You want to see me lose control but, honey, if I do, you definitely won't want to be there."

She had riled him, and knowing it sent pleasure rippling through her. She had an urge to laugh, but didn't think it wise and settled for a grin. "Russ, it may not please you to know it, but you cannot possibly frighten me—that is, not unless you jumped from behind a bush on a dark road late at night. I think of you as protective."

"Really! Protective wasn't one of the words you used when you were being fresh with me. Any other notions you have of me?"

She put both hands behind her head and winked at him.

"Uh huh. I think you're sweet as sugar. Uh . . . I'd better check on Tara."

"Don't worry. Grant Roundtree and his father came for Tara a few minutes before you came downstairs. She's going ice skating with Grant and spending the day with him. So you can sit here and back up your statement."

"I don't remember what I said." When he stared at her, she said, "Honest, I don't remember the exact words."

He leaned back in his chair, let his gaze brush over her and lowered his lashes. If he had wanted to send her blood rushing through her veins, he succeeded admirably. If that weren't reminder enough of the way he could make her feel, his full bottom lip crooked in a slow grin and wound its way over his face until he erupted in a laugh.

"You think you handcuffed me by telling me I'm honorable. Well, only one perfect person ever walked this earth, so I can slip up occasionally and still bear the title." He rubbed the back of his neck, pushed back his chair and stood. "If I decide to make you remember your exact words, that won't change your opinion of me, will it?"

"Who's that laughing in—?" Henry walked into the breakfast room with his fruit and cereal and stopped when it was clear to him that Russ was the only other man in the room. "Drake ain't back from Barbados yet, so . . ." He scratched his head as if in wonder. "That wasn't you laughing, Russ."

"Oh, but it was," she said. "Hearing Russ laugh strikes my ears as birds singing in early spring."

Henry put his food on the table, went back to the kitchen and returned with a cup of coffee. "Soon as I eat this I'll be out of the way. Next, somebody'll tell me pigs fly."

Russ went to the kitchen, returned with the coffee pot, filled Velma's cup and his own and took the pot back to the kitchen. "You're not out of trouble, Miss Brighton," he said.

"You owe me, and I will collect. Trust me. If either of you needs me, I'll be at the warehouse most of the day."

Her gaze trailed him as he strolled out of the breakfast room and headed for the stairs. With him away from the house, she would be able to work. In three weeks, she had to pull off a gala for some New Orleans society women. She phoned her local contact to confirm her menu and seating arrangements. Then, she made certain that her usual New Orleans supplier could give her beige cloths and burnt-orange napkins with beige trim for fifty round tables that seated ten people. With hotel reservations, flight and chauffeur arrangements confirmed, she put on her coat and went for a walk along the Monacacy River a quarter mile from Harrington House.

She was thinking how glad she was that Russ had provoked her into buying pants and sweaters, when she saw him, a lone figure in the gray mist of the afternoon standing with his hands in his pants pockets and gazing out at the river. Her first impulse was to leave him to his solitude, to get away before he saw her. But she couldn't will herself to walk away, for he seemed shrouded in loneliness. She had not thought of him as a lonely man, but how well did she know him? With plodding steps, she walked toward him, hoping he wouldn't resent the intrusion. Ten feet away, she stopped and waited for him to acknowledge her presence.

He didn't know how long he stood there. Time had come for him to make changes in his life, changes that would alter the lives of those closest to him. He loved his family, Alexis and Tara included, and he couldn't think of any place other than Harrington House as home. But to his way of thinking, Alexis was mistress of Harrington House—indeed, she had been since the minute she entered its door—and she should have the right to run it as she pleased. That meant she shouldn't have to deal with his idiosyncrasies or with Drake's antics, likeable although they usually were. And it was time he went out on his own, away from the safe umbrella of family love.

He wanted a family, but he was already thirty-four, and he'd probably be near sixty when his oldest child was graduated from college. If he was lucky enough to have three children, his seventieth birthday wouldn't be far away when the last one got an undergraduate degree, and that meant he'd be working until he was ready to fall into his grave.

Velma. He liked so many things about her, not the least of which was the way she made him laugh, their similar taste in music, her pranks, and the way she got fresh with him whenever it suited her. He loved her candidness, and how hot she got whenever he put his hands on her. He'd never come close to feeling for another woman what he felt for her, but did he want to deal with her hang-ups, her wobbly self-esteem?

He already knew one thing about his feelings for Velma: he didn't want another man to have her. He had resisted telling Dolphe to shut up and stop tomcatting at Velma, and doing so had drained him emotionally. But he wasn't ready to show his hand and raise both Velma and Henry's expectations.

His mind wandered back over the years and the comfort he had always found in the love, camaraderie and, later, professional successes with Telford and Drake. They had been together all their lives, and now, he would be the one to split up the trio. He didn't have to guess how his decision would set with his brothers, but he had to leave the comfort of that cocoon and make a life of his own. Chills skittered through his body as a feeling of loneliness enveloped him.

A snap as if something stepped on a dry twig or stick brought his head quickly around expecting to see a wild animal. "Velma! What are you doing here? How long have you been here?"

"I came out for a walk. Walking is my favorite sport, and I love to walk alone in the woods when I have the chance. When I saw you, my first impulse was to turn back, not to intrude upon your privacy. But seeing you alone out here on a day like this, I . . . I couldn't. If you'd rather be alone, I'll understand."

He didn't tell her that she appeared at the moment he needed her, and he didn't feel like emptying his heart to her. He reached for her hand to let her know he welcomed her.

"This is one of my favorite places. In the summer, I often sit by the river for hours, working or just straightening things out in my head. I walk in these woods mainly during winter when the foliage is sparse and I can see my surroundings. When I heard your footstep, I prepared myself to deal with a bear, reindeer or some other wild animal. Be careful out here alone."

He slipped an arm around her shoulder. "It's getting cloudier. Let's go home." As he said the last three words, his gut tightened, but he hoped she attached no significance to it.

When they reached the house, he opened the front door, closed it and looked down at her. "I'm leaving for Baltimore around seven tomorrow morning to meet Telford and Alexis." He stuck his hands in the back pockets of his jeans and looked into the distance. She deserves to know first, he told himself.

"I'd appreciate your confidence in respect to what I'm about to say." She nodded, an expression of worry clouding her face. "When you visit here again, I will probably have moved into a place of my own, most likely in Baltimore. It's time I was on my own, and Telford and Alexis need privacy to work on their marriage. I want them to succeed."

"How strange," she said, and he thought her bottom lip quivered, meaning she wasn't certain he would like what she had to say. "I'm giving up my apartment in Wilmington, Delaware, and moving to Baltimore so I can be closer to Alexis and Tara. I signed papers with my real-estate agent yesterday. He's looking for either a house or a co-operative apartment. It's time I settled all my interests in once place."

He certainly had not expected that, but it made sense to move nearer to her only relatives. "What part of the city are you considering?"

"The areas close to Druid Hill Park. I love those big old houses and elegant apartment buildings."

"Good choice. I'm thinking of the area near the armory. We would almost be neighbors. Let me know if I can help in any way. I'd be glad to examine the building for structural soundness, wiring, plumbing, and the like."

She gazed up at him, eyes wide and lips parted. "You would? Really?"

"Of course. Have you forgotten that I'm an architect?"

She shook her head. "I just didn't connect that with my buying a house. Thanks. You don't know how much better I feel about it. I'll call my agent Monday morning and tell him, so he'll know he'd better not try any hanky panky with little Velma."

He leaned forward and kissed her cheek. "I doubt he'd try to hoodwink one of the Harrington brothers. See you later."

She looked at him for what seemed like a long time, then braced one hand on his shoulder and the other at his nape, tiptoed and kissed his lips. "See you at supper."

Before he could grab her and settle her against him, she turned away and dashed up the stairs. He hadn't meant to kiss her and start a fire in his loins, but she wanted the kiss and took it. He lifted his shoulder in a slight shrug. *I can handle that. She has as much right to what she wants as I have to what I want. When a woman wants me, she should let me know it. If I like what she's offering, she won't regret it.*

She spent a while digesting what Russ had just told her. She understood that when she chanced upon him by the river he was ruminating about his life. It no longer surprised her that he had seemed lonely, for he had been. The decision to separate himself from those he loved so dearly—even if he didn't wear that love on his sleeve—had unsettled him. He might be living within ten blocks of her, walking distance, and it could mean everything or nothing for their relationship. It occurred to her that he was turning over a new leaf and she might not be on the next page. Well, what would be, would be.

She showered, resisted the urge to weigh herself and settled down to finish the last chapter of *Blues From Down Deep.* If only her life would smooth out as Regina and Justin's did, she mused after finishing the story, she'd be a happy woman. But no longer in daily close proximity to Russ, she doubted that she stood a chance.

I've been let down before. I didn't care nearly as much; I was five years younger, and I bounced back without a whimper. But . . . She thought for a minute. *If I plot my own course and follow it, I'll have no regrets, and I'll have everybody's respect, my own foremost.*

At ten after one the following afternoon, Sunday, she answered her cell phone. "Russ speaking. I'll be there in three minutes. Please alert Tara and Henry." He hung up before she could respond. She dashed down to Alexis' room and pulled Tara away from the piano.

"How long is three minutes?" Tara asked her.

"Less time than it takes to count to fifty. Come with me." Tara scooted off the piano bench, clapping her hands. "My mummy is coming home right now."

She stopped by the kitchen and told Henry. "Let's wait for them at the front door." Henry looked at her as one would an unwanted stranger. "You want me to stand out there in the cold on those steps?" At that moment, she heard the toot of Russ' Mercedes, and she and Tara bolted for the front door.

"Mummy! Mummy!" Tara shouted and raced to the car. Telford headed around the car to open the door for Alexis, but she was out of it before he got there, picked up Tara and hugged her as the child plastered her face with kisses. Almost immediately, however, she wiggled out of her mother's arms and ran to Telford. "Dad. I thought you and Mummy were never coming back." He picked her up and hugged her, swung her around and accepted the kisses that she poured all over his face. When he set her on her feet, he hunkered in front of her. "You've grown in just two weeks."

"Is it all right if I call you Dad?"

Velma's heart constricted at the smile of joy that covered his face. His love for that little girl shone in his eyes and in his whole face.

"That's the most precious thing you have ever said to me. It's what I want you to call me."

Giggles tumbled out of Tara. "Did you find out what is a honeymoon, Dad?"

"Did I . . . ?"

"Uh . . . yeah . . . I did. It uh . . ."

Velma couldn't help casting a glance at Russ who succumbed to the mirth he felt and let the laughter pour out of him.

Telford cocked his head in Russ' direction. "What on earth? Well, I never . . ."

"No need to be shocked," Henry said. "He's been doing

that lately. Darned near frightened the devil out of me first time I heard it."

In spite of the needling, Russ couldn't seem to stop laughing. Tara capped it when she said to Telford, "Now that you're my dad, Mr. Russ is my best friend."

"What about Grant?" Henry asked her.

"I like to be with Grant, 'cause he's my friend, but I love Mr. Russ."

Velma saw the expression of humility on Russ' face. What a complicated man! Tough as he was, his tenderness went deep. At the astonished expressions on Telford's and Alexis' faces, Velma intervened. "Explanation is simple. As long as he had Telford for competition, Russ didn't stand a chance. Let's go inside before I freeze."

She stood near the bottom of the stairs and watched as Telford lifted Alexis and carried her up the stairs to his room. She glanced at Henry, whose gaze had fixed itself on her as if he waited for her to acknowledge the validity of one of his pronouncements. She shook her head, denying it, but he had said the love Telford and Alexis showed for each other would shock her into acknowledging what she needed and didn't have. She looked away from him, blinking back a tear, and her glance fell on Russ, who stared at her with such hunger that she grabbed her chest as if to slow her heart beat.

To save face, she grabbed Tara's hand and started toward the rooms Alexis had shared with her child. "Your mummy and dad will be down here in a few minutes, so practice your music so you can play for them."

Velma closed her eyes and let the notes of Brahms "Lullaby" float over her. Lost in the music, she nearly jumped from the chair when familiar lips closed over hers, warm, sweet and loving.

"Russ," she whispered, as her fingers clung to his shirt. "Please don't do things like this to me. You're not even ready to find out whether we've got anything going for us. I—"

His lips cut off her words. When he stopped kissing her, she looked up at him, not doubting that her face represented a big question mark.

"I couldn't help it," he said. "I felt what you felt, and I needed what you needed. Let's walk out into the hall." They left the room, but the music followed them.

"You're right. I haven't decided where I'm headed, but neither have you. And I haven't decided because it will be written in stone when I do. If I tell you something, you can put your life on it. I can say this much: You're important to me, and I won't knowingly do anything to hurt you."

She appreciated his words, but they didn't satisfy her. "When I catered that gala celebrating the Harrington brothers' success as builders, I sat at a table with you, your two brothers and the women you brought with you, plus Adam Roundtree, Wayne Banks and their wives. All the men were your type, and all the women except me were beautiful, tall and had flawless figures. You associate with those men and others like them. It's like a club of successful men and their women. I can't convince myself that I belong there or that you want me too. If that's what's holding you back, believe me, a few kisses do not obligate a man. At least not to me."

He grabbed her shoulders. "When in hell did you get this fixation on how you look, and what a washout you are? I could have taken any of several women to that gala. I took you, and I was not doing you or Alexis a favor. I was doing what pleased me. You can be so sweet, so convivial, charming and loving, and then you can say something like that to me. It's getting to be painful."

"I'm sorry, Russ. You can't understand, because you're

the equal of your brothers in every way and in some respects you're their better."

"It seems that way to you, perhaps, but you didn't grow up in the shadow of Drake Harrington. From the time he could crawl, the word he heard most often from strangers and neighbors was *cute*. He smiled and whatever he wanted, he got it. After our father died, Telford and I both catered to Drake's every wish. Women, old and young, raved over him. He could grin and get anything he wanted. He still can."

How could he make her see his point? "Look. What I'm saying is that he got the girls when he wasn't old enough to date. In college, he was a poster boy. But I do not resent or envy my brother. I love Drake, and I know that no matter where in the world I am, if I let him know I need him, he'll drop everything—no matter how important—and come to me at once. I'm proud of him and of the man he has made of himself. I thank Henry for keeping Drake grounded, and for being a father to my brothers and me. He treated the three of us exactly the same, without exception.

"Velma, you are wrong to envy your sister. Love her and love yourself. Telford and Drake are closer to each other than either of them is to me, but they love me as much as they love each other. Let it go. It's weighing you down."

She put a hand on his arm, more to establish intimacy than to detain him. "I don't envy Alexis, and even though I'm not quite two years her senior, I always took care of her, because our mother wasn't a nurturer. I don't expect to be like her, but I want to be proud of the way I look. She's the model to which I aspire."

"Try not to let it take over. By the way, prepare to be the subject of conversation at dinner tonight."

"I thought the newlyweds would have that honor. Why me?"

"Because you'll have poached chicken or fish, and everybody else will have a decent meal."

She gazed up at him, a plaintive expression on her face. "You won't deride me, so I'll have at least one ally."

He could feel the grin spreading over his face. "Hadn't you better first find out what that will cost you?"

"You mean your support?"

"That's exactly what I mean. If you want me to take sides against my family . . ." He let the idea hang.

She laid her head to one side and narrowed her left eye. "Shoot your best shot, and we'll see what I come up with."

"Keep me supplied with roast pork and that fancy dessert—what was it? . . . oh, yes, crème Courvoisier—that you said was fit for a king."

"Make it convenient, and I will."

He'd walked right into that one. Her eyes widened when he said, "I can do that. You bet I can."

She seemed unsure as to their bargain, so he took pleasure in explaining it. "You agreed to cook those two dishes if I made it convenient. That's the bargain."

"Good. I'll decide when you've made it convenient."

Walking back toward the living room, he said, "If you think you're going to wiggle out of making me two of the best dishes I ever tasted, get real. It won't happen."

Telford ducked out of the kitchen carrying a package of cheddar cheese sticks and stopped when he saw them.

"Tara's practicing for your inspection," Velma said.

"Yes. I hear her, and I can hardly believe she plays so well. I'll get down there in a few minutes. I see you two are getting along well. I had hoped you would."

"Yeah," Russ said. "As if the one thing that will make me happy is to have other people plan my life. You mean well, but butt out."

"Gotcha," Telford said. "I'm a little overwhelmed right

now. Would you mind waiting until tomorrow to bring me up
to date on things here?"

"Fine with me. At supper, I'll be interested in how you
answer Tara's question about whether you found out what a
honeymoon is." The thought brought a burst of laughter
from him, and he leaned against the stair railing and let it
flow.

"This is something I'm going to have to get used to, and
you or somebody is going to explain to me how this body-
shaking laughter of yours has come about. In the thirty-four
years of your life, your biggest laugh was a grudging grin.
How'd it happen, man?"

"Long story, and if I tell you about it, I'll crack up all over
again."

Telford's eyebrows shot up. "Enough said. I'm beginning
to see the light, brother. Be back soon as I take these to
Alexis. She's hungry."

At supper that night, after Telford said grace, Russ looked
around the table at his new family. And there was a newness
about it, though the cast had not changed. Alexis was now
his sister-in-law and Tara his niece-in-law and he had a more
secure feeling about the love he had invested in both of
them. Drake should be there, he thought, to complete the circle.

"Now you can tell where you went on yer honeymoon,"
Henry said, after taking in a few spoons of hot leek soup. "I
know you musta told Russ, but he never lets a secret slip out
of him. Where'd you go?"

"Honolulu, and everything about it was perfect," Telford
said, his gaze lingering lovingly on his wife.

"It was pure paradise," Alexis added. "I'm still pinching
myself."

"I'm going to answer it," Tara said when the telephone

rang. "Hello. This is Tara speaking." Telford's eyebrow shot up as if to acknowledge that the child had matured in ways other than height and piano playing.

"Eeeeow. Mr. Drake. My mummy and my Dad are here. They just came back, and I'm playing Brahms, and Mr. Russ has been taking me places. Where are you?" Her giggles wafted through the otherwise silent room. "Barbady? Are you coming home tomorrow? Oh! When are you coming home?" She looked at Telford. "He's not coming home tomorrow."

Telford got up, took the phone as each person spoke with Drake, and Russ mused over his decision to leave the warmth of his family. He shrugged to shake himself out of the melancholia. He'd made up his mind, and he wouldn't change it.

"Did you find out what's a honeymoon, Dad?" Tara asked Telford. Is it in Hon . . . olu?"

"Honolulu," he corrected. "A honeymoon is the time when people who just got married go away together to . . . er . . . have fun all by themselves."

"Oh. Can't you have fun here?"

Russ wouldn't have laughed, at least not as hard, if Velma hadn't looked at him, wrinkled her nose and winked. Even Tara stared at him while he struggled without success to control the laughter.

"Russ, I've never known you to laugh with such gusto," Alexis said. "Your eyes light up and your whole face sparkles. It's delightful to watch."

"It must be a religious conversion," Telford said. "Beats all I ever saw."

"That ain't the only thing changed around here," Henry said. "Velma's given up eating, and is living on air and poached chicken. The two of 'em are having a strange effect on each other. No telling what would have happened if you'd stayed any longer. When Drake gets back, he'll think he's in the wrong place."

They bantered amiably throughout dinner, and he knew he would miss supper time with them most of all. It occurred to him that none of them would believe the mental anguish he was experiencing in anticipation of his move.

The next morning, alone with Telford at breakfast, he told him his plans. "It's time I went out on my own, Telford. I love this house and everybody who lives in it, but if I stay here, nothing in my life will change. You and Alexis need privacy to solidify your marriage, and I want you to succeed more than anything. I will hate being away from Tara and not watching her grow. She is such a loving child." He glanced away to shield his emotions, but he knew he hadn't succeeded when Telford's hand closed over his.

"You had responsibility for her, and she took your heart. She did that to me twenty minutes after I looked down at her for the first time. I can't advise you. This is your home. If you move away, you can always come back and claim your room. It'll be here for you. This might not sit well with Alexis."

"I know, but I've made up my mind. You ought to know that I had to take Tara to the hospital a couple of days after you left. She swallowed something her mother uses for mixing colors. Seems Tara thought it was a chocolate bar and tried to spit it out after she tasted it, but didn't quite manage. I'm sorry about that.

"I took her to Frederick General, and they pumped her stomach, let her rest for a couple of hours and released her. Before I left, I went up to see Uncle Fentress."

"How was he?"

"Not good. I'll get back there sometime this week. We're his only guests, so—"

"I'll get over there, too. Maybe he'd like to see our wedding pictures and some scenes from Honolulu. You don't want me to ask, but I'm going to anyway: What about Velma?"

"She means something to me, and we click in some important respects, but . . . well, I'm not there yet."

"You'll be careful with her, I hope."

"Of course I will."

Chapter Five

"How did you and Russ get on?" Alexis asked Velma as they sat together in Velma's room after breakfast on Alexis' first full day back at home. "He seems so different, so relaxed, even outgoing, and he intercepted Tara as Telford was about to take her to school, picked her up and hugged and kissed her. She plastered his face with kisses. I was ready to faint."

"He's been taking stock of his life, I guess," she told her sister. "I thought I was responsible for Tara while you were gone, but he immediately assumed the role of head of the house and responsibility for all of us, especially Tara. They became very close."

"Oh, I knew he'd take charge in Telford's absence; he's always done that, but there's more. I'll never get used to his robust laughter."

"It began when we were on the way home after taking you and Telford to the airport." She related her escapade in the roadside restaurant. "He laughed till I got worried. I think he discovered that he liked it."

"Maybe," Alexis said. "But he's always been a loner, not out of step, but not quite in tune with his brothers. Cynical and serious. Something happened, and I pray it was you."

"He lit a fire in me, all right. Honey, in that man's arms is heaven and hell, ecstasy and pure torture. All he has to do is touch me, and I'm ready to incinerate, but he's got the self-control of an anointed saint."

"So it hasn't gone all the way?"

She shook her head. "I'm not sure I want it to. He won't even tell me how he feels about me, but he behaves as if he cares a lot."

"Well, if you can't resist him, stay out of his way. Give him some work to do."

"I just got a call from my real-estate agent in Baltimore, and if I like the town house he found for me, I'll be leaving here very soon. I'm also looking to settle my business in Baltimore; it's gotten too big to handle with a laptop and cell phone."

"Wonderful. That means we can see each other more often, and at least I'll know where you are. When you come back next time, the guest room will be where my quarters were, and Tara will have the room you're in. Telford is going to put her piano in it."

"Can I borrow your car? I need to get started for Baltimore."

"Sure. First, you're going to tell me what prompted your new eating and dress habits."

"Russ, Henry and Lydia. Russ and Henry told me they hated my caftans, and that I looked best in the kind of dress—you know, fitted—that I wore at your wedding. They needled me till I bought some dresses like this one, and some casual clothes. If I had a nice slim figure, maybe Russ wouldn't be so reluctant to develop a real relationship with me. I went on a diet for a week and gained three pounds, so I went to see

Lydia, and she prescribed a diet. I'm hungry all the time, and I've lost half a pound."

"Back up there," Alexis said. "Did Russ suggest that he didn't like the way you look?"

"No. He discouraged me from worrying about my weight; in fact, I think the subject annoyed him. But I want to be proud of my appearance."

"I didn't know you felt this way."

She sat down beside Alexis and draped an arm around her shoulder. "I never talked about it. But when I saw how you looked in your wedding gown and the way Telford adored you, I wanted to look like that. I started wearing the caftans to hide my figure."

"Do you like yourself in the dress you're wearing?"

"I confess I do. It's fitted, but it looks nice. I'm not changing for anyone but myself."

"As long as you're happy. My car keys are hanging behind—"

"They're in my handbag."

"Okay. Drive carefully, and try to get back before dark."

The telephone rang as she passed it in the hall, and she stopped to answer it. "Hello. Harrington residence."

"Hello," a southern male voice said and, remembering Dolphe Andrews' thick southern drawl, she was immediately apprehensive. "Is Russ there?"

"Just a minute. I'll call him."

"Velma? Is this Velma?"

"This is Velma. Please hold on while I call Russ."

"Wait a minute. This is Dolphe. I want a straight answer. Is there any chance you and I could get together?"

"Are you serious? I thought you and Russ were friends."

"He didn't say there was anything between you, and you didn't come right out and say it."

She bristled at his effrontery; Henry told him and she

confirmed it. "Mr. Andrews, if I kiss a man, I do not kiss his friend the minute his back is turned."

"Give me that." He had the phone in his hand before she realized he was in the vicinity. "Dolphe, this is Russ. Man, what's the matter with you? She said she's not interested." She watched him grind his teeth as he listened. "I let her speak for herself, but if that isn't enough for you, I'll enforce her wishes, and you know it."

His fingers worried the curls on the back of his head, and he looked at her. "You want to say something to him?"

"Yes," she said and reached for the receiver. "Grow up, Mr. Andrews."

She dropped the receiver on the table and headed for the kitchen to speak with Henry. "Can I bring you anything from the Lexington Market? I'm going to Baltimore now."

"You sure can. I want three pounds of good country-rope sausage, sage sausage. Tel's back now, and that's all he wants for breakfast—that, grits, biscuits and scrambled eggs. And bring a gallon of milk. Thanks."

In Baltimore, she went with her real-estate agent to look at the town house, but as they drove in her car, she experienced neither eagerness to see the house, nor excitement at the prospect of finally owning her own home.

"Most people can hardly contain themselves when they go to look at a house, but you're behaving as if you're barely interested."

She turned into the street and slowed down when she saw a squad car. "I don't count my money until it's in my hand."

"You're gonna like this one," he said.

And she did. She parked in front of the gray brick structure, similar in design to several others, but of a different color. "This is it," he said. "Two floors, two-thirds of a basement and a large plot out back."

She got out of the car and stared up at the house. The

kitchen, large, airy and ultramodern, sealed it for her. Large living room, dining room, pantry and bath on the first floor, plus three bedrooms and three baths on the second floor. She would use the smaller bedroom for her office. After checking the finished basement and the closets, she told the agent, "I'd like my friend, an architect, to check the building."

"Fine. Who is he and where can I reach him?"

"Russell Harrington. He'll call you."

"One of the Harrington brothers, the building company?" She nodded. "I'll be delighted to meet him."

"If he approves, I'll take it."

She drove the agent back to his office and headed for the Lexington Market to shop for Henry but, unable to contain her excitement about the possibility of owning the house, she dialed Russ' cell phone number.

"Russ Harrington. What can I do for you?"

"Hi, Russ. This is Velma." She told him about the house. "Will you inspect it for me?"

"Of course. I'll do it tomorrow. You like it?"

"Oh, Russ. I love it. I'll be so unhappy if you find anything wrong with it."

"Scratch that. You'll be happy if I find anything wrong with it, because the builder will repair it before you put your money down. Got that?"

Realizing that he would steer her properly, she thanked him and relaxed. "Now, all you need to do is find a house or an apartment."

"Right. I want an apartment, so I don't have to worry about outside upkeep or protecting the place when I'm traveling. I'm glad you like it so much, Velma. By the way, where are you?"

"In Baltimore. Where are you?

"In Frederick. Drive carefully on the way home."

"You, too. Bye."

* * *

"We'll sleep in your room tonight," Telford said to Alexis at lunch, "because I don't want Tara down there alone."

"Right." She told him of Velma's plans, and her eyes widened when she learned that Russ intended to move.

"There's plenty of room for him. I don't like thinking that I've broken up this wonderful family. Is he staying with the firm?"

"Definitely. I think he's looking toward a family of his own, maybe not immediately, but he wants to stand on his feet, run his own household, direct his own life. He has always walked alone, although he walked along with us. He's, well . . . he's independent, a natural loner. But whatever he does, he has my support, and whenever he comes back here, his room will be waiting for him."

"I hope you made him understand that."

"He does, and he appreciates it."

"What do you make of these . . . er . . . changes in him? This ebullience and . . . well, his attachment to Tara?"

He fingered his chin and remembered that his father used to do that. "Velma. Whether he knows it or not, she's inside of him. As for Tara, she was in trouble and he feared for her life. That's an experience guaranteed to teach you what a person means to you."

Alexis seemed doubtful. "Velma said they were holding hands earlier than that, even before our plane landed in Honolulu. Now, Tara says you're not her best friend because you're her dad, so Russ is her best friend."

"What about Grant?"

Her eyes sparkled in that way he loved so much. "What five-year-old can compete with Russ Harrington?"

Like a day dawning, her face flowered into an expression of awareness. "I think we should leave Russ and Velma to heaven. Apparently independently of each other, they decided to move to Baltimore, so I have a hunch they're destined to be together."

He allowed himself a hearty laugh. "I think Russ has that hunch too, and that's why he's fighting his feelings."

"You did that at first," she said, glancing at him from beneath lowered lashes.

"Not anymore than you did," he reminded her. "Maybe it's a good sign. By the way, what will we do about Bennie? She's supposed to work a full day three times a week, but when I'm here, she comes at nine, spends the next hour and a half in the kitchen eating the breakfast Henry cooks for her, and she's ready to leave at three."

"I know. She doesn't work long enough to clean all of the venetian blinds."

"I'll shake her up," he said. "I've known for a long while that she's more interested in Henry than she is in doing her work. If she can build a fire under him, I'll genuflect every time I'm near her."

At about that time, Henry was also weighing on Russ's mind as he wavered between building a house of his own near Henry's cottage and setting it up the hill near the warehouse. He almost preferred having it near Henry's place, but was certain that Henry wouldn't like it. He bought some flowers, the *Maryland Journal* and a box of chocolates and drove to the Frederick General to visit his uncle. More than once, he had thought how pleasant it would have been to have an uncle with whom to share thoughts, problems and dreams when he was growing up.

He parked, went inside, got a visitor's pass and went up to his uncle's room. "I never know what to bring you," he said. "How's it going today?"

"Good as you could expect." He looked at the chocolates.

"The doctor said I shouldn't eat too many sweets, but I figure that at this point in my life, I can eat anything I can swallow. I'll live three days or a week less. Thanks for the chocolates. I always had a weakness for 'em. Sit down, won't you. You think the Ravens will win the Superbowl?"

He stared at the pale, fragile man, his age-induced blackness highlighted by the white sheets and pillow cases that surrounded him. And then he laughed. It rolled out of him, and still he laughed. After a few minutes, he looked at Fentress Sparkman. First time he ever saw a smile on the old man's face.

"Rang your bell with that one, did I?" Fentress asked him. "And I'm glad to know you weren't born solemn and straight-faced."

"I'm beginning to think I've had a reputation for either solemnity or piousness; I hope nobody thought me pious."

Fentress laughed aloud and raised himself up a bit. "You won't remember too much about your father, but you're more like him than your brothers are. Not so much in looks, but you got his disposition. He had tough guts and whatever he told you was like law. You'll go far, Russ. He wasn't the one carrying the grudge that separated us all his lifetime; I was, and when I see how you and your brothers have accepted me, I'm not a bit proud of myself."

"That's water under the bridge, Uncle Fentress. I don't believe in living in the past."

"You're right; it's a waste of your life. That was a fine-looking woman you brought here last week. She's got class."

"Thanks. Tell me, what do you know about my mother? When I needed her, I couldn't depend on her, here one day, gone the next. She came back permanently after Dad died, but I no longer cared whether she stayed or went."

He looked in the distance and shook his head as he remembered. "First time I heard of a black girl having a coming-out party was when Etta Clark's family threw that shindig for her. Spent more money on that party than I had the first twenty-five years of my life. She went after your daddy because his father had money—money and status that he denied me, his illegitimate son. I was envious, but not for long. She soon found marriage wasn't the parties and games she thought and took off. I guess she didn't grow up, but don't blame her, Russ; she lived as she was raised."

They talked for more than two hours. "I'll get back soon as I can," Russ said. "Telford and his wife returned yesterday, but Drake is in Barbados till the middle of February."

"I know. He came to see me the day before he left. I don't deserve the contentment I have these last days of my life, but I do thank you and your brothers for this peace of mind."

He gazed down at the man who brought back to him memories of the father he'd loved so much. "If you think of anything you need, call me."

With washed-out, teary eyes, Fentress Sparkman thanked his nephew, the one who had moved closest to his heart. "Not much chance of that, but thank you."

He went to a toy shop to find something for Tara, and saw in the display window a toy grand piano with a little figurine of a black girl sitting on the stool in front of it. He looked under it, saw a key and wound it. Immediately, the little girl began playing "Songs My Mother Taught Me." He bought it in spite of its hefty price and listened to the remainder of the songs: "Summer time," "The Waltz You Saved for Me," "I Hope You Dance," and "Singing in the Rain." Something for everyone, he thought, and wished he'd bought one for Velma.

Velma. He dialed her cell phone number. "What time are you getting back to Eagle Park?" he asked her.

"About four. Why?"

"Instead of going home, how about meeting me at Third and Elk?"

"What's there?"

"The street corner, babe. I'll park there and wait for you."

"Okay, Mr. Smarty. Be there a few minutes before four."

He'd been there less than ten minutes when she parked behind him. He started back to her car, and she got out and waited for him.

"I'm learning a lot about you, Russ."

He couldn't help grinning because he knew what she referred to. "Something new?"

"Only you would know how long you've been a smart mouth."

"I try not to pass up opportunities, and you provided a good one. I want some ice cream other than black cherry. Let's go to—"

"Now, Russ, you know I can't—"

"I don't know any such thing. This place has at least twenty varieties of no-fat ice cream and even more flavors made with pure cream. Come on." He knew from the light in her eyes that she couldn't wait to sample it.

"A big scoop each of no-fat peach, praline and strawberry," she said, rubbing her hands together in anticipatory delight.

He put a hand on her arm. "Hold it. Don't you think you're overdoing it?"

She looked hard at him. "For dinner, I will have poached chicken, broccoli and a salad with no dressing. I'm eating every bit of this ice cream."

"We have a special," the waiter said, "four scoops for seven fifty."

She didn't hesitate. "I'll take the special."

He shook his head. "When you hit that scale tomorrow morning, don't come at me with one of your stiletto shoe heels."

"Not to worry. I believe in taking my medicine."

"I just visited my uncle at the hospital."

"How is he?"

"He's weak, but he has all his faculties, and I . . . I really enjoyed that time with him. He told me a lot of things I didn't know, important things."

The waiter arrived with their dishes of ice cream with which came assorted wafers. Her face relaxed into a smile, lights twinkled in her warm-brown eyes and she rimmed her lips with the tip of her tongue. He wanted to grab her and love her senseless. A sensual woman if he ever saw one.

"Hmmm," she said, savoring a spoonful of praline. "This is decadent, plain sinful."

"It doesn't take a lot to make you happy, I see."

She didn't look at him, but focused on the ice cream. "In terms of quantity, no." She stopped eating then and looked up at him. "What hooks me is quality."

He decided to pick his way carefully. "Well, I admit this is first class ice cream. I haven't eaten better."

She put the spoon down and looked him in the eye. "I'm not talking about ice cream, and you know it. Neither are you."

On the verge of laughing, he said, "I am not going to laugh at your antics, Velma, so don't try to push me into it. Got that?"

She savored the banana, the fourth flavor. "Russ, do you swim?"

"Do I . . . of course I swim. In mid-summer, I live in that pool at home."

"Good. The complex I'm about to move into—provided you find the house is sound—has an olympic-size swimming pool, and I don't swim."

"Alexis swims like a fish. What happened to you?"

"She liked showing off in a bathing suit; I never had the nerve to put one on."

"You have the nerve now?"

"No, but I will by the time the swimming season comes."

He stopped eating and looked at her. After a moment, he decided to avoid an unpleasantness and keep peace with her. "I'll be glad to teach you whenever you're ready."

After eating the ice cream, they walked out into the late-January afternoon with its bright sunlight, calm wind and biting cold.

"What'll we do now?" she asked, and he had been wondering the same thing, unwilling as he was to end their first casual outing together. From the corner of his eye, he saw the street light change and the reflection of red in a window across the street.

"Do you ice skate?" he asked her.

"I did, but I haven't had on a pair of skates in, let's see, thirteen years. I left the skates home when I went to college."

"It's been a couple of years longer than that since I skated," he said, "but, hey, let's try it. The worst that can happen is that we fall down."

"That could hurt, if I remember."

"Yeah, but you've got a hell of a lot nicer cushion to land on than I have." She laughed, then looked at him with eyes wide and a drooping lower lip.

"What is it?"

"In my whole life, that's the first time I ever laughed about my size."

With her hand in his, he started across the street. "You're going to do a lot more of that, because I am not going to pussyfoot around the topic just because you're hung up on it. You look good to me, and especially in those slacks and that sweater, so as far as I'm concerned that settles it."

He rented the skates and a locker for her handbag, their coats and shoes, looked down at her and grinned. "Better let me take a lap, get the hang of it, so that if you fall, I'll have enough balance to catch you."

"No sir. Who's going to catch you while you're getting the hang of it? If we go down, we go down together."

They put on their skates, got on the ice and steadied themselves. He didn't like feeling as if he had cloven hoofs, but it seemed that way at first. However, he soon got his bearings and looked around for Velma. After searching the crowd and not finding her, he was about to decide that she was sitting on the bench, when saw her burnt-orange sweater breezing along ahead of him as skillfully as if she skated every day. He caught her as she turned to come back.

"Woman, did you lie to me about your skating prowess?"

She smiled the smile of a sated feline. "No. I just forgot how good at it I used to be."

As they skated together, he realized that he didn't allow himself time for fun and relaxation, that in the ten years since he received his masters degree in architectural design, he hadn't done ten foolish things. He loved football, but hadn't been to more than a couple of games. Success had come at the price of his youth and his youthfulness.

He grasped Velma's hand and guided them to the edge of the rink. "That was a lot more fun than I remembered, and I'd be willing to continue, but my sister-in-law frowns on straggling in to dinner after seven o'clock."

"I know. I was having fun, too. She looked up at him, her smile at once innocent and beguiling. "Can we do this again?"

The hell with convention. He hugged her and tweaked her nose. "Sure. Let's buy our own skates."

She reached up and brushed the side of his face with her left hand, and he had to dig into himself for control as he gazed at the tenderness that shown in her eyes. *If they were*

*any place other than a public arena, any place that afforded
a modicum of privacy, he would have wrapped her in his
arms and betrayed himself.*

She gasped when they walked out of the building into the
darkness. "Ooops! I promised Alexis I'd be home before
dark so she wouldn't worry."

"I'll call them." He took out his cell phone and dialed
Telford's home phone number.

"Say," Telford said after greeting him. "We don't know
what happened to Velma. She was due back before dark, and
she didn't answer her cell phone."

"That's why I'm calling. She's with me. We're in Frederick
and headed home. Tell Alexis not to worry."

"Thanks for letting me know. See you shortly."

As they walked to their cars, he told her, "Your sister
managed to regiment me where everybody else who ever
knew me failed."

"I'd like to know how she did it."

He checked the tires on the car and opened the drivers'
door for her. "Gourmet meals. Along with her 'you're-in-
the-army-now' house rules, she taught Henry how to cook,
did a lot of it herself and always set a table that made your
mouth water just looking at it. And she did it with such
grace. She made that house a home."

She got in the car, rolled down the window and ignited
the engine. "So feeding you is the key to getting you to behave."

He didn't know what got into him, but he had a desire to
see her back down, and he equated it with wickedness. "That
depends on the woman and what I want, or need, from her.
For some, good food would do it; for another . . ." He could
feel his bottom lip curling into a grin, "food, gourmet or not,
wouldn't cut it. But if she fired up like lightning every time I
put my hands on her . . ." He let her imagine the rest.

She didn't take him up on it. "Get into your car, Russ, and let's go before you find yourself testing your theory."

"That's no theory, that's fact. You tail me. If you have a problem, flash your lights."

"I ought to pray more," Velma said to herself as she rushed up the stairs to shower and change in the thirty-three minutes remaining before seven o'clock. "I need that guy. He's such a sweet man. He may not want to be, but he is. I know he thinks I'm off-the-wall with this diet, but I'm not going to stop until I can buy my clothes in the misses section." She chose a long-sleeved lavender dress, scoop-necked and with a flounced hem, combed her hair down and increased her fire power with a dab of Hermès perfume behind her ears and at her cleavage.

She took her seat at the table with seconds to spare. They joined hands, and as soon as Telford said grace, Tara smiled. "Mummy, Mr. Henry forgot the candles when you were in the honeywell."

"You mean when I was on my honeymoon."

"I forgot that word," Tara said, "but Mr. Henry put whipped cream on my apple pie. I love whipped cream. I love Mr. Henry, too."

Velma couldn't help glancing toward Russ, whose face bore a smile not unlike parental indulgence. He loved Tara so much. Surely he would want children of his own to love and care for.

"Did you forget Tel's breakfast?" Henry asked her.

"No. Thanks for reminding me. It's in a cool bag in the trunk of Alexis' car."

"I'll get it later," Russ said, and when she saw the quick, sharp incline of Telford's eyebrows, she knew that speculation was rife about Russ and her and decided to fuel it.

"Can you ice skate?" she asked Tara.

"A little bit. My school took us to skate three times. I loved it."

"Velma skates very well," Russ added. "I mean, she's good. At first, I was hard pressed to keep up with her."

Telford placed his fork on the edge of his plate, finished chewing his mouthful of food and leaned back in his chair. "You're telling me, Russ, that you went ice skating this afternoon?"

"Yeah. We filled up on ice cream, looked around for something else to do, and my gaze caught that red neon sign over the skating arena, so we went skating."

Henry cleared his throat. "Yer taken to laughing like a hyena, now yer ice skating on a weekday afternoon. Next, somebody'll tell me you been sky diving. There's hope for ya yet."

"Thanks, Henry. Your approval means a lot to me."

"If I didn't know you meant that, I'd think you were being sarcastic."

She looked at Russ for a gauge as to the seriousness of the exchange, saw a smile on his face and relaxed as he said, "Of course I meant it. And if I prove to be a rascal, give yourself the credit for that as well. By the way, I dropped by to see Uncle Fentress today. He was jovial and clear headed, and we talked for a couple of hours, but I can't see him lingering indefinitely."

"Alexis and I are going to see him day after tomorrow, when the pictures are ready. I'm going to call the hospital to find out whether Tara can go with us. Ten minutes with her would brighten his life."

"What's the matter with him, Dad?"

"He's sick. He's in the same hospital that Russ took you to."

"Oh. Everybody will be nice to him and give him a teddy bear."

"Give the old fellah me regards," Henry said.

Telford nodded. "I will. Takes me back nineteen years every time I visit him; it's almost like reliving those last days with my father." He looked at his wife. "You preached to me about the burden of hatred, and you were right. Caring about him gives me a lot of pleasure; hating him was a source of unhappiness."

Alexis walked with Velma to the kitchen, carrying plates and glasses. "If I had known you planned to spend the afternoon with Russ, I wouldn't have worried," she said to Velma. "From the looks of you both, I think you had a good time."

"We did, and we decided to do it again." She heard the note of pride in her voice and decided not to care about the message sent to her sister.

However, Alexis interpreted the remark and her sister's tone when she spoke as evidence of Velma's deepening involvement with Russ.

"I want you to be happy, hon," Alexis said, "but for all the time I've known Russ, seen him in this house day after day, he remains an enigma to me. Nobody would have made me believe that Russ Harrington would spend a Tuesday afternoon ice skating. He has always seemed driven to work, to succeed. Something's going on inside of him, and it's important. Be aware."

They joined the others in the den for after-dinner drinks, coffee and sweets, as was the custom in the Harrington family. She sat on the sofa, avoiding the chair she knew Alexis preferred. To her astonishment, Russ sat on the floor beside her, his shoulder rubbing her thigh.

"I'll be in Baltimore tomorrow," he said. "I'm going to inspect the house Velma wants after which I'll want to look at an apartment for myself." She thought the silence unusually loud, for there was no response except the glances that Henry,

Telford and Alexis exchanged. She had never witnessed such a morose moment in that house.

Finally, Telford said, "If you want to move anything, I'll be glad to help you."

Half leaning against her thigh, Russ told him, "What is here belongs here and will remain here. I'll be here most weekends, and I'd rather not sleep in an empty room." He looked up at Velma. "Excuse me for a minute." A minute later, she heard the kitchen door open, and remembered that he said he would get the cool box out of the trunk of Alexis' car. She had forgotten it.

"Tara," he called from the hall. She raced to him and immediately, her squeals filled the house.

"Mummy, look what Mr. Russ brought me. Come look. Along with Telford, Alexis and Henry, she hurried to see the source of Tara's excitement, a twenty-four inch replica of a grand piano to which was attached a bench and a little black girl with long pigtails. Russ plugged in the electric cord, turned the switch and the little girl began to play "Songs My Mother Taught Me."

"I know that. I play that song, Mr. Russ." She hugged his knees, slapped her hands together and giggled with delight.

"It was in the window of a toy shop," Russ said. "It looked just like Tara. I couldn't leave it there." He hunkered beside her and hugged her. "I'm glad you like it."

"I love it. I'm going to name her Cookie because Mr. Henry teaches me how to make cookies."

"Russ, this is so lovely, and she truly likes it." Alexis blinked back a tear. "The love that my child receives in this house . . . I . . . I didn't know I could be so happy."

Russ straightened up and walked over to Velma. "May I speak with you privately for a minute?"

She walked with him into the living room. "What is it?"

"Want to ride into Baltimore with me tomorrow? You'll

learn a lot if you're with me while I inspect the building and fixtures, and you can go with me to look at that apartment. Want to?"

She didn't hesitate. "I'd love that. And Russ, that was such a sweet thing you did, buying that toy for Tara. It's the perfect toy for her, but wasn't it pricey?"

"I didn't mind that. She's special to me."

"You will be a wonderful father," she said, and could have bitten her tongue. Never give a man the idea that you're anxious to settle down with him unless you want to get rid of him, her twice-married, thirty-year-old friend Lydia preached. And she could see the merit of that advice.

However, Russ apparently didn't attach any significance to the remark. "Thanks. I'm looking forward to cherishing my children and guiding them to be men and women I can be proud of and who will be proud of what they've made of themselves."

"If they are like you, you can't ask for more."

He looked at her for a long time, until she felt as if he was dissecting and analyzing her. When his eyelids fluttered and his eyes took on that dreamy look that never failed to heat her blood, she swallowed hard and tried to break the force that his gaze exerted, sapping her will, making her pliable and hungry for him.

His left hand circled her upper right arm, and she could feel that pull to him, that anticipation of the thrill that always shot through her when he folded her into his arms. As if he knew he had sparked that cord of lightning that shot through her, his eyes darkened with the turbulence of a howling storm, and he sucked in his breath.

Did he pull her to him, or did her body move automatically toward the music that made her soul dance? She only knew that he touched her, and that her lips immediately parted themselves for the entry of his sweet, loving tongue.

And then, he was inside of her, dipping, tasting, twirling, mining the gold he found in every crevice of her mouth.

His grip on her tightened, the scent of his male heat attacked her olfactory senses, and every nerve in her body clamored for the friction that would soothe and sate them. Her breathing shortened, and when her nipples began to ache and pain her, she grabbed his left hand and placed it on her right breast.

"Russ. Oh, my Lord," she moaned as he squeezed and pinched the beaded areola. "Honey, please."

He had to know that he had taken it as far as it could go, for he put both arms around her and then gently stroked her back.

"Sweetheart," he whispered, "we're going to have to do something about this."

She rested her head on his chest. "But you don't want anything to happen between us. You don't want a relationship with me, but every time we get together like this, you pull me in deeper."

He kissed her eyes, brushed his lips across her cheek, and pressed his lips to hers. "Shhh," he whispered. "I know, and I'm not foolish. This isn't a simple thing that either of us can wish away. It explodes when we don't expect it. I look at you and . . . Hell, I don't know. You want a cooling off period, see how it works?"

No. She didn't want any such thing, but he would never know it. "That may be a good idea. You don't put your hands on me, and I won't put mine on you."

When he laughed, she imagined the satisfaction she'd get from giving him a good sock. "Let me in on what's so funny."

His grin widened. "We are. I give it till the next time we're alone."

She stepped back and looked at him. Damned if she liked having her nerves fried every time he touched her and then left to blister. Even plants needed cool rain after a good sun scorching. "What about that famous self-control of yours?" she asked, being careful to keep her tone warm and even.

The lights in his eyes danced a mischievous twinkle, and she realized there wasn't much chance of getting him into a serious mood.

"I hope I'm not required to use more self-control than I applied a minute ago." His gaze drifted to her breast, still beaded and tingling with hunger for the feel of his warm mouth. "I guess I'd manage if I had to, but I sure as hell wouldn't be happy about it."

"You're serious, aren't you?"

"I told you. I don't say things that I don't mean."

"Then where does that leave me?" she asked him.

"We're in this together, babe. If you fall, I'll catch you, and I hope you would do the same for me." When she raised an eyebrow, he added, "I wouldn't mind having some help with this control business. You make the prospect of losing it seem like what Sir Edmund Hillary must have felt when he got to the top of Mount Everest."

She didn't know why, but something in her—maybe it was the devil—told her to test it. When her tongue pressed the right side of her cheek, she was duly warned, that having been a signal of recklessness for as long as she could remember. Her gaze swept upward from his feet to the hair on his head in a sexy come-on, but when her gaze settled on his face, she knew she had made the wrong move. His face bore as stern an expression as she had ever seen on it.

"I'm sorry, Russ. It's a wicked streak that I have yet to conquer."

"Don't conquer it; just learn when and when not to let it have sway."

Her hand caressed his wrist, and oh, how she loved touching him. "Am I forgiven?"

"Nothing to forgive. You have to learn what works with me and what doesn't, just as I have to get to know you."

"I'm as transparent as glass," she said.

"You couldn't be serious."

"I was. Say, where did they go? I thought they'd join us in the den after a while."

He took her hand and walked with her to the den. "None of them would have gone in here as long as we were outside there together. They're in their rooms for the night." He winked at her. "So behave yourself. Want a glass of wine?"

"I'd love it."

He poured each of them a glass of wine, placed it on the table beside his favorite chair. "Sit here?" She did, and he sat on the footstool beside the chair. "What time do you want to leave for Baltimore tomorrow?" he asked her.

"Around nine."

"Then, meet you for breakfast at eight."

"Oh, I don't need that much time. Ten minutes is enough for me."

A frown clouded his face. "It isn't enough. You need more sustenance than you can get from half a grapefruit and a cup of black coffee. I hate this whole thing." He drained his glass. "I'd better turn in. What about you?"

"Right," she said, filling her voice with false gaiety. Whenever the subject of her size or her diet arose, he shifted from sweet to indifferent with the speed a thoroughbred smelling the finish line.

She leaned over, kissed his forehead and jumped up from the chair. "See you in the morning."

"You bet," he said in a listless tone that suggested he might have been miles away.

* * *

Maybe he was missing something important. She looked good to him, and when Dolphe behaved like an adolescent over her in that fitted dress, that should have told her something. He fluffed up the pillow on the sofa, stopped in the act of putting the footstool where Alexis kept it, and put his knotted fists on his hips. "What the devil is coming over me? I don't give a hoot whether these pillows are straight, and I don't care where this stool sits." Disgusted with himself and his absentminded acquiescence to rules for which he had no use, he showed his contempt for *la politesse* by getting a bottle of beer, uncapping it and taking a swig from the bottle as he headed up the stairs.

Just before he reached Telford's bedroom, the door opened and Telford stepped out into the hall. "I just wanted to thank you for telling Alexis that you're not moving your things. I'd understand if you did that, but she was more upset at your leaving than I thought." He dug his toe in the carpet. "She appreciates that you need your own life, but she wants you where she can keep an eye on you . . . uh, look after you. Don't laugh now. I'm discovering that she is a nurturer."

"Hell, man. You always knew that. I did. Tell her she'll see so much of me that she'll forget I don't live here. Eventually, I hope to build a house up the hill. That way, I'll still be here. And I'll situate it so that there's still plenty of private space if Drake decides he wants to do the same."

"Good. She'll be happy to hear it." He ran his hands over the curls at the back of his head. "Russ, can you tell me what the problem is with Velma? Can I help in any way?"

He'd never shared intimacies with Telford or Drake as he suspected they had with each other, and doing it then made him uncomfortable. Yet he realized that their behavior no doubt seemed odd to onlookers.

"I'm having a hard time accepting her shaky self-confidence. She has decided she doesn't like the way she looks, and she doesn't believe she's attractive. With a lot of help from Henry, I suspect, I finally got her to stop wearing those mammy caftans and put on some normal clothes." He shrugged because he had a sense of defeat. "She looks great in them," he went on, "but she doesn't believe it. I like her the way she is. Maybe I'm unfair, but I find vanity about looks tiresome and shallow. Every time something good happens between us, you can bet the topic of diet or size will crop up and dampen the mood. Much as I like her, I know I'm going to get fed up with it."

Telford's arm draped across his shoulder, as it had so many times over the years when big brother let him know he was there if needed. "I'm surprised. When did you notice this?"

"That night after your wedding. She wants to be slim and willowy like Alexis."

"But you've never shown an interest in tall, slim women."

"There've been a couple, but nothing significant and the attraction wasn't strong. Anyway, I told her Alexis was your type, not mine, but she's fixated on that all-American ideal, and I'm tired of it."

"Take it slow there, brother. She wants you, so she'll find herself."

"If she doesn't, I'm out of here."

Chapter Six

"My first impression of this house is that it's a reasonably good buy for the money," Russ told Velma as they walked through the building. "I also like the layout. You check out the kitchen to see whether it contains everything you need in the place that's most convenient, go through the storage, clothes and linen closets and be sure to check the amount of storage space in the basement. I'll do the same later, but it's important that you're satisfied. Did you bring any notepaper?" She showed him the lined, yellow tablet. "Okay, I'm starting with the roof. See you later."

After deciding that the builder should put screens over the drainpipes to prevent tree leaves from clogging them, he okayed the roof and exterior of the house. His biggest job would be the plumbing, so he worked at that next.

"It's already one o'clock," she told him. "I'd better get us something to eat. What would you like?"

He looked down on her from his perch on the rung of a ladder. "Some Maryland crab cakes, homemade biscuits, apple pie and coffee. Lots of coffee." He stepped down from the ladder, opened his wallet and handed her two twenty-dollar bills.

"What's all this for?"

"I want four crab cakes, and if you get them at Frannie's over near the Armory, that alone will be twenty bucks. What're you having? Lettuce?"

"I'll be back as soon as possible, and you watch your mouth. This is going to be a lovely, productive day, and we're not going to provoke each other."

"If you get yourself a couple of crab cakes, we won't."

"Oh, pooh," she said. "See you later."

Shortly after four o'clock, he washed his face and hands, filled out his report to the real-estate agent, signed it and gave her a copy for herself. "A couple of things have to be corrected, but they are not major, and the builder will take care of it. It's a good house. Solid. I like it."

"I don't know how to thank you," she said.

"And you shouldn't. It's the least I'd do for you. Let's go. I want to show you the apartment I'm considering."

They had spent the day working together, laughing and teasing, and although he'd done strenuous work, he'd hardly been aware of the energy he expended. "She's good for me in so many ways," he said to himself as they drove along Swan Drive to skirt the park. Something other than having a model of womanhood for a sister gnawed at her sense of self. He needed to find out what it was, and he promised himself that he would.

"I love this neighborhood," Velma said when he parked in front of an old, but elegant, apartment building.

"Me too. It isn't nicer than your area, just older and different. This won't take long."

"It's more than I need," he said of the thirty-foot step-down living room and two large bedrooms.

"I like the dining area and balustrade on the level with the entrance and foyer," she said.

"Yeah. It is nice, but what am I going to with a dining room, or that big kitchen? I'm planning to use that second bedroom for an office. There's a gourmet take-out and delivery shop less than two blocks away. That'll take care of my eating needs."

"You'll miss that great food Henry and Alexis serve up every evening."

"You promised to cook me a gourmet treat if I made it convenient. Remember?"

She looked around the unfurnished apartment and then at him, and it occurred to him that she was a natural flirt. "Yes. I remember."

His first thought was that he'd never made love to a woman on a bare floor, and that he wouldn't like to test that with Velma. "Let's not go to meltdown," he said, certain that the remark would send her back up. "Wait till I get the place furnished."

She stared at him for a long time, her expression unreadable. And then she laughed. At first, it sounded like bubbles forcing themselves out of a bottle, but the more she laughed the more gaiety poured out of her until he was caught up in it and laughed with her.

When they at last controlled the mirth, he put his hand on her shoulders. "Sometimes, like right now, you're so precious and I think you're the one woman in this world for me. Let me inside of your feelings and thinking. Let me understand you, because I don't, and I want to. Let me love you, Velma."

"Do you want to?" she whispered. "Do you really want to? From my early childhood, I've smiled through so much hurt. I . . ." She looked away. "I'm sorry. I never drop my problems on other people, not even my sister, who has always been the person closest to me."

He put his arms around her. "Closer that your parents?"

"We were closest to each other because of them. I think I told you this. Alexis says they loved us, but they didn't. I protected her, acted as a buffer between her and them, but there was no cushion between them and me."

He glanced around the open room. Here was the opportunity to get behind the person she so carefully hid, but without one chair or a means of relaxing and making her comfortable, he knew it wasn't the time for it.

"Will you tell me about it? Not now, but at a convenient time and place?"

"If I can."

"I'll remind you, and I'll help you. You care for me; that is not in question. But how can you care for a man if you don't trust him? If I tell you you're beautiful and that I like you just as you are, you won't believe me."

"I want to, Russ, but I'm so accustomed to . . . to seeing everything that's wrong with me that—"

"All right. I don't want us to get into that. Let's go home." As he drove, he realized that his attitude toward a relationship with her was changing, and he made up his mind to help her see herself as she appeared to him.

"I'm going to love my new home, especially since I'll be closer to Alexis and Tara."

"Is that all, woman? Have you forgotten that you'll be only eleven little blocks from me? I'm crushed."

"You poor baby," she said. "I will definitely make amends."

"Oh, you will." When her eyebrow shot up, he said, "I've already told you that my punishments are enjoyable. Just one mild one, and you'll be clamoring for more. Knocking down my door."

"Are we talking about something that can be discussed in the presence of a ten-year-old?"

"Not in the presence of *my* ten-year-old, if I had one. Why?"

"Just checking on the location of your mind."

"You make me laugh without trying, and it's a great feeling, laughter. I can't believe I lived thirty-four years without realizing what a cathartic it is."

She patted the hand that rested on the steering wheel. "Every time I see you laugh, I feel so good. The transformation that takes place in you is like the metamorphosis of a deity. Total and wonderful."

"It's as strange to me as it is to you."

"I'm planning a gala in New Orleans next week, so I'll be leaving this weekend. I'm looking forward to it; I could use a respite from this cold weather."

"Do you have everything in place?"

"Everything. Trust me, it wasn't easy, but I'm satisfied that my clients will be pleased."

"How do you manage that business, catering parties and social affairs all over the country, with only a laptop and a cell phone?"

"That's all I need. I use local services and suppliers."

"I'll be working in Philadelphia while you're away, and I suspect, for a while after you return. But you have my cell phone number," he said.

They discussed everything but themselves and skirted issues guaranteed to push them apart. "I'm kissing you right here," he said and drove into the garage.

She slid closer to him and wet her lips with the tip of her tongue. "Hold the dynamite, honey," she said with a grin, "I'm running on empty. I may not punish, but I do collect what's coming to me."

"Music to my ears, because I always pay my bills; in your case, I'd pay with relish."

Her arms went around him, and she brushed his mouth

with her lips closed. To his astonishment, her lips trailed over his eyes, cheeks, the side of his neck and only briefly lingered on his mouth. All the while, her fingers moved lightly over the back of his head, his nape and the side of his face. He moved away and stared at her.

"What are you telling me?" It wasn't the earth-shaking explosion she usually generated in him, but a kiss of love and tenderness. A kiss without passion.

"I . . . I just . . . It's the way I feel," she said in barely audible tones. He had to get out of that car before he did something foolish like telling her he loved her. He wrapped his arms around her and held her until he heard the door to the kitchen open.

"That you, Tel?"

"Russ." He answered Henry. "I'll be inside in a minute."

He brushed her lips with his own. "I'll get back to this," he said to Velma. "It may be a week or even two, but I'll finish this. You understand?"

Her smile warmed him. "Yes."

He got out of the car, opened the passenger door and guided her into the kitchen, avoiding the concrete steps over which he had stumbled many times.

"What you sitting out there for?" Henry asked him. "Ain't a soul in this house but me. It's time some of you came home. I had Bennie hanging around my neck all day, and she ain't done ten minutes of work. Place looks like it did when she walked in here this morning. Only way I could get rid of her was to go over to my place and lock the door, so you ain't getting a big supper tonight."

"Long as it's not cabbage stew. Tell Bennie you're not interested in her."

Henry propped his fists on the bones that served as his hips. *Tell her? I ain't done nothing but showed her for the last ten years. The woman's got the hide of an elephant.*

Russ didn't laugh for he knew that, in his present mood, Henry would use any excuse to cook cabbage stew. "If you'd like me to speak with her, just tell me."

"Suppose I asked you to shoot her?"

He worked hard at controlling the laughter that threatened to burst out of him. "Henry, there aren't many things you can ask of me that I'd hesitate to do, but . . . Look. Don't cook her breakfast or her lunch, and maybe she'll catch on. She might also do some work."

"She butters me up about how good me cooking is. Next time she sits down there and *orders* pancakes like she was in a restaurant, I'm going to spill a bottle of Angostura bitters in the batter. That ought to fix her."

The laughing began with Velma, who leaned against him and let it roll out of her. Watching her was more than enough to provoke his own outpouring of mirth.

"Ain't a bit funny," Henry said, but immediately gave the lie to his remark and joined them, laughing and holding his side as he did so.

"What's going on in here?"

He spun around toward the door, glimpsing the tears on Velma's face as he did so. "Hi," he said to Telford and Alexis, glanced at Henry and resumed the laughing orgy.

Henry recovered first. "Ain't nothing wrong with us, Tel. Just the thought of Russ shooting Bennie on my behalf. And in case you want to know why, she trailed me everywhere I went today, ain't done a bit of work, just gazing up at me like a moonstruck heifer. Never saw the beat of it. And if you find it funny, look for cabbage soup tonight."

"I never expected to see a scene like that one, you and Russ laughing uncontrollably," Telford said. "I'm all for joy, but by damn, this is almost frightening. First Russ and now Henry." He put an arm around his wife and left the kitchen with her.

"If the rest of you didn't have to eat it, I'd give him cabbage stew anyway," Henry grumbled.

"Where's Tara?" Russ asked him.

"Spending the night with Grant. Adam Roundtree's taking them to some kind of reading competition for five-year-olds. Grant will be six in a couple of weeks, so this is his only chance."

"I'll help you cook dinner, Henry," Velma said. "You fix some potatoes and vegetables, and I'll fry some catfish."

"Where're you going to get catfish?" he asked her.

"In the cool box in Russ' car." She looked at Russ. "I got it when I went to get our lunch."

"Now that's food," Henry said. "Ain't had no catfish since Alexis elevated the menus."

After dinner that night, Velma excused herself, went to her room and tallied her financial obligations. *I can buy my house and the warehouse, too. In a year from now, people will know about Brighton Food and Entertainment Services.* She hugged herself, rolled over on the bed and laughed. She could do it.

However, her joy was short lived, as her mind wandered back to Russ and the questions he would have about her parents and how they affected her. She didn't want to open those old wounds, to remember her loneliness, the hours of dread and fear, and that last night . . . She slapped her hands on the sides of her head to blot out the memory of it.

Two weeks later, she moved into her new town house at Eighty Eutaw Drive, a short walk from Druid Lake. "Where are you?" she asked Russ after answering her cellular phone around noon of the day she moved in.

"I'm in my apartment."

"What you doing there this time of day on a Tuesday?"

"Looks like the flu. I got drenched yesterday morning at our project in Philadelphia, and I already had a cold."

"Do you have a fever?"

"Looks that way. I can't seem to get warm enough."

"I'll be over shortly. Do you have any bed linen, any glasses? What's there?"

"Living room furniture, my bed, my desk and chair, and kitchen basics. You shouldn't come over, because this is probably contagious."

"I'll wear a mouth and nose guard, and I won't kiss you."

"You will so."

"I'll be over there in an hour, so don't go to sleep. You'll have to open the door."

In one week, she had to leave for New Orleans. "I can't go off and leave him here if he's sick," she told herself. She shopped for groceries and arrived at his apartment with two bags that she could barely carry.

"What's all this?" he asked when he opened the door.

"Food. What have you eaten today?"

"Nothing much. I'm not hungry. I think I'll lie down."

She put her hand on his hot forehead and agreed with him. "I'll bring you some soup and a couple of aspirin in a minute."

Gratified that he ate all of the chicken soup and noodles, she debated whether she should call Telford and tell him. "Don't you think I should let him know you're not well?"

"What can he do other than eat up all that food you brought me? You can tell him, but discourage his coming here. He's got other things to do."

She sat beside him at the head of his bed, and he managed to get his head into her lap and go to sleep. Her fingers stroked his hair, and when he breathed more deeply, she leaned against the headboard and slept.

Darkness had set in when she awoke, her dress damp

from his perspiration. When she tried to ease up, he wrapped his arms around her, pressed his face to her belly and seemed to sleep more soundly. His forehead was still warmer than normal, and she wanted to give him juice and another aspirin, but he wouldn't release her.

"He's the same man asleep that he is when he's awake," she murmured. "Stubborn."

He rolled over and looked up at her. "Am I making you uncomfortable?"

"You devil. You were awake." She stroked his face. "Of course I'm not uncomfortable. I slept for several hours, but I wanted to get up and get you an aspirin and some juice, and you wouldn't let me. You still have a fever."

"Maybe." She brought a cold towel, and he wiped his face and the back of his neck. "You can't imagine how good that felt. Thanks." After he took the aspirin and drank two glasses of orange juice, he remained propped up in bed.

"Did you call Eagle Park?"

"She shook her head. I decided to wait and find out how you reacted to the aspirin, but I went to sleep."

He slid over and patted the space beside him. "You mind sitting here?"

She sat beside him with the headboard supporting her back. "I know I should have gone to Eagle Park this morning, but I didn't want Alexis to have to take care of me. I want her to spend her caring on Telford. Velma, you can't know how important it is to me that they succeed.

"He needs Alexis, needs to know she's there for him. I didn't shed a tear when my mother died, because I had long since stopped caring about her. She abandoned us whenever it suited her and as often as she liked. She wasn't there my first day in school and never saw me in a school play. When I got a cold, it was Henry who wiped my nose, because our father worked long hours. Even so, he tried to make up for our mother's flightiness. I still miss him."

As she listened to him, she understood that he attributed to Telford his own needs in a woman, thanks to his mother's irresponsible behavior. "He's tender inside," she thought, understanding now why he placed such a high value on loyalty, even in little things.

"You should be unpacking and settling into your new home, and you have to get ready for your job in New Orleans, but you came when I needed you. You came, and you stayed."

"I couldn't have done differently, Russ."

"Good grief, I wrinkled your dress, and I don't have an iron. This is terrible."

"The only person who'll notice will be your doorman, and I won't spend any time worrying about his opinion. I'd better fix your supper and head home."

"Cook enough for both of us and we can eat together."

She cooked rice, broiled the shish kabob that she bought ready to cook and sauteed fresh spinach in garlic and olive oil. She couldn't find a tray, so she improvised, folding a white towel over an *Ebony* magazine.

"This is delicious, but it doesn't excuse you from cooking me that gourmet meal when I make it convenient."

"You're beginning to sound like yourself, so I can leave you without feeling guilty. I'll call you when I get home."

She got home after ten o'clock that night, exhausted but happy. She made up her bed, took a shower and crawled between the sheets. But sleep eluded her. She imagined that if she made one false step with Russ, he'd tell her good bye and stick to it.

* * *

One month had passed, and she dreaded going to see Lydia. She had followed the diet faithfully, but after four weeks, she had gained two pounds. She phoned Russ that morning, learned that he was up, had eaten breakfast and thought he no longer had a fever.

She didn't tell him that she intended to see her nutritionist, only that she had an appointment and would call him later.

"Are you certain that you followed the diet correctly?" Lydia asked.

"I did, and I hope I never see poached chicken again."

"This diet always works unless there's a medical reason why it shouldn't."

Velma sat forward. "What do you mean?"

"I mean I want you to see this endocrinologist."

"All right, but not till I come back from New Orleans. Whatever's wrong with me has been wrong for years, and taking care of it can wait a couple of weeks." She thanked Lydia and left. Pictures of heaping cones of rich, strawberry ice cream flitted through her mind, and she could almost taste the Cajun praline cheesecake that teased her in her mind's eye. She stopped at the gourmet deli near Russ's apartment house and bought a quart of vanilla ice cream and two pints of strawberries.

"Hi, I brought you something," she said when he opened the door, and handed him the ice cream. "How do you feel?"

"Surprisingly normal."

"I brought us some ice cream and strawberries."

He gazed down at her. "What happened to the diet?"

"I'm off that for the time being, but who knows—"

"Are you telling everything?"

She shook her head. "No, but when I know *everything*, I'll share it." She hulled the berries, sliced and sweetened them and served them over the ice cream.

"I don't know why you did this," he said, "but it hits the spot. Thanks."

After a half-hour visit, she said, "You're no longer my patient," pronounced him well, kissed his cheek and left him gaping at her as she dashed out of his apartment. She didn't plan on making such visits a habit.

For the remainder of the week, she worked at getting her house in order and contracted for future catering jobs. She knew that Russ had gone back to Philadelphia—probably earlier than he should have—to work on his plans for a building that complemented the Griffith-Joyner house that the Harrington brothers had built the previous year. Sometime earlier, he suggested that they cool off their relationship, but he then laughed at the idea. He hadn't called, and she didn't intend to call him.

She had felt closer to him than ever when he lay sick with his head on her lap and when he told her about his mother, but none of it translated into a commitment. At least she understood one of the reasons why he found trusting his emotions to a woman so difficult. She suspected that she could blame herself, too. Hadn't he asked her to open up and let him love her? But how could she face all that pain and hurt? She blinked back a tear and telephoned Alexis.

"Hi. Got any place for me to sleep this weekend? I thought I'd drop by Saturday afternoon and leave early Sunday."

"Wonderful. We've turned my old rooms into guest quarters, and Tara sleeps in the room you always used."

"Where's her piano?"

"In her room. Please bring Henry some of those sausages you got for him last time. They're great. Are you driving or what?"

"I'll rent a car and drive, but I'm thinking of buying one. We'll talk about that when I see you. Bye."

"See you Saturday."

Velma thought that over for a few seconds after she hung up. Already, her sister had settled into the role of wife and mistress of Harrington House. Russ needn't worry about that marriage; Alexis loved Telford and couldn't help appreciating how different her life was from what it had been with Jack.

With every muscle screaming for help after she pulled and pushed boxes and furniture most of the day, she crawled into bed, moaning relief as she did so. Sleep, precious sleep, was all she wanted. But as she began to doze off, the telephone rang.

"Hello," she murmured, only half asleep.

"Hi. This is Russ. It seems as if I awakened you. It's early. Are you all right?"

"Me? All right? I guess so. Have a seat."

"Hey. Are you asleep, or . . . ?"

"Who is this?"

"Russ."

"Hmmm. Hi, love."

He nearly skidded off the elbow of the highway. Hearing that low, sultry voice sent a message straight to his loins. "I'll hang up and let you get back to sleep."

"I don't wanna sleep, I wanna be with you."

He saw a rest stop for trucks up ahead, slowed down, pulled in and parked. He didn't want to miss such conversation as she could muster in her present state, but he couldn't risk hearing it while driving.

"You want to be with me?"

"Uh huh."

"When? What did you have in mind?"

"Stop teasing me. You're so sweet. Hmmm." Silence.

"Velma, are you asleep?"

"Why don't you ever kiss me? I love the way you kiss . . . Hmmm."

It wasn't fair to invade her privacy, asking intimate questions that she didn't know she was answering, but as tight lipped as she was, he refused to feel guilty.

"What do you like about it?"

"You taste good and you make me feel so good, but I'm too big and you can't hold me close like I want you to. I'm so . . ."

He listened for the rest of her sentence, realized she'd fallen into deep sleep and hung up. He eased back onto the highway and headed for Baltimore.

Even half asleep and in a sensuous mood, what she looked like was paramount in her thoughts. A capable, successful woman who let herself be a captive to the size dress she wore. He sucked air through his front teeth in dismay. If she was hell bent on suffering about it, too bad. As much as he cared for her, he wasn't prepared to deal with her feelings of personal inadequacy. He'd been around enough self-denigrating men and women to know he didn't want an intimate relationship with a woman who didn't love herself as she was. He glanced over his left shoulder and moved into the center lane. *If she would only let herself accept what a wonderful person she is, beautiful, intelligent, accomplished and witty. And loyal. Precisely what I like in a woman.*

"Oh, what the hell!"

When he arrived at Harrington House Saturday afternoon and saw the gray Pontiac parked in the circle, he wondered whether Dolphe had come back to test his luck with Velma, and took pleasure in thinking how disappointed his friend must be. He streaked up the steps and pushed the door open as quickly as he could, escaping the biting cold.

"Eeeowww!" Tara squealed when she saw him. "Mr. Russ! Mr. Russ, come see my new room. My dad put my piano in it." She lifted her arms, and he picked her up and folded her little body to his chest. Only two weeks, and he'd missed her more that he would have imagined.

"Where's everybody else?" he asked, walking up the stairs with her in his arms. "Dad went to meet Mr. Drake, and my mummy and Aunt Velma are in the guest room talking low so I won't know what they're saying. Mr. Henry said I should call you Uncle Russ. Can I call you Uncle Russ?"

"You certainly can. I'd like that a lot."

She kissed his cheek several times. "I like it, too."

"Whose gray car is that in front of the house?"

"Aunt Velma's. She had to bring Mr. Henry some sausages."

He couldn't help grinning. He knew of nothing so refreshing as a child's innocence, and Tara coupled hers with the charming way she had of telling everything she knew.

So Velma and he were destined to meet whether or not they planned it. To discourage Tara's free talk, he changed the subject. "What are you planning to call Drake?"

"Uncle Drake, like Mr. Henry said."

"I like your room," he told her of the sunny yellow-and-white color scheme, and attractive child's furniture. "Play something."

She played Kreisler's "Caprice Venoise," then folded her hands in her lap and looked at him. "Did you like it, Uncle Russ?"

"It was beautiful. I'm proud of you."

"I better practice," she said and was soon lost in the sounds she made.

He gave himself a good talking to and convinced himself that he shouldn't look for Velma. He went instead to the kitchen and greeted Henry.

"How do you like picking up after yerself?" Henry asked him.

He allowed himself a laugh and patted Henry's shoulder. "Haven't had any experience with that yet."

"Then yer place must look like a pig pen."

"Not really. I limit my kitchen activities to making coffee and putting a few waffles in the toaster. The dishwasher takes care of clean-up."

"What about the bath and the bedroom? That gets dirty, too."

"It's a big apartment, Henry. When it piles up, I'll get a cleaning service."

"Don't wait till you get a dispossess notice."

He draped an arm around Henry's shoulder. "I'm not that bad. I may create clutter, but I can't stand filth. Where's Velma?"

"Down the hall there with Alexis. She come in here looking good. What's with you two? That fellah Andrews called here two or three times asking for you. I finally told him you and Velma had moved, and he acted like I shot him. Did my soul good. A man that won't take no for an answer is either silly or dangerous."

"Think I'll mosey down the hall and break up that sisterly confab."

He felt less sanguine about it than his words suggested. He could hardly wait to see her, but then what? He knocked on the door and waited.

"Oh!" she claimed. "Russ. Oh, dear. I didn't know you'd be hear this weekend. Come on in. Alexis and I are just catching up."

She turned to leave, and he detained her with a slight grip on her hand. "I won't come in, but I'll be in the den for a while, if you'd like to talk. How are you, Alexis?" he called out.

As he expected, she came to the door. "Fine. No trace of the flu? I hate the thought of your being sick alone in that apartment."

He couldn't resist planting a few questions in Alexis' mind. It would serve Velma right for not telling him she'd be in Eagle Park for the weekend. "Thanks, but I wasn't alone. Velma took care of me." He looked at Velma. "Don't forget to give me the bill for that dress I ruined. I liked that dress. You think the cleaners can straighten it out?"

At first, she seemed surprised, then she narrowed her right eye and poked out her chin. "You didn't ruin the dress. I had it cleaned and wore it here today. Perspiration won't harm first quality silk."

"Give me the cleaning bill."

"Of course not; it was my pleasure. I'll join you in the den in a minute."

With her eyes shooting sparks and her demeanor that of one about to spit fire, he wasn't sure he wanted to go to the den. But what he said to her was, "Would you like me to fix you a drink of some kind in the meantime?"

"I'd love a lemonade mist."

"A . . ." He caught himself. "My pleasure."

He strode down the hall and into the kitchen. "Henry, what's a lemonade mist?"

"Never heard of it. Is that what she said she wants?" He nodded, wondering how Henry managed to read his thoughts. "Don't worry about it. Put some shaved ice in a glass and pour lemonade over it. Another way to water down perfectly good lemonade."

He made the drink and set it on the bar. Understanding a woman was a full-time occupation. She entered the door smiling, walked over to him and kissed his cheek. But when she would have moved away, his left arm shot out, encircled her waist and drew her into his embrace.

"You want to play?" he asked her.

"The . . . Somebody may walk in here."

"Let them. Open your mouth and let me in."

"Russ. Honey."

"Yes. Yes." He slipped between her parted lips, trembling as she sucked his tongue and caressed his face and neck. Her nipples beaded against his chest, and he caressed her left breast, pinched and teased it until his mouth watered, and he lifted her to fit him. Her hips began to weave and undulate against him, and he tried to move her from him. But she locked her legs around his and let herself feel his bulk.

"Velma! For heaven's sake, do you want us both scandalized? Sweetheart, let go."

He set her on her feet, but she wouldn't look at him. He put an arm around her, moved to the sofa and sat down with her. "I know I precipitated that," he said, "but were you teaching me a lesson? Was that it?"

"Alexis probably thinks you made love to me while I was dressed. I wanted to sock you."

"So you asked for a drink that didn't exist." He stifled a laugh. "I made it anyway. It's over there. What else?"

"It's always that way when you . . . I mean when we kiss. I never want it to stop."

"Do you remember my calling you a couple of nights ago when you'd just gone to bed?"

"Vaguely. I woke up the next morning and saw that the phone was off the hook. I recalled your saying 'This is Russ,' or something like that. Why?"

He repeated the conversation to her. "You said I don't kiss you, and I wondered where you were those times we heated up the atmosphere. And if you wanted to be with me, why didn't you tell me you would be here this weekend so we could drive over together?"

"You didn't tell me you were coming, either."

"But I was going home, and you were visiting my home. There's a difference."

"Oh, stop splitting hairs. One is noon and the other is twelve o'clock at midday."

"All right. Let's start again. Are you angry with me?"

She looked directly into his eyes. "You're kidding. The only answer to that is a good yawn. How could I be angry with you after what happened here a minute ago?"

"Search me. I decided today that I don't understand women, and I'm opening myself up to learn." She laughed, and it was a good thing, because he had to laugh at his own foolishness. "I'd suggest we see a movie, but Drake will be here soon, and I'd like to be home to welcome him. I haven't seen him for over six or seven weeks."

"Then let's watch the national ice skating competitions. Want to?"

He got up, got the glass of rapidly melting lemonade mist and handed it to her. "If you don't drink this, I may not forgive you."

She sipped the drink, put the remainder on the coffee table and lay her head against his shoulder. He liked it when she took liberties with him and welcomed her into the circle of his arms.

As they watched the skaters, he thought how much he had changed since Telford's marriage to Alexis, how less sure he was that the woman in his arms wasn't for him. He needed to make love with her, but doing that would be a commitment to at least work toward a lasting relationship. And he suspected that if he ever got inside of her, he wouldn't want to leave. She heated up easily, and he hadn't even begun to mold her into the ball of fire he knew she could become. If she would only let him know her.

"Whoops. That was too bad," she said when a skater fell during the free-style program. She always empathized with anyone in trouble, and he liked that about her.

The doorbell rang. "Excuse me, sweetheart. That must be Drake."

He rushed to the door, unlocked it and opened his arms to his younger brother. "Welcome. Glad you're back here safe." He picked up Drake's bags. "I'll take them up to your room."

"I didn't realize you'd be here, man. This is great. Soon as I get out of these clothes, we'll catch up. Who else is here?"

"Velma's in the den."

"Things okay with you two?"

"We've more ground to cover but . . . well, so far so good."

"Glad to hear it. I like her. Is that Tara playing the piano?" He nodded. "I'll be damned. She's moving fast."

The music stopped, and Tara came barrelling down the hall. "Mr. Drake. I mean, Uncle Drake. I been listening for you."

Drake picked her up and swung her around. "How's my best girl?"

"I'm getting big." She giggled and kissed his cheek. "Mr. Henry said I have to call you Uncle Drake. Can I call you that?"

"That's what you're supposed to call me. If Telford's your dad, I'm your uncle."

They settled into a happy convivial evening. He was happy to be at home with his family, but getting a place of his own was the right thing. He talked with his brothers late into the night, discussing their projects, planning and exchanging ideas, each reporting on his aspect of the work.

"Velma and I made a frightening discovery while you both were away. I've been dealing with it, but all three of us will have to work at this." They were immediately alert and listened intently as he described the discrepancies between bills of laden and the content of the unopened containers, as well as between items in opened cases and those listed in the records.

"Who's guilty?" Drake asked.

"That's the problem, seems to be an outside problem in some cases and an inside job in others. Think we can have a look at it tomorrow morning? I didn't think of checking unopened cases, but Velma did, and almost everyone of them was short a carton or two."

He arose early and went down for breakfast. "How are you?" he asked Velma, leaned over and kissed her quickly on the mouth. "It didn't occur to me that you'd be eating alone. How'd it happen?" He stared at her plate. "Back on the diet, I see."

"After the meal I ate last night, it's a wise decision. If I keep that up, I'll pop out of all those new clothes I bought."

"Those clothes that you look so beautiful in."

"Thanks," she said.

"When are you leaving for New Orleans, and when will you be back? I'd like to meet your plane, if possible."

"I'll give you my flight schedule before I leave. Pray that it goes off without a hitch. I haven't worked previously with the supplier I'm using. I use top-quality materials and appointments, but if he tries to cheat . . ."

"Don't you have a couple of firms you can use at the last minute if you have to?"

"One, but I'm getting another. I'll get there a week earlier, to deal with surprises."

"Don't be taken in by the southern charm. All business and no small talk will earn you the respect you deserve. If you need me, you have my cell phone number." She raised an eyebrow. "It's three hours by plane," he added. "If you need me, call."

* * *

She stepped out of the Louis Armstrong New Orleans International Airport into the stifling and muggy heat, thankful for the air-conditioned limousine that awaited her. After checking into the Omni Hotel, she left her bags on the bed and went straight to her supplier of linens and banquet accessories.

The tall man, Creole from his curly hair to his high-polished black shoes, looked at her the way a cattleman sizes up a prize-winning heifer. Affronted, she said, "May I see the linens first and then the porcelain. If I don't like the linens, we can't do business, contract or no contract."

"Right this way, Miss Brighton. Everything you wanted is here."

She checked the porcelain, silverware, candles, candle holders and vases. "Be sure to shine up those candle holders. And I want a bowl of . . . Are callas in season?"

"Why yes. We have them year-round. Any particular color?"

"Our colors are lavender and pink, so let's stick with that for the flowers. I want a large bowl in the middle of each table. I ordered thirty tables, each seating ten."

"Yes ma'am. It'll all be there, in place. I can't tell you what a pleasure it is to work with a professional."

"Thank you. I'm staying at the Omni if you need me."

She took a deep breath and headed for the food caterer. She knew at once that she needn't have worried; everything about the establishment was the personification of order and efficiency. The head chef sat with her, went over the menu and the service. She couldn't have been more pleased.

She left after an hour and a half and went back to the Omni in the air-conditioned limousine. "Now that I've made my points," she said to herself, "I can travel by taxi." Inside her hotel room, she kicked off her shoes, hung up her clothes and telephoned Russ. After relating her experiences with the supplier and the food caterer, she said, "Now if you were here, we could go sightseeing."

"I'd join you, but Drake will only be here a week, and we want to straighten out our inventory records."

"Can you do that in a week?"

"I can devote only two days to it, although they'll work at it full time. But if you need me, I'll be there."

"And you would, too. You have so many ways of endearing yourself to me."

"You're not bad at that yourself. Excuse me, I'd better speak with Bennie. She's driving Henry out of his mind."

"Bennie?"

"The woman who comes three times a week to clean. After working here for years, she's suddenly taken a shine to Henry, and right now, he's mad enough to choke her."

"Well, I'll be. Cupid usually does a better job than that. If he stings one, he stings the other. Give Henry my regards."

"I will. How about a kiss?"

She made the sound of a kiss. "Bye, love."

Calling him that was presumptuous, but it would make him think. She took a shower, got a copy of *If You Walked in My Shoes* and got in bed to read. "Presumptuous or not," she thought, "might as well call it what it is."

Chapter Seven

Russ parked in the garage beneath the apartment building in which he lived and took the elevator to the tenth floor. As he walked toward his apartment, his steps slowed and a feeling of apprehension settled over him. He went inside, dropped his briefcase on the first chair he passed, walked over to the picture window and looked out on the park in the distance, made unappealing by the dark, ominous clouds. He gazed, unseeing, at the scene before him until the ring of his cellular phone startled him.

"Hello?"

"Russ, this is Drake. I'm in Frederick, at the hospital."

His body stiffened, and his senses jumped to alert. "What is it?"

"It doesn't look good for Uncle Fentress. I was on my way to the airport, decided to stop by, and I'm glad I did. He's not going to make it, Russ, and he asked for you over and over. Telford's on his way here now. Where are you?"

"Home. Just stepped through the door. I'll be there in an hour and a half, provided it doesn't rain or sleet."

"Drive carefully. I'll be here when you get here."

He got a half-pint container of milk from the refrigerator, put two slices of raisin bread in a Ziploc bag, grabbed his briefcase and headed for the garage and his car. While he waited for the elevator, he dialed Velma's cellular phone.

"I'll call you from there," he told her after giving her the news he received from Drake.

"I'll pray for the best. Please don't drive too fast."

"I won't. Be in touch."

He got in his car, put the milk and raisin bread on the bucket seat beside him and headed for Frederick. In the two short months he'd known his uncle, he had developed an affection for him, a man he had learned as a child to dislike. Not that he ever encountered Fentress or even recognized him before he was in his late teens; it was the name Sparkman that came to represent all that was unethical and unscrupulous, an attitude passed from his father to Telford to him.

He had made it a point to visit his uncle often, making up for lost time as it were, and he cherished the hours he had spent talking with the old man. Hours during which he learned precious things about his father, came to understand his mother better and got an idea of his heritage that no one else, including Henry, could have given him. He slowed down to the speed limit in order to exit off the curved ramp. What could he offer Fentress Sparkman other than the comfort of knowing his nephew cared?

An hour and twenty minutes after leaving Baltimore, he parked in a space provided for visitors to the hospital and rushed to his uncle's room. Memories of his dash to the bedside of his beloved father in that same hospital over twenty years earlier filled him with uneasiness and dread. He joined Telford and Drake at his uncle's bed and took the old man's still warm but weak hand.

"Uncle Fentress, this is Russ. How are you feeling?"

Fentress opened his eyes and made an effort to smile. Almost like looking down at my father, he thought. "So glad you got here, Russ. Your brothers are here somewhere. I . . . I want you to build something lasting that has Josh's name on it, and I want you three to stay together. If you do that, you'll always be successful. You made my last days happy." He lifted his hand, but it fell to the bed. "All of you. Everything's with Casper Richard, my lawyer. Russ, I'm leaving it to you to see that my wishes are carried out. You hear?"

"Yes, sir. I'll do my best."

"Telford, you did a great job raising the boys and yourself. And . . . and you took this little three-man company and made it a name to be . . . reckoned with. Wish I'd had Drake with me. I'm getting tired. Too bad Josh couldn't see what fine men you are." His voice weakened and Russ bent toward him.

"What did he say?" Drake asked.

"He said, 'would someone say a prayer?' I can't . . ." He bowed his head and said the Twenty-third Psalm and, to his surprise, Drake followed it with the Lord's Prayer. By the time Drake finished, Fentress Sparkman had slipped away.

The next morning, Russ contacted Casper Richards and learned that he was executor of his uncle's will. "Sparkman made that change a couple of weeks ago," the lawyer said. "You and your two brothers come to my office this afternoon, and I'll read the will and turn everything over to you."

The Harrington brothers had made themselves wealthy by their brains and sweat, but Fentress Sparkman made them rich, leaving each of them two million dollars, as well as a vast amount of property to be divided equally among them. After the funeral and burial in Eagle Park, Russ, Telford and Drake sat in the Harrington House basement recreation room sharing their feelings about their uncle, what he gave them and how different their lives might have been had he been a part of it when they lost their father. They agreed to name the apartment complex Russ was designing for construction in Philadelphia "the Joshua Harrington-Fentress Sparkman Manor" and to upgrade the structure to luxury level, ensuring its longevity.

"Have you spoken with Velma in the last couple of days?" Russ asked Alexis after he left his brothers.

"Yes. She said you told her Fentress passed, and she accepted that you were caught up in the things that had to be done, but Russ, don't shut out the person you need. When people who love you know you hurt, they need to help you heal."

He let the wall take his weight. "I know you're right, and I need her, but she has an enormous load down there in New Orleans, and I didn't want to add to it by dumping my feelings on her."

Alexis treated him to a withering look. "She won't appreciate that; at least I wouldn't. When a woman loves a man, she wants to be there for him when he needs her."

His heart seemed to leap frog in his chest. "You're suggesting something that she hasn't confirmed."

Both hands went to her hips and immediately dropped to her sides. "What? Well, if she hasn't, it must be because you haven't encouraged it. I wish one of you would tell me what's keeping you apart. Maybe I can help?"

"You can if you find out why she can't trust me fully, can't let me know who she is deep inside. I haven't the slightest idea what will make her cry, and she's hung up on the way she looks. She refuses to see that she is beautiful, hates her size and God only knows what else. It's a foolish vanity that has begun to test my patience."

She stared at him, wide-eyed. "I had no idea. I'll get to the bottom of this."

He went to his room and dialed Velma's cellular phone number. "Russ here. How's it going down there in New Orleans?" he asked when she answered.

"Great so far. The gala is tonight, and after this job, my reputation is going to soar. Everything is in place and perfect. Now, tell me about you. How are you handling this? I know you cared a lot for your uncle, and I'm sorry I couldn't be with you."

"Thanks. I appreciate that. I'll bring you up to date when I see you Sunday."

"You still planning to meet me Sunday?"

"Of course. If I tell you I'm going to do something, I do it unless it's not humanly possible."

"I know, and it's just one more thing that sets you apart. I'm looking forward to seeing you."

"Me too."

Two days later, he awaited her as she emerged from the airport's security area. He knew his face was one big grin, and he did nothing to squelch his obvious pleasure in seeing her. "You got some suntan," he teased and wrapped her in his arms. "You're just what my eyes need to see." Realizing how deeply he meant it gave him a moment's pause, because every word came from his heart.

She squeezed him to her, reached up and caressed his cheek, a gesture he had begun to anticipate from her. He relished the tenderness and caring that it conveyed.

"Thanks for coming. Because you're so sweet, I'll cook you a nice dinner."

"Not after your long flight, but I'll take a rain check on it. That makes two you owe me, and I am going to enjoy collecting, but tonight, I'm taking you to dinner. You've probably had enough seafood for a while. If you like Italian food, let's go to the Ristorante Panzini."

"I love it. What's the atmosphere like?"

"Jacket and tie. Sedate."

She rubbed her left cheek. "All right. I can do that."

He hugged her a little tighter and wished he was some place where he could sample the sweetness he always found when she opened up to him. "I'll be at your place around six." He picked up her suitcase, took her right hand in his left one and made his way with her to his car.

"You'll be warm in a minute. It heats up quickly," he said of his 2004 Mercedes. "If you don't mind seeing some blighted areas, I'll take a short cut to your place."

"This must be one of the worse," she said, as they drove through Dolphin Street. "All these boarded-up houses, crumbling steps and broken windows on both sides of the street."

He drove around the remnants of a discarded sofa bed and nearly hit an old automobile tire. "I forgot it was this bad," he said.

"With all the abandoned houses and thousands of people sleeping on the streets, you'd think somebody would—"

"Wait a minute," he said, cutting her off, "I'm going through some of these side streets to see how they look. I just had an idea."

When she opened the door that evening, it pleased him to see that she wore a fitted lavender dress with long sleeves and a flirtatious hem that suggested he'd find what he was looking for if he lifted it.

"I haven't gotten this place straight yet," she said.

He walked around, observing her taste. "I like what you've done so far," he said of the beige velvet sectional sofa and the Doris Price paintings that hung above it.

"I can't seem to find a coffee table."

"Get two of 'em. They don't even have to match," he said.

"If you find a couple that you like, use them. I don't believe in fashion. Do what makes you feel good."

She raised an eyebrow and laid her head to the side as if contemplating a newly perceived idea. "You wouldn't be a nonconformist?"

The thought amused him. If you kept your own counsel and did things according to your own desires, you could expect that label or that question. "If you mean, do I follow my own counsel, then I'm a nonconformist from my head to my toes. But I don't do anything just for the hell of it. That would be professional suicide for an architect."

"And for any other professional. What do you think of my getting a Persian carpet for this room?"

"I wouldn't cover this great hardwood floor completely. I'd put a colorful carpet, preferably a beige-tone Tabriz, in front of this sofa and smaller ones in the same family elsewhere in the room. To me, that gives a more inviting and more elegant look. But . . . some other scheme might suit you better."

"I like that. I like it a lot." She left the room and returned with her scarf and a pair of gloves.

"Where's your purse?" he asked her.

She handed him her door keys. "I don't need it tonight, do I?"

He looked at the keys. "Never can tell," he said, juggling them in his hand. "This may give me ideas."

She walked to the closet in the foyer, got her coat and handed it to him. "Honey, if I trust you with my life when you're driving on a highway, I can certainly trust you with my door keys. Besides, your pride won't let you do anything unseemly."

The seriousness of her facial expression nearly provoked him to laugh, but he managed to maintain a straight face when he said, "Your confidence gives me strength."

She looked hard at him for a minute before giving in to the mirth that suddenly erupted from her, and then his laughter joined hers, binding them in a joyous frivolous moment.

They walked arm-in-arm to his car, and he realized that she was becoming a fixture, an important part of his life, and in spite of his reservations, he admitted to himself that he'd rather be with her than away from her. He ignited the engine, felt her leg beside his, warm and assuring and switched off the engine. She looked up at him, her expression questioning.

"Were you serious when you said you missed me, or just making talk?"

She turned fully to face him. "I missed you. I always miss you when I'm not with you." Her hand caressed the side of his face, communicating her feelings in a sweeter, more loving way than her words had managed.

He stared down at her almost unwilling to believe what was happening to him. Her gaze met his steadily, unflinching, and when she opened her arms, tremors streaked through him and he gripped her body to his own. Then, with a groan that he knew signaled his capitulation, he plunged his tongue between her parted lips and gave himself to her. She took him and loved him until he trembled in her arms. Stunned at the strength of his feelings, he relaxed his hold on her and leaned back in his seat.

With her head against his shoulder, she said, "Does this mean you missed me?"

"Definitely," he said, igniting the engine again, "whenever you're not with me."

At dinner that evening, she listened, fascinated, as he told her about his inheritance and the plan for its use that had begun to unfold in his thoughts.

An Important Message From The ARABESQUE Publisher

Dear Arabesque Reader,

I invite you to join the club! The Arabesque book club delivers four novels each month right to your front door! It's easy, and you will never miss a romance by one of our award-winning authors!

With upcoming novels featuring strong, sexy women, and African-American heroes that are charming, loving and true… you won't want to miss a single release. Our authors fill each page with exceptional dialogue, exciting plot twists, and enough sizzling romance to keep you riveted until the satisfying end! To receive novels by bestselling authors such as Gwynne Forster, Janice Sims, Angela Winters and others, I encourage you to join now!

Read about the men we love… in the pages of Arabesque!

Linda Gill
PUBLISHER, ARABESQUE ROMANCE NOVELS

*P.S. Watch out for the next Summer Series **"Ports Of Call"** that will take you to the exotic locales of Venice, Fiji, the Caribbean and Ghana! You won't need a passport to travel, just collect all four novels to enjoy romance around the world! For more details, visit us at www.BET.com.*

SPECIAL OFFER! 4 BOOKS FREE!

BET BOOKS™

www.BET.com

A SPECIAL "THANK YOU" FROM ARABESQUE JUST FOR YOU!

Send this card back and you'll receive 4 FREE Arabesque Novels—a $25.96 value—absolutely FREE!

The introductory 4 Arabesque Romance books are yours FREE (plus $1.99 shipping & handling). If you wish to continue to receive 4 books every month, do nothing. Each month, we will send you 4 New Arabesque Romance Novels for your free examination. If you wish to keep them, pay just $18* (plus, $1.99 shipping & handling). If you decide not to continue, you owe nothing!

- Send no money now.
- Never an obligation.
- Books delivered to your door!

We hope that after receiving your FREE books you'll want to remain an Arabesque subscriber, but the choice is yours! So why not take advantage of this Arabesque offer, with no risk of any kind. You'll be glad you did!

In fact, we're so sure you will love your Arabesque novels, that we will send you an Arabesque Tote Bag FREE with your first paid shipment.

* PRICES SUBJECT TO CHANGE.

YOU'LL GET 4 SELECT ROMANCES PLUS THIS FABULOUS TOTE BAG!

Visit us at:
www.BET.com

THE "THANK YOU" GIFT INCLUDES:

- 4 books absolutely FREE (plus $1.99 for shipping and handling).
- A FREE newsletter, *Arabesque Romance News*, filled with author interviews, book previews, special offers, and more!
- No risks or obligations. You're free to cancel whenever you wish with no questions asked.

INTRODUCTORY OFFER CERTIFICATE

Yes! Please send me 4 FREE Arabesque novels (plus $1.99 for shipping & handling). I understand I am under no obligation to purchase any books, as explained on the back of this card. Send my free tote bag after my first regular paid shipment.

NAME _____

ADDRESS _____ APT. _____

CITY _____ STATE _____ ZIP _____

TELEPHONE ( ) _____

E-MAIL _____

SIGNATURE _____

Offer limited to one per household and not valid to current subscribers. All orders subject to approval. Terms, offer, & price subject to change. Tote bags available while supplies last.

Thank You!

AN025A

ARABESQUE

Accepting the four introductory books for FREE (plus $1.99 to offset the cost of shipping & handling) places you under no obligation to buy anything. You may keep the books and return the shipping statement marked "cancelled". If you do not cancel, about a month later we will send 4 additional Arabesque novels, and you will be billed the preferred subscriber's price of just $4.50 per title. That's $18.00* for all 4 books for a savings of almost 30% off the cover price (Plus $1.99 for shipping and handling). You may cancel at any time, but if you choose to continue, every month we'll send you 4 more books, which you may either purchase at the preferred discount price. . . or return to us and cancel your subscription.

THE ARABESQUE ROMANCE CLUB: HERE'S HOW IT WORKS

THE ARABESQUE ROMANCE BOOK CLUB
P.O. BOX 5214
CLIFTON NJ 07015-5214

PLACE
STAMP
HERE

"Uncle Fentress wanted me to build a monument to my father, because he felt responsible for dad's failure and his early death. But as I see it, my father was responsible for his own mistakes, for being too trusting and not watching his back. Still, I was closer to my father than to anyone else and his passing broke me up, so I'm happy to erect a lasting monument to him."

"Do you have anything in mind?"

"You gave me an idea as we drove through Dolphin Street. A couple of blocks from there, we saw a row of abandoned but sturdy houses of similar architecture. I'm going to try to buy those buildings, renovate them and make them into apartments for homeless people. Uncle Fentress left me far more than enough for that."

"Russ, that's a wonderful idea. If I can help, will you let me?"

"Of course I will. I'm pleased that you want to help. I'll show you the plans, but first I have to buy the property."

After a meal of the crab soup, veal marsala, fluted mushroom, tiny parsleyed potatoes, broccoli raab, green salad and gorgonzola cheese, she didn't want dessert. However, she didn't want to cast a pall over their first real date, and a loving one at that, so she ate the *pere e cioccolata* or pears with chocolate and raspberry sauce.

"This taxes you a bit," he said, savoring the dessert, "but you're a good sport. Besides—" his eyes twinkled with mischief—"You loved it, didn't you?"

"I did. It's really special." *And you'll pay for it*, her conscience nagged.

"One of my favorites. This stuff kicks serious butt. A smart woman would learn how to make this."

She couldn't help grinning. An opportunity to top Russ came rarely. "This smart woman already knows how to make it."

He leaned back in his chair and looked at her, his face the picture of delight. "Touché. Keep it up; you won't be able to get rid of me."

"I'm asking myself why I would want to, but nothing comes to mind right now. Of course, you never can tell."

His evident love of a challenge seemed to trigger his entire demeanor, as he sat forward, strummed his long, lean fingers on the white tablecloth, and exposed his teeth in a grin that held less mirth than she would have expected.

"Think hard."

"Say, I was teasing."

He sat back, relaxed. "Good you told me. If you're teasing, at least smile. What I see makes as much of an impression as what I hear. Want to dance after we leave here?"

She had to remember the advice that Drake, Henry and Alexis gave her about Russ, and his own words: "I'm serious even when I tease."

"I love to dance, and I can't think of a better way to end this wonderful evening."

He stood, signed the check, put a bill on the table and took her hand. "Then we'll dance. Sure you aren't tired? It's been a long day for you."

"I'd dance unless I was bedridden, and even then, my spirit would dance."

"Now we really are soul mates. I haven't danced much since I left graduate school. As I think back, I realize I've done hardly anything other than work." He grinned. "Hell, I haven't even chased my share of women."

If he could be serious in his teasing, so could she. "Well, honey, you missed your chance."

As if enjoying that conversation, he poked his tongue in the left side of his jaw. "Good thing I'm not prone to accepting dares. That was a dare, you know."

"Explain these things to me, hon; I'm not used to bantering with men. As a rule, I just talk to them. That was meant to be a simple statement of fact, not a challenge."

He held the car door while she seated herself and then fastened her seat belt. "Hmmm. You mean I can't sow my wild oats? You are a cruel woman." He got into the car, fastened his own seat belt, and cast her a side glance, grinning as he did so. "I wouldn't have thought you the type to rob a man of his birthright."

"I surprise myself sometimes." And no matter what she expected, he certainly surprised her.

He found them a table as soon as they entered the lounge, took their coats to the cloakroom, came back to her and extended his hand. "The music isn't too bad, although I'd rather hear a saxophone right now than a trumpet," he said. "If a trumpeter isn't a boss, I don't want to hear him."

She didn't know the tune, and it didn't matter; she fitted her steps to those of the man who held her in his arms, and moved with him.

"Dreaming?"

She opened her eyes. "Gee. I didn't know the music stopped. You're a terrific dancer. Honey, if you want to sow any wild oats, plant 'em right here."

"Starting when? I like to think I'm sowing on fertile ground."

"You've been cultivating and fertilizing for months now, but I always heard that spring is planting time, and this is just late winter."

"Ever heard of winter wheat? You're getting sassy."

A baritone saxophone began to growl the opening notes of "Lover Man;" he opened his arms and she stepped into them. Slow and sensuous, the jazz man played and Russ danced the man's tune and mood. He held her so close to him that her breasts began their tell-tale ache against his chest, and when arousal snaked toward her loins, she missed a step.

"Sorry," she murmured, not trusting her voice.

"Give in to it, sweetheart. Let yourself go."

"I can't with you holding me like this in front of all these people."

"They're living their own lives," he said, but he danced a little farther away. "Are you all right?"

She squinted up at him. "After what you just did to me, don't you dare ask."

She had thought he would smile, but his solemn face told her that he understood how she felt and that his experience had been similar.

"This is nothing to play with, Velma. I have to accept that, and so do you." At that moment, the band struck up a Latin number, and his face brightened into a broad smile, exposing his perfect white teeth. "Let's go for it, sweetheart."

She was sure her bottom lip dropped when he moved to the Latin beat, his hips swaying and twisting with the rhythm of his dancing feet.

Get with it, girl, she told herself and swung with him into her favorite dance. The music played until she was breathless and wondering if the band leader had a grudge against her. She looked around and saw that the other dancers had moved aside to give Russ and her space and that the band was playing only for them.

She moved close to Russ. "Tell the band leader to cut it off, please."

"Had enough?" he asked looking and dancing as fresh as when they arrived.

"No, but my feet are asking for relief."

At his signal, the band leader ended the music, and the other patrons treated them to a long and loud applause. His eyes widened at that. "You mean we were the only ones dancing?" He walked with her back to their table.

"Looks like it. When these men saw that they couldn't keep up with you, they gave you the floor. What would Drake say if he'd seen us?"

He scratched the back of his neck in a way that suggested perplexity. "Drake? He'd probably faint."

"Are you going to tell me sometime why you aren't what your family perceives you to be? You three brothers are so close, yet they don't really know you."

His quick shrug didn't fool her; she knew him well enough then to understand that his words gave him pause.

"They know the person I've always been. I suppose you're seeing the man who is reacting to you and who is relishing these changes he sees in himself. Until that night in that roadside restaurant when you pretended to be a bride, I never imagined that laughter—I mean a good belly roll—could make a person feel so good.

"As I think of it, there was never that much laughter in our home. Alexis, and especially Tara, changed our lives. They brought joy into that house." He beckoned the waiter. "What would you like to drink?" he asked her.

"Maybe a spritzer. Anything stronger will put me out."

He tipped the waiter. "Thanks, but I think we'll leave now." To her he said, "It's almost midnight. You need to rest."

She couldn't argue with that statement. She'd left her hotel at seven that morning, and exhaustion had finally begun to set in. On the drive home, she struggled to keep her eyes open until he said, "Lay your head against my shoulder and sleep if you want to."

He parked in her driveway, walked with her to her door, unlocked it and handed her the key. "Mind if I come in for a minute?"

She didn't mind and said as much. "I enjoyed the evening,"

she said. "Sorry I pooped out at the end." She turned to go into her living room, but he detained her with an arm across her shoulder.

"I've waited days for this." He drew her into his arms and looked down into her face, vulnerable and raw as she had never seen him. At that moment, she would have given him whatever he asked, for he was deep in her heart. She lifted her arms to him for the kiss that would blot out her senses, but he didn't ask for passion.

His lips moved over hers so gently and so sweetly that her heart constricted with the love she felt for him. "Russ," she whispered. "What kind of message are you sending me? You are uncertain where you want this to lead, if anywhere at all, yet you're tying me in knots."

"I was uncertain, and I fought it, but I know I need you in my life."

"Think, Russ. You're not satisfied with me. You—"

"You have problems, but they are no longer an issue with me. I will help you deal with them, because I am not going to let you scuttle the best thing that has ever happened to me."

"But Russ—"

"I asked you to trust me, to believe in me and to let me love you. Now, I'm asking you to let me help you move the barrier between us. I think you're beautiful as you are. Don't let frivolous notions rob you of your self-confidence, your charm. If there's something important that I don't know, tell me what it is, and I'll do anything I can to help you deal with it. I'm in deep with you, Velma. Are you listening to me?"

She could barely whisper the words. "I trust you, and I'm . . . I'm so happy when I'm with you. You're in here." She pointed to her heart. "Right here."

His hands moved along her back in lingering strokes. "Will you let me know who you are, what hurts you, makes you cry, makes you do devilish things, angers you? I need to know you."

"I'll try. From childhood, I bottled everything up inside of me; it won't be easy."

"I know that, and I promise patience." His left hand caressed the side of her face. "I hadn't planned to stay this long, and I'd better leave so you can get to bed."

She raised an eyebrow. "Now that's a new twist."

"What do you mean by that?" he growled.

She couldn't help laughing, and she let herself enjoy it. "I don't have the energy to battle wits with you. But when you hand me an opening like that, well . . . just think of what came to my mind that I *didn't* say."

"I can imagine." He drew her into his arms again. "Kiss me, sweetheart."

He flicked his tongue across the seam of her closed lips, and when she parted them he slipped inside darting and tasting the nectar he found there. A rush of blood zoomed straight to her loins, and her long-denied libido betrayed her, hardening her nipples and causing a warm throbbing in her love canal. Unconsciously, to increase the pleasure, she tightened her buttocks as if she were doing isometrics, and he stepped back from her. Knowing, and sympathetic.

"We have to do something about this, but not until you've settled a few things within yourself."

"I know."

He kissed her quickly and left. She stood there for a while going over the evening, remembering all he said, and marveling that he had shared with her information about his inheritance and the financial implications. Tomorrow, she would dance for joy, but right then she was almost too tired to crawl into bed. She looked toward heaven. Maybe God would smile on her after all.

The next morning, she dragged herself out of bed and

into the kitchen for a fortifying cup of coffee. She had promised Lydia that when she came back from New Orleans, she would see the endocrinologist. But how she dreaded it. Maybe she'd just stay as she was; Russ liked her that way.

"No. I have to like myself," she said aloud, went for the mobile phone and dialed the doctor's office.

Several days and as many tests later, she left the doctor's office with a prescription for a synthroid pill and the information that she had a hypothyroid condition. She didn't know whether to be happy or sad. "Take one a day," the doctor had told her, "and you have to take a TSH test periodically so I'll know you're getting the right dosage."

"Will I lose weight?" she'd asked him.

His "If you want to" had not filled her with joy. "It's not enough to eat less. Get out more, do things like hiking, riding, swimming," he added. She told him she didn't know how to swim. "Get a young, muscular guy to teach you," he'd said. "I want to see you again in two weeks."

Now, I guess it's up to me. At least it isn't my fault, and I'm doing something about it.

Russ tightened his coat collar as he ran the few steps from Velma's house to his car. He ignited the engine and waited for it to warm up. March couldn't come too soon. After a few minutes, he eased the Mercedes from the curb and headed to his apartment. The past ten hours had changed him irrevocably. When she walked through that gate at the airport and smiled when she saw him, it was as if he'd seen the sunshine after years of darkness. But sitting in the car, looking at her while she caressed his face with such gentleness, such sweetness and tenderness, confessing that she missed him whenever she was away from him, he'd fallen in love with her.

He knew it wouldn't be easy for them, because he had no intention of letting her sell herself short. To his mind, she was the equal of any woman and superior to most.

"I'm not letting her go," he said aloud. "Never."

The next morning, he telephoned her, and could hardly believe the extent of his disappointment when he heard her recorded answer. He left a message saying he was leaving for Eagle Park the next day for a conference with his brothers and would probably be there through the weekend.

"I was taking a walk," she told him when she returned his call. "I have a lot to tell you, so maybe we can steal a few minutes this weekend. I want to talk with Alexis, too."

"Is what you have to tell me good or bad?"

"It has potential for good. You said you'd teach me how to swim. When can we start?"

"In the dead of winter? Our pool isn't enclosed."

"Then, let's join a sports club here in Baltimore. Want to?"

He had promised to help her work through her problems, and if it meant joining a sports club, he would do that. "All right, I'll find a good one. When will you get to Eagle Park?"

"Sometime before dark on Friday. I have appointments here Friday morning, so I can't leave before three. Find out if Henry wants anything and let me know, will you?"

"I will. Drive carefully, sweetheart."

"You, too, love."

Before Russ cut the motor in front of Harrington House, Telford stepped out of the front door to welcome him. "It's good to see you," he said to Russ as they embraced. "Drake went into town, but he should be back in an hour."

"When's he going back to Barbados?"

"As soon as he takes care of his affairs. You've probably

learned that it's one thing to inherit a lot of money, and another thing to put it in the right places."

"That's one of the things I want to discuss with you and Drake. I'll wait till he gets back. Where's everybody else?"

"Tara's in school, Alexis is grocery shopping and Henry's wherever Henry is this time of day."

The comment about Henry struck him as funny, and he laughed. Telford stared at him. "What's come over you, Russ? Don't misunderstand me. Whatever it is, I like it. We all do. But seeing you break into a laugh is so damned strange. You should see how your face and your eyes light up when you laugh."

He lifted his right shoulder in a quick shrug. "Nothing and nobody stays the same. Not even you."

"Damn straight. I'm changing before my own eyes."

Velma would laugh at that, Russ thought, and she'd have something witty to say about it. "You're happy, Telford, and you can't imagine how glad I am for you. Alexis is as different from Mama as sugar is from salt."

"I didn't realize that still bothered you. Knowing what Alexis sacrificed for Tara, and seeing how she loves and cares for her child helped me get over Mama and her selfishness."

"Uncle Fentress told me why she behaved as she did. That didn't excuse her, but it helped me to understand her. It doesn't cut as badly."

They walked toward the kitchen, looked in and didn't see Henry and went down to the basement recreation room. "I'd like to know what he said, but it hardly matters. I've put it behind me; if I hadn't, I wouldn't have been able to love Alexis. Tell you what . . . Let's throw a few darts," Telford said, "It's been ages since I beat you at this."

Drake found them there. "How's it going, brother?" he asked Russ, his arms open in their usual greeting.

"Haven't got a thing to complain about. Life's good."

Drake stepped back and looked at Russ. "Same old sourpuss. You're looking fit, man."

"Don't be so sure about the sourpuss," Telford said.

After they discussed their projects, and each reported on his aspect of the work, Russ sat against the arm of the leather sofa and crossed his knees. "I've decided to take a part of the money Uncle Fentress left me and restore a row of boarded-up, vacant houses in Baltimore. Of course, I'll have to purchase them. They're on the edge of a slum neighborhood, but if I do what I'm planning, the area is bound to undergo some gentrification. I'll make the housing available to homeless families, so I'm not after financial returns. They'll be known as the Joshua Harrington Victory Homes. The owner abandoned the property, so it belongs to the city. I put in a bid this morning, and I got the impression they're eager to unload it. Since I'm developing it for homeless families, the cost will depend on the plans I submit."

"I take it you'll be the architect," Drake said.

He nodded. "That's the biggest outlay."

Telford stood, stuck his hands in the back pockets of his jeans and walked to the other end of the room and back. "All right, you're laying out the money for the property, materials and manpower, but you need a builder, so why not use me?"

"Right," Drake said. "Let Harrington Brothers do the job. You'll get what you want, and we'll all honor our dad. What are we going to do about the Sparkman holdings in Eagle Park and Frederick?"

"According to his accountant, it's all income-generating property," Russ told them. "Why don't we change the titles to Harrington Brothers, maintain the property and split the monthly yield?"

"Works for me," Telford said.

"Me, too," Drake assured them, "and dealing with it this

way is less of a hassle. Besides, the value of good real estate increases."

Russ threw the dart that remained in his hand and missed the bull's eye. "I forgot to mention that I'm giving Henry a substantial amount. Who knows? If Bennie ever catches him, he'll need every penny he can lay his hands on."

Drake stared at him as if he were from outer space. "*Bennie?* You're kidding."

"No I'm not. Henry can hardly stand her. He suggested he wouldn't mind if I shot her."

Remembering the conversation, he threw his head back and laughed. Visions of Bennie chasing Henry flooded his mind, and he laughed until he almost lost his breath.

"Sorry," he said when he could control his laughter, "Bennie with Henry makes as much sense as a toy poodle with a greyhound. Not to worry though, Bennie's chasing the wind."

He noticed that Drake stared at him. "This is the second time I knew you to laugh this way. Keep it up. I'm told laughter makes you live longer."

"Yeah," Telford said, "and if we're all nice to Henry, maybe he'll forget how to make cabbage stew."

"Don't even think it," Russ said. "We're always nice to Henry, and he always does as he pleases." He heard the wistful note in his voice. "Still, I wouldn't exchange him for anything."

"Neither would I," his brothers said in unison, and then announced that they also planned to give some of their inheritance to Henry.

"And he'll leave it all to Tara," Russ said, "but if that will give him pleasure, it's fine with me."

"Seen Velma?" Drake asked him.

"Uh . . . she'll be here Friday."

"So you've seen her," Drake insisted.

"Yes."

"Now look, brother, nobody every accused you of being talkative, but why so taciturn? If you want me to back off, just say so."

"I know you have my interest at heart, Drake, and I appreciate it," Russ said, "but I'm treading through a veritable minefield right now, and I don't want anybody's ideas and feelings to influence me but my own."

"Just answer this," Drake persisted, "are you living with her?"

"No way. Trial marriage isn't for me. I wouldn't invest myself to that extent without a firm commitment from the woman, and shacking up implies the opposite."

"Considering how conservative you are, I don't know why I asked."

"Conservative? I wonder what you'd have said if you'd seen me at the Silvertone Lounge in Baltimore night before last."

Drake sat forward. "You were in the Silvertone?"

Russ nodded. "Sure was, and I had a ball."

"Next, somebody's going to tell me you danced half the night," Drake said.

He didn't know when he had so enjoyed rattling Drake. "Not quite that long. About three hours. The music was mind boggling."

"And so was the woman, I'll bet," Telford said. "I hope she doesn't prove to be as close mouthed as you."

"Considering the changes that have come over him," Drake said to Telford, "I'd welcome the woman with open arms even if she made a living collecting cans and didn't have a tooth in her head."

He didn't know why, but aggravating Drake—the certified Harrington lover man—was sweet music to his soul.

"Don't get carried away, Brother," he said to Drake, "You and Telford are not the only Harrington men who can make a woman weak in the knees."

"*What?*" they asked in unison.

"Are you sure you're all right?" Telford asked.

He crossed his heart and grinned just to exasperate them further. "Never felt better. Life is sweet."

"I'm going to wake up and find this is a prank someone's playing at my expense," Drake said. "I can't wait till Friday. I bet she'll talk."

"I have no fear of that." Russ said. "Look, I have to work on my plans for renovating those houses. I should have something to show you in a couple of days." He started up the stairs, turned and looked back at them. "Don't bother to speculate; any idea you get will be the wrong one."

"What do you make of it?" Drake asked his older brother. "He's a different man. Not only is he giving out all this laughter, but he's downright talkative. If you weren't witnessing it along with me, I might think I was losing my sanity."

"Oh, come on. Russ is in love, and furthermore, I'm sure he knows it."

"You think so? I was leaning toward that, too. I hope it's Velma."

Telford patted Drake's shoulder. "Not to worry; of course it's Velma. But I'm a little surprised; he intimated that he had some reservations about her."

"If she can bring this out in him, he's probably decided that whatever he didn't like isn't important."

"Not Russ," Telford said. "He may be besotted with her, but his eyes are wide open. That brother doesn't allow himself to get hoodwinked by anybody, Drake; not even you or me."

"She's good for him," Drake said, "and I'm rooting for her."

"And she will need all the support she can get. Beneath this new facade is the old Russ. He can't discard thirty-four years of himself overnight, unless he got amnesia, and that hasn't happened."

Velma turned into Number Ten, John Brown Drive as nightfall set in, parked in the circle and walked back to the trunk of the car to remove her suitcase and the items she brought for Henry. But as she opened the trunk, his arms encircled her.

"I'll get that for you; come on inside, it's very cold out here." He hugged her. "I'd kiss you if I didn't think we'd have icicles dripping off our chins. If Drake saw that, he'd be a nuisance for the remainder of my life."

"Then how about a nice little dry kiss?"

"Yeah. Why not?" He kissed her nose, then brushed his lips over hers. "I'd as soon wait; it's too cold to feel anything. Come on."

He hung her coat in the hall closet. "Wait here while I get your bag."

"There's also a shopping bag of food for Henry, and a wrapped package for Tara."

"Go on down to your room, and I'll bring them. Oh yes. Rub a towel over your face until you warm it up."

His laughter warmed her, set her clock to ticking properly. "And you rub yours," she said. "Cold lips aren't much more inviting than cold stew, unless, of course, you're short of opportunities."

"I've been four days without opportunities," he grumbled.

"I know, darling, but we can fix that."

He eyed her with a stern facial expression. "Is that another one of your *double entendres?*"

With a playful slap on his buttocks, she said, "Hurry back. I want to get out of these clothes. I've had them on since seven this morning."

"Right. Be back in a minute."

Inside the guest room, she kicked off her shoes and sat down in the overstuffed chair that Alexis had covered in gold, antique satin. There was no denying her sister's exquisite taste. "But I no longer think that way," she said to herself. She rushed to answer his knock, and he dropped the suitcase beside her feet and pulled her into his arms.

"Don't overdo it, baby," he said. "When I walk out of here, I have to go straight to my brothers, and that will be tantamount to passing military inspection."

"Telford, too?"

"Sure. They're both curious about what's going on with me."

"And you didn't tell them." She didn't question him, but stated a fact.

"I figured they'd have more fun guessing." His lips, warm, firm and sweet pressed her mouth, and she opened to him, took him in and feasted on the loving he gave her. "When can we talk? I'm anxious to know what you have to tell me."

"About half an hour. Can we meet in the den? I . . . I hope you'll see it my way."

She could see that he forced the smile. "I hope so, too."

Chapter Eight

"It's not a good time for us to get into anything deep," Russ told her when she met him in the den as she'd promised. "Telford just told me that our foreman will be joining us for dinner and later to discuss our projects in Philadelphia and Eagle Park. Drake's leaving Monday for Barbados, and we need this conference."

She understood, and maybe she'd better wait to tell him what the doctor said, for he had as much as warned her that the treatment alone wouldn't insure a loss of weight.

"I just got a plum of a job right there in Baltimore," she told him. "It's a national fraternity that scoffs at Greek letters, a society of intellectuals, and they didn't question the cost."

"Where in Baltimore?"

"They're renting the Horseshoe Club, and from what I can gather, that's class."

"It definitely is that. That job will probably bring you some good business."

"That's what I'm hoping."

He didn't seem disappointed that what she told him had no direct bearing on their relationship, and she let herself relax. Alexis peeped into the room.

"Drake told me you were here," Alexis said, spreading her arms to welcome her older sister. "My, but you're looking great."

"She always looks good," Russ said, precipitating the sharp rise of Alexis' eyebrows.

"Can't argue with that. The brothers are having a conference after dinner, so you and I will have a chance to catch up."

"Seems like it," Velma said, to which Alexis replied, "But you'd rather be with someone else. I certainly don't blame you."

Russ' arm slid across her shoulder, warming her from her head to the bottom of her feet, and she automatically leaned closer him. Her sister's knowing look sent a rush of heat to her face, and she stopped herself just before she turned and buried her face in Russ' shoulder.

"You're closer to him than when you were last here," Alexis said to Velma as they sat in Velma's room sipping after-dinner coffee. "I know he cares for you, but has he told you?"

"In so many words, yes. I just can't seem to open up to him. I want to, and I trust him completely, but I can't seem to—"

"Let him see your shortcomings," she finished for Velma. "Until you do, and until the two of you can discuss the most intimate and painful things and still love and respect each other, you're not going anywhere. Russ is ready for that, and he isn't going to wait forever until you get there."

"He said he would be patient with me while I fumble my way."

"But he didn't give you until forever, I'll bet?" Alexis'

pause indicated a diffidence not usually associated with her self-assured sister. "He . . . uh . . . I think he's refusing to cast his lot with a woman who doesn't like herself and who isn't self-confident enough to accept and appreciate his feelings about her. There! I said it."

"What? He said *that?* When?"

"Several weeks ago. He seemed unhappy as well as adamant, but today, something's changed."

"I suppose he's hopeful. I lay off my diet when I'm with him, but I've made up my mind to lose weight, and that's that."

"That's your right, but you shouldn't do that because you think someone else looks better than you do. Besides, Russ likes what he sees when he looks at you and what he feels when he holds you."

"You can talk. Just look at you, Alexis. There isn't a model in this world who looks better than you do."

"Nor one who holds Russ Harrington's interest."

"This isn't about Russ; it's about me. Okay?"

"All right, but this goes deeper than your weight. If you packed away your caftans, and bought a wardrobe of lovely, flattering clothes, your weight isn't the core of the problem. And you'll discover that I'm right."

"I appreciate that you're telling me this because you care about me, and maybe you're right, but I have to find my own way."

"I know, and I'll always be here for you, no matter what."

She hugged Alexis, for nearly her entire life, the one source of love and affection that she could count on. "That's the one thing I'm sure of."

They sat quietly for a few minutes, each in her own thoughts. She had to straighten out her life. Already thirty-one years old, if she was going to have a family of her own, she'd better get started. Thoughts of Tara and the joy she gave to everyone who knew her prompted her to ask, "Does Tara spend the night away from home often?"

"Oh, dear, no. Grant Roundtree's having a pajama party for five of his friends, and Tara would have raised a ruckus if we'd refused to let her go. She needed a playmate, Grant doesn't live too far away, and they've grown very close."

"I noticed that at your wedding. That little boy is as protective of her as a man is of his woman."

"He copies his father's behavior with his mother. Adam is a strong family man and a devoted husband." She locked her hands behind her head and released a sigh. "But Telford doesn't like to come into this house and find that Tara isn't here. She lights up his life."

"Well, those guys will talk all night, and I won't get my kiss, so I might as well turn in."

"Play your cards right, and you can soon kiss him, turn over and go to sleep," Alexis said.

"Oh yeah? I might kiss him and turn over, but you can bet I wouldn't be going to sleep."

Alexis' throaty, sexy laugh reminded her of the sound of their mother's giggles when she was alone with their father, intimate times more often followed by bickering and loud accusations. Quickly, she shut out the memory, kissed her sister good night and watched her as she glided down the hall, a tall, willowy slip of elegance.

"I'll never be tall," she said to herself, "but one day, I'll wear a size twelve or fourteen."

After breakfast the following morning, Saturday, she dressed in pants, two sweaters and walking shoes, put on a cap, scarf, and gloves, got her coat and started out to brave the brisk late February cold. She knew from the conversation the previous evening at dinner that the brothers would spend the day trying to find out who was stealing their tools and supplies. Russ felt as if he should spend time with her, entertain her, but she wasn't a child and she let him know it. She'd be there when he and his brothers finished their work.

She returned to the house around ten, her face feeling like a glacier, and went into the kitchen intending to get a hot drink. The doorbell rang. "I'll get it," Henry said, left her and took his time getting to the door.

"I want to speak with Russ Harrington." The voice, soft, cultured and feminine, got her attention, and she forgot about the hot drink.

"What you want with him?" Henry asked. "He's not here."

"It's personal, and I'm not leaving until I speak with him."

"I said he ain't here. You planning to camp out here on the steps in the cold?"

He closed the door and nearly knocked Velma down, causing her to wonder at the source of his anger. She wanted a look at the woman, but decided she had better not risk opening the door. Instead, she called Alexis.

"You mean he closed the door in her face?" Alexis asked as she rushed down the stairs.

"I didn't interfere," Velma said, "because Henry usually has a reason for being obstinate."

"You're right, but no matter who she is or what she wants, I can't let her stand out there in this freezing weather."

Velma wanted nothing to do with the woman, so she started to her room, but stopped when she heard Henry speaking on the telephone.

"I don't know who she is, Russ; as far as I know, she ain't never been here before. She's maybe an inch taller than Velma, don't seem to weigh too much, lean face and looks like she might be a Native American. "All right, but that's gonna cause more trouble than you wanna deal with." After a long pause, Henry continued. "It's no matter. Alexis let her in and gave her a seat in the living room. Yeah? All right, I'll tell her."

He stopped in front of Velma. "Yer headed to the right place. Whatever this is, it ain't nothing Russ done wrong. There ain't a crooked bone in his body."

"Thanks" was as much as she could manage, and she went on to her room.

Shortly after one, she decided that whatever was going to happen had happened, refreshed her makeup, combed out her hair and headed to the kitchen for a sandwich and tea.

"That's the biggest damned lie I ever heard," she heard Russ say, his voice low with controlled anger. "Where do you get off coming here, upsetting my family with this nonsense? We had a one-night affair, and I made certain that you didn't get pregnant. 'No commitments, no promises, no regrets, just tonight,' you said. I was needy, and I took what you offered, but I am not a fool. I put on not one but two condoms, didn't trust even that, and withdrew."

She nearly dropped the sandwich on the floor as she grabbed the edge of the counter for support. She didn't consider it eavesdropping, as no one made an effort to whisper, so she continued to listen. At last, unable to resist getting a look at the woman, she made herself walk to the living-room door, leaned against the wall and sucked in her breath.

The woman's beauty met any standard, taller than she and much slimmer. She wanted to turn away, but couldn't and stood rooted to the spot.

"I want a DNA test, and I want it Monday," Russ said. "I would support my child because it was mine, but you're not sticking me with responsibility for another man's stupidity. I'll meet you at the courthouse in Eagle Park Monday morning at nine. If you're not there with that child, I will sue you for slander. And bring the birth certificate; I want to see who you listed as the father."

"When were you with her?" Telford asked, with the calmness of one discussing a balmy day.

"The third day of January before last, fourteen months ago."

"How old is your child, Miss?"

"Parker," she said. "Iris Parker. Almost five months. I didn't carry him quite full term."

"I see," Telford said. "I believe Russ when he says he made a special effort to protect you. He doesn't lie. But if, by chance, that child is a Harrington, we're behind you one hundred percent. If you're lying, you'll hear from me."

"And from me, too," Drake said. "I don't believe for one minute that you have a child by my brother. Why didn't you tell him you were pregnant? Not every man wants to father an illegitimate child. If it was his, he had a right to the choice."

He walked over and faced her. "You know what I think, Miss Parker? You read in *The Maryland Journal* that Russ inherited a lot of money. Right? Well, remember this: there isn't one fool in this house."

Alexis rose from the big beige leather chair that she favored. "I'll see you to the door, Miss Parker. Don't forget to be at the courthouse with your son at nine o'clock Monday morning." She opened the front door. "Good bye."

Velma met her sister in the hall. "Why would she lie, Alexis?"

"For the reason Drake gave her. This has nothing to do with your relationship with Russ."

"Of course not. That is, not unless it's really his, then—"

"Then nothing. It happened before he knew you existed."

She peeped out of the oval window beside the front door. "Hmmm. A Chevrolet." She turned to her sister. "Alexis, did you see how that woman looked? A real beauty queen. Flawless. I wouldn't like to be compared to her."

"But you're already doing it. You come with me."

She grabbed Velma by the arm and walked with her to her room. "Did he marry her? Wasn't he so sure he didn't want a relationship with her that went to great lengths to make sure he didn't *have* to marry her? Velma, don't start comparing yourself with that woman."

"But if that's the type he chose, it's the type he likes, otherwise why did he take her to bed?"

Alexis blew out a long breath. "You are being deliberately dense. You know darned well that a man can take care of his needs and not have an iota of affection for the woman."

"Yes, I know, but she's—"

"She's to be pitied. Be careful how you treat Russ about this."

She was sure that her mouth fell open. What was wrong with Alexis? "How *would* I treat him? I believe every word Russ said. He would never lie about a thing like that. It's just that fate can be nasty sometimes."

Alexis released a long breath. "Thank the Lord. I was afraid you were losing your common sense."

Velma couldn't help grinning. "Fear not; the important thing is what I *am* on the verge of losing."

Alexis threw up her hands. "Don't tell me. I don't want to know about it."

"Why not? I may one day be able to wear your sleek clothes."

"Will you please stop dwelling on your size? Focus on this new situation, and remember that Russ loves *you*."

"If so, that makes you and him the only people who ever loved me."

"Velma, please don't say that. Our parents loved us. I know they did."

"I don't need that kind of love. If what you say is true, why did Papa walk off the day after Mama died leaving me, an eighteen-year-old kid right out of high school, to take care of the funeral and look after you and me? I remember his note verbatim: 'I'm sorry, but I'm leaving. I just can't stay here now. Sell the house. The money ought to see you through school. Papa.' The note was on my pillow in an envelope with thirty-six hundred dollars cash.

"I let you believe he was broken hearted, because I didn't want you to hurt the way I hurt. Well, maybe he was, but not as much as I was having lost both of my parents in two days."

"Oh, Velma. Forgive him. He was only human."

"I will, but not until I confront him. No man who loved his teenaged daughters would be that cruel."

"You aren't going to—"

"I just made up my mind, and nothing you can say will stop me. Right now, I'm going to find Russ."

He didn't see her when she entered the den, but he sensed her presence seconds before her telltale perfume confirmed that she stood beside him. If she didn't stand with him now, if she didn't believe in him, he wanted no part of her. With sharpened senses, he looked down at her not knowing what to expect. She reached up, eased her hand behind his neck and urged him closer.

"Why don't we run into Eagle Park and ice skate for a while," she whispered. "You could use a change of environment."

He had to be certain. "You know what happened in here a few minutes ago?"

She nodded. "I was standing in the doorway."

"And?"

"I believe you. Every word you said. You would never knowingly do anything dishonorable. Come on and let's go skate."

He turned toward his brothers. "We're going into Eagle Park to the skating rink. See you in a couple of hours."

"Wait a minute," Drake said. "You're going *where?*" He repeated it. Drake got up and walked over to Velma. "Have you been sprinkling some kind of dust over my brother? He's taken to laughing like it's going out of style, bops at The Silvertone, and now, he's going ice skating."

She gazed up at Drake, her face shrouded in innocence. "Where do you find that dust you're talking about? I can definitely use some. This man isn't easy to handle. What's the name of it?"

At the look of confusion on Drake's face, priceless and real, Russ' throat rumbled with mirth, and the more Drake stared at her, the harder he struggled to contain it.

"Damn," Drake said, and Russ let the laughter roll out of him.

Telford leaned against the back of the sofa and stretched his long legs out in front of him. "If you ask me, it's Brighton dust, and she's not the first person to spread it around."

"Maybe I ought to thank God there're only two of 'em," Drake said.

"Wrong," Russ said. "I would think you'd be sorry there aren't three. After all, you already know that this pattern is unbeatable." He eased his left arm around Velma's waist and walked with her to her room.

"I don't know how long it'll take me to clear myself of these charges. If she doesn't meet me at the courthouse, I'll have to sue her, and I don't know where she lives."

"Don't worry about that. I saw her license plate, and it's INP 2003. Must be her car, since the plate had her initials."

He pulled her into his arms. "If I kissed you like I want to right now, I'd probably cause a spontaneous combustion."

"Oh, honey. Give in to it, and let's see what happens."

With her lips warm, welcoming, glistening, and beckoning

him, heat plowed through him and with a hoarse groan, he slipped his tongue through her parted lips. She pulled him into her, firing his passion with the sucking motion that he knew would one day catapult him into ecstasy. Her breasts began rubbing across his chest while her hips undulated against him. Nearing full arousal, he kicked the door open, stepped inside the room with her and closed the door with his foot.

"I want you more than I want to breathe, but I know that if I bury myself deep inside of you, I won't want to walk away. I'm not going to settle for less than I know we could have together, and for that we need a bare, no-holds-barred discussion. Do you understand?" Her body quivered, and he closed his eyes as desire pelted him.

"Woman, you don't want me on these terms. Give us a chance, so I can be everything I can be and want to be to you."

She stepped back from him. "Did I start this, Russ? I was almost minding my own business when you—"

He ran his hands ruthlessly over the back of his neck. She wasn't real. "You can't make a joke out of something this important, Velma."

"Joke? I was trying to tell the truth. If I hadn't turned it on a little bit, we'd probably be at the skating rink by now."

"Oh, hell." He put his arms around her. "Baby, there're two of us rowing this boat. Put on something warm and meet me at the bottom of the stairs in ten minutes, okay?"

She reached up, kissed him on the mouth and said, "Be gone with you." He turned to open the door and felt a slap on his buttocks. *Get out of here, man. She doesn't need to know what she just did.* After a long, penetrating look at her, he hurried down the hall and dashed up the stairs to his room. Thank God for a little exercise!

* * *

She didn't know why she had suggested they ice skate, except that she knew he needed to do something different, even exciting, before he shifted back to the old Russ, the solemn man who almost never found anything sufficiently amusing to laugh at it. It proved a tonic for her as well.

"Let's sit over there on that bench," he said, "and I'll help you with your skates."

Velma didn't need help with her skates, and seconds before telling him so, a window of wisdom flooded her mind with insight, and she realized that he needed to do something for her. Kneeling on one knee, he slipped on her skates, tied the shoes and looked up at her.

"Have you ever been engaged?" he asked her.

She tried to imagine how that question came to his mind. "No. You're the first man I haven't managed to . . . to discourage, And I may succeed with you, yet."

He didn't smile, and when she felt his hand on her left knee, possessive, and therefore not by accident, she knew he hadn't liked her answer.

"All right," she conceded, "I haven't agreed to marry, because I have never loved a man that much. Did anybody ever ask me? Yes, but I didn't even consider it seriously."

"I see." He straightened up and sat beside her. "And you didn't allow yourself to love anyone because you thought you weren't perfect, that you might be rejected."

"I didn't say that."

"You didn't have to say it. You love Alexis, and you're proud of her. I can see that sibling envy can affect a person's feelings about himself, but that usually translates into dislike and even meanness toward that sibling. But you would defend Alexis with your life. So there's more to it."

"I've never tried to understand my feelings about myself, Russ, because I have always accepted them. By the time I was old enough to go to school, I looked upon Alexis as my responsibility. She idolized me, followed me everywhere, and that seemed to please our parents and, as I look back, especially our mother. As we grew older, I protected her from the ugliness that was our world. A world of self-centered parents who often behaved as if they had no children.

"I was about eight the first time I was aware that one of their verbal brawls ended in loud sex. And until my mother died and my father disappeared, that was their pattern. One day, when I was about eleven, I asked my father if he would move Alexis to the guest room, and when he asked why, I told him. He said nothing, but he changed her room and left me to deal with the situation as best I could. I don't think they could relate to each other in any other way."

"So you sheltered her and took the brunt of it yourself."

"I guess you'd say that. She was the most popular girl in our school, got the leading role in school plays, was a drum majorette, everything that goes with being beautiful."

"But that didn't bother you until she married."

"That's the night I saw the difference between her and me, and that was when I realized I'd never have what I want so badly."

His hand wrapped around hers, as if to encourage her. "Go on."

She blinked back the moisture that threatened to drop from her eyes. "I . . . I wanted what she had . . . the love of a wonderful man and a houseful of people who cared deeply for her and—"

"And what?"

"Children of my own. My own family." The tears came then, and she couldn't stop them as they rolled down her cheeks.

"This was the wrong time for us to start this," he said and wrapped his arm around her. "Your life hasn't been easy, and we could say the same of Alexis. But she has put it behind her, and I want you to try and do the same." He hugged her. "If I did what I feel like doing right now, I'd probably get locked up."

She wiped her eyes and looked at him, unable, even in her sadness, to resist putting words to the image in her mind's eye. "You? They'd probably pull me in first, 'cause, honey, you can make a woman think and feel sin."

"Sin? Is that what they call it these days?" He stood, grasped her hand and moved onto the rink. Repeat after me: 'I am Russ Harrington's woman, and he knows I am perfect.' "

She couldn't help laughing and thought her heart would overflow with joy. "You are totally nuts, but you are number one with me."

As they skated, she began to notice the women who gazed at him. "Serves her right," she said beneath her breath when one woman tripped over her skates as she passed Russ. A glance at him and she knew he hadn't seen the woman or the incident. He didn't seem to mind forwardness in a woman, and that was probably a good thing, since she possessed a talent for self-assertion, but breaking your neck to make a man notice you somehow didn't make sense.

"We'd better pack it in," he said. "It's six o'clock, and I'll need to change before dinner."

"So will I."

In the locker room, she sat on a bench to remove her skates and, to her surprise, he knelt in front of her, untied her shoes and slipped them off her feet.

"Thanks," she said, awed by the thought that struck her. He was kneeling before her, putting on her skates when he suddenly asked her if she had ever been engaged. She didn't have to be an Einstein to make the connection: the thought of asking her to marry him or maybe swearing he would never do it had crossed his mind. She'd give anything to know which.

Tara raced to meet them when they walked into the house. "Uncle Russ, Aunt Velma, guess what?"

"What?" they asked in unison.

"Grant is going to be my partner in the school play, and he's going to be George Washington and I'm going to be Martha Washington. Grant's daddy said thank God we wouldn't be Republicans. Is my dad going to mind?"

"I don't know," Russ said. "Didn't you ask him?"

"No, because I don't know what a Republican is."

"But you won't be one, so don't worry."

Her bottom lip dropped. "But Uncle Russ, we don't know who George Washington is."

He lifted her and hugged her, his face softening with love and warmth. "Was. He's not here any longer. When he was here, he was a wonderful man, the father of our country."

"Oh. Who was the mother?"

Velma nearly laughed at the perplexed expression on Russ' face. "Uh . . . his wife, I suppose."

She scampered down. "I'm going to telephone Grant. He doesn't know that, and he's worried."

A frown flitted across Russ' face. "Worried about who was the mother of our country?"

She appeared confused, but only for a second. "He wanted Martha Washington to be George Washington's wife in the play."

Russ stared at Velma, as if asking for guidance. Then, he said, "Tell him not to worry. You'll be his wife in the play."

She clapped her hands, hugged Russ' leg, and ran up the stairs, obviously with the intent of telephoning Grant. Russ looked toward the stairs and back at Velma. "Was life ever that simple?"

"Or that sweet?" she answered.

"I'd better get upstairs and freshen up," he said, "or Alexis will have my head. Thanks for being there for me when I needed you, and for opening up to me the way you did. See you later." His lips brushed hers. Then he gazed down at her for a long time before turning and dashing up the stairs.

She awakened at about three o'clock the next morning, dampened with sweat and panting for breath. Slowly, she remembered with crystal clarity the vision of Iris Parker chasing her until she stumbled and the woman stared down at her, laughing. "He's mine," Iris sneered, "and he will always be mine. Look at me. Can *you* take a man away from *me?*"

She got up, straightened the rumpled bedding and crawled back in bed, but insofar as rest was concerned, the night was shot, and she could only blame herself and her sensitivity to the way she looked.

"I'm going to take that medicine, follow my diet and get some exercise every day, and I'm going to a spa and treat myself well. I deserve it," she said aloud and began waiting for seven o'clock.

"Are you going to work at the warehouse with your brothers this morning?" Velma asked Russ at breakfast.

"I have to," he said, and she thought she detected a tone of regret in his voice. "Drake leaves tomorrow morning, so it will be some time before we can work on that inventory again."

"Found any clues as to who's ripping you off?"

"No, but we're able to determine who is not doing it, and that's important."

"Then I'll catch up with you in Baltimore. I have to prepare for that party I told you about."

"You mean the fraternity that doesn't use Greek letters? When is the affair?"

"Saturday night."

"They didn't give you much time to prepare for it."

"I know, and I'm charging them for that."

"I wish you could wait until this afternoon, and I'd tail you home."

"It would be nice. Thanks for the thought."

Saturday came too soon. The number of last-minute chores was almost too demanding for one person to handle. "I'll be glad when I open my office and have a place to store my own merchandise," she told the woman she'd hired to assist her.

"Be sure and remember me when you start hiring," the woman said.

"If we get on well here, I will," she said.

She didn't remember a more elegant, perfectly served dinner, but almost as soon as the coffee and aperitifs were served, guests at table after table lit a joint, and she was sickened by the aroma and the inhalation of the smoke. Because she was responsible for everything in the room, from glassware to the chairs on which the people sat, she was reluctant to leave. She noticed a change in the type of drugs used and, in desperation, called her sister and explained her dilemma.

"I'm responsible for all these things I rented," she told Alexis, "and I can't decide whether to walk out or stay here and protect my financial interest and risk being arrested."

"I hope I never have to bail you out of jail, hon. Go near the front door, so you can get out if things get worse. And have your coat and your pocketbook close by."

She enjoyed a challenge, and right then, she faced a serious one, but if she stayed and was arrested on a felony charge, she could say goodbye to her business.

"I'm leaving," she said to herself. "After all, everything I rented is insured." She rushed to the cloakroom, got her wrap and briefcase and headed for the door. But as she reached for the doorknob, the door opened with such force that she fell backward and nearly toppled to the floor.

"Sorry, I . . ."

Thinking that a policeman had stormed in, she stood behind the door waiting for a chance to slip away. However, the intruder, realizing that he had hit something or someone, pulled the door as if to close it.

"What the . . . Velma! For Pete's sake, did I hit you with this door?"

She stared up at Russ, too dumbfounded to speak and wondering how and why he was there. "Let's get out of this place," he said, taking her briefcase in one hand and her elbow in the other one. "I smell that weed all the way out here."

"How did you know about this? Did Alexis tell you?"

"Indeed, she did, and it's what you should have done."

"I was leaving when you almost knocked me unconscious, wasn't I?"

"I know how you must feel about this, so I'm not going to react if you decide to chew me out for coming here to get you." As startled as she was, she recognized the change in his voice from outrage to gentle caring. "Will you let me take you home?"

He settled her in his car before getting in and fastening his own seat belt. "Where to?"

By then, her alarm was turning to anger. "Home, please. All that scrumptious gourmet food, and I had to leave without tasting even a crumb of it. I have never been so disgusted."

He rested his forearms on the steering wheel. "Run that past me again."

When she repeated it, he said, "If I ever learn how your mind works, I'll give myself a medal and I will deserve it. If you're hungry, we can go to a restaurant, to my apartment where I may be able to find a sandwich, or to your house, and I'll cook whatever I can find there."

"How about take-out?" she asked him.

"Whatever you want."

"Surprise me with something from that gourmet take-out shop."

He bought two veal cordon bleu dinners, a quart of pecan praline ice cream and a bottle on Pinot Griglio wine. "We are going to have a feast," he told her and headed the car for her house.

"You set the table, and I'll put the food out," he said. "Where do you keep your serving plates?"

"What the heck?" she said to herself and led him to the cabinet that held her fine porcelain. "He bought the dinner, but we're eating it in my house." She set the table with white linen placemats, crystal wine goblets, sterling silver flatware, and white candles in silver candlesticks. Not satisfied, she took the bowl of yellow snap dragons from the coffee table in the living room and placed them in the center of her dining room table.

"There," she said, lit the candles and dimmed the chandelier.

"Hey! What's all . . . Were you expecting dinner guests?" he asked her.

"I set the table while you were doing whatever you were doing in there."

"Woman, your mouth is going to be your ruin."

"I'm sure that with your help it can learn to be . . . uh . . . gratifying rather than ruinous."

"I am not going to touch that. The table is lovely. You and Alexis have a penchant for elegance, and it suits you both, or maybe I should say you wear it like your skin."

"Thanks. Hadn't you better say the grace? I can imagine what Tara would do if she saw us sit down and immediately begin to eat."

"Don't mention Tara and grace in the same sentence. She's the reason I started saying it at home. By the time she finished saying the grace, the food was cold. She was four years old, first time I had that experience, and she blessed everybody she ever heard of."

She didn't think it wise to eat the ice cream following that caloric meal, but a feeling, warm and sensuous, washed over her when she looked first at the double scoop that he served her and then into his dark eyes. Eyes that sparkled with warmth, affection and mischievousness.

"Anything I give you will be good for you," he said with a grin that spread over his entire face.

"Anything?" A ten-year-old would have detected the sexual overtone in that one word. In an attempt to cover that brazenness, she smiled and added, "Don't get me wrong; I don't doubt it."

He set the ice cream down in front of her and handed her a spoon. "It's a good thing you don't, because nothing revs my engine like a good challenge."

She thought it best not to push the envelope further, to resist being clever and enjoy the evening with him. "I don't put these dishes in the dishwasher," she said, "so let's stack them in the sink."

"Nope. We'll clean the kitchen properly."

She stared at him. "You're ruining your reputation as a sloppy person."

"No, I'm not. I'm sloppy, but I am very clean, and I don't like to look at dirty dishes." They hand-washed the dishes and glasses and put the silverware in the dishwasher. "Now, you won't face it tomorrow morning." He took her hand and walked with her to the living room.

"Would be nice if we had a fire in that fireplace," he said. "It's what I miss most about being away from Harrington House."

"It won't take but a minute," she said and lit the kindling.

"Come over here?" he asked when she would have sat opposite him, and patted the place beside him on the sofa. His arms slid around her; she inched closer to him and rested her head on his shoulder.

"You ate with gusto tonight."

"And I'll pay for it."

"Do you believe that the only thing about you that attracts me is what I see?"

"Whether you'd walk away from me and whether you would still care for me aren't the same thing."

He tightened his arms around her, leaned over her and gazed into her eyes saying nothing, wordlessly communicating to her what she needed so badly to hear him put into words.

"Tell me," she whispered. "Russ, tell me you care for me."

"Don't you know that I do? When we're together like this, can't you feel it? I care deeply for you."

His heat enveloped her, firing up every nerve in her body, and heating the blood that rushed to her vagina like lemmings toward the sea. She swallowed the moisture that accumulated in her mouth and lowered her gaze. But he tipped up her chin with his index finger.

"Look at me."

The hard, masculine man in him seemed to jump at her, lassoing her the way a cattleman ropes a steer. She couldn't stand the intensity of his gaze and the sensual storm raging in his eyes sent shivers coursing through her body. "Honey," she whispered as her breathing became pants, "hold me."

Her left hand brushed the side of his face and slid up to the back of his head, but still he gazed at her, seeking she didn't know what. When she could no longer bear it, she said, "I need you, Russ. Just like you need me, I need you."

The words had barely escaped her lips when she felt his mouth hard and urgent on hers. "Open, baby. Open to me."

His tongue drove into her mouth and she welcomed his passion, pulling him deeper, sucking on it, feasting, satisfying her hunger to have him inside of her in any way possible. He slowed the pace, and brushed his lips over her eyes, her cheeks and her neck.

"Kiss me. Kiss me," she moaned, and he ran his tongue along the seam of her lips before finding his home inside, darting, searching and claiming her. She was going mad, she just knew it, when her nipples began to ache and the discomfort between her legs made her want to cross her knees and create a friction of her own.

"Russ, please." She grabbed his hand and rubbed it across the nipple of her left breast.

He unzipped the back of her dress and pulled it down to her waist, tore off her bra, bent to her breast and covered it with his warm lips. Screams tore out of her as he suckled her, teasing the nipple with the tip of his sweet, loving tongue and pulling on her as if his life depended on it. Her hips began to move, and when he stopped, she held his head to her, moaning as he kissed, nipped and suckled.

"Honey . . . oh, Lord."

The suckling ceased, and she looked up to find him gazing down at her. "Do you want me? Now? This minute?"

"Yes. Yes. *Oh yes!*"

"If we take this step," he said in a voice she hardly recognized, "there won't be any turning back for me. So if you're not sure I'm the man for you . . ."

"I love you, Russ. I fell in love with you Christmas Eve. You're it for me."

He zipped up her dress, took her hand and climbed the stairs with her. In her bedroom, he took her in his arms and asked her, "Are you sure?"

For an answer, she unbuttoned his shirt and reached for his belt, but he stilled her hand. "Let me." In seconds he'd stripped her of everything but her bikini underwear, threw back the bed covers, lifted her and lay her between the pink satin sheets. He stood gazing down at her, and when she tried to cover her body with her hands, he stopped her.

"This minute is mine. Let me enjoy it."

She reached out her arms to him and he moved to the edge of the bed, unbuckling his pants as he did so. He let them drop to the floor and stood before her nude but for the G-string that cupped him. She had never dreamed that a man's body could be so beautiful, lean, tapered and muscular.

She wanted to touch him, to feel him, and when she ran her hands over the treasure before her, he jumped to full readiness. She realized that she licked her lips though she was a little scared at the size of him. When he put one knee on the bed, she opened her arms to him in a gesture as old as time. Her legs spread as if of their own volition, for she could think of nothing but getting him inside of her.

"Will you let me lead us in this?" he asked, leaning over her.

For an answer, she nodded, but her fingers itched to stroke him, to make love to him and she moved her hand over his left pectoral. "Too soon for that," he said and brushed her lips with the tip of his tongue. And then he was lying on top of her, and she could feel his strength as she parted her lips for his kiss. But he didn't linger there. His mouth cherished her ears, eyes, nose, neck and throat.

If only she could feel his lips warm and moist pulling at her nipple! But even as she tried to rub her breasts against his chest, he denied her.

"Russ. Honey, please."

"Please what. Tell me what you want. I want to please you."

"I want your mouth on my nipple. I want . . . Oh," she moaned as he suckled her left breast and rolled the nipple of her right one between his fingers. Rivulets of heat cascaded through her body and zoomed straight to her love canal. Her hips undulated and she reached for him, but he moved away from her.

"Russ."

He moved downward, and she felt his lips on her navel, kissing her belly as his fingers skimmed the inside of her thighs. She tried to cross her knees, but he held her open and vulnerable to him, kissing her thighs and beneath her knees until she thought she would incinerate. Suddenly, he gripped her legs, rested them on his shoulders and parted her delicate folds. She held her breath, and then the tip of his tongue sent fire shooting through her. Her moans filled the room as he kissed and sucked until she let out a keening cry.

"Get inside of me. *Honey, get in me.*"

He kissed his way slowly up her body. "Open your eyes, and look at me." She felt his fingers dip into her folds and stroke the nub of her passion until the liquid of love flowed freely from her. If he didn't get inside of her she'd die. He reached down and handed her a condom. "Can you . . . ?" She snatched it from him, took him in her hands and rolled it on him.

"This first time is important for us," he said. "I want you to trust me."

"I do. I do. Please."

He kissed her nose, and let her feel the tip of his penis, but frustrated and anxious, she grabbed his buttocks and swung up to him, taking him inside of her.

"Are you all right?"

She nodded. The feel of him. Oh, the feeling of having him inside of her. Slowly he began to move and as she joined his rhythm, the pulsating began. He increased the tempo, moving in and out and from side to side, filling her to the point of explosion but not letting her burst.

"Russ, I'm dying. I want to burst."

"You will. Be patient and give yourself to me."

"I am. I do."

"All right. Move with me now." He reached between them and stroked her. She couldn't bear it. Suddenly, heat seared the bottom of her feet, her thighs trembled and the squeezing, pumping and clinching began in her vagina.

"Oh, God," he groaned. "Baby!"

The heaven-and-hell pleasure gripped her and she threw out her arms in surrender as her cries of passion echoed through the bedroom. The unearthly sensation plunged her to the depths and then flung her up to ecstasy.

"Oh, Russ. I love you. I love you so much."

The wind seemed to seep out of her, but then she wrapped her weakened arms around him and met his thrusts as he raised his head from her breast, and drove into her, pumping furiously. With a groan, he tightened his buttocks, then let out a fierce shout and gave her the essence of himself.

"Velma. Sweetheart. Mine. Mine."

Open and more vulnerable than he had ever been in his life, he braced himself on his elbows and gave her as much of his weight as he dared. Drained. She had drained him of more than the fluid that left his body, more than his energy and strength; she took from him the part of himself that had always propelled him to walk alone. The quiet of the room, broken only by the sound of their breathing, seemed to him as noisy as the loneliness he had sometimes felt. He couldn't find himself. Still buried within her, still a captive of the drug that gripped him as nothing ever had, he couldn't do the one thing at which he had always excelled: think. He couldn't think straight. When she stirred beneath him, he raised up with his elbows for support and looked down into her face. Her sweet, loving face.

"I love you," he said. "I don't have to ask whether you had an orgasm, because the strength of it nearly wrung me out of socket. Ah, Velma. Velma." Her lips, glistening and pouting, beckoned to him and he bent to taste their sweetness.

"I love you, too. And I want you to know that I never felt anything like that before in my life. I don't think I knew who I was, until now."

He rubbed her nose with his own. "I certainly never had an experience like that one. If I had, only the Lord knows what kind of wild oats I'd have been sowing." He felt a playful slap on his buttocks.

"You no longer know or understand what wild oats are. They're out of fashion. Got that?"

Soul-warming laughter poured out of him. "As long as I can sow my oats with you, I don't care about the wild ones."

She raised her arms and stretched like a cat, and he stared down at her until she drew up her knees, bathed her lips with the tip of her tongue and asked him, "Any more where that came from?"

He grinned, partly because her words amused him and

partly because just knowing that she loved to make love with him turned him on.

"For you, it's like an eternal flame, a spring that can't dry up. Why? Interested?"

The shock of her teeth on his left pectoral sent a shot of adrenalin straight to his groin, and he hardened within her. Pride suffused him when her eyes widened, her lower lip dropped and her eyes then took on the glaze he recognized as desire. She bucked beneath him, and an indefinable, gut-searing sensation plowed through him.

Her fingers dug into his buttocks, urging him to move, and he bent to her breast and sucked her nipple into his mouth. Her muscles tightened around him and he put a hand beneath her hip and carried them on a fast, wild ride to sweet paradise.

He lay buried inside of her, as drunk on her as if he had too much hard liquor. Emotionally and physically depleted. Many times, he had imagined what it would be like to have her fitted to him as a glove fit his fingers. The first touch of her portal had been the kiss of sunshine, the awakening of every nerve ending in his body. And then he was deep inside of her. Home. Heaven. He didn't know how he survived the thrill of it, the shattering, heavenly torture of her explosive release. He kissed her eyes and put his head on the pillow beside her. She didn't know it, but he was hers.

When he awoke an hour later, he wondered how he would react if she lapsed into self-doubt and, with it, the inability to give freely of herself. He knew it was possible, because she still had the image of Alexis always before her, and she still believed that her parents had never loved her—both potentially lethal.

"No matter what else is on your agenda, I want you to make time for us. I'll do the same. I want us to find out if we can make it together. Do you agree to that?"

"I'm glad, because that's what I want. Oh, Russ, I . . . I feel like a stranger to myself."

He tightened his arms around her. "Maybe that's what I was feeling a moment ago. I just couldn't get in touch with myself."

Chapter Nine

Russ drove home slowly, deep in his thoughts. The mechanics of driving his Mercedes from Velma's house to his apartment were far from his mind. A few days earlier, he would have been able to tell himself that he cared for Velma and wanted her and that there was little else to it. And he would have been close to the truth. That was before her acceptance of his explanation about Iris Parker, before she further endeared herself to him with her simple faith and trust, her belief in his integrity as a man.

And then, the sweet, loving way that she received him into her body—giving him all that he asked for and more and shaking him to the roots of his soul—had hurtled him beyond the caring and physical want and into a deeper and more serious, more binding realm. For the first time in his life, he loved a woman and needed her.

In spite of all that, however, he didn't see how he could forego the kind of bond with his woman that he knew was essential to him. And although she had shared things about herself that allowed him to see her vulnerability and to empathize with her, she hadn't given the part of herself that would let him feel that nothing separated them. He needed it, and they could have it. With love and patience, he would lead her to it.

When Velma awoke the next morning lying on her belly, her left knee drawn a little toward her chest, she slid her right hand over the sheet to the empty space next to where she lay—searching. She rolled over, kissed and caressed the pillow that had cradled his head and breathed deeply of the musky male scent that overwhelmed the odor of their lovemaking.

She hadn't wanted him to leave her, but she hadn't articulated her feelings. Female clinging vines—which was how she thought of possessive women—were not among those she admired, and she was danged well not going to become one. She didn't doubt that when they left the Horseshoe Club, lovemaking was not uppermost on Russ's mind any more than it was on hers. They had responded to the moment, and she would never be sorry. How could she be? He gave her the love and loving she never expected to receive—complete fulfillment. And for that, she took greater pride than ever in her womanhood. Memories of that moment when he splintered in her arms, undeniably hers, would never leave her.

She stuck her big right toe out from underneath the covers to test the air, grimaced and dragged herself out of bed. No one would relish the task facing her; she could only guess at the shape in which she would find the Horseshoe Club. After waiting forty minutes for a taxi, she resolved to buy a car. At last she stood in front of the building. From the outer facade, it appeared that the club hadn't suffered any damage. However, she wouldn't let herself relax until *after* she spoke with the manager and examined the things she had rented.

"Yes ma'am, may I help you?" the porter asked Velma when he opened the door.

She glanced around, saw nothing untoward and allowed herself to breathe normally. "May I please see the manager?"

"Right this way, ma'am."

"What happened?" she asked the manager after explaining why she left the club without supervising the cleanup and packing.

"Nothing much, Miss Brighton. The maître d' took care of everything. A few of the rowdies got hauled off in the Baltimore Express to spend the night in jail."

She gaped at him. "You mean the police *did* come?"

"If I hadn't called 'em, the place would have been a wreck. There wasn't a sober person in here, male or female. 'No smoking' signs everywhere, and they perfumed the place with marijuana." He shook his head. "They may call themselves intellectuals, but with the stuff they were using, I bet they burned up their brain cells long ago."

"This is the first and the last time I cater for that bunch."

His perfect composure was not what one would expect of a man whose place of business could have been permanently shut down owing to his customers' disregard of the law, and it irritated her. She took the job primarily on the strength of the Horseshoe Club's reputation as a place catering to an elegant clientele.

As if he read her mind, he explained, "They paid in advance and didn't question the price. Fooled me, but it won't happen again."

"I've never been around such people. From angels to devils in less than two hours."

"Well, I've been in business a long time, but I still make a mistake now and then. We have refined people coming here, people who appreciate the kind of service you render, and I'll be glad to recommend you."

She thanked him, inspected the items she had rented and breathed deeply, relieved that she had accounted for everything and found nothing damaged. "Last time I'm doing this for a group that doesn't give me impeccable references," she told him.

"Makes two of us." He handed her his card. "Don't forget: we rent for wedding receptions, sororities, fraternities, graduation parties, you name it. And the customers almost always ask me to recommend a caterer."

"You never cater these affairs?"

He shrugged. "Never. I could make a lot more money doing it, but I don't need that kind of stress."

She left the club with the intention of visiting her real estate agent, but instead impulsively made a visit to see her friend, Lydia.

"My goodness," Lydia said, "you've gained four pounds. Didn't you go to see that endocrinologist I recommended?"

In spite of Velma's effort to appear nonchalant, learning that she continued to gain weight darkened her mood the way a sudden black cloud blots out the sunshine. Until that moment, she had been happy, she realized, and not even the prospect of facing disorder in the Horseshoe Club had dampened her spirit.

"Maybe this is just my lot in life," she said, unwilling to take on the burden of yet another diet or to follow her current one more rigorously.

"Nonsense," Lydia said. "That's a pile of baloney, and you know it. What did Dr. Klee say?"

"I have a hypothyroid condition. He gave me some pills, but I still have to watch what I eat. When I'm with . . . with Russ, I just eat whatever I want. He thinks people who are preoccupied with the way they look are vain and frivolous."

"And he's right, but controlling your weight is the intelligent thing to do. He's got other reasons for saying that."

She wanted to get off the subject. "I know," Velma said, and she did, but she wasn't ready to deal with those reasons. "I just stopped by to say hello. See you another time."

Half an hour later, she sat in the office of the real estate agent, half happy and half worried. The warehouse he found suited her needs perfectly, but it was defaulted property that belonged to the city, and getting permits represented hurdles she hadn't counted on.

"We have to demonstrate to the city that your business will enhance that neighborhood and provide jobs for the locals. Can you write a good proposal?" the agent asked. The warehouse had probably been vacant for years, but as soon as someone showed interest in buying it, impediments popped up like mushrooms after rain.

"I'll do my best," she told him. "Anybody else bidding on that property?"

He shrugged. "They never tell you that."

She knew she had several strikes against her: no previous ownership of business property, a small business with very few employees, and a business unrelated to the neighborhood's needs. Well, she would write a proposal that would make the buildings commissioner take favorable notice. She couldn't afford to fail, and she wouldn't.

Russ left the movie feeling upbeat. An hour and a half of relaxation without a single murder or shot fired. It was a light story about a guy who loved his horse. He could have used more entertainment of that type. He'd laughed uncontrollably when the horse bit the guy's backside. Relaxed and mellow, he draped his arm around Velma's shoulder.

"Were you serious when you offered to go to the courthouse with me tomorrow morning?" he asked.

"Of course I was serious," Velma replied. "I'll go unless you'd rather I didn't. No telling whether she'll bring along one of those friends of the court, or whatever they're called."

"Television stuff. I'll be glad if you come, but it won't matter whom she brings. I'll accept the results of a DNA test or nothing."

"It's your right to insist on that. I just want to be there for you."

She had so many ways of endearing herself to him, of touching that place in his heart that had once been hard, if not locked, but that softened more every time he saw her and whenever any part of his body made contact with hers. How could one woman bring about so many changes in him so consistently and so swiftly? Time was when he would have considered himself a softie, less than a man, if he opened himself up completely not only to a woman, but to anyone. He didn't have to be told that those years merely prepared him for the transformation he saw in himself, changes that he embraced with pride.

"I'll be here at eight thirty in the morning," he told her when he took her home. "I want to be at the courthouse no later than nine."

"I'll be ready." She had a habit of giving him her door key so that he unlocked her door and opened it. At first, he thought it unusual, but he'd come to like it. He unlocked the door and followed her inside.

"Do I get a kiss?" he asked her.

She said nothing, but clicked on the light switch, and he thought he detected an expression of concern on her face. Still, she looked up at him, lifted her arms to his shoulders and lowered her lashes. She hadn't meant to be seductive, he knew, but the gesture seemed to say, "Do with me as you wish." He knew what would happen if he let himself give in to his feelings, and he wanted to avoid a heated exchange, but he controlled the impulse to back away, lest she misunderstand. With his arms around her, he brought her close to his body, inhaled the dizzying perfume she wore and let her woman's warmth seep into him.

"You're so sweet," he whispered. "Kiss me and let me get out of here."

As if it were the most natural move she could make, her right hand caressed his left cheek, and then her parted lips, soft and glistening, welcomed him. His arms tightened around her as he sipped the sweetness she offered. And like a hummingbird drinking the nectar of a flower, he lingered. Lingered and supped until the heat began its treacherous journey to his loins. Then, he stepped away from her. And that pleased her, he saw, for she registered neither surprise nor displeasure.

"Thanks for such a lovely evening," she said. "See you in my dreams."

Velma didn't want to drift into an affair with Russ, but she knew that, considering the way she felt about him and their mutual explosive reaction to every kiss, no matter how simple or how fleeting, if she wasn't careful she would wake up one morning to find either her clothes in his closet or his clothes in hers. And as much as she had wanted to feel his arms around her and to have his lips and tongue drain her of her will, she couldn't allow their times together always to end in lovemaking. If she had so much as looked into his slumberous eyes when he asked for a kiss, they would have been in her bed that minute.

And if I start to think of what he did to me and the way he made me feel that night, I'll still be awake come daybreak.

She arose early and remembered to say her prayers, for she didn't know what the morning would bring. "I won't let myself contemplate anything unpleasant," she said aloud to herself as she tripped down the stairs on her way to the kitchen. "I didn't offer to go with him because I was curious, but because I love him," she continued.

She opened the door before the echo of the doorbell died away. "Hi, hon," she said, her face bright with a smile that welcomed him. "My goodness, you're dressed to the nines."

He leaned down and kissed her. "You're not looking bad yourself. You look great in that," he said of the dark orange suit. "I always wonder why the sisters wear those drab colors. Nothing beats a dark-skinned woman in just the right autumn color."

"Thanks. If you need coffee, the pot's still hot."

He didn't move away from the door. "I appreciate the thought, but I just had a cup. Ready?"

After he helped her into her coat, she wrapped a long mustard-colored wool scarf around her neck, slipped on her gloves and slung the straps of her pocketbook across her shoulder.

"Let's go."

To his amazement, Iris Parker was sitting in the waiting room when they arrived, rolling a baby carriage with her foot, suitably dressed for a visit to Buckingham Palace.

"Hi. I'm so glad we could meet away from . . ." It was then that she saw Velma.

"Good morning, Miss Parker," Velma said in a tone pleasant enough but without pretending to be friendly. He stifled a laugh when Velma solved the seating problem by sitting in a different section of the waiting room, beating Iris Parker at her own game.

After a brief court hearing, during which each side stated their position as to the child's parentage, the judge ordered the tests. Russ wondered why any woman would subject herself and her child to that kind of scrutiny knowing that she would lose the case.

"You'll get the results at the end of the week," the technician told him.

Holding Velma's hand, he walked over to Iris, but didn't look at the child. He didn't need to, because he knew it had none of his genes. "I don't see how you could subject yourself and your child to this knowing that the result will be negative. Aren't you aware that there is now a court file on you and your son? Did you bring the birth certificate?"

"Couldn't we go somewhere and talk . . . uh . . . privately?"

"That isn't necessary. Ms. Brighton knows all about this, and she won't discuss this with anyone, so go ahead and talk." She winced at that, but he'd only told the truth.

"Well . . . I'm, uh . . . things aren't going too well right now, so—"

He cut her off. "Did you bring a copy of the birth certificate?"

He could see her confidence slipping away like melting winter snow from the limbs of trees in the afternoon sunlight. "I forgot it. I had so many things to remember, formula, Pampers, a bracelet for motion sickness . . . Matt sometimes gets sick in a moving vehicle. Well . . . you know."

"Next time, Iris, pick an easier target."

Her smile weakened, and she bent down to the carriage to adjust something, but she didn't respond to his taunt. He wondered what that misadventure would cost him as he watched Velma concentrate her attention on Iris Parker.

* * *

How do you feel?" Velma asked Russ as they walked down the courthouse steps. "If I were you, I'd be furious."

She didn't see how a woman would have the gall to accuse a man of paternity knowing that it wasn't true. Her perusal of the child and of Iris made her wonder about the woman's motive, especially since it was obvious that the child's only resemblance to Russ was in its humanity. *Iris wanted Russ and, evidently, would do whatever it took to get him.*

"Naturally, I'm annoyed," he said, frowning. "There's the inconvenience as well as the stigma—the accusation itself and my name on a court docket. If I'm furious with anybody, it's with myself. I thought I'd picked an intelligent, modern woman who had as much to lose as I did, a woman who took care of her needs with no strings attached, as she claimed. What a laugh!"

She squeezed his arm. "Don't beat yourself up about it. You did the responsible thing and protected her. After you get the test results, this incident will be history."

He stopped walking and looked into the distance. "True. But I can't help feeling for that poor child. No father and a mother whose responsibleness I seriously question. My brothers and I suffered the effects of a flaky mother. But our father did all he could to make up for it."

Velma was getting used to his shrugs and gestures that could mislead anyone to believe that his words had only been verbal musings, of no import. Knowing that, his shrug did nothing to lessen her concern that he might feel more for Iris Parker—a tall, beautiful and elegant woman—than he realized.

His hand rested gently on her shoulder. "After I take you home, I'm going to the housing commissioner's office to sign the papers for that property on Reese Street. Tomorrow, we start work on the renovations."

If only she could be that fortunate and get permission to acquire the warehouse she wanted so badly. "I'm happy for you," she told him, and she meant it. "Have you finished your design for the interior?"

"They're rowhouses with identical structures, built by the same builder, so I only had to develop one design and I've finished that."

"So you're ready to begin."

"Right. By the time we rip out the interior, Drake will be back and we can begin rebuilding. Velma, I'm more excited about this project than about anything I've done in a long time."

"I suppose you are. Fourteen families that are now homeless will have a decent place to live."

"Twenty-eight. Two families per house, but they'll have separate entrances. It's . . . well, I've never done anything that gives me so much pleasure." He parked in front of her house. "I won't forget what you did this morning."

At a loss for words, she merely leaned toward him, kissed him on the mouth and got out of the car as quickly as she could. She needed privacy to deal with her conflicting emotions.

She sat down on her living room sofa with a glass of ginger ale and an almond biscotti, kicked off her shoes and ruminated over the morning's events.

Russ, a big man with a big heart. A child who had his sympathy. And a beautiful woman who had possessed him, if only once. Could a man with Russ's willpower, honor and strength avoid the quagmire that this scenario represented? She went to the bathroom, washed the makeup off her face and marveled that Russ Harrington had rejected Iris Parker but chose her.

She finished the sketch of a furnished dining room, complete with decorative items and china, crystal, silverware and table linen suggestions. It was the second such job she'd done for an architect, and she couldn't wait to show it to Russ. Delighted with her accomplishment, she got the urge to celebrate with a new hairdo and something smart to wear and telephoned her hairdresser for an appointment.

"What you having today?" Bea Hobson asked her as she walked into the shop.

"Something different. And very modern. Anything as long as it's new and I'll look good."

"What about braids?" She showed her an intricate design. "If you don't like it, I can always take them out."

She chose the braids. On the way home, after trying on several suits that were either too small or the skirt was too long, she bought an elegant rust-colored suede one. Not because she needed it, but because it looked good on her and she felt like treating herself.

Her next stop was Lydia's office, less for checking up on her weight than to gauge her friend's reaction to the braids. "How do I look?" she asked of the new hair style.

Lydia appraised her at length, twisted her mouth slightly to one side and then lifted her right shoulder in a gesture of disregard. "Next, I guess you'll have your stomach taped and your ears pinned back."

"Aw, Lydia. I thought I'd do something different. You don't like my braids?"

"If I liked 'em, I'd wear 'em. They look great on a lot of African American women. But, honey, if you want my opinion, you're not one of 'em." As if it were a hopeless subject, she threw up her hands. "But if that's what mills your wheat . . . Let's see how the weight's coming along. Hmm. Three pounds down. Not bad."

"You mean I lost three pounds?"

"Yep. Stay on that diet and take your medicine. If you exercise properly and regularly, you ought to see substantial results."

Velma let out a long sigh. "Thanks a lot," she said to herself. "In other words, keep on starving myself."

To Lydia, she said, "Whatever you say." She'd wasted her time stopping to see Lydia, and she didn't dare think of Russ's reaction.

Lydia got up from her desk, walked over to Velma and put an arm around her shoulder. "Listen, friend. You and I have been buddies since we were college freshmen. When we were roommates, you were always binging, eating this month and starving yourself the next. But you didn't seem to worry about your weight."

She went over to the window and looked out, giving notice that what she was about to say next would neither be easy for her nor pleasant for Velma. "I used to wonder how you could be so irresolute about your weight and so doggedly persistent about everything else. Another thing, I've never heard you say a kind word about either of your parents. As students of psychology, that tells both you and me that you have some deep-seated problems, and it's time you got to the core of them."

"Look, I know you mean well, Lydia, but—"

"But, honey, when we're dealing with your weight, we're only treating the symptom, not the cause."

"But it's a medical condition."

"Velma, not every person with a hypothyroid has the problem you have controlling your weight. Talk to Alexis and figure out what happened in your youth that didn't happen in hers."

Those words stayed with Velma long after she left Lydia's office. She didn't have to discuss it with Alexis, because she knew the answer. As the older of the two, she had been the shield between her sister and the turbulence and selfishness that she herself witnessed in their parents. Toward late evening, she managed to concentrate on the banquet she had agreed to plan for a teachers' conference. She was able to do that because she had made up her mind to follow Lydia's advice.

The next morning, she went to her safe deposit box and took out the bundle of papers marked "Family Affairs." Sitting in the little room that the bank provided for its box holders, she sifted through papers she hadn't looked at in thirteen years, not since she was eighteen and became head of her household and caretaker of sixteen-year-old Alexis.

High school diplomas, their mother's death certificate, old property deeds, bills of sale for their house and her father's automobile, the marriage certificates of her parents and grandparents, all brought back memories—mostly bitter ones—and tears to her eyes. At last she found what she sought: her father's letter to her telling her he was leaving, leaving her with responsibility for her mother's funeral and for the education of herself and Alexis. The note said he was going to Canada, which was as good as telling her nothing, since Canada was one large, vast land area. She was on her own.

Two days later, Russ called Velma and suggested that they go ice skating for an hour that evening. Although they had talked, she hadn't seen him since the morning she went with him to the courthouse.

"Before dinner or after?" she asked.

"Before. Then I'll fix supper for you. What do you say?"

"Sounds good to me. What will you cook?"

Was she implying that he might not be able to turn out a decent meal? "Playing it safe, eh? Well, I don't ask you that when you're the cook, do I? I'll be at your place around six. Okay?"

*   *   *

"What on earth?" He gaped at her as she stood in the door wearing an expression of expectancy. Yes, expectancy. What else could he call it?

"Hi," she said.

"Hi. What happened to your hair?"

A frown slid across her face and then settled there. "Come on in. That's about the worst thing a man could say to a woman. Well, one of the worst. I had it braided, as you can see."

"But why, for Pete's sake? I thought it looked nice the way you wore it."

"You don't like it?"

He gazed down at her, thinking that he'd just blown his chance to get that welcoming kiss. Heck. He wasn't going to lie. "Did you expect me to?"

"Sorry," she said, her shrug of indifference belying her real feelings. "I felt like something different."

"And you definitely got it. Do I rate a kiss?"

She stroked his cheek, stepped close and took him into her warm, sweet mouth.

"Let's go, before you start an explosion. Woman, you're dynamite."

"This is the one thing I like about winter," she said as they glided over the ice.

"Don't you like Christmas?"

She slowed down. "I was about to give you a glib answer: *Of course I like Christmas. Doesn't everybody?"* The phrase was on the tip of my tongue, she thought, *because the truth was so painful.*

"Christmas in our home was never the glorious time for me that it seemed to be for everyone else. I grew up praying that it would pass without a blowout. The only wonderful Christmas I ever knew was the one I spent last year in your home. That's when I knew what Christmas could be."

He had a powerful urge to hold her to protect her from the demon that he realized still haunted her. With her hand in his, he skated to the edge of the rink and sat with her on a bench.

"You tell me things like that when we're among a bunch of strangers, and I can't hold you the way I want to."

"I didn't plan to say it. And I didn't know the thoughts were so near the surface of my mind."

"You had to handle too much at too early an age, and you've buried your feelings about your parents and your childhood." He was dealing with an unfamiliar sense of helplessness, and he felt crippled. "Trust me to be here for you no matter what your problem is and whenever you need an ear." He dared not say more, for whenever he probed, she closed up.

She patted his hand.

"I'm dealing with it, Russ. It won't beat me down."

"Were you dealing with it when you got your hair braided?" It was a tough question, but it came out of him honestly and required as much of her.

"I'm not sure. I finished a terrific design for a furnished dining room complete with appointments, and I was so happy with it that I treated myself to something different."

She may have believed that explanation, but he didn't. Most women would buy a new dress or a new pair of shoes. He changed the subject. "I didn't know you designed interiors. Will you show it to me?"

Her face bloomed with delight. "I want you to see it. It's my second assignment for an architect, and I think I did a good job. I'd like your opinion. Could we stop by my house?"

He swung his arms across her shoulder and urged her

closer to him. "Tell you what. I'll wait in the car while you go inside and get it."

Her eyes widened, a frown settled on her face and she poked her right index finger in his chest. "Chicken. Nothing will happen to you in my house that you don't want to happen."

Laughter bubbled up in his throat and then spilled out. He threw back his head and gave it full rein. "Velma, that's a man's line."

"I know," she said, "and I used it because I figured you'd understand it."

When he finally stopped laughing, he said, "In the future, if I say that to you, I'll know you'll get the full import of my meaning." He realized that his left eye narrowed. "You can dish out a lot of sass, babe."

The grin that settled around her mouth and the sparkles that lit her eyes heated his blood, and he had to force himself not to pull her into his arms.

"You call it sass? I call it telling it like it is."

"Come on, sweetheart," he said. "Let's go. I've had enough ice."

He would have expected anything but that long, slow wink she gave him. "You didn't get any ice from me," she said, in a tone suited to her wink. "I'm a warm blanket on a freezing night."

He had a feeling that she was toying with him and enjoying it, not that he minded. He could give as good as he got. "You don't have to remind me," he said. "My memory is as good as the next person's. And trust me, no blanket, however warm, can generate half as much heat as you can." He ignored her narrowed right eye and gaping mouth, stood and held out his hand to her. "It's getting late, and we have to stop by your place."

Chicken or not, he waited in the car while she went inside

her house to get the design. If her work was credible, it meant that they had one more important thing in common. He opened the passenger door, and she climbed in, obviously out of breath.

"You didn't have to run. I'd wait for you indefinitely. No. Cancel that."

"You mean you wouldn't wait for me indefinitely?"

He pulled away from the curb and glanced at her. "You think you have to ask that?"

"I guess not." She seemed subdued, but he didn't know why. Anyone who knew him was familiar with his impatience. He'd exercised more patience with her than he had in all the thirty-three and a half years before he met her.

"I didn't want to mislead you because my patience is not infinite."

"I know."

As soon as they stepped inside his foyer, she handed him a large brown envelope. "What do you think?"

He walked over to the table, turned on the light and opened the envelope. "Hmm. This is . . . I'd say it's excellent. Contemporary all the way. Very imaginative and no cute stuff. I like it."

"Gosh. I'm stunned. You hurled my ego halfway to the moon." She clasped her hands tightly and pressed them against her breast, and he didn't doubt that his appraisal of her work gave her a boost.

"No need for that. It's a really fine job. Who's the architect?"

"Peck and Crawford. About a year ago, I decorated a family room for them for a model home. I don't plan to solicit this kind of business. I'm good at planning parties, receptions and galas, and I intend to stick with that. What are you cooking? May I help?"

"Steak, baked potatoes and asparagus. Ice cream for dessert. Nothing could be simpler. You can wash the asparagus."

After eating, they cleaned the kitchen. Russ made coffee and carried it into the living room. They sipped quietly, occasionally smiling at each other. Then he put their cups and saucers in the dishwasher, turned it on and closed the kitchen door.

"Sit over here with me," he said, patting the spot beside where he sat on the sofa. "I wanted to tell you this when we were alone and in a peaceful environment. I called the courthouse in Frederick this morning, and the clerk faxed the report to me. The DNA tests were negative, as I knew they would be. Iris Parker will receive a copy of the report.

"I can't figure out why she would get herself into such a mess. Drake says she came after me because she read about my inheritance. Oh, well. Want to ride with me to Eagle Park tomorrow?"

"Will we have time to shop for Henry at the Lexington Market?"

"Sure. It's on the way out of Baltimore. Say, you haven't said a word about the test results."

"It's what I expected, Russ. Look. I'm going to ask you something, and it's going to make you mad."

"Then don't ask it."

"I need the answer. Do you have any further interest in Iris Parker? Or her child?"

"Wait a minute." He began rubbing the back of his neck, a sure sign that he was displeased. He took a deep breath. It was a reasonable question. "I am not, nor have I ever been interested in Iris Parker. I lectured to a group at the YWCA, and she was present. She came up to me later and suggested we have a drink and talk about a project she had in mind. That same night, I slept with her in her apartment. The next time I saw her she was in Harrington House accusing me of fathering her child.

"As for her son, I feel sorry for him, because he's got nothing going for him. I also feel sorry for the farmers whose crops were flooded last summer, but that doesn't mean I'm going to rush out to save them."

"All right. All right. Don't get your dander up. I had a right to know."

"I agree. Anyway, it's myself that I'm annoyed with, not you. I'd better take you home before—"

"Before I fall asleep," she finished for him. "What time are we meeting tomorrow?"

"Is eight too early?"

She shook her head. "Fine with me."

"What the devil did you do to yerself?" Henry asked Velma when she walked into the kitchen around noon that Saturday to give him the sausages and double-smoked bacon that he preferred. "You look like a plucked chicken."

"Oh, Henry. That's not a nice thing to say."

"Don't matter if it ain't. You managed to get rid of one of the prettiest faces I ever saw with those pickaninny things on yer head."

"I guess that means you don't like it," she said, feeling an urge to get out of the kitchen.

Henry sucked his teeth and looked toward the ceiling. "And I ain't the only one that don't like it. I bet you that. If you don't like yerself, how do you expect other people to like you? Did Russ tell you how pretty you look with them cornrows?"

"Oh, Henry. You make it sound awful."

"And I ain't overstating it either. Alexis is a pretty woman that's tall and thin, and you're a pretty woman that's short and round. God knew just what he was doing when he made both kinds, and you shouldn't go around second guessing him."

She walked over to Henry and patted his shoulder, realizing that she would have hugged him if she'd had the nerve. "Why do you think my size has anything to do with my hair?"

"Cause I'm on to you. You ain't been yerself since the wedding, and you better watch yer step."

"There you are." Russ strolled into the kitchen and didn't stop until he had both arms around her. "I'd like to talk with you for a few minutes," he said to Henry.

"What about? I got to fix lunch seeing as how you brought company with you. We can talk while you peel these potatoes, that is, providing yer hands ain't stuck where they are."

Russ brought her closer to his body. "No problem. I can hold her while she peels the potatoes."

"You beginning to sound like Drake," Henry said. "But in your case, it's a welcome sign."

"I'll peel the potatoes," Velma said, and to her surprise, Russ kept both arms around her while she stood at the sink and began peeling them.

"Velma already knows about this," Russ said to Henry. "You know Uncle Fentress left me a lot of money."

"Yeah. I sure do."

Russ told him his plans for the Josh Harrington Victory Homes in Baltimore and added, "Two hundred and fifty thousand goes to you, so if you'll give me a deposit slip, I'll put it in your bank."

"Are the three of you out of yer minds?" Henry asked him. "What am I going to do with two hundred and fifty thousand dollars? You built me a house, you pay me too much, you feed me. I don't even have to buy an aspirin. Once a year, I spend three hundred dollars to go to Florida, stay with my sister for two weeks and fish. Every five or six years, I buy a few trousers and some shirts."

She heard a catch in Henry's voice, glanced at him and saw the unshed tears glimmering in his eyes. "The three of you are like me own sons," he said. "You give meaning to my life. I don't need money."

"I don't care what you do with it," Russ said. "I'm giving it to you. If we're like your sons, you're like our father. So please give me the deposit slip."

"I ain't got any heirs except you boys. Well, there's Tara, of course. Maybe you should be saving it for yer own kids." He looked at her. "You want some, don't you?"

Though flushed with embarrassment, she resisted lowering her head, but looked him in the eye. "Of course I do, Henry, but don't you think you've overstepped a line?"

The sound of Russ' laughter so surprised her that she dropped the vegetable peeler on the counter and turned to look at him. "I thought you knew that Henry says whatever he wants to. Telford, Drake and I are never allowed to doubt Henry's opinions of us and what we're doing. Get used to it."

She didn't know how to take that. He seemed to be admitting to Henry that their relationship would be permanent. But she knew you couldn't draw water until the well was sunk, so she didn't dwell on it. Still . . . it seemed out of character for Russ. When she turned back to the counter to continue peeling potatoes, she felt Russ at her back as he slid both arms around her and nuzzled her neck. Joy suffused her and, as much as she disliked peeling potatoes, she would willingly have peeled them for hours.

A short while later, Telford and Alexis found them that way. "I was hoping you'd get here this weekend," Telford said to Russ; then, he walked over and kissed Velma's cheek. If Russ saw the grin on his brother's face, he didn't mention it. She noticed that Alexis stayed in the background as if she wanted to avoid spoiling what must have seemed like an unspoken love between Russ and herself.

"Any problems?" Russ asked, though he didn't move his arms from her waist.

"None, but I wanted to talk over the renovation of the Joshua Harrington houses."

"We can do that now." Russ turned to Henry. "I want that deposit slip, and I don't want any trouble out of you about it." He tightened his arms around her in what everyone present had to recognize as an expression of caring. "I'll see you later," he said for her ears alone, walked over to Telford and said, "Come on."

"I see you've been making progress," Henry said to her after the two men left the kitchen. "You'd make more if you used yer head for something other than them corn rows."

She washed the potatoes, put the peelings in the garbage can, washed and dried her hands and looked at Henry. "My deep affection for you is not enough to prevent me from telling you to mind your business, Henry."

Alexis gasped, but Henry's response was to suck his teeth. "Say anything you want to, but I bet you'll pay attention to my words. Thanks for peeling the potatoes."

She kissed his cheek. "You can't imagine what a pleasure it was."

"I'll bet. You shouldn't have to peel potatoes in order to get next to him."

She knew Alexis would follow her to her room, so she locked arms with her sister. "Where's Tara?"

"In her room. She's being punished for refusing to speak to her father. He called, although he didn't ask for her, but I told her to come to the phone and say hello to him. Would you believe she flatly refused? Said he didn't come to see her, so she didn't want to talk with him."

"Doesn't he have visitation rights?"

"He has no rights, because he gave me full custody in exchange for my share of our common property. Millions. You know that. Still . . . I asked him to visit her once a week, but he hasn't been here since a couple of days after Christmas."

"Then I don't blame her," Velma said. "Children are gifted at identifying a phony, especially if it's a parent."

"I'm not going to entertain that idea, because I know it will take us straight to your feelings about our parents." They walked into Velma's room and closed the door. "What did Russ say about your hair?"

She sat on the chaise lounge, crossed her leg and folded her arms. "Now don't you start."

"So he didn't like it any more than Henry does. Of course, Henry's from the old school."

"What about you?"

Alexis sat beside her and draped an arm across her shoulder. "I suppose you're going through a phase, though I don't see why it should have this effect considering how tight you are with Russ. He made love to you, didn't he?"

"What? Why do you say that?"

"Because I remember how Telford was with me after he took me to bed. He was always loving. But after that, he couldn't keep his hands off me. You're not as pretty in the braids as you are with your hair hanging around your face."

"Henry said I ruined my face, and Russ wanted to know what I'd done to myself."

"Whatever's eating you, hon, get it straightened out as fast as you can. You're important to Russ. Don't let him decide he's put his eggs in the wrong basket. Did he get the DNA results?"

"Yes, and of course the results were negative. I went to the hearing with him. Oh, Alexis, I love him so much."

"Does he know it?"

She nodded. "He knows it."

"Work on it."

"I will," she said, and as soon as Alexis left the room, she picked up the telephone and dialed her lawyer.

Chapter Ten

"Thirteen years is a long time," the lawyer told Velma over the phone, "so don't expect too much. I have a man with an excellent record of finding missing people. What can you tell me about your father?"

She read her father's letter to the lawyer: "I'm sorry, but I'm leaving for Canada. I just can't stay here now. It's too much. Sell the car and the house. The money ought to see you both through school."

"That was all?"

"That and the nearly four thousand dollars cash that he put in the envelope. He was a distinguished university professor, wrote many papers on molecular biology and was at one time president of his professional society. I forgot its name."

"If you have any of his published papers, send me a couple. If he's working, this shouldn't be too difficult."

After hanging up, she found several of her father's professional papers in a trunk where she kept painful mementos of the distant past and mailed them to the lawyer along with a photocopy of her father's handwritten letter to her. Having taken that step, she had to deal with the anxiety and jangled nerves that set in at once. Nonetheless, she managed to concentrate sufficiently to develop and present to the city housing commissioner her proposal for use of the warehouse she wanted to buy, and to outline its potential benefits for the neighborhood in which it was located.

She returned home from the commissioner's office anxious to shower and recover some mental energy, for the man's assistant had exhausted her with rapid-fire questions that she had not anticipated. However, before she could begin to unwind, the phone rang.

"Hello."

"Hi. This is Russ." As if she wouldn't know his voice awakening from a hundred years' sleep. "Want to do a good deed?"

"How good?"

"The local chapter of my fraternity has its annual dinner-dance next Friday night, and I forgot about it until I saw this notice in the mail that's been here at least six weeks. Will you go with me?"

"Six weeks? I'd like to see what your desk looks like."

"My desk is neat; it's my in-box that's overflowing. Will you go?"

"Of course. I'd love to go. What will you wear?"

"Tux."

"What color is your cummerbund? I don't want to wear a dress that clashes with it."

She thought she heard a snicker or a laugh. "I have a few. White, red, gray, something called burgundy, mauve—"

Her bottom lip dropped. "Where did I get the idea that you're conservative? You're a social butterfly."

His deep sonorous laugh sent darts zinging through her limbs. "Me? To think of myself as a butterfly, social or otherwise, boggles my mind. Most of the occasions on which I've worn this tux have been business related. I didn't even consider attending previous fraternity parties, but I figured it would be pleasant to go with you because you're such a good dancer."

She thought for a minute. Something didn't add up. "Russ, I guess I'm surprised that you joined a fraternity. I would have thought that you wouldn't tolerate the hazing."

"I barely made it, but from my great grandfather down to Telford, Harrington men had been Omegas, and I didn't want to be the one to break the chain."

"What about Drake?"

"He's a born Omega. Let me know what you'd like me to wear. Okay?"

"In a couple of days."

After searching for hours the next day, she found a dark peach-colored, one-shoulder chiffon gown fitted to the hips with a set-in flair that flattered her figure.

"It's the perfect style for you," the saleswoman said, "and the color is flattering, so I don't know what's wrong with it. Wait a minute."

She left and returned with an off-black wig that had straight hair that curved beneath the chin. "Try this on, and let's see how you look."

Velma stared at the effect. "I'll take the dress."

"What about the wig?"

She shook her head. "No thanks. My own hair is longer than this." Thursday morning, she would get a new hair style, but only because long hair made her look better in her new evening gown. And Russ had better not comment. She told him what she bought, and he replied that he'd wear white accessories.

When she opened the door for him that Friday evening, he sent a long, sharp whistle through her house. "All this for me? Baby, you're a dream, and I'm a lucky man. Can I have a hug?"

She stared up at him, tall and resplendent, a man to make any woman feel like a queen just to walk beside him. His eyes darkened, and she took a step backward.

"A hug, yes, but nothing more or I'll have to redo my makeup."

He opened his arms. "I didn't know you were wearing any." His arms closed around her, and she clasped him as tightly to her as she could. He looked down at her, his gaze devoid of passion. "You take my breath away. Let's go before I lose the will to leave here."

Inside the elegant Wyndham Baltimore Inner Harbor Hotel, he checked their wraps in the cloak room and headed for the mezzanine and the fraternity's pre-dinner cocktails.

He recognized his feeling of accomplishment—yes, and completeness—as he strolled with Velma into the reception room, and he understood that feeling. Although he had become an architect known for the high quality and imaginativeness of his work and a member of a respected firm, he had never felt successful; indeed, he hadn't given it serious thought. As one of the Harrington brothers, he had always accepted his identity as a man to be reckoned with, but hadn't considered the implications.

He looked down at Velma and realized that he saw himself at last as a whole man, separate from his brothers, on his own and with a woman he loved and who loved him. Perhaps that accounted for the changes he saw in himself. The lessening of the alienation, the distance from others that he'd lived with as long as he'd known himself, and a contentment he hadn't known he lacked.

"Now this is a pleasant surprise," a fraternity brother and Howard University classmate said to him. "It's been years, man. I didn't even know you lived around here."

"Same here," Russ said. "It was worth coming just to see you." He put an arm around Velma's waist in a gesture that he knew signified possessiveness, but the smile on her face said she didn't mind. "Miss Brighton, this is John Gandy, a buddy from my undergraduate days."

"I'm glad to meet you," she said and extended her hand. It seemed to him that John held Velma's hand a bit too long, but he didn't share his thought.

"I'm going to move toward the bar and get us a drink," he told John, "but I want your phone number."

John handed him a card. "And I want yours. Right here in Baltimore and I didn't know it. I don't want to lose you again," he said, pocketing Russ's business card.

To his mind, the dinner didn't differ much from dozens he had eaten at conferences, conventions, and assorted events, and he said as much to Velma.

"I have a contract to cater this affair year after next, and you won't eat chicken à la king. Do they always have these banal speeches?"

"Always. I can't wait for the dancing."

Later, when the first notes of "Everything I Have Is Yours" wafted through the room, he rose and extended his hand to Velma. "Dance with me."

She stood at once, a warm welcoming smile lighting her face, and he walked with her to the dance floor, holding her hand as he weaved his way past tables and standees. He loved the way she moved into his arms, knowing that she belonged there, and caught his rhythm at once. Caught it and swung with him the way she did that time they made love. He told himself to think of something else, but her feminine scent and soft, yielding body made it difficult for him to think of anything other than the thrill after thrill of loving her, of being buried deep within her body.

He felt a tap on his shoulder, turned and stopped dancing. "What is it, Dolphe?"

Dolphe Andrews grinned in triumph. "You know the rules. Yield, man."

He narrowed both eyes. "When it comes to my woman, *I* make the rules. Do you want to dance with this man?" he asked Velma.

"No. I don't want to dance with him. I don't want him to touch me," she said.

"All right, Dolphe. This is one woman you can't have, so let this be the last time you hit on her. If you're foolish enough to try it again, you will deal with me, and I will be merciless." He resumed dancing. "Oh yes. And don't call my home in Eagle Park again. You understand?"

Dolphe's face dissolved into a quizzical frown. "Look, Russ. I'm sorry, man. I hope there are no hard feelings. You probably won't believe me, but this is the truth. I'm not tom-catting. The first time I laid eyes on Ms. Brighton, I was a goner, and it never happened to me before. I wish you the best, man." He walked away without waiting for a reply.

"Well, hell!" Russ said under his breath. To Velma he said, "If he hadn't trampled on so many girls when we were at Howard, I'd feel sorry for him, but you can't treat people that way without paying for it."

The music ended, and he stood in the middle of the dance floor looking at Velma. "I'm sorry. If I'd had any idea that this would happen, you never would have met him in my home."

"He must have been the campus Romeo."

"He was a good student, and we got on well enough, although we were never tight. I wanted the grades that would get me into graduate school, and he wanted the girls."

The band struck up a calypso, and with Velma swinging her hips and twirling around him, he quickly forgot about Dolphe Andrews. They danced until the lights blinked, and he couldn't remember a time when he had enjoyed a social occasion so much.

"Are you tired?" he asked Velma.

"Not one bit. Why?"

"Let's go over to Hunt's Club, get some coffee and maybe dance some more. I mainly want an excuse not to end the evening."

"We'll be together tomorrow, won't we? I told Alexis that I'd see her this weekend."

"I'm not sure I can get there. I spent so much time at the Joshua Harrington houses here in Baltimore that I neglected the Florence Griffith Joyner apartments in Philadelphia. And with Drake not here to supervise the work, I should be there. Tell you what. I'll get there later Saturday. Okay?"

She assured him that it was, and it occurred to him that Velma didn't nag and never asked him to inconvenience himself. With a start, he realized that he'd do anything for her short of violating his principles or breaking his neck.

On the way to the cloak room later, he saw John Gandy waiting beside the women's lounge. "What ever happened to Amelia?" he asked John of his college sweetheart.

John nodded toward the women's lounge. "She's in there. She's also the mother of my three-year-old son. Can you wait till she comes out?"

He looked at Velma, who nodded in agreement. "So you two got married. That's great. I'd love to see her. Is she still hooked on Dr. Pepper?"

As he expected, John laughed. "She stopped drinking it when she was pregnant. Here she is."

"Honey, I'm sorry, but there are a lot of women in there. I

know you don't like . . . Russ Harrington! My goodness, what a wonderful surprise."

Russ leaned down and kissed her cheek, then introduced her to Velma and watched with pleasure as the two women greeted each other warmly.

"I want you two to come over for a good visit," Amelia said. "How about Saturday next week, at about six for dinner? It'll be just the four of us, so we can talk."

"I'd like that," he said. "Will you be free then, Velma?"

"Yes, and I'll look forward to it. Thank you for asking me, Amelia."

Later, as he and Velma ate almond-cream wafers and sipped espresso coffee at the Hunt Club, he surprised himself by saying, "You don't have a coy bone in your body, and you can't imagine how refreshing that is."

For a moment, she seemed perplexed. Then she shrugged and said, "Me? Coy? You're right. I guess I'm too frank for that. In my case, being cute would send the wrong message."

He ignored that, not wanting to enter into a discussion of her weight and figure. A man had just made a spectacle of himself over her, and she still didn't believe she had an attractive figure.

"I've heard better dance music," he said, "but it's passable. Want to dance?" She agreed, and they joined the other dancers in a slow two-step.

After an hour, he tired of what he thought of as the imitation jazz music, and suggested that they leave. Standing in her foyer later, he put his arms around her and held her as close as he dared, for he wanted to avoid the fireworks that ensued whenever they came together. He let his mouth brush hers, but she parted her lips and, unable to reject what she gave, he opened himself to her loving and let himself cherish her as he longed to do.

"You don't want to take this any further tonight," he said,

having caught her signal, "so I'd better leave. You . . . you're lovely, and I enjoyed being with you." He winked, hoping to lighten the effect of the words he felt impelled to utter. "You suit me in every way. You understand?" He kissed her nose and left.

Velma turned the car into number 10 John Brown Drive and suddenly wished she had stayed in Baltimore, for her relationship with Russ would be the focal point of her sister's conversation. That and whether she had stopped dieting. She rushed up the stone walkway, rang the doorbell and rubbed her hands together to create warmth. She soon heard footsteps.

"Velma, honey, come on in. You look as if you you're freezing," Alexis said as she embraced her sister. "Other than that, you look great, even serene."

Velma hugged Alexis, relishing the love that was always there for her. "Marriage certainly goes well with you. How're you spending your time?" she asked her sister as they headed for the guest room, which they all thought of as Velma's room.

"I do chores in the mornings, and in the afternoons I work at sculpting. Drake found a gallery that's interested in my work, and I'll have a show there next November. I'm very excited about it. Any progress with the warehouse?"

"I put in a bid, along with a proposal, and now I have to . . . well . . . wait and see."

"Doesn't Russ know anybody in the housing commissioner's office?"

"Uh . . . I haven't told him about this yet. I'm not leaning on him."

"What? Oh, well. I hope you know what you're doing."

"Who knows? I'll bring it up at a convenient time."

Alexis stopped walking. "Why do you need to pick a time? The two of you are very close. He's your lover. If you keep secrets from him, you'll make the same mistake I made with Telford. And the longer you keep it, the harder it is to reveal it, and the greater difficulty he will have accepting and understanding it."

"My lover? It's only happened once. Anyway, I haven't deliberately withheld anything from him."

Thoughts of those minutes in Russ' arms weakened her, and she sank into a chair. "Alexis, he was so wonderful, so loving and tender. He made me realize that I didn't know myself. I've never been so . . . so completely swept away, so overwhelmed. I can't describe it."

Alexis' face bloomed into a smile, and she rushed over and hugged Velma. "I'm so happy for you. I knew he'd be like that, because he puts himself wholeheartedly into whatever he does, and I could see how much he wanted you." She stood up, frowning. "Why has it happened only once?"

"Because I am not going to drift into an affair with him. He's used to working for what he gets, and I don't want to test that old adage—"easy come, easy go'."

It occurred to her that, although she had told Alexis she intended to find their father, she hadn't confided to her sister that she had begun the search. Alexis had a stake in the result of that search, but she would nonetheless ask her to call it off.

"I can't, and I won't do it," Velma said to herself.

She walked over to her sister and put an arm around her. "I have to tell *you* something. My lawyer has a man looking for our father. When the man finds him, I'm going to him, no matter where he is, because he is the only person who can answer the question that looms over me like a black cloud."

"You still don't believe our parents loved us, do you?"

Alexis asked, and Velma could feel the sadness that enveloped her. "For years, I've tried to convince you, but I guess you need to hear it from his lips. I wish you'd let sleeping dogs lie, because nothing good can come of it."

She didn't know how to make Alexis understand, and wasn't sure she should burden her sister with facts that could devastate her. She had always shielded her from it, and she would continue to do it.

"Mummy?" Tara's voice calling Alexis signaled an end to their tête à tête, for which Velma gave silent thanks. She unpacked and, unable to figure out why she felt lonely and ill at ease, she telephoned Russ.

"Russ Harrington. What may I do for you?"

"Hi. This is Velma."

"Hi, sweetheart. Where are you?" She told him. "I think I detect something forlorn in you voice. What's the matter?"

"Nothing. I mean, well I—"

"Anything wrong there?" His voice carried an urgency that let her know he was well attuned to her.

"No. There're a couple of things I think I should tell you, and I missed some opportunities to do it."

"And it's bothering you? From my watch, you can't have been in Eagle Park more than half an hour. What brought this on?"

"I realized I hadn't told Alexis, and I should have, and then—"

"All right. I'll knock off here early, and I'll see you tonight. Tell Henry that if I'm not there by seven, save dinner for me, and warn Alexis." Almost immediately after mentioning Alexis' name, she could hear his chuckle through the wire. He adored his sister-in-law to the extent that he didn't let her house rules faze him, a feat on Alexis' part, considering how Russ hated being regimented and usually didn't allow it.

"I'll be happy to see you," she said, as if she hadn't seen him for weeks. "Please be careful and don't drive fast."

"I'll take care. And don't worry about how you think I'll react to what you have to tell me. You hear?"

"I won't. Kisses."

"Kisses."

She put her clothes away, then went to give Henry the meat she brought for him.

"I thought you planned to ignore me," Henry said. "Thanks for the sausage and bacon."

"I brought you some good maple syrup, too."

She thought she saw a smile cross his face. "You did? Now, that's right nice of ya. Tara's going to love her breakfast in the morning. The child loves pancakes as much as she loves to play that piano."

"Russ said he'd be home for dinner, and if he can't make it by seven, save him some."

"Good thing you told me. I thought he wouldn't be here till tomorrow evening. Least, that's what he told Tel."

"He just changed his mind."

"Humph. Does that mean you're getting a little sense?"

She patted his shoulder. "I'll see you later."

She met Alexis on the stairs. "Russ will be home for dinner, but he may not get here by seven."

Alexis gazed at her older sister for what seemed to Velma like ages. Then, she said, "That's not a problem. We'll save his dinner. Did you call him?"

"Yes."

"Good. When you need him, let him know it, and he'll be there for you. I was a long time learning that, but once I knew it, I've been a happier woman."

"Thanks. I'll keep that in mind. I wanted to see Tara, but I wouldn't like to interfere with her practice."

"You'll see her at dinner. I'll send up a few prayers for

you and Russ." They walked down the stairs arm in arm, and Velma wondered if finding and contacting her father would shatter the peace that had always seemed to envelop her younger sister.

Unable to conquer her restlessness, she dressed warmly, told Henry she was going for a walk and headed toward the Monacacy River. She walked at a swift pace along the road toward the river, and as no wind stirred to rustle the branches of the trees, she heard only the crunching of her footsteps upon the twigs and leaves. She reached the banks of the river and stopped, for only then did she remember Russ' caution about being in the woods alone.

She retraced her steps at twice the speed, traveling just short of a trot until she reached the open road. It was then that she saw the man approaching with his German shepherd by his side and his steps slow and heavy. Harrington House loomed in the distance, but seeing it did not banish her fears.

Facing the man whose eyes seemed dim and reddened with age, she made herself smile when he stopped. "Good evening, miss. How far do you think I am from Beaver Ridge?" he asked in a voice strong, but gravelly.

Taken aback, she replied, "Good evening, sir. I'm afraid that's a long way from here, around twelve miles. It'll be dark hours before you get there."

"That's no problem."

"I think you're headed in the wrong direction, too. When you get to that big house down there, walk to the end of John Brown Drive, turn left and continue in that direction. But it's really too far for you to walk."

"I'll be just fine. Come on, boy." He patted his dog and turned back toward the house. "You live there?" he asked, pointing toward Harrington House and settling into stride with her.

"No, sir. My sister lives there. I'm visiting her."

"You look like you'd fit well in a place like that one. Good manners. Nice carriage and a lovely face. And you're well spoken, too."

"Thank you, sir." As slowly as he'd been walking when she met him, he seemed to have no trouble matching her strides, but she gave that only passing thought.

"Oh, don't thank me," he said. "You have some fine traits. Give God the credit for that."

"I certainly can't credit my parents," she heard herself say and with a bitterness that shocked her.

"They couldn't have been all bad, considering how you turned out. A man would be proud to have you for a daughter, and let me tell you that the man who wins your hand will be fortunate indeed."

"How do you know that?" she asked, aware that they were nearing Harrington House. "Would you . . . like to come in for a cup of coffee or tea? You've a long way to go."

His faced creased into a smile. "How do I know? Only a gentle, loving woman would spend time with an old man, a stranger with nothing to offer her but his good will. Your young man is fortunate, and he knows it, but you don't. Well, I'll be on my way. Thank you for your company and for the offer of a hot drink."

"Uh . . . I could drive you there, sir."

He shook his head. "Thank you, but I'll be just fine."

She stood at the front door and watched him as he walked on with the German shepherd, though unleashed, close by his side. In the twilight, the street lamp lit up just as he should have reached the corner, but she didn't see him.

"I guess he decided to walk faster," she told herself. Bemused and unaccountably shaken, she opened the door and went inside.

* . * . *

Russ parked in front of Harrington House at seven-twenty that evening, thanks to his disregard of the speed limits. He figured he would have been there half an hour sooner if he hadn't taken the time to search for a small gift. Somehow, it seemed an appropriate, if not the best way to re-assure Velma. He hadn't wasted time worrying about what she would tell him, because he wanted an open mind. And most of all, he wanted her to know that if she shared personal things with him, no matter how painful, she would only draw them closer together. If she had been at her home in Baltimore, he would have brought her flowers. He left the box in his Mercedes, deciding to get it when he was ready for it, and at dinner with his family was not the time.

For the first time in his memory, he didn't use his key, but rang the doorbell. "Now, I've *really* left home," he told himself when he realized what he'd done.

"What's this? Did you lose your key?" Telford asked while wrapping him in the familiar embrace with which the brothers always greeted each other.

He evaded the question. "If I had used it, nobody would have greeted me at the door. A little attention never hurt anybody."

Telford's eyebrows shot up. "For the last two months, I've been watching the metamorphosis of Russell Orwell Harrington. Let me know when it's complete, brother."

"Man, you're getting fanciful."

When they reached the breakfast room, his eyes searched for Velma, but Tara claimed him. "Eeeeeow, Uncle Russ. I thought you weren't coming." He lifted her, swung her around, and knew again the exhilarating effect of the love that the child expressed in her own inimitable way.

"My dad said you were coming tomorrow. Then my mummy said you changed your mind and you were coming tonight, but Aunt Velma didn't know what time." She hugged him and kissed his cheek. "When is Uncle Drake coming?"

He set her down beside her chair. "Next week, I think."

He straightened up to let his gaze find Velma and for a brief, poignant moment, as tension gathered in him, the expression in her eyes nearly unglued him. He didn't care about the silence, and he knew that everyone at the table, including Tara, watched him. That didn't bother him either. He walked around to her, stood behind her chair, placed his right hand on her right cheek, bent down and kissed the side of her mouth.

"Hi," she said.

"Hi. If you had turned around, I'd have done it right."

Her right hand caressed the hand that rested on her left shoulder. "I'm kinda slow tonight. Did you speed?"

He knew that question was a reflection more of her nervousness than of anxiety about his driving.

"A little. It isn't often I get to eat Henry's cooking." He patted Henry's shoulder. "Don't get up. I know where the stove is. Sorry I'm a little late," he said to Alexis, after kissing her cheek, "but I got here as fast as I could."

"Don't apologize. We're glad you're here. Sit down. I'll put some warm food on the table. Actually, we just started. Tara insisted that we wait for you."

He looked over at Tara. "That's my girl."

"No. I'm Uncle Drake's girl. I'm your best friend."

"That's right," Telford said. "Let's keep these relationships straight."

He sat where he could look at Velma, and seeing her put a hefty slice of roast pork on her plate made him wonder if she had come to terms with herself. He hoped so.

"Henry, man, this is food for the Gods," he said after tasting the stuffed roast pork, hash brown potatoes and red cabbage with chestnuts.

"Nothing better than potatoes and onions cooked right," Henry said. "Alexis gave me the idea, and when I got to thinking about it, I just fried some bacon and onions, sliced some baked potatoes, put that in the pan and browned the whole thing. Salt and lots of black pepper. Tastes good if I do say so myself."

He waited impatiently through the meal and the hour the family usually spent in the den, sipping coffee and after-dinner drinks and bonding with each other. Finally, Alexis announced that she had better put Tara to bed and, as if taking their cue from her, Telford and Henry said good night and left them alone.

"Excuse me a minute," he said. "I'll be right back."

He dashed out to his car for the box he'd left on the front seat. "I hope you like it," he said when he handed it to her. She looked at the box, then at him, put the box on the chair and opened her arms to him.

With her warm, soft body tight in his arms, he told himself that as much as he longed to give himself to her, letting go wouldn't be wise. He wanted nothing to sidetrack her, to give her an excuse not to open up to him as she had wanted to do, had felt the need to do when she called him earlier in the day. He bent to her mouth and tasted her sweetness. Then he set her away from him.

"Don't you want to know what's in it?" he asked her, pointing to the oblong box that was wrapped in shimmering mauve paper and secured with a large purple bow.

"It's beautiful, Russ. I hate to unwrap it."

Her gasp of excitement when she saw the Degas ballerina atop the round music box was all the thanks he needed. She sat down, apparently speechless, and looked at it, turning it around and over, examining it and shaking her head as if in wonder.

"I'll cherish this for the rest of my life," she said speaking to herself, he realized, more than to him.

"Push that little button on the side." She did and heard the strains of Irving Berlin's "Always."

"Do you know the words to that song?" he asked her.

She nodded. "Yes. I know every word of it."

He had unnerved her, and that wasn't his intention; he had only wanted to let her know what she meant to him, and that nothing she told him would change what he felt for her.

"This means more to me than . . . Russ, I don't know how to express what I'm feeling right now."

"Just trust me to be with you through whatever you're facing."

She rested her head against the back of the chair, folded her hands in her lap and closed her eyes.

"What is it? Don't you feel well?"

"Sorry," she said, sitting forward and looking directly at him. "I'm fine. I don't want to give you the wrong impression, but before we get to what was on my mind when I called you, I have to tell you what happened to me just before dark this afternoon, around five, or so. I hope you'll believe me, because I'm having trouble believing it myself."

He dragged the hassock over to her chair and sat down beside her. "Go on. I'll believe you."

He listened to her incredible story of the old man and his German shepherd. "You weren't frightened?"

"No. I invited him in for coffee or tea, which he declined, and then I offered to drive him to Beaver Ridge, but he refused that offer as well."

Holding both of her hands in his, he ruminated over what she told him. Finally, after thrashing it around in his mind for a while, he said, "Isn't there a lesson in this? I mean, it's as if you were getting divine guidance."

"Maybe. I guess so. But hold that thought until after I tell you what I called you about."

He got up, poured her a glass of Chardonnay and opened

a beer for himself, then he sat on the hassock and said, "I'm listening."

"First, I should have told you that I'm trying to purchase a building, a place where I can locate my business. It has to be large enough for an office, a testing kitchen, and storage space for my standard supplies. Something like a warehouse. I have a real-estate agent handling it. It's something I should have discussed with you before I took the first step."

"I'm glad you're doing this. Why didn't you tell me?"

"I guess because I'm not used to sharing my personal and business activities. I've always worked alone. I hope you understand."

"I do. Will you tell me more about it? Not now, but before you sign anything."

"I will," she said, "and I . . . I may even ask you to look it over."

"I'll be glad to do that. What was the other thing?"

"Well, that's about me. On the advice of my nutritionist, I was examined by a medical doctor, and after some tests, he said I have a hypothyroid that makes if difficult for me to lose weight and easy for me to gain. I'm taking medicine for it, but that alone won't keep me from gaining. I'll still have to eat sensibly and exercise daily, but I won't blow up every time I eat a bowl of grits."

He wanted to ask her how long she'd known that, but decided that she might consider the question provocative. Instead, he asked her how she felt about herself after learning that what she had considered a weight problem could be a health condition.

"Does knowing that make a difference in the way you feel about yourself?" he asked.

"I don't know. Uh, my nutritionist is a buddy from my college days. We were roommates. She thinks . . . Well—"

"Tell me. Don't hold back. Let me be with you in this."

She didn't look directly at him, but seemed to have found something interesting just over his left shoulder. "Lydia—that's her name—Lydia said I never worried about my weight when I was in college, and Alexis said that whatever is going on with me now is . . . uh, deeper than . . . than how I look."

He'd thought that all along. "Do you . . . plan to get help with this?"

"Yes. I'm working on it." She paused, as if in thought. "I'm thinking about what that old man said: 'Any man would be proud to have me for a daughter.' "

Remembering that part of her strange story gave him a slight chill. "He was right, but I wonder how he knew."

Her shrug was barely noticeable, but it told him that she was equally perplexed. "I'm beginning to like your idea that I was getting divine guidance. I can use some more of that."

For the first time, she sipped the wine, but when he looked at his beer, he saw that it had no foam. He discarded it in the kitchen and got another one.

"I appreciate your telling me this. By taking me into your confidence, you're telling me that I'm important to you."

Her gaze held a quizzical expression. "Didn't you know that? Do you think I would make love with a man who wasn't important to me, that I could enjoy such intimacy with a man I didn't care deeply for? Are you serious?"

"I don't think it's the same thing," he began, but as if her words had triggered a reminder of what they experienced that long night of loving, she rimmed her lips with the tip of her tongue and her eyes took on the dark, shimmering glaze that he'd come to recognize in her as desire. Desire for *him*. And like a river seeking its sea, his blood plowed headlong toward his loins.

He put the beer on the floor beside the hassock, took the

glass of wine from her fingers and placed it beside the beer. "I need you."

She stood and held out her right hand to him. In a second, he was on his feet with his arms around her and his fingers gripping her tightly to his body. Her lips parted, and his tongue found its home in the sweet warmth of her mouth.

"So long," she murmured against his lips when he released her. "It's been so long."

He gazed down into her face, knowing that the most essential question between man and woman blazed on his. "I don't want to take you upstairs."

Her arm draped around his waist, holding him as if she feared releasing him. "Come with me."

He wanted to pick her up and carry her to her bed, but he knew she would begin thinking about her weight, and he wanted that as far from her thoughts as possible. Arm and arm, they walked down the hall to her room. Henry and Alexis wouldn't like finding a wine glass and beer tankard on the floor, but the throbbing in his loins made every thing or person other than Velma insignificant.

As he had sat at her feet, first holding her hands and then gripping her knees, his gaze pinned on her, she had hardly been able to think of what she wanted to tell him. With his gentle acceptance of her shortcoming as a friend, if not as a lover, love bloomed in her heart for him as never before. He hadn't questioned her failure to tell him of the doctor's diagnosis, and he had a right to know that, if nothing else. A man might not want to be saddled with a woman who had health problems when she was barely thirty. Without warning, every atom and molecule in her body responded to him, and he knew it. Somehow, her body communicated to him its needs.

She controlled the urge to run with him to her room, but she wanted to, for frissons of heat swirled around in her igniting ever nerve end in her body. He closed the door behind them, and she turned to him with lips parted and took him in. But she knew at once that he was as hungry as she, when he trapped her between himself and the wall, twirling his tongue in and out of her mouth in a certain promise and pressing his bulging need against her belly. She thought she would scream in her impatience to know again the pleasure of his thrusts within her.

"Easy, sweetheart," he said. "I need a little help here, or I'll explode."

"I want you the way you are and the way you have to be. Just love me, Russ. That's all I need."

"Can you slow down now, and let me lead us? I want it to work for both of us. Later, whatever you want and whatever you do will suit me."

She didn't answer. She couldn't, for his hand had snaked down to her bosom, and his fingers were teasing his nipple while his tongue danced in her mouth. She reached up until she could touch his head.

"What do you want?" The words seemed torn from him.

"I want your mouth on my breast," she said, freeing it from the rounded neckline of her dress before he could manage it.

When he looked down at the glistening brown areola and licked his lips, she sucked in her breath and waited for the pleasure of feeling his mouth on her. He lowered his head, sucked her into his mouth and feasted there until tremors shook her. He stopped, unzipped her dress and, when she stepped out of it, tossed it across a chair. He picked her up and lay her on the bed. Then, with fingers that trembled, he unhooked her garters, rolled down her stockings and pulled off the garter belt.

"Help me with this thing," he said of her brassiere that fastened in the back. She unhooked it, and he leaned over her, spreading kisses over her face, neck and ears until she moaned, "You know what I want. Don't tease." She thought she would bounce off the bed when his tongue began twirling around her right areola and his fingers slid up her thigh, parted her folds and began their magic.

"Please, honey. Take off your clothes. I'm going out of my mind." She unfastened his belt, yanked it off and tugged at his sweater. Within seconds he stripped himself and removed her bikini panties.

"Now," she said. "Now."

But he resumed the tease and torture, suckling her and letting his talented fingers dance at the entrance of her love portal, strumming her the way a master lyrist plays the lyre. Her belly quivered and her legs trembled until, nearly wild in her passion, she swung her body up to him, took him in her hands and pressed upward until she had him within her.

With one hand beneath her hips and the other one around her shoulder, he moved within her, stroking and twisting, until she tightened around him and every part of her, every pore in her body, opened to him.

"I can't bear it," she moaned. "I'm so full."

He increased the pace, rocking her until she felt the heat at the bottom of her feet and the pumping and squeezing in her vagina. And then she howled in release, sinking to the depths, while he stroked her, dragging her from the abyss of her orgasm and catapulting her to the pinnacle of ecstasy.

Flinging her arms wide, she cried out. "Oh, Lord. Oh, Lord."

"Is it good to you?" he asked her. "Is it? Is it?"

"Yes. Yes."

"Do you want anybody else? Do you?"

"Only you," she moaned. "I only want you."

He gripped her to him, rocked her, lost his body, mind and soul in the valley of her passion and gave her the essence of himself.

Chapter Eleven

A couple of hours before daylight, Russ made it upstairs to his room by the force of more willpower than he remembered ever having exerted. Leaving her had nearly killed him, but he couldn't afford to expose her by allowing his family to know he hadn't slept in his bed.

He loved her. Oh, how he loved her, but the knowledge that another human being had the ability to control him, to bend him, sent chills through his body. He stripped, threw himself across his bed, buried his face in the pillow and groaned. If he was as much like his father as his Uncle Fentress proclaimed, would he also be a doormat for the woman he loved? He believed in himself, in his strength as a man, but the knowledge was of little comfort; he knew that generation after generation, history repeated itself.

He tossed for a while, then got up, slid beneath the covers and waited for daylight. It seemed to him that the wind had never howled so fiercely or so noisily, but he knew it wasn't the wind but his troubled mind that made him too restless to fall asleep.

At the first streak of dawn, he rolled out of bed, donned a robe and went to the bathroom. With both Alexis and Tara living on the second floor, he could no longer stroll around naked. The shower refreshed his body but left his emotions seriously in need of repair. He walked into the breakfast room, saw that the table hadn't been set and went to the kitchen to find Henry.

"What happened to you?" Henry asked him, measuring the flour for biscuit dough. "Ya sick? It's a quarter past six in the morning."

"Must have looked at the clock wrong. I'll set the table."

Henry put the bag of flour aside and stared at Russ, "I knowed you since before you turned seven, and I never knowed ya to lie. As late as you always sleep, yer body's clock shoulda told you it wasn't nine o'clock. Something ain't right with ya."

He wasn't up to hassling with Henry. "I'm going in there to set the table. Hurry up with those biscuits."

"And when did you start doing housework? You ain't like yerself."

He knew Henry cared deeply for him, but he was in no mood for the man's pungent observations. "I have an apartment, as you well know, and I live alone. Who do you think does the housework?"

"You don't. Probably looks like a pig pen. Here're some clean napkins. Bennie ironed them yesterday."

He was supposed to respond with a witty remark to the mention of Bennie, but he didn't feel like it. He put the napkins on a tray beside the glasses. "Thanks. Glad to hear she did some work."

Placing the napkins, glasses and flatware mechanically, his thoughts elsewhere, he didn't hear footsteps, so he whirled around, nearly dropping a glass when Telford said, "What's this? Man, I didn't know you knew how to set a table."

"Why shouldn't I know how? I've been eating at tables since I was three."

He didn't look up, but he could feel his brother's hard stare when he said, "What wildcat did you . . . Say, what's the matter? It isn't even six-thirty."

"I know what time it is, Telford," he said, wishing he'd stayed in his room and realizing that with every word he uttered, he increased suspicions about himself. He glanced up to see a troubled expression on his brother's face and wanted to apologize, but if he did that, he'd get a battery of questions.

It occurred to him that his laughter, joking and lightheartedness of the past weeks had led his family to expect that of him, but he was behaving as he had before Velma taught him to laugh, to enjoy just being alive. Too bad. He didn't feel like being frivolous.

"Is Henry in the kitchen?" Telford asked him.

"Yeah. He's making biscuits."

"Thank God that's *one* thing I can count on around here," Telford said, spun around and headed for the kitchen.

He finished setting the table and considered sitting down at his usual place and waiting for breakfast, but he thought better of it, got a mackinaw from the closet in the foyer and went outside.

He walked down the road, feeling the invigorating bite of the late winter wind in the early dawn, and when a fawn scrambled across his path, he stopped, knowing that the doe would follow, putting him in danger if he was between her and her calf. While he waited, he slipped his hands into his pants pockets for warmth, and his fingers settled on his keys.

As if propelled by a force outside of himself, he turned back, got into his Mercedes and drove off. With no destination in mind, he headed toward the sunrise. Two hours later, he sat on the banks of the Patapsco River, drinking coffee from a paper cup and shuffling through the pages of his mind. Some new pages and some tattered and yellowed with age.

Was it reasonable for a man to lose himself so completely in a woman? Three times the night before, he'd given her all of himself. Everything. As vulnerable to her as a newborn baby. And then, when he'd thought himself sapped of energy and drained of desire, she settled herself atop him, loved and kissed him from head to foot and, if that hadn't nearly disintegrated him, she then took him, all of him, his essence, stripping him of himself.

He would never forget soaring unfettered and uncontrolled, his manhood fully and finally glorified to the utmost. He swallowed the last of the coffee and pitched the cup into a nearby refuse basket. The memory of it would remain with him for as long as he lived, and he would love her for just as long.

"Say, buddy. That your car parked over there in that no-parking area?"

He looked up into the face of a Maryland highway patrolman. "Yes. It's mine. I didn't realize parking here is prohibited."

"Let's see your papers."

Russ got up and stood facing the man. "They're in my car behind the visor. Officer, are you married?"

"Been married for eleven years. Good years. Why?" the man asked, as if getting such a question was not unusual in his normal working day.

You could say things to a stranger that you wouldn't dare mention to anyone else, because he would never see you again. Russ looked the officer in the eye, wanting to be certain that the answer he got was the truth.

"Did you ever feel as if you didn't own yourself?" he asked the man. "That you didn't belong to your *own* self? I mean when the woman you love *really* loves you, do you have to lose your insides?"

The officer braced his hands against his hips and looked hard at Russ. "Hadn't thought of it that way, but I can remember a couple of times when it sure seemed like that, when I gave up everything, including my *self*. That was a while back. I wouldn't mind if it happened now two or three times a week, if I get your meaning. *Say!* You weren't thinking of jumping into this river, were you?"

Russ stared at the man. "Good Lord, no. But that a woman could have that much control over me—"

"Not to worry, friend. The good thing about it is that she doesn't know it. Trust me, she's so busy doubting herself that she would never believe it."

They walked together to the car, and Russ opened the door and gave the officer his papers.

"They seem in order," the patrolman said. Then his gaze bore into Russ. "You can start worrying when she no longer gives you an opportunity to lose yourself. Until then, consider yourself a lucky man. And watch where you park."

That no-parking sign wasn't there when he got out of the car, and he'd swear to it, but he thought it wise not to voice his thoughts. He got into the Mercedes, ignited the engine and looked back to wave at the patrolman, but didn't see him or his car. He switched off the engine and brushed his hand across his forehead, wondering whether the patrolman had anything in common with the old man and the German shepherd.

"Maybe yes, maybe no," he said aloud, "but one thing is certain; I'm in one hell of a spot with Velma." He ignited the engine and headed for Eagle Park.

"You mean he just went off without a word to anybody?" Alexis asked Telford when she joined him for breakfast.

"That's right. I wonder if he and Velma had a fight."

"Just like he used to be. Tight lipped and sharp tongued," Henry said and sat down with them to eat his regular breakfast of fresh fruit, cereal and coffee. Henry didn't believe in clogging his arteries with biscuits, sausage, eggs, and bacon. "I wonder what coulda happened. When we left them in the den last night, they didn't look like two people likely to get into a fight." Henry added, "course it won't be the first time I was wrong."

"I'm going down there and find out why Velma hasn't come to breakfast," Alexis said. "This isn't one bit like Russ. Maybe I can help."

"Just a minute," Velma said in answer to Alexis' knock. Velma opened the door and her mouth dropped open seconds before her lashes covered her eyes. Alexis didn't doubt that her sister expected her visitor to be Russ.

"Hi," she said with a breeziness intended to cover the awkwardness of the situation. "Aren't you coming to breakfast?"

Velma's face darkened into a frown. "Why, yes, but it's not quite eight-thirty. Any . . . uh problems?"

"Well," Alexis said, temporarily at a loss for words, "you usually eat early. I wanted to be sure you're all right."

"I got to sleep late."

"Nothing wrong, I hope." Even to herself, she sounded as if she was fishing for information.

But Velma's face transformed itself into a brilliant smile. "No indeed. It was the most wonderful night of my life. Oh, Alexis. I can't begin to tell you how I feel. Russ is . . . he's wonderful. He . . . he's precious to me."

"No help here," Alexis said to herself. "Honey, I'm happy for you. Nothing compares with the love of a wonderful man. It was a long time coming, but you have it now, and you're very fortunate. So is he. I'd better finish my breakfast."

"You stopped eating to come see if I was all right?"

She patted Velma's shoulder. "When you're a creature of habit, expect such things. We let Tara sleep late on Saturdays, and she'll be down in a few minutes. She'll want pancakes, too, and I'm not sure Henry made the batter. See you later."

Polite, meaningless chatter. She hated making talk, but how else could she have closed the conversation without raising her sister's suspicions? She went back to the breakfast room to finish her meal.

"I take it she was alone," Telford said, after Henry left the table.

"Alone and floating on the clouds. They were together last night, and they definitely did not have a fight. That makes his disappearance even more inexplicable."

"Depends on how his mind's working. He won't let too much time pass without giving me a call," Telford said.

She braced her right elbow on the arm of her chair, took several sips of coffee and studied her husband's face. "If he's got his thinking cap on, he'll call Velma. She's the one he's going to have to deal with."

At about two o'clock that afternoon, Velma began to pack. Henry, Telford, Alexis and Tara had each found a reason to stay in their room or, at least, to keep out of her sight. She saw nothing that she could kick, slam or throw, and with no outlet for her anger, she decided to leave. Russ had a reason for his behavior, but she didn't care to know what it was.

"Mind if I come in?" Alexis asked, already walking through the door. "Hey, what are you doing?"

"Just what it looks like. I'm going home. I don't need to

be here to find out what he's got to say. I don't want to hear it, and I'm not going to listen. He owes me better than this. Dammit, he can't love me out of my senses and then walk off as if I don't exist. Damn him!"

"I think you should sit down and calm yourself. Convict him after you let him have his say. And leave anger and self-pride out of it. If he made you so happy, what do you think you did to him? You don't know what happened to him in that bed with you last night. Until he tells you that, hold your tongue, because saying you're sorry will be wasted on Russ."

Velma put her hands on her hips and glared at her sister. "And his sorry will be wasted on me, too."

When Alexis put both arms around her, she had to fight back the tears. "He did a real job on me last night, Sis. I couldn't forget him if my life depended on it, but that doesn't mean I have to accept this. I won't."

At the soft knock on the door, both of their heads snapped up, and when Velma didn't speak, Alexis answered.

"Yes?"

"Open the door, please, Velma."

Velma sucked in her breath and grabbed her chest as if that would slow down her heartbeat.

"Good luck," Alexis said, rushed to the door and opened it. "You've got your work cut out for you," she said to Russ and headed down the hall.

"Don't I know it!"

She stood rooted in the spot as he walked in and closed the door behind him. "I see you're packing. You have every right to be angry. Yes, and hurt. I didn't do it deliberately."

"How can you say that? Did somebody put a gun in your back?"

When he didn't respond to that remark, she braced herself for words that she would probably rather not hear.

"What we did in this room, in that bed last night knocked the stuffing out of me," he said without preliminaries. "I'd never had such an experience. Never. You made me king of the world. What I was feeling for you when I stumbled out of this room at four-thirty this morning scared the living hell out of me. I knew I loved you and that you loved me, but I didn't have a clue as to what that meant until last night."

She wasn't prepared for that, and his confession rocked her, settled deep inside, down in the pit of her where she lived. She had to sit down lest her legs desert her, and she groped toward the edge of the bed, sat there and looked up at him.

"When I woke up this morning, every atom of my being loved you. I loved the whole world. I cried because I was so happy that I couldn't contain what I was feeling for you. I wallowed in the bed, kissing and hugging the pillow on which you had laid your head. I kissed the air. I sang in the shower, and I danced until I was exhausted. Then I dressed, went to the breakfast room, sat down, and Henry said, 'We don't know where he went.' It was downhill from there."

He walked over to the window that faced the garden, turned and walked back to her. "It may sound trite, but you must know that I'd rather hurt myself than you. I was sitting at the edge of the Patapsco River down near Sykesville trying to deal with . . ." He threw up his hands. "With us. When I finally got a grip on myself, my first thought was that I'd hurt you, that I'd probably damaged what was most precious to me. If you can't forgive me, I'll have to accept it, but I don't know how I'll live with it."

In her unhappiness, she had considered every scenario except that he was trying to find his way out of the tidal wave of loving that had engulfed them, that he was actually trying to find his way back to her.

"Are you still scared of what . . . of your feelings for me?"

"Not as much as I was, but I won't lie. I'm just learning what it means to be a part of another person, to give up my aloneness and to accept that I need another person as much as I need to breathe. Can you understand that?"

She wanted to hold on to her anger and hurt, but her heart wouldn't let her. "I think so, but the next time you feel undone, at least tell me you're going for a spin, and make it a short one. If you had walked into this house half an hour later, I'd have been on my way home."

He hunkered before her and rested his hands on her knees. "I doubt I can ever feel that way again. I don't see how it can happen twice, but I promise to share my feelings with you as best I can. I'm not used to this level of sharing, but I'm going to try."

His hands moved up from her knees to her bare thighs, ignoring the dress that covered them. But she knew the difference between seduction and possessiveness, and he was—consciously or not—telling her that she belonged to him. She kept her mind on the importance of the issue at hand. She had to.

"But you've always claimed that I don't share things with you," she said.

"I know, and I realize now that I've been thinking of incidents and situations in our pasts, telling each other about that, and about our attitudes, people and things, things outside of us that affect us. Giving assurance that we loved and cared for each other. Telling each other such things was my idea of sharing." He shook his head as though rejecting the thought. "Last night and this morning, I found out what sharing is, what it means to share . . . to give oneself, holding back nothing. I may have more to learn about that than you have."

"Maybe it's all those things you mentioned. You and I are

alike in a lot of ways, but it's too bad we both have a hard time revealing our deepest feelings. I'm going to try too, Russ."

His gaze locked on hers, and his finger slid further up her thighs. For a moment, she held her breath, mesmerized by his darkened eyes, their turbulence telling her that he knew her, knew what she could give him and that he wanted it.

She shook herself out of the trance. "Honey, we don't want Telford or Alexis to come down here thinking we were both so angry that one of us might have killed the other, only to find us locked together in this bed. I'd never get over that."

The thought of it made her laugh, a nervous tension-relieving laugh perhaps, but it brought a smile from him. A smile that dissolved into a grin. When she opened her arms to him, he pushed her backward and rolled with her on the bed. Tears rolled down her cheeks as he hugged and kissed her, whispering "I love you" over and over. She thought her heart would bounce out of her chest.

"I love you, too, but I'm hungry," she said, hoping to stave off the throttling grip of passion in an attempt at levity. "Did you eat lunch?"

"Lunch?" He rolled her over on her back and sat up. "I haven't even had breakfast." He looked at his watch. "Two-forty. I hope Henry's gone to his house by now. I don't feel like fending off his meddlesome comments. Come on."

They walked hand-in-hand to the kitchen. "Well what do you know?" Russ said, "Henry left us some food." He took the plate of ham and chicken sandwiches and the string bean and tomato salad over to the table in the corner.

"What'll we drink?" he asked, more to himself than to her. He returned to the table with a bottle of ginger ale for her and a glass of milk for himself.

Telford walked in, joined them at the table and began speaking as if the day had not been one of unusual events.

"Think you can give me an hour or so before dinner, Russ? I'd like us to check inventory, if you can spare the time." Russ looked at her, not for permission she well knew, but for understanding.

"If you need an extra hand, I don't have anything more important to do," she hastened to say.

"Great," Telford said. "I appreciate this, Velma." He looked at Russ. "Whenever you're ready."

Russ got a pair of pliers and began removing the industrial-weight staples on the wooden boxes. He'd bet they had lost thousands of dollars because of that scheme. Every carton was short at least one box.

"You two want to work on those last three cases together while I check the accountant's audit?" Telford asked Russ.

"No," Velma said, and Russ' head jerked around. "This requires concentration," she explained before he could ask why.

Telford looked at her, his eyes sparkling with devilment and, Russ realized, happiness. "I've been thinking in terms of Brighton power. Are you suggesting there might be such a thing as Harrington power?"

He couldn't believe it. Velma lowered her lashes and let her gaze sweep Telford at snail speed from his shoes to his head. "If you don't know it, won't do you a bit of good for me to tell you. You know? I once had a puppy that used to sit and stare at himself in the mirror, sitting there and thumping his tail. He was one happy little puppy."

Russ threw his head back and let the laughter pour out of him, good cleansing and stress-releasing laughter. "Don't look at me," he said to his brother when Telford stared at him, his whole demeanor a question mark. "She can swap wit with the best of them."

"Yeah. And I can see why you laugh so much these days."

They worked at their separate tasks for over an hour before Russ called to Telford. "Case number A-39002 from Worth Tool Company. Packer 33. Four cartons missing from an unopened case. What's in the audit?"

After a minute during which he assumed Telford was doing a computer search, he heard the words that would lead them to the answer they sought.

"Sixty-four cartons. Weight: three hundred and twenty pounds, same as the other cases in this series. The auditor didn't open the case, but he certainly supervised the weighing of those boxes."

Russ walked over to Telford and looked at the computer screen. "Maybe the accountant put it on the spread sheet and the auditor was too lazy to check."

"I don't think so," Telford said. "We changed that. Remember, the accountant merely logs in what he sees on the invoice after checking to see that there's a package or case that matches the invoice."

"You're right. So we go after Packer 33 and the auditor."

"Is the packer's ID on all of these cases?" Velma asked them.

"Sometimes it's on a slip inside, and we haven't been too careful about examining it. But that's all in the past. Let's see what else we can find."

"All the ones I have from Worth Tool have a carton or two missing, and they all have Packer 33 stamped on them."

Russ sat on the floor and wrapped his hands around his knees. "Let's quit for the day. No one man packed all of these cases. In fact, Worth probably doesn't have a packer with that number. We need a lawyer. How about Schyler Henderson or Wade Maloy?"

Telford signed off the computer and covered the screen as

protection against dust. "Henderson is in nearby Baltimore, and contact's much easier. What do you say?"

"Works for me," Russ said.

"Are you going to sue the company?" Velma asked.

"With a vengeance. And they'll pay," Russ said. "If this is their practice, they won't want every one of their customers to bring suit and put them out of business. I doubt the case will go to trial."

"Telephone call for you, Russ," Henry said as they walked into the house. "It's a woman, and if I ain't mistaken, I've heard that voice before."

He didn't like the sound of it. Hoping to avoid a misunderstanding, he took Velma's hand, walked to the hall table and lifted the receiver. "Russ Harrington speaking."

"I need to see you, Russ, please. It's terribly important."

The expression on his face must have been worth a good laugh. He closed his mouth and let the wall take his weight. "What? What do you want from me? The court sent you the results of the DNA tests, although you knew all the time what the tests would show. You didn't succeed in tricking me into supporting you and your child, so what do you want now? I have no intention of being your fairy godfather."

"I'm about to be dispossessed, and I don't have anyone to turn to. My folks are dirt poor, and besides my father isn't going to forgive me for having an OW."

He ran his hand over his hair. "If you had come to me like an honest person and told me your plight, I might have been inclined to help you, but you didn't do that. No woman will ever accuse me of impregnating her and not offering to marry her *before* the child is born, that is, if she intends to give birth to it. I wish you luck."

He hung up, but the thought of a five- or six-month-old baby on the street, homeless, didn't sit well with him. "That's one experience I wish I'd never had," he said to Velma, who looked at him without expression.

"What does she want now? Money?"

His shrug belied his concern. "I suppose so. She's about to be dispossessed. It isn't that I don't want to help a human being in trouble; I just don't want any involvement with her."

"It would be good to have the name of a social agency that you can refer her to if she calls you again."

"Yeah. But I hope she doesn't call." In one day, he'd gone from euphoria to the depths, back up and down again. He let out a long breath. At least they knew how they were being cheated of their building supplies.

"Do you want to eat dinner here, or would you like to drive into Frederick?"

"I'll be happy eating here," she said, "but if you want to get away—"

"Oh, no. I'd rather eat here, but I wanted to give you your choice. I'll be in my room." He kissed her on the mouth and dashed up the stairs.

What a roller coaster! He showered, put on a robe, lay down on his belly and wrapped his arms around his pillow. Every muscle in his body reminded him that he had stayed in that bed less than an hour and a half the night before, and without intending to, he dozed off to sleep.

An insistent knock on his door awakened him. He opened the door, looked straight ahead and then let his gaze drop until it fixed on Tara. "Gee, Uncle Russ, were you sleeping? It's almost seven o'clock, and I didn't see you anywhere. My mummy, my dad and Mr. Henry were worried 'cause you didn't come to breakfast and nobody knew where you went. I didn't want you to get into trouble 'cause you didn't come to dinner on time."

He picked her up and hugged her. "I'm glad you knocked, because I was sound asleep." He looked at his watch. "A quarter of seven. Thanks a lot. Say, I didn't know you could tell time."

Her smile, so warm and sweet, blessed him. "I been telling time since I was in church school. My mummy and my dad taught me how." A frown marred her face. "Uncle Russ, did you make it up with Aunt Velma? Was she still mad at you?"

If you wanted anything broadcast, let Tara know about it. "Your Aunt Velma and I are not angry with each other. We're friends."

Her frown deepened. "When I get mad at Grant, I stay mad a long time."

He worked hard at controlling the laugh that wanted to spill out of him. "How long does it take you to stop being mad?"

"I don't know. Sometimes it takes a whole hour. Grant's mother told Mr. Adam that I'm very femi . . . fem—"

"Feminine." He could attest to that. "But you *do* forgive Grant. Right?"

She nodded. "He's my friend, but you're my best friend."

He put her down. "If your best friend doesn't hurry, he'll be late for dinner."

She kissed his cheek. "I'll go tell Aunt Velma you're her friend."

He stood at the door and watched her scoot down the stairs. What he wouldn't give for several children of his own with her intelligence, joy and love for everyone around her!

As he started down the stairs, his cell phone rang, and he started to let it ring, but he thought better of it and answered. "Russ Harrington. What can I do for you?"

"Russ, buddy, this is Sam Jenkins."

"Well what do you know. This is a surprise, and a pleasant one. What's up?"

"Got a minute?"

"Actually, no. Dinner will be served in two minutes."

"Then I'll make it brief. You told me that whenever I'm ready to stretch myself and build a building for my gym business, you'd draw up the plans. I'm calling you on it."

"Where do you intend to open the gym?"

"In Baltimore. I'm looking for the right piece of property, and I'll need an architect to redesign the interior."

"My word is my bond, brother. I'll get back to you Monday."

He hung up and headed for the breakfast room. "I told everybody you were on your way, Uncle Russ," Tara said, "and he didn't think he had ever seen her so pleased with herself.

"When will you be six, Tara?" he asked her after Telford said the grace.

"In May when my dad has a birthday. Grant's already six, and he thinks he knows more than me."

"More than I. He may know more than you about some things," Telford said, "but I am sure that you know more than he does about some other things. Next time, remind him that when it comes to playing the piano, he's no match for you."

She clapped her hands. "Oh, goody, I will. Mummy, can I—"

"No, Tara, you may not leave the table to call Grant."

"Oh. Sorry."

Russ wondered how he'd lived over thirty years without seeing the love and warmth all around him. He loved his brothers and Henry, but he hadn't realized what he drew from the love they gave him. It struck him forcibly that he needed them all in his life; his brothers, Alexis, Henry and Tara. Yes, and Velma. Maybe that explained his angst early that morning. The word, *need,* and what it meant still made him uneasy, but he could live with it. Hadn't Tara awakened him because she needed to know that he wouldn't suffer what she considered the embarrassment of being late for dinner? Yes, he needed them.

He put his fork aside. "I wonder if there's another family anywhere like this one." When the adults stopped eating and looked at him, he said what he felt. "The happiest time of my day is dinnertime at this table. Too bad Drake isn't here."

As if sensing his vulnerability, Velma stepped in. "I thought Drake would be here this weekend."

"Next Wednesday," Tara said. "That's what he told me when I talked to him this morning."

"Ain't nothing like having all the boys here together," Henry said. "After all these years, the only thing changed is Russ talks and picks up after himself. Never thought I'd live to see it. Passed his room this morning and it looked like Bennie had just straightened it up. Me hat's off to ya, Velma."

He knew someone would eventually get to the subject of Velma and himself. "I hate to disappoint you, Henry," Russ said, "but the room was straight this morning because I was awake so early that I wasn't my normal self. If you're going to give Velma credit for something, be sure it isn't my neatness."

"I've only been in his apartment three times," Velma said, "and each time it was clean when I got there. The kitchen was spotless."

Henry stopped on his way to the kitchen, turned around and looked at Velma. "Three times? You're joking. I give both of ya more credit than that."

He listened to the patter, hardly hearing it, not needing to hear it, for he knew that kindness would coat every word spoken. When the phone rang, Henry answered it.

"She's right here," he said. "Phone for you, Velma."

"I had my calls transferred here," she said and left the table to go to the telephone. "This is Velma Brighton."

"Hello, Ms. Brighton. This is Alvin Crooks. My man says he's found your father, but he hasn't spoken with him or written him. He wants to know what's next."

She thought her knees would collapse, as the telephone table swayed and the chandelier seemed to triple in number. "Just give me all the information you have, including his address and telephone number, what he's doing for a living and the best time and place for me to reach him. Send me the bill."

"Will do, ma'am. If you have any trouble with this, you know my phone number."

She thanked the lawyer and hung up. Now what? Should she tell Alexis and get more discouragement, or should she contact him, try to get the answers and then tell her sister? After her experience of sharing with Russ, she figured she should let her sister know that their father was alive, but if she did that, Alexis would immediately discourage her pursuit of information about their parents. She decided not to tell Alexis until after she spoke with their father.

"Want to go see an old movie?" Russ asked when she returned to the table.

"Which one?" she asked. "I love just about all of them except the ones with slapstick comedy. I never could stand pie throwing and that stuff. Cheap way to get laughs." With those words she succeeded in diverting attention from her phone call; the discussion at once centered on movies and what they offered.

"Are we really going to the movies?" she asked him after dinner, sitting beside him on the sofa in the den.

"Yeah. If Henry will keep an eye on Tara, maybe those old married people over there will go along with us."

"I heard that," Henry said. "Mind you, Drake won't be calling you an old married man a year from now. I'll sleep in my little room back there tonight and watch out for Tara, Alexis, if you want to go with them."

"Thanks Henry," Alexis said, looking directly into her husband's eyes, "but we . . . uh . . . we'll go with them another time."

"Why didn't I know that?" Russ asked, his tone just short of mocking.

"Am I missing something here?" Velma asked no one in particular. She didn't want to see a movie unless it was on television. And speaking of television, the house contained several, but she didn't recall having seen anyone watching them.

Russ stroked her nose with his right index finger. "If you had to ask that question, you are definitely missing something."

She rubbed her cheek against his hand. "Let's just stay home and talk."

"Oh. Oh," Henry said. "First time I ever knowed a plain old fever to be catching. Must be some new virus. If nobody's going out, I guess I'll get on down to me house and feed me puppies."

Telford stood and took Alexis' hand. "We're turning in. See you tomorrow morning."

Alexis released his hand, hugged Velma and then put an arm around her husband. "If you're not having breakfast," she said to them, "please leave a note where I can find it. You two have a nice evening."

"I wish you the same," Russ said.

A glance at him confirmed the jovial mood that accompanied his dry comment to her sister. "You should be sleepy," Velma said to Russ.

He leaned back against the sofa and closed his eyes. "I should be and I am. Will you feel deserted if I go to bed?"

"No, indeed. How long had you been asleep when Tara woke you up?"

"About half an hour or so. She's a wonderful little girl. She woke me up because she didn't want me to be late for dinner. I gather she heard the conversation this morning concerning my whereabouts, and she didn't want me to be the subject of discussion this evening. Or something like that."

"Pretty close to it. She came down and announced that you were on your way. I understand that you're rest broken, so let's say good night."

He walked with her to her room. "I'm not going in, and I am definitely not getting into any heavy-duty necking with you." His lips settled lightly on hers, but when she parted them to receive him, he broke the kiss. "I owe you one. Sleep well."

"You, too, and pleasant dreams."

A few minutes later her phone rang. "I forgot to tell you that John and Amelia want us over at their place next Saturday. I hope you can make it, because I want to get reacquainted with John. We were good buddies when we were undergrads. You'll like him."

"I liked what I saw. I have a reception next Friday, but I'm free Saturday, so I'd love to go with you. Night."

"Good night, sweetheart."

After a quick shower, she fell asleep almost as soon as she touched the bed.

At about nine o'clock Monday morning, she phoned her lawyer. "Anymore news? I didn't have the privacy to ask questions when we spoke Saturday evening. Does your contact know where my father lives and how he supports himself?"

"He isn't working in his profession as a molecular biologist, but he has a fine job teaching medical engineering at the university. He leaves his apartment only to shop for food and other essentials, to go to the university and to go to the dry cleaners. Nothing else. Doesn't seem to have any friends. You won't have any trouble finding him; he lives in the heart of Montreal. The report and the bill are in the mail." She thanked him and hung up. She would chart her next move after she read the report.

"You must have written a strong proposal," her real-estate agent said when she telephoned him. "The commissioner's office is considering your bid. If it's accepted, you're gonna have to either begin renovation or occupy the place within a month. So prepare yourself."

She checked her suppliers for the Sepia Sweethearts' annual gala. After coaching the disc jockey as to the kind of music the group wanted, she attended a rehearsal of the exotic dancers and the jazz singer and combo that made up the evening's entertainment. She preferred to organize parties and galas for which entertainment was excluded, but she'd work with what she had.

Come Friday evening, she surveyed the ballroom at Muti's Entertainment Center, found everything in order and told the manager that he could open the doors. The oohs and aahs of the attendees as they entered gave her a feeling of pride and reinforced her sense that she was good at her profession. At the gala's end, the president of Sepia Sweethearts called her to the podium, thanked her for planning their best gala ever and gave her a citation and an honorary membership.

"From now on, our own Sepia sister will cater all of our parties and galas," the woman said to thunderous applause.

With one of her most gratifying jobs behind her, Velma walked out of Muti's in high spirits and crossed the street to her car. However, as she reached for the door on the driver's side to open it, a man jumped from the second-floor balcony of the building in front of where she'd parked her car. He stumbled for a minute, then looked around and ran down the street. Almost immediately, a woman leaned out of the window and shouted, "Police! Police!"

After standing there dumbfounded for a second, she used her cell phone to call 911, reported what she saw and added that a woman was calling for the police. That done, she drove home.

"Do you think that man saw me?" she asked Russ that night when they spoke by phone.

"I doubt it. He was in too big a hurry. Anyway, you're not in that neighborhood often, so I wouldn't worry about it." But she did worry; only a criminal or a person pursued by one would take a chance on jumping from a balcony onto a concrete sidewalk.

"What do I wear to John and Amelia's house tomorrow?" she asked him. "Is it a party, or what?"

"Amelia said it would be just the four of us. Remember? So wear whatever you like. I'll have on a business suit. That dress you had on Sunday was nice. You looked beautiful in it."

She wished he wouldn't say that. She'd never been beautiful a day in her life. "Thanks, but you're proof positive that love is blind."

"Are we back to that, for Pete's sake?"

"All right. All right. I stand corrected."

She heard him suck his teeth, and wondered if she had disgusted him, because she hadn't previously heard him do that. "The correction you need is inside yourself. Do you think you have to be perfect in your own eyes before anyone can love you? What did you eat for dinner?"

It sounded as if he had changed the subject, but she knew he hadn't. "Filet mignon, roast tiny red potatoes, asparagus, stilton cheese and espresso. I substituted the cheese for the desert. Would you believe the president of the group that held the reception read me a citation? Then, they made me a member. From now on, I'll do all their events."

"That's wonderful. I know you're good at what you do, and I'm trying to get my fraternity to hire you for the national gala. Of course, if they have it at a hotel, you can't do it. But we'll see."

They talked for another half hour, saying nothing, just touching each other in the only way possible at the moment. "I'll be at your house at five-thirty," he said. "Kiss me?"

She made the sound of a kiss. " 'Night, love."

"Sleep well, sweetheart."

Saturday afternoon melted into four-thirty, and she had to find something to wear to dinner with Russ and his friends. She shuffled the dresses in her closet, pushed them aside and looked at her suits. "Oh well," she said after having wrestled with the problem for about a quarter of an hour. "He said he liked that dress, so I'll wear it. And he'd better remember that he asked me to choose it."

He rang her bell at five-twenty-five. She started toward the door at breakneck speed, then told herself she shouldn't seem so anxious to see him and slowed down. Reflecting on her behavior, laughter bubbled up in her throat and threatened to spill out at about the time she opened the door. His look of surprise at her demeanor brought the laugh out in full and, unable to control it, she took his arm and urged him inside.

He rested the back of his right hand on his hip and gazed down at her. "What're you up to?"

She managed to control the laughter and said, "I was laughing at myself." She explained why and added, "All that posturing, and you couldn't even see me."

He rubbed the fingers of his left hand over his temple and a frown settled on his face. "So you play pranks on yourself? You were anxious to see me, but you didn't think it a good idea to let me know it, but a minute after I'm in here, you spill the whole thing." His arms went around her, and his kiss held just enough pressure to make her long for more.

"I'll get my stole," she said having decided she wouldn't need a coat.

The first thing she noticed when she walked into the Gandy home was the Steinway grand. "Who plays?" she asked John, who met them at the door.

"Amelia, when she has time. She'll be with us as soon as she gets Jay straightened out. At three, he's a real handful." He led them toward the back of the house to a large, cozy family room. "Make yourselves comfortable. I'm going for some ice."

They sat in the family room awaiting their hosts, but they could have been anywhere, for their thoughts remained focused on the mutual love that grew in their hearts.

"If you hadn't rocked me on my heels when you opened your door," Russ said when she smiled at him, "I would have told you how lovely you look. I really like that dress."

"Thanks. I wore it because you said you like it."

He spread his knees, rested his forearms on his thighs and looked at her until her nerves seemed to want to rearrange themselves. "Do you like to please me?" he finally asked.

"I'm always happy when I know I've pleased you."

He sat up, crossed his left knee over his right one and winked at her. "That's not quite what I meant, but knowing you, I'll take what I can get."

At the sound of footsteps, Russ stood. Shock reverberated through her when Amelia walked into the room. When they met, she didn't notice the woman's obvious limp nor her thick waistline. She jumped to her feet, and walked to meet their hostess, her mind swirling with questions that she couldn't ask. They embraced each other.

"I'm glad you could come, Velma," Amelia said. "Russ, John and I were close during college, and I want us to resume our friendship. Of course, we can't do that unless you like being with John and me." She pressed her bottom lip down with her index finger, and Velma found that a fetching mannerism.

She didn't want to tell the woman that she and Russ didn't have a permanent arrangement, so she made herself smile. "I appreciated your invitation. Something tells me you're a really good pianist. That so?" she asked, hoping to change the subject. When she glanced at Russ, he let her know that he understood her mood.

"She was really good," John said, "until we went into the Peace Corps, and she didn't practice for the two and a half years we spent in East Africa. When we came back, music wasn't her priority; she had to get a master's degree as quickly as possible, so we could start on our family. Since we've had Jay, she plays, but whenever she goes to the piano, Jay wants to play, too. So her playing isn't what it was when we finished Howard."

"Now I realize how we lost touch with each other," Russ said. "You left the country. I finally gave up trying to find you."

She listened as they reminisced, enjoying their camaraderie and the opportunity to share in Russ' past. John Gandy sat beside his wife, put his left arm around her shoulder and held her right hand with his other hand. His left hand teased her hair, stroked her cheek and caressed her shoulder. It was never still, but continuously fondled her, communicating to his wife that he loved and adored her.

After a dinner of roasted cornish hens, broiled mushrooms, string beans and rice, with vanilla ice cream under raspberry sauce for dessert, Amelia left them and returned with three-year-old Jay. When introduced to the child, Velma said, "Hello, how are you, Jay?" to which he replied, "I'm sleepy."

She didn't know why she did it, but she opened her arms to the boy, and he responded by crawling into her lap. She cradled him, and within minutes, he was asleep.

After using all of her willpower to avoid looking at Russ, his voice reached her from across the room. "I wish I had a camera. That's the most perfect picture I ever saw."

She looked at him then and had to stifle a gasp, for his eyes communicated to her the depth of his feelings.

Later, as he drove them to her house, she asked the question that had nagged at her all evening. "When I first met Amelia, I didn't realize that she's handicapped. Did it happen while she was in Africa?"

"She's been that way since birth. She usually wears a shoe that camouflages it."

"Have they been married long?"

"About eight years, but they've been together since they were eighteen, and they're both my age, thirty-four."

He parked in front of her door, cut the motor and got out of the car. She was hardly aware of the open passenger door, for her mind remained on Amelia Gandy. A woman with a flawed figure, and one shorter leg, who limped badly, had a handsome six-foot-three-inches-tall husband who hadn't seemed able to keep his hands off her, though he'd been her lover for sixteen years. She released a long breath of air, grasped Russ' hand and stepped onto the sidewalk.

Inside her foyer, he let her know at once that he wouldn't stay long and when she looked at him inquiringly, he said, "Amelia is a beautiful woman. Inside, she is pure gold, a loving person of unquestionable loyalty. She's all that and much more. You've been wondering how it is that a handsome, successful man like John loves her—and it's so clear that he does—when she is not perfect to the beholder."

He slapped his balled right fist into his left palm and shook his head as if there was something he didn't understand. "Now you know that a man can adore a woman whose body doesn't meet *Vogue* magazine's standard of beauty. Velma, let it go. Please, for your sake and mine, learn that you're worth any man's attention. You're lovable, and I love you, but if you don't accept this fact, and especially after last Friday night, what do we have going for us? You think about this."

He kissed her quickly and left. She trudged up the stairs to her bedroom, her heart heavy and her feet dragging. She merely asked some questions, and he knew the basis for them. It didn't escape her that, although Russ Harrington loved her, he would walk away from her if she didn't deal with her . . . she hated to say it . . . her insecurity. She sat in the dark for an hour ruminating about her life and the mess she might make of it. Thoroughly chastened, she told herself, "I'm calling that lawyer first thing Monday morning. I don't have to wait for his letter. I'm going to see my father."

Chapter Twelve

Shortly after nine Monday morning, Velma telephoned Alexis, more out of guilt, since she planned to do something of which she knew Alexis disapproved. However, when she learned that Alexis wasn't feeling well, she postponed speaking with Alvin Crooks, her lawyer, and drove to Eagle Park.

"My Lord," she said to herself as she parked in front of Harrington House, "I didn't tell Russ I was coming here. He's piqued at me anyhow, and this will only make it worse."

"Some kind of virus," Telford explained when he opened the door for her.

"I thought she might be pregnant," Velma said. "You sure?"

"If I thought she was, I wouldn't be standing here. I'd be up there in the clouds somewhere. No. When that happens, it will be a planned event."

She bounded up the stairs to the room Alexis shared with her husband. "How're you feeling, hon?"

"Lousy. I must have the flu. I ached something awful last night. We didn't want Tara to get this, so Telford got her ready for school. She told Henry that men should learn how to braid because both Russ and Telford made a mess of her hair."

"I can imagine. I thought you might be pregnant, but Telford said you're not. Are you?"

"No. It's really the flu. I don't think it's good to begin a marriage with a pregnancy if you can avoid it."

Laughter poured out of Velma. "You sound as if you don't know if there's a way to avoid it."

Alexis rolled over, reached for the glass of orange juice on the night table and took a sip. "Promise me you won't make any jokes. I don't feel like laughing. How are things with you and my brother-in-law?"

"Sometimes, he's the most wonderful man, and I can actually feel with every nerve in my body and with my five senses how much he loves me. Then I can do or say something, and he withdraws. Like Saturday night." She told Alexis about their visit with John and Amelia Gandy, her reaction to Amelia, and the questions she asked Russ later.

"Would you believe he knew I was comparing her to beautiful women with perfect bodies and wondering how a man like John Gandy could be besotted with her after sixteen years, first as her lover and later as her husband? He said I wondered about it because I believe that an imperfect woman isn't lovable. And I think I'm imperfect. He took it personally. Then he passed his lips across my mouth—dutifully, I felt—and left me."

"From my discussion with you these past several months, I suspect there's some truth in what he said. And I'll bet that's the only thing that gets between you."

"He'd probably agree with you, but I don't know. I'm sick of being dissected and analyzed. I'm going downstairs to say hello to Henry, because I definitely don't want cabbage stew for supper."

"You shoulda stayed in Baltimore and looked after yer

man," Henry said after accepting her kiss on his cheek. "Before I leave this world, I want to see all the boys married to good women. You're a lot slower than yer sister."

She patted his shoulder and accepted the buttered buscuit that he handed her. She bit into it. "Hmm. This is fabulous, even by your high standards. I'm probably faster than Alexis, but I suspect Russ is to Telford as a saddle horse is to a thoroughbred. That man is deliberate, and he takes his time."

"Tell me something I don't know. Is Russ coming this weekend?"

"I guess so. Drake will be home, so I can't imagine he won't come to see him."

Henry put some utensils in the dishwasher and grabbed his back as he straightened up. "Now, you listen to me, young lady. That ain't no way to deal with Russ. I bet he don't even know you're here. If he don't, get on that phone and call him. You're hell bent on wrecking this thing, both of ya. Did you bring me sausages?"

"Of course I did. And don't worry about Russ and me, there's a problem, and I'm working on it."

"At least you're dressing like a fine woman, and yer hair's back to normal. The braids didn't look bad on you. Not a bit. But you're prettier with your hair down. Piling it on top of yer head don't make you look taller. Makes ya look like a short woman with her hair piled on top of her head. If ya want it to look short, cut it."

She accepted another biscuit, though she knew the scales would punish her for it. "Henry, I didn't dream that you paid this much attention to women."

He treated her to a dismissive glance. "I ain't always been old; I was a man of me time, and I had me a fine wife, God rest her soul."

She heard a wobble in his voice and saw the unshed tears glistening in his eyes. Though she knew he shied away from intimacy, she put an arm around him. "And I know you were a wonderful husband to her. Take comfort in that."

"I try," he whispered, "but sometimes that ain't much comfort. I been without her for the last thirty of me sixty years." She didn't remove her arm, and his behavior didn't suggest that he wanted her to. "You take care with Russ. Being married to a man who loves you and who you love is a blessed state. There's nothing else like it."

"I will. He means everything to me."

"I know that. You just make sure he knows it. If you got a lot of time on yer hands, you can French these string beans."

She sat on the stool that Henry used, washed and prepared the beans and stored them in the refrigerator. "Anything else I can do?"

"Well, if you don't mind, you could take Alexis a couple of aspirins and some hot tea with lemon and sugar." He made the tea, and she took that and the aspirin to Alexis.

"Does Russ know you're here?" Alexis asked.

She slapped the side of her face. "Oh, goodness. I meant to call him. See you later."

She headed for her room, and as she walked in, she heard her cell phone ringing. "Hello. Velma Brighton speaking."

"This is Captain Hawkins, police department. Did you witness a man running from a balcony last Friday night? We'd like to talk with you."

"I did, sir, but I'm in Eagle Park right now, and later this week, I'm scheduled to go to Canada for a couple of days."

"Where's Eagle Park?"

"About a twenty-minute drive from Frederick. I can go there and give a deposition, if you'd like."

"That may work. Could you identify the man, if you saw him?"

"Only by size, color and height, sir. I didn't get a good look at his face. He was a swarthy white man, dark haired, slightly built and about five-nine or five-ten. And Captain, that man could really run, so I suspect he was rather young."

"Thanks, Miss Brighton, this is a big help. If we need you, we'll let you know."

She hung up and stared at the phone. They'd traced the call to her. Not that she minded, but she hoped she wouldn't have to testify in court. She sat down and dialed Russ' cellular phone number.

"Russ Harrington. How may I help you?"

"Russ, this is Velma. I'm in Eagle Park, and I—"

"Hi. What're you doing there? Is Alexis all right?"

"I called her this morning, and when I learned that she has the flu, I came straight here. Drake will be home day after tomorrow. If you're coming, I'll stay till you get here."

"I won't be able to leave here till Friday afternoon."

"Then, if Alexis doesn't get worse, I'll leave sometime Wednesday. Where are you?"

"We're gutting these houses, and I'm in a hard-hat area, so I have to be careful of loose wires. If you get back here Wednesday, I want to see you."

"Okay. But we'll talk before then. Be careful. Love ya. Bye."

"Throw it over there," he said to someone. "Back at you," he said to her. "I'll fix that Wednesday night."

She couldn't help laughing. He didn't have privacy to speak, so she needled him. "Well, you'd better bring all your tools. This . . . uh . . . house right here is in bad shape and has been since Friday night."

"Bad . . . what?" His laughter, a sound that she adored, reached her through the wire, and she joined him in it.

"You'll pay," he said. "And I hope you remember what the punishment is like."

The laughter seemed to float out of her of its own volition. "Do I ever. I can hardly wait."

"You little imp," he said. "I'll bring the tools, alright. See you."

After she hung up, she realized that she had tied up her week and her weekend. Another week would pass before she could confront her father.

Wednesday afternoon at four-thirty, Russ hung up his hard hat, noted that the steps had been removed and jumped from the open door of a house to the pavement below. The last of the houses had been gutted, and a big crane was shoveling up what was left of the debris. He phoned Allen Krenner, the Harrington brothers' foreman.

"We'll start the renovations tomorrow morning, Allen, but unless Telford says otherwise, we won't need more than half a dozen men here for the remainder of the week. Drake gets in from Barbados today, and he may have something to say about this, but as far as I'm concerned, we're ready to go."

He washed up in the trailer, changed his clothes and headed home. Bring all of his tools, eh? She'd be screaming "uncle" before he got through with her. He telephoned her. "I'll be by your house at seven, and I expect I'll be starved, so suppose we go somewhere for a quick bite?"

"Quick bite? Why quick?"

"You've got a world-class imagination, sweetheart. Now's a good time to use it. See you in a couple of hours."

At seven, she opened her door to him, her face blooming in a smile. He stepped inside, pulled her into his arms and lowered his head. He felt the pressure of her hands on the back of his neck and his body quickened in anticipation of what was to come. Her lips parted, and he sank into her, starved for what he found there. When she showed no sign of easing up, he forced himself to stop and stand back.

"I think we'd better go somewhere and eat," he said. "I only had a sandwich for lunch." He looked hard at her. "Is . . . uh . . . that something you wear out in the street?" he asked of the silk pants and knee-length tunic she wore.

"Some women might, but I wouldn't."

He studied that cryptic remark. She had a way of talking around an issue and letting you figure out the meaning, but he had plans for the evening, and didn't intend to have them squashed by a misunderstanding.

So he asked her, "Are we eating out, or do you plan to have something brought in?"

"Neither," she said. "Here I am all decked out in this sexy thing, and you're talking about food."

"Damn straight, I am. I'm practically starved."

Her face creased into a grin. "Really. Well, I'll do my best to take care of that. Come on."

She led him to her dining room. "I cooked for you. I even roasted a pair of pork filets. Would I let you starve?"

He pointed to the table where broiled grapefruit halves awaited him, the smell of the cognac teasing his nostrils. "With stuff like that, no, but otherwise, I can't say. You haven't been tested."

She patted his buttock. "Sit down, please. Just for that smart remark, you'll have to say the grace."

"You'd make me say it anyway." He took her hand, and suddenly felt impelled to thank the Lord, not for the food, but for the joy he found in their relationship.

When he finished, she raised her head and looked at him. "You're a blessing in my life."

And may it always be that way, he thought. He savored the roast pork, potato pancakes, string beans and the tomato salad. "Velma, this is good stuff. I'm speaking first-class."

"Well, you said you were starved, and that makes you easy to please."

He waved the fork in her direction, laughing to himself at the thought of what Henry would say if he saw him do that. "Woman, let this be the last time I have to tell you that I am well acquainted with my mind. So I know what I think. I say this is good food, and it would be good even if I wasn't hungry. So just thank me nicely." She folded her hands in her lap and lowered her lashes, and he could see that he'd pleased her.

"Sorry I didn't have time to make a snappy desert, so you'll have ice cream."

"Works for me. I love ice cream about as much as Tara loves it. Vanilla and raspberry mixed?" he asked.

"Close. Vanilla with raspberry sauce."

"Your Brownie points are piling up. When did you do all this? I called you a little after four-thirty."

"After we spoke, I went to the butcher and bought the filets, bought the ice cream and a package of frozen raspberries. I had the other things here. It's a simple meal and didn't take long to cook."

He finished the ice cream, leaned back in the chair and patted his belly. "For cooking like this, I have a feeling that if I didn't already love you, I'd be falling fast right now. Let's clean the kitchen."

"I think you're a slave driver," she said in jest, or at least he hoped she wasn't serious. Some of his workers had accused him of that, but he'd only been asking for an honest day's work.

"Maybe, but when you wake up tomorrow morning, you won't have to face a sinkful of dirty dishes, and you won't have to ruin your pretty hands with this steel wool I'm using to scrub this pot."

They teased and bantered until he turned on the dishwasher, flicked out the light, took her hand and walked out of the kitchen. She looked at her watch. "There's an old Paul

Robeson movie on tonight, and its just beginning. Let's watch it."

He stared down at her. "I hope you're kidding."

"Why?"

He didn't believe anybody could fake that kind of innocence. "Oh, hell," he said, picked her up and carried her upstairs to her bedroom. "You still want to know why?"

Her shrug was as elegant a gesture as he'd ever seen. "Me? You blustered about bringing all your tools, but I haven't seen any, so I figured we'd watch a movie. And that's fine with me."

She had the ability to drive him up the wall. He let her see a grin on his face before he lifted her to fit him, locked an arm around her shoulder and the other one around her buttocks and stared down into her face.

"Have you found anything lacking with the tools I've got?"

She bit her bottom lip and swallowed visibly. "Uh . . . no."

"Do you want me to leave?"

"No," she whispered.

"Then let me know you want me to stay."

She locked her arms around his back and parted her lips. "Ah yes," he said and plunged into her mouth.

Her short pants and the quiver of her thighs around his body told him that her desire was headed toward its apex. He placed her on her bed, leaned over her and ran his hand over her body while he twirled his tongue in her welcoming mouth. When she began to shift and rock, he released her right breast from the tunic's rounded neckline, pulled her nipple into his mouth and sucked it. Her loud cry sent shivers through his body and he hardened, then stripped himself and Velma, found his home inside of her body and rode with her to a world of their own.

* * *

The next two days came and went with Velma floating on air, barely aware of the passage of time, happy in the love she shared with Russ. She no longer considered the possibility that the cloud on which she floated might burst. The whole world was hers.

"Life would be perfect," she told herself that Saturday morning as she headed for Eagle Park, "if I knew I'd live with him forever, if I had three of his children, and if I wore a size twelve." She laughed at her daydreaming, contenting herself with the knowledge that she had lost six pounds, and that after their earth-shattering lovemaking the previous Wednesday night, Russ would have to bring up the subject of marriage.

A little animal skittered across the highway, and she swerved to avoid hitting it. "If he doesn't mention it, I will," she said aloud. "That's why I have a mouth."

Russ had gone home the previous evening, but she had catered a Friday-night reception and couldn't accompany him. She parked in the circle that constituted the gateway to Harrington House, and Russ stepped from the front door to meet her.

"I thought you'd never get here. Traffic must have been heavy," he said, folded her in his arms and held her, kissing and caressing her. She locked him as tightly in her arms as she could. Words didn't seem to matter.

At last, he released her, but continued holding her hands. "One of my former college roommates is here this weekend to talk business with me. I hope he doesn't get Brighton disease."

She might have been perplexed if she hadn't seen the twinkle in his eyes. "Brighton what?"

"According to Telford, that's a contagious virus that has infected Harrington house. You want to disagree with that?"

He smiled as he said it, besotting her, pushing air beneath her feet. She felt as if she were flying.

"I wonder if that virus works equally well on all the occupants." She turned toward the kitchen when she heard footsteps heavier than Henry's would be. However, she knew another man approached before she saw him, because Russ' arm pulled her flush to his side, though he didn't look toward the intruder, but directly down at her.

"Sam, this is Velma Brighton," he said, still looking down at her, making certain that the man got the correct definition of their relationship.

"How are you, Miss Brighton?"

Good manners dictated that she at least look at the man, but Russ seemed determined to prevent it. "Hello, Sam," she said, not bothering to control the grin. "I'd better get on to my room so you two can talk."

"Nice meeting you." Sam's words came out almost as a question. "What was that all about?" he asked Russ as she walked off.

"What did it look like?"

She could hardly control the laughter until she was safely inside her room. Even as she laughed, one thought simmered in her head: *Russ Harrington, your days as a loner are over.*

She and Russ spent very little time together. Drake and Telford needed briefing about the status of and plans for the Joshua Harrington Houses in Baltimore, and the brothers discussed progress on Fisherman's Village in Barbados. She spent Sunday morning with her sister and her niece.

She tried to make herself tell her sister that before the coming week ended, she hoped to see their father and to have a candid, soul-cleansing talk with him.

"You seem a little preoccupied," Alexis said. "Are you all right? I can see that it's going well with Russ. He's a different man. Open. Brimming with laughter and . . . Velma, Russ is happy."

"Yes. I love being with him when he's this way. I realize I'll do most anything to make him laugh. Seeing him break up gives me the biggest charge."

"See that he stays that way."

Tara bounded into the room with Biscuit trailing behind her. "Come hear me play, Aunt Velma. My dad is teaching me a new piece. It's a waltz, and Chopin wrote it. If I learn that real good, he's going to teach me some ragtime. What did he call it, Mummy?"

"Something by Scott Joplin. I forgot the name."

She didn't envy Alexis her happiness, but as she gazed at her niece—a beautiful, well-mannered, and intelligent child— she wondered when she would hold her own son or daughter. Fearing that she might develop melancholia, she grasped Tara's hand.

"Let's go to your room. I want to hear you play."

They nearly bumped into Russ as he stepped out of his room. "I thought you and Sam were talking business," she said to him. "And you were in your room asleep."

"Mr. Sam is in Mr. Henry's room," Tara explained.

"Right. Sam's asleep. We talked most of the night. What time are you leaving?"

"Around four, I guess."

"If Telford and Drake get back here within the next half hour, I'll trail you. We have to talk with Allen before I leave."

"She has to listen to me play, Uncle Russ. She promised."

"And she will." He pulled Tara's braid. "What will you play for her?

" 'Barcarole' by Offen . . . What's his name, Mummy?

"Jacques Offenback."

She looked at Russ, perplexed. "That's his name, Uncle Russ."

After Tara played the piece several times, Alexis joined them. "Henry has sandwiches, fruit, sodas and coffee in the breakfast room. Serve yourself."

"Can I have ice cream, Mummy?" She paused for a second. "No thanks. I'll ask Mr. Henry." With that, she headed for the kitchen.

The two sisters walked down the stairs arm in arm, and as they reached the bottom, Drake and Telford entered the foyer. "Well, well," Drake said to Velma, "I wondered whether I'd get to see you." He favored them with a sample of his famous charm, his grin infectious and his long-lashed brown eyes sparkling. "I see you've been making progress."

Both of her eyebrows went up. "You know something that I don't?"

"No indeed. You know this, and you know it well. Keep it up; you've made a brand-new man of him."

She wished she thought it. For Drake's ears, she decided that diffidence was better. "As long as he's happy."

That brought a laugh from Drake who, she had learned, was close to being the most discerning person she'd ever known. "I'm not buying that, and neither would he. If it were true, he wouldn't even know where you live."

"Guilty as charged," she said. "Let's eat."

In the kitchen, she selected a pastrami sandwich and a Mitsu apple and took her plate to the breakfast room, where she joined Henry, Alexis and Tara. She ate most of the sandwich and went back to the kitchen for a glass of lemonade.

"I hope this warehouse is located near Reese Street," she heard Russ say, and at the mention of the word *warehouse,* her antenna shot up. "I'm renovating some houses there, and your project would help raise the level of the area." She stopped in her tracks, every nerve in her body on edge.

"Sorry I can't accommodate you, man. It's about ten blocks down on Bricker, between Just and Hornet." She groped for the doorjamb and let it take her weight. Her ware-house. Sam Jenkins was bidding for her warehouse.

"I'll stop by there tomorrow sometime," Russ said, "and have a look at it. I'd like to get an idea of what you'd need in the way of renovation and redesign. Warehouses can be tricky; they're not always what they look like."

Her knees shook and perspiration poured from her, but she managed to get down the hall to her room, though she would never know how she did it. She had to calm herself and tell Russ that she had a bid in for that warehouse, that her real-estate agent had canvassed Baltimore and that ware-house was the only one that suited both her needs and her bank book. He had to tell his friend to back off.

"Where's Velma?" Russ asked nobody in particular as he sat down to eat his lunch. "I thought she was in here."

"I thought she was in the kitchen," Alexis said. "She went to get a glass of lemonade."

She hadn't come into the kitchen or he'd have seen her. "Excuse me." He left the table and headed for her room. "I thought you were eating lunch," he said when she opened the door. "What's wrong?" He didn't like her demeanor, slumped in the chair like a defeated person.

"Eat your lunch," she said. "We can talk about this later."

So there *was* a problem. He sat down on the chaise lounge, facing her. "We'll talk about it now. What is it?"

He didn't know whether she realized that she was wring-ing her hands, but she had to hear the unsteadiness in her voice. He braced himself for the unpleasant. And she deliv-ered it.

"That warehouse Sam's bidding on is the one I'm trying to get."

He jumped up from the chaise lounge and stood over her, wanting to be certain that he heard her correctly. *"What did you say?"*

She looked at him with an expression of defeat in her eyes. "I said—"

He sat down. "Never mind. I heard you. This puts me between a rock and a hard place, Velma. If it wasn't for Sam Jenkins, I wouldn't be here, I wouldn't be an architect and there would be no Harrington, Inc., Architects, Engineers and Builders. One of our classmates stole my graduating term paper the night before the deadline for handing it in. If my professor hadn't received that paper on time, I wouldn't have graduated. The student who stole it was at the bottom of the class, and with that paper, I would graduate at the top. The guy was in a bar on Georgia Avenue around midnight that night, bragging that he knew he was going to pass. The more he drank the more he bragged. Sam was in the bar, and he knew someone had stolen my paper. He got his uncle, a judge, out of bed and asked him to issue a search warrant for the guy's room. The campus police went in at six the next morning and found the term paper on the poor fool's desk. I told Sam that if he ever needed me, I'd be there for him. I thought he was joking when he said, 'I'd like you to design the first building I own,' but I shook hands on it."

"Where does that leave me?"

"I'll help you find another one."

"My real-estate agent knows Baltimore better than you or I, and this is all he could find that I can afford. If I don't get that building—"

"Don't say it. We'll find something for you. I gave Sam my word, and I have to honor it. Who knows, maybe he won't win the bid, and you will."

"But your design will practically guarantee that he wins it, because you will do your best."

"Let's not worry about it right now. Come on back and eat your lunch."

"Just . . . give me a few minutes. You go on."

He leaned over her and kissed her mouth. "All right."

Velma sat as he'd left her, contemplating the latest turn of fate in her life. The more she thought about it, the more deeply and sharply the pain sliced through her. He wouldn't renege on his word to his friend, but didn't he owe her—his lover, the woman he said he loved—as much as he owed Sam?

"Damned if I'm putting up with this," she said, grabbed her overnight bag, threw her things in it, wrote a note to Alexis and, although she felt like a sneak doing it, she slipped out of Harrington House, got into her car and headed home. The next move was his, and if he didn't make the right one, he could forget she existed.

At home, she checked her answering machine and called her sister. "I'm fine, hon. I just decided the best place for me was home. I'll call Tara tomorrow and explain. If you need to know any more, ask Russ. I'm turning off my phone."

"I don't like the sound of this."

"Neither do I. I'll talk with you when I feel more like it." She hung up, turned off the telephone, ate a ham sandwich, drank a cup of herbal tea and went to bed.

The next morning, Monday, at eight-thirty, she telephoned her lawyer and told him that Sam Jenkins had bid on the warehouse.

"We'll work with that. I'll get as much information as I can about him and what he plans to do with the property. Leave it to me." What choice did she have?

"I want the information on my father. You said you sent me a letter, but I haven't received it."

"I sent it certified mail, so it'll come back to me if it isn't delivered. Here's the deal on your father."

She wrote down the information and then read it back to him. "I'm leaving here tomorrow morning on the first plane I can get."

"I don't give personal advice, Ms. Brighton, but I've lived a few years, and I think you should be careful. Try not to give him too big a shock. No telling what shape his heart is in."

She thanked him, hung up and began searching the internet for flight information and hotel reservations. The next morning found her on Air Canada en route to Montreal.

She didn't know what she had expected, but it wasn't the tall but gaunt man with thinning white hair peering at her over a pair of rimless glasses.

"Who is it?" he asked.

"I know you're not expecting me, Father," she said in hopes of easing the shock, "I'm—"

"Oh, my God! *Mildred,*" he said, staring at her.

She wondered whether he was ill. Mildred was her mother's name. She inhaled a deep breath. "Papa, this is your older daughter, Velma. May I come in?"

He flicked on the light and stepped back into the apartment. "For a minute, I thought . . ." He shook his head as if denying something. "She's never far from my mind. Always, she's with me. Yes. Yes. Come on in."

He waited until she walked into the house, then stepped behind her and closed the door. "I . . . I can't imagine . . . This takes some getting used to. Have a seat. I'll make some coffee."

She didn't want any coffee, but she knew he had to stall, to pull himself together. While waiting for him to bring the coffee, she looked around at what she could see of the house.

The foyer was neat and the living room comfortable, though without a particular personality. Functional. The years had not been kind to him. He no longer stood ramrod straight, nor was he robust with a thick chest, and his deeply lined face was that of a man seventy-five rather than sixty-one years of age.

She didn't hear him come back into the living room. "After all these years, why have you come?"

Where should she begin? She had pictured herself telling off a younger, strapping man, and hadn't counted on the damage that years and circumstances had inflicted. She plunged in without preliminaries.

"I don't like myself, and I have a hard time believing that anybody other than Alexis could love me. I figured you could make me understand why I'm this way."

He sipped his coffee—black and without sugar—seemingly glad to have an excuse not to look at her. "Is Alexis all right?"

"She fine, but I didn't come here to talk about her. Why didn't you and mama love me and my sister?"

He nearly dropped the cup. "How can you ask me such a question?"

"Because you didn't, and the way you left me to handle that funeral . . . I didn't even know what one was like or why people had them."

He put the cup in the saucer and rubbed his left hand across his forehead. "I know it was hard for you, but I couldn't stay there another minute. She was everywhere. When I saw you at the door, I nearly fainted until you spoke. You look just like her, but your voice is soft where hers had become harsh."

"Why, Papa?"

He inhaled deeply and blew out a long breath as if resigned. "Your mother hated intimacy, and we fought constantly about that. She wouldn't have minded if I had taken a mistress, but it never once occurred to me to commit adultery. I loved her." He leaned back and closed his eyes. "Oh, I loved that woman. I soon learned that she was more accommodating after a bitter fight, and I staged them. I know it was sick. It was a neurosis of hers, and I fueled it.

"She wanted to send you and Alexis to a boarding school, but I wouldn't agree. A really ugly fight ensued, one that I didn't stage. She scratched and bit me, finally telling me she was going to kill herself. Furious as I was, I told her to suit herself, that I didn't care what she did.

"She ran out of the house wearing a nightgown, raincoat and bedroom slippers. I thought she was going to drive somewhere, but she didn't get in the car. You know the rest.

"I loved my daughters, but the older you got, the more ashamed I was. I knew you listened to the unsavory things that went on between your mother and me. I couldn't change that, so I withdrew and saw as little of my children as possible."

Velma wanted to cover her ears, to stop him and save him the embarrassment of telling his daughter such personal things. But he continued talking, and she could see that, the more he spoke, the less pain the revelations appeared to cause him.

"I had to leave there, Velma. She was everywhere, all over the house. And I knew she was dead before they found her. I couldn't stand the guilt, knowing I could have stopped her. I had to go. I knew you would take care of Alexis; you always had."

His eyes pleaded with her. "If I had stayed there, I would have killed myself. You may say that I deserted you, but don't ever say that I didn't love you."

She stood, but realizing that she was unsteady, she sat

down again. "Thanks for talking to me. I . . . uh . . . I'd better leave now."

He held out his hand to her and then quickly withdrew it. "Don't ever say I didn't love you," he croaked out. "A hundred nights I walked the floor with you when you were a baby. And you were so smart, and I was so proud of you."

"Then how could you do what you did?"

He closed his eyes as tears rolled down his face. "Guilt. Yes, and fear. She was everything to me, young and beautiful like you are now, and I was so scared she'd leave me. She was always threatening to leave me.

"It was an awful environment for two girls. She . . . she walked out that night in twelve-degree temperature, knowing she would freeze. And she did. Guilt. Not an hour has passed in the last fourteen years that I didn't think of her. Right in the middle of a lecture, she's there before me. I live in hell."

"I'm so sorry, Papa. Terribly sorry." And she was; she hurt for him.

"Are you?" She nodded. "Well, thanks for that redemption. Do you have a picture of Alexis?"

"No sir, but I have one of her daughter, Tara. She's five and precious."

He looked at the picture of his granddaughter. "She's beautiful. I've missed so much. Do you have children?"

"No, sir. I've never married."

"I don't ask the two of you to forgive me, but please try to understand."

If she didn't get out of there, she would come apart, and she didn't want him to see her crumble. "Yes, sir," she said. "I'll try, and I'll tell Alexis."

He thanked her for coming to see him, though he hadn't once asked her how she found him. They said goodbye, and she stepped out into the twilight. So much to digest, piled on her like wood on a wood pile. She hadn't guessed what a miserable family they had been, and as she blinked back the tears, she almost wished she hadn't found out. A glance at her watch confirmed that it was a quarter of six. With luck . . . She phoned the airline, got a reservation on a seven-forty flight to Baltimore, canceled her hotel reservation and walked into her house at midnight.

She got ready for bed, slid under the covers and began to shake as tremors plowed through her. She tried to hold back the tears, but they came, escalating into sobs.

"Russ. Russ, I need you," she whispered, but for her, there was no Russ, and she cried herself to sleep.

"I can't believe she just walked out without a word," Russ said to Alexis after he'd searched the house, the grounds and the banks of the Monacacy River.

He'd never known Alexis to appear dumbfounded, but nothing else would explain her demeanor. "She called a minute ago," Alexis said. "I hadn't seen the note she left, but I found it after I talked with her."

"Why did she leave?" It was a rhetorical question, because he was increasingly certain that he knew the answer and that Alexis didn't.

"It'll sort itself out, Russ. You're bound to have little misunderstandings," Telford said in an obvious attempt to reassure him.

He didn't want to be consoled, because it wouldn't help. "There's nothing little about this, Telford. I've hurt her. I couldn't help it, and I don't see how I can repair it."

He felt Tara's little arms hugging his leg. "Didn't you kiss her, Uncle Russ? My dad kisses my mummy after he upsets her."

He looked down at the precious little girl. "Didn't I . . . She didn't give me a chance." As badly as he hurt, he couldn't help laughing. Tara illumined his life. Immediately, his thoughts returned to Velma, and he wondered if he would ever laugh again without thinking of her, the woman who taught him the joy of laughter.

"I'm heading out of here," he told them. "Be seeing you." He threw his overnight bag into the trunk of his car and headed for Baltimore. She didn't answer her cellular phone, and her house phone didn't ring. "I'll get through this," he promised himself. "Six months from now, I hope I won't give a damn."

He threw himself into rebuilding the house that bore his father's name. Telford and Drake stayed closer to him than usual, in their quiet way, giving him moral support as they had always done when he needed them. The full crew of twenty-three men finished the work in three weeks, and the landscapers began beautifying the lawns. He should have been happy.

Where Russ was out of sorts, Velma used her misery to push herself toward her goal. She worked out in a gym daily, took her medicine and ate properly. However, two weeks of that regimen netted her a loss of only one pound and a half.

"I'm through torturing myself," she told her gym instructor when he begged her not to discontinue her exercise program. "I'm fine just like I am," she informed him in an in-your-face manner that she knew was not typical of her. "I don't have to be a string bean." While she dressed, rebellion welled up in her. "I'm going to be the way that suits me," she said to herself, left the gym and went to the hairdresser.

"I want a pixie cut and style, Bea. I'm tired of this long hair."

Bea shrugged and got the scissors. "It's past time."

She admired the results in the mirror, left the hairdresser and stopped at the first shoe store that she saw. "I want a pair of dress shoes with one-inch heels, size seven and a half." She wore the new shoes and dropped the three-inch-heel slippers into the first refuse bin she saw.

"Thank God my silly years are over. Now, I can walk a block without my feet killing me."

"This silence has continued long enough," Alexis said to her in a phone call one morning not long after Velma's epiphany. "This isn't like you. You promised to talk, but you chat about everything except why you don't come here and what happened between you and Russ. And he's become as tight lipped as he was the day I met him."

"All right. I wanted to wait till we were together, but too much time has already passed. I was content with myself, or thought I was, till I fell in love with Russ, saw you in your wedding dress and how Telford adores you. No one but you had ever loved me, and I couldn't accept that a man would love me and want me for himself alone when there were so many tall, beautiful women like you that he could choose from. Russ was impatient with it.

"Two professionals told me that my problem went much deeper, and I know enough psychology to grant them their point. I went to Montreal to talk with our father." She related her experience during that visit, adding, "I don't know when it started after that meeting, but I've begun to see myself differently. I don't want to look like anybody but me, and I've changed me to suit myself."

"I had a feeling you'd done that, but I didn't ask for fear

the news would be bad. I wish you'd told me; I'd have gone with you."

"I know, but I had to settle something with him. I have his telephone number if you want to call him." She read it to her.

She heard her sister's sigh of relief. "Good. I'll use it. I wish you would make up with Russ. He's not happy."

"Neither am I. For me, happiness is a man named Russ. We'll talk."

"Call Russ. You're the one who walked out."

"What will be, will be, Sis."

Several hours later, she received a call from her real-estate agent. "Nine o'clock Thursday morning, we have to appear at the housing commissioner's office. Bring your proposal. I have pictures of the warehouse and the neighborhood."

"I'll be there." But her thoughts were not of the warehouse, but of Russ, whether he would be there to witness for Sam Jenkins, and what he would say to her if she lost the bid.

That Thursday morning, she walked into the office of the commissioner looking like a new woman, in a knee length flounce skirt, one-inch patent leather shoes and her new short pixie hairstyle. Russ sat with Sam and another man in the official's twelve-by-twelve-foot office, the intimacy of the setting giving her no privacy from him. He nodded to her, but she couldn't respond; they were boxers in opposing corners of a ring.

Sam spoke as a man accustomed to having his way. In answer to the official's questions, Sam said he would hire twenty-two to thirty workers; she would hire a maximum of twelve. With each comparison, she lost to Sam.

Exasperated, she asked Sam, "Why would upper-class people want to join a health club in that neighborhood? Why do you want that warehouse?"

"Why not? I'm starting a business."

"In addition to my business there, I'm planning to give six-month cooking classes twice yearly for up to eighteen students who live in the neighborhood. What will *you* give to the neighborhood?"

"Jobs."

To each of the official's remaining questions, Sam bested her. She saw herself losing the warehouse and turned her back so that Russ wouldn't see her without her composure. Her real-estate agent placed his arms around her in an attempt to comfort her, and she leaned to him.

"Did you try to find another building, Sam?"

At the sound of Russ' voice, dark and angry, her head snapped around.

"What's with you, man?" Sam asked Russ. "As I explained to you, I don't want to lay out a lot of money to have a real-estate agent canvass Baltimore for a site."

"Ms. Brighton paid me to do precisely that," her agent said.

Russ stood and looked down at his friend. "Try to find another place, man."

"What's with you, Russ? Who's side are you on?"

His eyes narrowed and he slammed his right fist into his left palm. "*Hers, dammit.* I gave you my word, Sam, but you're demanding too much. I love this woman. She's my soul mate, and you're asking me to deprive her of something she needs for her livelihood. I can't do it. I won't do it." He looked directly at her. "Give him the warehouse. I'll find a spot and build whatever you want."

She stared at him in wonder, excited and afraid that her ears had misled her. "Are you . . . Do you mean that?" She moved out of her agent's arms. "Do you?"

"You bet I mean it." He turned to Sam. "I'll always be

grateful for what you did for me when we were in college, but Sam, don't ask this of me. I can't hurt her like that."

"Sorry, Russ. I didn't realize it was so serious. I'm sure I can find a place in a more suitable neighborhood." He threw up his hand for a high five. "Don't let grass grow under your feet, brother. She's choice."

"Don't I know it! Let me know when you find a place, and I'll redesign it for you."

"Will do. Be seeing you, Ms. Brighton."

She thought she nodded; she wasn't sure. Every nerve in her body jumped to alert as Russ walked toward her, slowly, as if measuring his steps. "I'd like you to leave with me. Will you?"

She turned to the real-estate agent and thanked him. "I'd love to," she then said to Russ, "but who gets the warehouse?"

"It's yours, Ms. Brighton," the official said. "Step in the office across the hall, and you can sign the papers."

She didn't move. How could she? He stood within a foot of her, reaching for her hand. "Let's go sign those papers."

She signed the papers, accepted a copy of the deed and the key to the warehouse and walked out of the municipal building with Russ holding her hand.

"I want us to go some place where we can talk," he said.

"My house?"

"Fine, but let's sit on the back porch." She wondered at that but didn't comment. "Have you forgiven me, Velma?"

Sitting with him on the porch in the late-winter breeze, contentment enveloped her. "How could I not forgive you after you confessed publicly that you love me?"

He shrugged as if that were of no import. "I should have done that a good while ago." He let his gaze roam over her. "So that's it. You did something to your hair. You cut it."

She settled in the chair and stuck out both feet. "Yep, and

I also tossed out my spiked heel shoes. I'm through with needless suffering."

Russ leaned forward, hope springing to life within him. "Why? What prompted this? Tell me."

She looked him in the eye, making a point, he thought. "I decided that I am who I am, and if somebody doesn't like it, *tough!*"

He could hardly contain the happiness that bubbled within him. "What brought this on? It's what I've longed to hear, mind you, but how did you come to this?"

He listened to her story of her visit with her father and her reason for finding him. He had thought his own mother flaky, but compared to Velma's mother, she was not so bad.

"Do you plan to see your father again?"

"I suppose so. I couldn't help feeling his pain. Imagine living with that guilt and grief." She paused, suddenly far away.

"What is it? What are you feeling?" he asked her.

"He . . . father said, 'She—mama—was so beautiful, just as you are right now.' I had forgotten that. And he said I looked just like her."

He understood then why Velma had not been able to believe that he found her beautiful and physically attractive. "Of course, he loved you. He loved your mother, and he said you were just like her." He walked to the edge of the porch and peered through the screen at two squirrels frolicking in the grass, walked back and sat on the porch swing beside her. "Does this mean you're off that diet?"

Her fingers stroked his knee in a rhythmic fashion, communicating to him contentment, even as her smile did. "I am going to take my medicine and eat sensibly, but I have spent my last minute in that torture cell that goes by the name of gym, and as far as I am concerned, chicken breasts are extinct."

He reveled in his own joy and laughter. Twenty-four hours earlier, he'd had no hope for reconciliation. "It's past lunchtime," he said. "Let's phone for something to eat."

"I could enjoy some fried catfish and baked cornbread," Velma said.

"Great." He placed their orders, went to the kitchen and made a pot of coffee, explaining that he hadn't had anything in his mouth all day except toothpaste.

"I was miserable, Velma. I didn't know how I could bear it if you lost that bid. When I realized he would win it, I couldn't stand it. Then that guy put his friggin' arms around you, comforting you as I should have been doing. Hell, I don't want to think about that."

They ate in silence, she apparently as deep in thought as he. "I'd better get to work," he said when they finished lunch. "Can we see each other this evening?"

When she cocked her head to one side and smiled at him, he rocked back on his heels and waited for a bit of sauciness. "Who said you have to go back to work?"

His pulse accelerated, and water began to accumulate in his mouth. "Nobody. Why?"

"Then, stay."

He looked hard at her. "Are you aware that it's been three weeks and four days since I last saw you?"

Her hands moved up and down her sides, rubbing, evidence of her agitation. "I thought it was longer than that, but if you insist on leaving, at least kiss me good bye."

"I don't insist." A grin played around her lips, and he couldn't get at her fast enough. "Challenge me, will you?" he asked her.

Her face bloomed into a big smile. "Why not? It always

works." She reached for his shoulders, parted her lips, and his tongue found its home between them.

Several hours later, as he lay buried deep inside of her with her legs snug around his hips, she said, "This has developed into an affair, and I am not happy having an affair with you."

"We can always get married," he said, as if he hadn't thought of it constantly during the past three weeks.

"I know we . . . what? What kind of proposal is that?"

He separated them, slid off the bed and knelt beside it. "I love you, and I want to marry you. Will you do me the honor of being my wife?"

She rolled off the bed and knelt beside him. "Oh yes. Yes. That is, if we can have three children."

He thought his heart would explode from the joy that filled him. "It's what I want, honey. A family. I'll take as many as you'll give me. Boys or girls, I don't care which or in what combination. I just want a family."

"Russ, love, you can't know how happy I am."

"I am too." He attempted at first to control the mirth, for the moment was a serious one. But the laughter spilled out of him unimpeded.

"What's funny?"

"Us. We must look a sight kneeling here like this. When can we get married?"

"Six weeks. Okay?"

He nodded. "I wouldn't mind if it was earlier. I'd better tell you something. I sent Iris two thousand dollars through my lawyer. Telford told me he saw her sitting with her child on the street, her things stacked around her. She's nothing to me; I did the humane thing."

She gripped his hand. "This gentle sweetness that you try to bury deep inside is one of the many reasons why I love you."

"I can't count the reasons why or the ways in which I love you. Life isn't long enough for that. I'll be a good husband to you, sweetheart. When you need me, I will always be there."

"I know that, darling, as well as I know my name."

He put her in the bed, crawled in beside her and rocked them both to ecstasy.

Dear Reader,

Many of you have read all of my twenty-four previous romance titles (as well as my mainstream novels), and I want to thank you for your loyal support. I have written *After The Loving,* the story of Russ Harrington, second oldest of the three Harrington brothers, because so many of you wrote and e-mailed me asking that I continue with this trilogy. Apart from Tara, Russ was always my favorite person in the Harrington household. Being a middle child myself, I not only empathized with him but understood his feelings and needs better than those of the other characters. I sincerely hope this is reflected in the story.

If you enjoyed this story and have not read *Once in a Lifetime,* you may want to read it for a better understanding of the characters in the Harrington household and to know the circumstances of Russ and Velma's first meeting. That book won many new readers for me.

I am currently at work on *Love Me or Leave Me,* Drake Harrington's story and the final book of this series (due out in September 2005). In it, you will also encounter Schyler Henderson, whom you first met in "Swept Away."

My thanks to those of you who made *Last Chance At Love* such a smashing success and who came out to meet me at my stops in and around Detroit and Idlewild, Michigan, where important scenes in the story take place.

If you would like to receive my bimonthly newsletter, please go to my website, http://www.gwynneforster.com, click newsletter and fill in the form. For current news, please join my internet group: VoicesForTheWrittenWord@yahoogroups.com.

I enjoy receiving mail and answer it as promptly as possible. E-mail: GwynneF@aol.com or P.O. Box 45, New York, NY 10044 with SASE if you would like a reply.

I wish you all good health and many blessings.

Sincerely yours,
Gwynne Forster

About the Author

Gwynne Forster is a national bestselling and award-winning author. She is the winner of the Black Writers Alliance 2001 Gold Pen award for Best Romance Novel, for *Beyond Desire*, a Doubleday Book Club, Literary Guild, and Black Expressions Book Club selection. Her 2001 romance novel *Scarlet Woman* was also a Black Expressions Book Club selection. That same year, Romance Slam Jam nominated Gwynne for three Emma awards and for its first Vivian Stephens Lifetime Achievement Award. In 1999, *Romantic Times* nominated Gwynne for a Lifetime Achievement award; that same year she was named Author of the Year by the on-line website Romance in Color. *Fools Rush In,* which was published by Arabesque in November, 1999, received the *Affaire De Coeur Magazine* Award for Best Romance with an African-American Hero and Heroine, and won the award the previous two years as well.

Gwynne's most recent romance, *Last Chance at Love,* has been a top seller. Her current novel, *After the Loving*, is a sequel to *Once in a Lifetime.* Look for Gwynne's next romance in September, 2005.

Gwynne holds bachelor's and master's degrees in sociology and a master's degree in economics/demography. As a demographer, she is widely published. She is formerly chief of nonmedical research in fertility and family planning in the population division of the United Nations in New York City and served for four years as chairperson of the International Programme Committee of the International Planned Parenthood Federation in London, England, positions that took her to sixty-three developed and developing nations. Gwynne sings in her church choir, loves to entertain, and is a gourmet cook and avid gardener. She lives with her husband in New York City.

She is represented by the Steel-Perkins Literary Agency, 26 Island Lane, Canandaigua, NY 14424. You can contact Gwynne Forster at P.O. Box 45, New York, NY 10044, or email her at *GwynneF@aol.com*. Visit her websites at *www.gwynneforster.com* and *www.tlt.com/authors/gforster.htm*.

BOOK YOUR PLACE ON OUR WEBSITE AND MAKE THE ARABESQUE ROMANCE CONNECTION!

We've created a customized website just for our very special Arabesque readers, where you can get the inside scoop on everything that's going on with Arabesque romance novels.

When you come online, you'll have the exciting opportunity to:

- View covers of upcoming books

- Learn about our future publishing schedule (listed by publication month and author)

- Find out when your favorite authors will be visiting a city near you

- Search for and order backlist books

- Check out author bios and background information

- Send e-mail to your favorite authors

- Join us in weekly chats with authors, readers and other guests

- Get writing guidelines

- AND MUCH MORE!

Visit our website at
http://www.arabesquebooks.com

COMING IN MARCH 2005 FROM
ARABESQUE ROMANCES

More Arabesque Romances by
Donna Hill